Books should be returned or renewed by the
last date stamped above

AF

TATE, J

FOR LOVE OR MONEY

For Love Or Money

Money

June Tate

headline

First published in 2003
by HEADLINE BOOK PUBLISHING

First published in paperback in 2004
by HEADLINE BOOK PUBLISHING

10 9 8 7 6 5 4 3 2

ISBN 0 7472 6550 X

Typeset in Times New Roman by
Letterpart Limited, Reigate, Surrey

Printed and bound in Great Britain by
Mackays of Chatham plc, Chatham, Kent

Papers and cover board used by Headline are natural, recyclable products
made from wood grown in sustainable forests.
The manufacturing processes conform
to the environmental regulations of the country of origin.

HEADLINE BOOK PUBLISHING
A division of Hodder Headline
338 Euston Road
LONDON NW1 3BH

www.headline.co.uk
www.hodderheadline.com

To my very special friend Heather . . . with love

Acknowledgements

To Shona, exotic Amy, Helena and Sherise, the 'team' at Headline. Many thanks for your stalwart work, girls!

With love to my two beautiful daughters, Beverley and Maxine. We are the 'Tate girls', and make a pretty dynamic team of our own!

Chapter One

Southampton, 1946

Connie Ryan stood in front of the mirror and studied her reflection. The fitted bodice of her sleeveless floral dress clung to her slim waist, which was encircled in a black patent belt; the full cotton skirt flounced as she spun round. She pushed her bust upwards but it made no difference. Opening the top drawer of her light oak dressing table, she reached for the roll of cotton wool and stuffed two wads into her bra, turning this way and that until she was satisfied.

'Who do you think you are, Jane Russell?' Her sister, Doreen, stood in the open doorway, staring at her with a bemused expression.

Connie blushed with embarrassment. 'Do you have to spy on me, our Dor?'

'Spy on you! I've got better things to do with my time, thank you very much. Fortunately I'm not vain like you. If you spent less time in front of the mirror, you might be a better daughter and give our mum a helping hand, instead of leaving everything for me to do!'

'You forget I have to prepare for my future,' said Connie earnestly. 'It's all right for you, you've got the faithful Eric panting at your heels. I don't want marriage and kids, I want stardom! Not everyone has been blessed with a voice like mine.'

Her sister, the elder by two years, laughed. 'You've sung at

1

Dad's Social Club a couple of times and all of a sudden you're bloody Vera Lynn!'

'Not her! She sounds as if she has a bad case of adenoids. *I* sound more like Anne Shelton: rich and mellow.'

'Well, at least *she* doesn't have to stuff her bra!' retorted Doreen as she left the room.

Connie continued to fuss in front of the mirror. Her shoulder-length hair was dark, with the slightest natural wave. She twisted it up onto the top of her head. How sophisticated it made her look. The Hollywood film stars wore it like this. She longed to be like Rita Hayworth with her endless legs, luxurious red hair, and looks a girl would kill for. She wasn't at all bad looking herself, she mused, pouting her lips and letting her hair loose. The boys thought so anyway. She knew just how to flirt, to tease them so they didn't know whether they were coming or going. She gave a chuckle. Stupid idiots!

She used her hairbrush as an imaginary microphone and started to sing 'All of Me', letting her natural ability as a singer tell the story of unrequited love in a deep, throaty voice. One day she would be a star. Have her name in lights. Be famous. Be someone.

Downstairs, her mother Freda was preparing her supper. She was not as tall as her daughters, but she was slim and nippy, bustling around the kitchen, testing the potatoes, opening the back door to let out the smell of fish. Turning to Doreen she asked, 'Is Madame Butterfly coming down to lay the table?'

'I didn't ask. She was primping in front of the mirror as usual. I just thought it would be quicker to do it myself.'

With a sigh Freda said, 'You should make her do her share.' She wiped her hands on a tea towel and smiled affectionately at her daughter. 'We are all at fault, letting Connie get away with murder. It isn't good for her. She's getting spoilt rotten. Your father doesn't help, encouraging her to sing at the Social Club.'

Doreen looked up from the table. Clutching the knives and

forks in her hand, she said, 'Well, you've got to admit, Mum, she does have a good voice.'

Freda frowned. 'I know that. She sings beautifully, but she's only eighteen. I don't want her head filled with impossible dreams. She'll only get hurt.'

Continuing to lay the table, Doreen pondered over the future of her younger sister. Although Connie drove her wild with her ambitions and plans, she was fond of her sibling. She also realised the strength of Connie's commitment, whereas she didn't think that their mother did. Connie was determined and stubborn, and she could be ruthless when she had a bee in her bonnet. By hook or by crook, she would do her utmost to fulfil her dreams, and that was what worried Doreen the most. Just how far would she go to reach her goal?

At that moment George Ryan arrived home from his job as store man at the fruit and vegetable wholesalers, Oakley and Watling. He was a genial man, who loved his family and worked hard to give them a decent living. He was a man of simple pleasures: an occasional bet laid with the bookie's runner; tending his allotment where he grew his own vegetables, with a couple of fruit trees to feed the family and eke out the rationing; spending some evenings and the weekend at his Social Club. But he was strict with his girls over their behaviour and had his own set of rules. He was fiercely proud of Connie and her voice, and encouraged her – in his own way.

'Hello, love,' he said, and kissed his wife on the cheek. 'What's for supper?'

'Fish pie, with cabbage and mashed swede. Suet pudding to follow, with custard. Will that please your Lordship?'

He slapped her playfully across her backside. 'Now don't get cheeky!' He hung his jacket and brown overall behind the door. 'I'll just go and wash up,' he said as he headed for the stairs.

The Ryans lived in a rented house in Orchard Lane with two bedrooms, bathroom, living room and kitchen. It suited George because it was just a short bike ride to work. In the summer months he would sometimes walk, but in the winter his bicycle saved him time. The wind and rain coming off the Solent River could be uncomfortable then, but with his trusty old oilskins, bought from a local fisherman, his short journey saved him from too much of a soaking.

At that moment, Connie came down the stairs. 'Can I do anything, Mum?' she asked.

Freda gave her a caustic smile. 'Your timing is, as always, impeccable. I don't know how you do it!'

'What do you mean?'

'You always manage to arrive when everything has been done. Well, you can do the washing up when we've eaten.'

'But I'm going to the pictures!' she protested.

'Then you'll have to be quick about it, won't you? And I want everything washed, dried *and* put away.'

'Mum!'

'Look, our Connie, if you had come down earlier, you would have done your share, so it's your own fault . . . and take that sulky look off your face! If the wind changes, you'll stay like that and what will your adoring public have to say then?'

Freda could be very cutting when she wanted to be. Connie didn't answer, knowing she was beaten at her own game.

As she washed the dishes, she hummed quietly to herself, thinking of the previous Saturday night when she'd performed at the Workman's Social Club in St Mary's. The audience was made up of working men and their wives hoping for a good evening out. Every Saturday someone took the stage in an effort to entertain. Sometimes it was a comedian with a natty line in smutty jokes, on others, a musician of sorts – an accordion player, perhaps, or a man with a ukulele, which enabled the gathering to sing along. That always went down well. Twice now Connie had appeared with the club pianist and had sung the latest songs.

She had a certain alluring quality of which she was unaware. She would lose herself in the lyrics of a love song, and the poignancy of her deep mellow voice held a certain magic which caught at the heartstrings. It stilled the chatter of her audience as they were drawn to the sound, and as she stood at the sink in her mother's kitchen and wiped a glass, she recalled the applause which had echoed round the hall at the end of her last performance.

'One day,' she murmured softly, 'I'm going to sing in a posh place with posh people listening to me, clamouring for my attention. I'm going to be famous.'

'Haven't you finished yet?' Her mother's sharp tone of voice interrupted her dreams.

'Yes, I have,' Connie snapped. 'Now I'm going to the pictures.' She laid the damp tea towel across the draining board and walked into the living room. Taking her coat from the peg behind the door, she said airily, 'I'll see you later.'

'Don't be late back!' Freda called after her.

Connie made her way to the Odeon cinema where she had arranged to meet her friend, Molly Baker, who worked along-side her in Sands', the hat shop in Above Bar. They got on well together, Molly was a bright, humorous girl with a mischievous smile and twinkling eyes, and both of them aspired to be as wealthy as the majority of their clients who dressed up their utility clothes by wearing smart and decorous hats, which were mercifully not on clothing coupons.

'I'll be an old man's darling,' Molly had stated one day whilst they were arranging the frivolous millinery. 'He can buy me furs and diamonds and set me up in a luxurious flat, where he can feed me expensive chocolates from an enormous box tied in gold ribbon!'

Connie had grinned at her and asked, 'And what are you going to do for him in exchange for all these luxuries?'

'Absolutely nothing! What sort of a girl do you think I am?'

'No man will do all that for nothing and well you know it.' She looked dreamily into the distance. 'I could never let an *old* man take care of me. I want someone young and handsome

5

who will adore me and take me to all my singing engagements and tell me how beautiful and wonderful I am.'

'That's not a man!' retorted Molly. 'That's a lapdog.'

As she approached the cinema, Connie caught sight of her friend standing in the queue for the upper circle. The film showing was *Caesar and Cleopatra*, starring Vivien Leigh and Claude Rains. A popular choice, looking at the length of the queue.

'You're late!' accused Molly as Connie joined her.

'Sorry, Mum made me wash and dry the dishes before I came out.'

'Well, you only just made it,' Molly grumbled as the queue began to move.

They settled in their seats and watched the trailers for the forthcoming week and the Pathé news showing the civil war breaking out in China under the Communist leader, Mao Tse-tung, followed by the plight of the Jewish refugees from Europe to Palestine, stranded in the port of Haifa. Finally, the credits rolled and they sat back to enjoy the big film.

During the interval, they discussed the film over the tubs of ice cream they had bought from the girl who came round with her tray slung round her neck with straps.

'That Stewart Granger,' Molly sighed. 'What a gorgeous-looking man.'

'I would have thought Caesar would have been more your type,' quipped Connie, 'knowing you want a sugar daddy to take care of you.'

Her friend looked at her and, licking the ice cream from the small wooden spoon, said, 'Are you crazy? With a man like Mark Anthony around!'

Whilst the house lights were on, Connie gazed around at the people in the front circle, the most expensive seats in the cinema. She spotted the figure of Les Baxter, the local bookie. Beside him sat a young woman. Connie wondered if it was his daughter, but as the lights began to dim, she saw him put an arm around the girl's shoulders. She is definitely an old man's darling, she thought, and then looked back at the screen as the second half began.

The following Saturday, Connie went with her parents to the Workman's Social Club. Doreen was going dancing with her friends but Connie declined the invitation to join them, thinking that it might pay dividends to be seen at the club – maybe they would ask her to appear again.

To her great disappointment nothing was said, but she was surprised when Les Baxter came into the club and, after ordering his drink, came over to the table.

'Good evening, George. How's your luck?'

George Ryan laughed. 'You should know, you've taken all my money these last two weeks.'

Les nodded to Freda, then, turning to Connie, said, 'I heard you sing the other week. You have a very good voice, you should do something about it.' With that, he walked back to the bar.

Connie looked at her father. 'What on earth does he mean?'

George shrugged. 'Beats me.'

George and Freda went to play darts with another married couple and Connie, seeing Les sitting alone at the bar, rose from her seat and walked over to him.

'What did you mean just now?'

He smiled benignly at her. 'You have no idea just how lucky you are, young lady. You're young, good-looking and the Lord has seen fit to give you a voice. You could really go places, you know.'

Connie sat on the bar stool beside him. 'I know,' she said, 'and I intend to get to the top one day.'

He burst out laughing. 'At least you have ambition and you're not backwards in coming forwards, I'll say that for you.'

'You know, Mr Baxter, you are the first person to take my singing seriously.'

'Is that so?'

'Yes. My family treat it all as a bit of a joke. They say I'm

7

full of dreams, but I have never been more serious in my life.'

The determination in her voice and the steely look in her eye as she spoke sparked an interest in the bookie. He thought for a moment and said, 'Give me a little while. I have a friend in show business; I'll have a word with him. I'll get back to you, Connie.'

She felt her heart pounding with excitement. 'Thank you, Mr Baxter. Thank you very much for taking an interest in me.' She got off the stool and walked back to the table. He knew somebody in show business! Why that should surprise her she didn't know. She had never spoken to Les Baxter before, but everyone knew about him. He was worth a bomb. He had bookie's runners all over Southampton taking bets for him, and during the war it was rumoured that he was big in the black market and had made a killing financially. And now he was taking an interest in her! She frowned. She wouldn't say anything to her family, they were sure to pour cold water on it, and it may come to nothing after all. But . . . on the other hand, who knows?

She looked over towards the bar and saw that Baxter was watching her. She smiled at him. He raised his glass to her and smiled back.

Chapter Two

At Sands' hat shop on Monday, both Connie and Molly were kept busy most of the morning, unpacking and displaying new stock, so there was no time to talk. Connie was bursting to tell her friend about Les Baxter, and could hardly contain herself. Eventually there was time for a break and a cup of coffee.

'What's on your mind?' asked Molly immediately they were alone.

'Whatever do you mean?'

'You've been jumping around this morning as if your tail was on fire, bursting to tell me something. I know you.'

'You'll never guess what happened at the Social Club last Saturday evening.'

'But you're going to tell me, I can feel it in my water.'

'Les Baxter told me I had a good voice and he's going to talk to a friend he has in show business.'

'About what?'

'Well, about me, of course.'

'What about you?'

Connie could feel resentment rising at her friend's lack of excitement. 'About my singing.'

Molly just looked at her. 'And?'

'What on earth's the matter with you?' Connie's temper rose. 'Les Baxter is interested in me, he thinks I've got a great voice and he's going to talk to someone he knows in show business!' She waited for some reaction, but Molly just looked puzzled.

9

'So what?'

It was as if someone had just burst her balloon, Connie felt so deflated. She glared at her friend. 'I thought *you* of all people would understand. Seems I was wrong.' She turned away and drank her coffee.

Molly, outspoken as always, said, 'If Les Baxter was interested in *me*, I'd be dead worried.'

Anger and disappointment made Connie spiteful. 'Why would he be interested in you – ever?'

The hurt expression on her friend's face made Connie feel guilty at her outburst but before she could apologise, Molly walked out of the staff room in a huff.

'Bugger!' Connie muttered angrily. Molly was the only one she could tell about the bookie, and now she'd upset her.

For the rest of the day Molly deliberately kept out of Connie's way, which only infuriated her even more, but as they both left the shop at the end of the day, Connie caught hold of her arm. 'Look, I'm sorry for what I said, but I was so excited and you couldn't care less.'

The disappointment in her voice touched Molly's kind heart. 'I'm sorry, but you know that anything that bookie is involved with is bound to be dodgy, that's all.'

'He's the only person apart from you who has taken my singing seriously,' said Connie, 'and that meant so much to me. Don't you see?'

'What else did he say?' Molly asked.

'Only that he would get back to me.'

'Just don't get your hopes up, Con. I wouldn't want you to be let down by expecting too much.'

As Connie walked home, she thought about her friend's advice. Maybe she was being foolish, pinning her hopes on what had been a very short conversation that hadn't really promised her anything. However, she knew that Les Baxter was a man with irons in lots of fires; if anyone could help her it would be someone like him. What did she care about his reputation? She wanted success and if he could get it for her what was she expected to say? 'Sorry, but you are a villain and I can't have anything to do with you.' Like hell she would!

But as the days passed and she heard nothing, Connie was so disappointed that she became short tempered, which was not acceptable to her mother at all.

'Don't use that tone of voice with me, Connie!' Freda snapped at her daughter as she was preparing a meal one evening. 'I don't know what's got into you lately, but don't bring your moods back to this house.'

Connie tried to explain. 'I'm really fed up, that's all. It's just that I want so much more from life than just working in a hat shop. I'm not like my friends, Mum. I want to be someone, not just get married and have a couple of kids, look after the home and wait hand and foot on some man. I want a man to wait on me.'

Freda's face flushed with indignation. 'I never felt I had missed anything by marrying your father and having you girls It's not easy being a wife and mother, trying to prepare meals when everything is so short, yet you brush it aside as if I'm nothing.'

'I didn't mean it like that. You're happy in what you do. I have more ambition, that's all.'

'All you want is to be the centre of attention! So, you can sing a bit. Don't imagine that will take you to the great heights you so desire, and anyway,' she added, 'being famous isn't all it's cracked up to be.'

Connie pushed back her chair. 'How would you know, Mother? What famous person are you familiar with? Tell me that!' Rising from the table, she walked out of the front door, slamming it behind her.

Freda put down the knife she was using to peel the potatoes, and let out a deep sigh. What was she going to do about Connie? she wondered. Her dreams were so ridiculous. Yes, she sang well, but to go from a working-class home to where she wanted to be was just a pipe dream. When would she

11

realise it? Shaking her head, she continued with her chores.

Les Baxter had, in fact, entirely forgotten his meeting with Connie. Later that month, he was in a London afternoon club doing a spot of business when across the bar he saw an old acquaintance of his who was a theatrical agent whom he knew through their shared love of horse racing, and it reminded him of his conversation with the kid in the Social Club back in Southampton. He walked over to the man.

'Jeremy, you old bastard, how the devil are you? I haven't seen you since that day at Ascot.'

'When I lost my money and almost the shirt off my bloody back, as I recall, whilst you coined it!' The agent grinned at him. 'That being so, you can at least buy me a drink.'

Les chuckled. 'Can't beat a bit of inside information. What's your poison – still brandy?'

'Yes, and make it a large one.'

The two men sat at a small table talking about horses, Jeremy Taylor being an inveterate gambler, and not without knowledge of the best bloodlines – learned from books and several owners he'd met through his theatrical connections.

They moved on to a small restaurant where their conversation turned to the various artists who were on Jeremy's books. He'd been in the business for several years, taking over the agency when his father had retired. He was now, like Les, in his late thirties, but better educated, sophisticated and although married, quite a man about town. It was part of the business to be seen at the right place at the right time and with the right people, but most important, he had a nose for talent.

As they finished their meal and ordered coffee and liqueurs, Les said, 'I need to pick your brains, Jeremy.'

His friend raised an eyebrow. 'Really? That sounds interesting. Fire away.'

'A few weeks ago I heard a girl sing in a club and she had an amazing voice. She wasn't professional, just an amateur, but she had something. What would you advise a girl like this to do to get on?'

Jeremy laughed at his friend. 'Good-looking, was she?' As Les nodded he added, 'So why don't you just take her to bed? You don't have to try and make a bloody star out of her first!'

'Don't be ridiculous, the kid's only eighteen!' He thought for a moment and said, 'There was something about her that held the audience. I sat and watched them. She had something – apart from a voice . . . and she's ambitious.'

Realising his friend was serious, the agent's attitude changed. 'If she really has a good voice she should have lessons. Without proper training, she could ruin it for the future. Is she a looker? Does she have a good figure?'

'Yes, she could be made into a real glamour girl with the right clothes, right hairdo. She has all the basic equipment to start with.'

'Take her to a singing teacher and get a professional opinion. It will save a lot of time. They'll soon tell you if the girl has *real* talent.' He took his card from an inner pocket of his jacket, wrote a name, address and telephone number on it and said, 'Take her here to Irene Vicario. She'll tell you after an hour. It will be money well spent.' Looking at his watch he said, 'I must be off. Give me a call when you're next in town, other than that I'll see you at the races sometime.'

Les glanced at the name on the card, remembering the fire in Connie's eyes when she spoke of her hopes of success. She did have something and it wouldn't hurt to do the kid a favour, and if she did have talent, then he could be on to a good thing. He'd seen the money to be made in show business. If the girl really was good, he could manage her, make sure she got the best deals, appeared at the right places. But first things first. He would have a word with George Ryan; see if he was agreeable to giving his daughter a chance.

On the following Saturday morning, George was as usual drinking in his local, studying the form for the day's racing, when to his surprise Les Baxter came and sat beside him. Looking up from his paper he asked, 'What are you trying to do, put the mockers on me for today?'

Les chuckled quietly. 'With the horses you fancy, my friend, you can do all that by yourself. I wanted to talk to you about your daughter, Connie.'

George was puzzled. 'Connie? What about Connie?'

'I'm sure you'll agree, George, she really does have a good voice. It seems a pity not to do something about it. I think the kid has talent, don't you?'

George was extremely proud of Connie and her voice and loved it when she sang at his club – it was a real thrill for him – but he had never thought about it beyond these narrow boundaries. He frowned and said, 'She's just a child, Les. Yes, she likes to sing and does it well, but—'

'I met a theatrical agent pal of mine in London the other day and had a word with him. His advice was to take Connie to a singing teacher to find out if she really does have talent. He gave me an address of a woman in London.'

This was all going far too fast for George. 'That's really nice of you, Les, to take an interest, but Connie is just eighteen, still growing up. Singing in the club is one thing, but professionally – well that's another. She's much too young for that, but thanks for taking the trouble.' And he returned to studying the paper.

Much to his surprise, Les Baxter was disappointed. He'd been thinking about this over the past two days, and planning in his own mind a campaign for young Connie, if the teacher agreed that she was talented. Now her father had dismissed the idea without a second thought. It seemed a shame. He bet if Connie knew, she'd be furious.

Les didn't enjoy having his plans thwarted and decided to take things a step further. He couldn't go against the wishes of a father, but he could do a little pushing – from another quarter, but that would have to wait. Business came first.

That Saturday he would be as busy as he was every race day.

14

He had a turf accountant's office where it was legal to accept bets over the telephone; he also had bookie's runners all over Southampton, who earned ten per cent of their takings. There were several meeting places overseen by trusted men in Les's organisation where the runners used to bring their bets in clock bags made of leather. When each bag closed, after the last bets were taken, it would set the clock, confirming the bets – written on scraps of paper with a *nom de plume* – had been made before the racing started.

Tonight, Les himself was working under a tarpaulin in the back yard of a local shop, where the owner had been slipped a few quid for his trouble. Bookies would arrive on foot, by bicycle and sometimes by taxi. It was a very lucrative business. There was no income tax, no betting duty. The only monies to be paid out, apart from the runners' ten per cent, was for bribes to the police to keep them off your back or to warn about a forthcoming raid.

Bookie's runners would automatically serve a prison term if they had a third offence, therefore if a raid *was* in the offing, the runners would quickly be changed. You had to be tough to stay in business, and able to protect yourself from predators. Les Baxter was well organised. He had his small band of heavies who dealt with those who occasionally got greedy. He was not a man to be crossed.

It was the following midweek before the bookie put his plan into action. He took his old mother into Sands' hat shop, much to her delight. Although in her sixties she liked to look smart. He smiled to himself as Connie came rushing over to serve him.

'Good morning, Mr Baxter. Can I help you?'

'This is my mother, Connie. Help her to find a hat, there's a good girl.'

Connie fussed over the old girl and Les watched her. There was no doubt about it; she did possess a natural charm. Her smile was radiant as she found a hat that his mother liked. The girl carried herself well, all she needed was a decent hairdo and some good clothes and she would be like Cinderella, waiting to go to the ball. If only her voice was as good as he hoped.

His mother called him over to get his opinion on her choice of hat. A smooth chocolate-brown velour, trimmed with colourful pheasant feathers. It was plain but smart. 'You look like a queen, Ma,' he said.

As he walked over to the counter with Connie to settle the bill he said casually, 'I didn't forget our conversation, you know. I did have a word with my friend in show business.'

Her eyes widened and shone with excitement.

'I told your father about it. I also have an address of a singing teacher for you to visit to find out if you really do have talent. Shame he won't let you go.'

'What?'

'Your dad, he thinks you're too young.' He put his wallet away. 'Pity really, now we'll never know if you are good enough, will we?' He smiled at her, put an arm round his mother and walked out of the shop, chuckling softly to himself. He wouldn't like to be in George's shoes tonight. That youngster really had a temper on her. He could see that by the thunderous expression on her face when he told her of the missed chance of a lifetime. He would even bet money that Connie would have a go tonight when she got home. All he had to do was wait.

Connie could not wait for the shop to close that day. She was so angry that her father had turned down Les Baxter's offer without consulting her, that she was hard pressed to be polite to her customers, and when it was time to go home, she could hardly wait to face him.

George Ryan was completely taken aback when he opened the front door of his house and was confronted by his daughter, ranting at him for spoiling her life.

'What on earth are you talking about?'

'Les Baxter brought his mother into the shop today. He told

me that he had an address of a singing teacher in London who could tell if I was good enough to be a professional . . . and you turned him down!'

As he took off his coat he said, 'Yes, that's right, I did.'

'How dare you!' Connie's face was puce with outrage. 'You didn't ask me what *I* wanted.'

'Connie, you are only eighteen.'

'What the hell has that got to do with it?'

'Now don't you speak to me like that.'

Freda by now had emerged from the kitchen and was listening to the heated exchange. 'What the devil is going on?' she asked.

Turning to her mother, Connie said, 'I've had the offer of a lifetime. Les Baxter wants to take me to London to see a singing teacher.'

'Whatever for?'

'To find out if I have a voice good enough to become a professional. He,' she nodded her head in George's direction, 'turned him down . . . without asking me what I wanted.'

At that moment Doreen arrived home. Seeing the look on Connie's face and sensing the atmosphere she asked, 'What's the matter?'

Freda told her.

Turning to her father, Doreen asked, 'Is that right? You turned Baxter's offer down, just like that?'

'Of course I did. Connie is still a child, much too young to even contemplate turning professional, even if she *had* the talent,' he said dismissively.

Connie looked at her sister, tears brimming in her eyes. 'You see, Dor, he doesn't think I can sing, not really.' She turned angrily to her father. 'You think I can sing well enough for your mates at the club though, don't you? I've seen you preening yourself when all the blokes say how good I am. I'm all right for that! Good enough to boost your ego, and for you to accept the free pints they offer you, because I was a good turn and you are my father.'

17

George looked nonplussed because of course she had spoken the truth. He did bask in her reflected glory, but when faced with the bare facts, he didn't like the picture of himself that Connie had painted.

Doreen, calm and fair-minded as ever, said, 'I don't see what harm it could do to let her find out if she really does have talent.' She looked hard at her father. 'You at least owe her that much!'

Connie was speechless at the unexpected support from her sister, and held her breath.

Outnumbered now, George turned to his wife for help. 'What do you think, love?'

Whilst all the shouting and arguing had been going on, Freda had been thinking. It would be best for Connie, in her opinion, to find out now that her dreams would never come to fruition. Then perhaps they would all have a more peaceful life.

'I think you should let her go,' she said firmly.

Chapter Three

Two weeks later, Connie was sitting in a train heading for Waterloo with Les Baxter. She was so excited she was twisting the gloves in her hand.

'For goodness' sake, Connie,' said the bookie, 'settle down or you won't be able to sing a note, you'll be too excited.'

'I know! I just can't believe I'm sitting here with you, going to see this woman.' She gazed at him with soulful eyes. 'What if she says I'm no good?'

Her innocence and vulnerability touched Les and he said, 'Do *you* think you're any good?'

There was a sudden determination about her mouth. 'Yes, I do. I *am* going to be a star one day, I just know it!'

'Then you keep that faith in yourself, because if you don't, you can't expect anyone else to believe it either.'

When they arrived at the station Les took her to the taxi rank and gave an address to the driver for somewhere in Maida Vale.

When the cab stopped, Connie got out of the vehicle and, as Les was paying the driver, she read the brass plate beside the front door: *Madame Irene Vicario*. There was nothing else. Nothing that gave any hint of her professional status. She felt a comforting hand on her arm as Les led her up the three steps to the front door.

'Take a deep breath,' he said as he rang the bell.

The teacher opened the door herself. 'Mr Baxter?'

'Madame Vicario?'

'Yes, you'd better come inside,' she said.

They entered a hallway which was covered with an elegant but worn rug. The walls were hung with framed pictures of Paris. Connie recognised the Eiffel Tower and the Champs-Elysées. There were also scenes of Parisian café society.

Irene invited them into a large drawing room, which was so full of furniture that to Connie it seemed like a furniture shop. There were touches of style and splashes of colours, the like of which she had never seen before.

Over a large leather sofa was a colourful shawl with fringes which were knotted. On a table behind the sofa, a vase of flowers, a pile of musical scores and a feather boa. The tall mantelpiece was filled with trinkets, figurines, small oval brass-framed photographs. Two easy chairs, covered in chintz, housed a tabby cat and newspapers. Yet there was such an air of comfort and warmth in the busy room that Connie felt she could stay there for ever.

Irene, seeing her interest, said, 'You like the room?'

'I've never seen one like it. It's fascinating.'

'It houses all my treasures. Sit down, we need to talk.'

Les sat in an armchair beside the fire, Connie in another and Madame Vicario on a high-backed chair beside a round table.

'I believe you have had no professional training, is that right?'

'Yes,' said Connie. 'I was in the school choir and I some-times sing in my dad's Social Club.'

'Do you read music?'

'No, I'm afraid I don't. Does that make a difference?'

Madame shrugged. 'It depends if you have a good ear. When I have made some tea for Mr Baxter, we will find out.' She got to her feet. 'Excuse me a moment, the kettle should be boiled by now.'

When they were alone, Connie said to Les, 'I don't know very much at all, do I?'

'Just be patient,' he said.

Madame returned with a tray of tea and two biscuits on a plate, telling Les to help himself, and beckoned Connie to follow her. 'We'll go into the music room,' she said.

This room was stark by comparison. It was not a large room and contained only a piano and stool, a tall table with a large aspidistra plant in one corner and a chair.

'This room is for work. Here we need no distractions,' said Irene. She stood in front of Connie and said, 'Now let's do some breathing exercises to open the lungs.' She placed one hand over Connie's abdomen and the other at her back. 'Do as I do,' she said, and took a deep breath, letting it out slowly.

Connie copied her.

'Breathe in . . . and now out.'

After a few minutes the woman sat at the piano. She ran her fingers over the keys and said, 'I am going to play a note. Listen carefully and then sing, haaa, like a laugh. Like this,' and she demonstrated what she meant.

Connie concentrated hard, listening to the resonance of the note, opened her mouth and sang, 'Haaa.'

'And another.'

This was repeated, several times, the notes creeping higher and higher until Irene said, 'This is called a scale. Now listen, then sing these notes one after another.'

Connie did as she was asked, relaxing as she did so.

The teacher moved up a semitone. 'Now sing, "Mmmmm".' Again she went up the scale, with Connie following with her voice. Eventually Madame Vicario said, 'Now take a break. Who is your favourite singer?'

'Anne Shelton,' replied Connie without hesitation.

'You know her signature tune, "Lili Marlene"?'

'Yes, Madame. I do.'

The teacher sorted through some sheet music on top of the piano and showed Connie the cover. It had Anne Shelton's picture on the front. 'Then sing it for me. Wait, I'll play the introduction.' Her fingers covered the keys with consummate ease, and she nodded to Connie when she wanted her to come in.

This was one of Connie's favourite songs and she forgot where she was and thought of the lyrics as she sang. Her voice was clear and filled with the poignancy of the words. When she had finished she looked hopefully towards the teacher who just picked up another sheet of music and asked, 'Do you know, "I'll Be Seeing You"?'

'Yes, although I'm not too sure of all the words.'

'Then stand behind me and read them over my shoulder.'

This she did and followed this with, 'Long Ago and Far Away'.

At the end of the song Madame Vicario told her to sit down. She looked at Connie and asked, 'Why have you come to me?'

'To find out if you think I have real talent.'

'Why is this important to you?'

Connie looked at the woman with her frilly blouse and long skirt, hair piled on top of her head, with a few wispy bits escaping down her neck, and realised for the first time what a good-looking woman she must have been in her youth. 'Because I want to be a star! I want success so badly it is almost too painful to bear.'

With an enigmatic smile the teacher said, 'Success doesn't always bring happiness, my dear. It can change your life so completely and in the end sometimes it takes control. It can devour you . . . eat you up.'

'How do you know this? Were you once famous?'

Irene Vicario nodded. 'My mother was French; I was born in Paris, my father was Italian. Both were singers and I became one too. I sang opera. I performed in La Scala in Milan, Covent Garden in London. I was very good,' she said without embarrassment.

'Did you ever marry?'

The smile faded and a small frown creased her brow. 'No. I loved a man once but I put my career first.' She paused. 'I shall regret it for the rest of my life!' She stared hard at Connie. 'Are you really certain a singing career is what you want?'

'More than anything in the world!'

'I am so sorry to hear you say that, but I can understand your need.' She rose from the piano stool. 'Let's go back to Mr Baxter.'

Connie, heart racing, followed her into the drawing room.

'Sit down,' she was told.

'Well, Mr Baxter,' Irene said slowly, 'this girl does have a good voice, but she needs to learn a great deal. She must learn how to breathe, how to phrase her words, how to use her voice, how to take care of it. But yes, she does have talent.'

Les grinned broadly. 'I knew it. I just knew it.' He beamed across at Connie who was sitting with a stunned expression. 'How do we go about this?' he asked.

'She must have lessons, of course. If she was to start singing now professionally, without guidance, she could ruin her voice, eventually.'

'How often should she have these lessons?'

Irene shrugged. 'It depends what you hope to achieve and how soon.'

'As soon as possible,' said Connie eagerly.

'My dear child, it takes years of training to be a true singer, four years at the very least.'

Connie felt her stomach plummet. 'Four years!'

Les quietly asked, 'Is there no other way?'

Irene shrugged. 'A crash course of six months, lessons twice a week, and then she could start, but the lessons would have to continue after, maybe once a week.'

Sitting listening to all this, Connie's excitement evaporated. What on earth was she thinking of? There was no way her parents could afford to pay for lessons, and so many. She was destined to sing occasionally at her father's club. There was to be no stardom for her. How ironic the situation was! Told by a professional that she did have talent, but without the wherewithal to make it happen. She was overcome with despair.

'I see,' said Les. 'But after six months, it would be all right for her to work?'

'If you could find work for her! It is always difficult with an unknown.'

'But in your opinion, Madame Vicario – and I want a straight answer – has Connie got what it takes, with help from you, to make it to the top?'

Irene glanced at the young girl and seeing the hunger and longing in her eyes, said, 'Oh, yes, Mr Baxter. She could go far with the right training, and the right contacts.'

The bookie rose from his seat, held out his hand and said, 'I can't thank you enough for your time. I'll be in touch.' He took out his wallet and handed over some notes. 'That's right, I think?'

The woman nodded. 'Thank you.'

Turning to Connie, Les said, 'Come along then. We have a train to catch.'

Connie stood up reluctantly. She didn't want to leave this house because she felt once she stepped through the door into the outside world, all her dreams would be left behind.

Irene took both Connie's hands in hers and said quietly, 'If you come back here to work with me, make very sure it is *really* what you want to do. If you turn professional, it will change your life. Think carefully before you take such a step.'

'Thank you, Madame,' said Connie. 'I did enjoy meeting you.'

'And I you, my child.'

Outside the house, Les hailed a passing taxi and they drove to the station in silence – Connie through deep sadness at a lost opportunity, and Les, whose mind was racing, calculating, scheming . . . planning.

When they arrived at Waterloo, he took Connie straight to

the buffet car and sat at a table. 'I'm starving, aren't you?' he asked.

'No, I couldn't eat a thing!'

Hearing the despondent note in her voice, he said, 'Why so gloomy? I thought you'd be over the moon, being told you have the talent to make your dream come true. Why the long face?'

With tears of frustration brimming she snapped, 'Because it's impossible! Dad couldn't afford to pay for lessons even if he believed in me, which he doesn't. I'm only good enough to please his mates. He doesn't look beyond that. I don't think he's ever had a dream in his entire life!'

Les started to laugh. 'That is the most apt description of your father I have ever heard.'

Consumed suddenly with guilt, Connie added, 'I still love him, of course. He's a decent man.'

'Of course he is. But don't you worry, today isn't a waste of time, I promise.'

She looked at him and asked, 'What do you mean? Of course it was, well in some ways anyway.'

'Connie! Listen to me. I thought you had something the moment I heard you sing.' He saw he had her attention and continued, 'I believe in you and I intend to see you realise your dream.'

'You do? How?'

'I am prepared to foot the bill for your training, cover your expenses and eventually make the right contacts for you to start your career as a professional.'

Connie looked at him and asked, 'Why would you do this? I'm nothing to you. What would you be getting out of it, Mr Baxter? What's in it for you?'

'For one so young, my dear, you are a bright girl, and you're right. This would be a business deal. I'll be your agent and manager.'

She gave him a calculating look. 'Which means what, exactly?'

'It means I will recover my expenses when you start to work and I'll take a percentage of all your earnings.'

'And that's all?' she asked, suspiciously.

He smothered a grin. 'I promise, that's all. Connie, you are a child as far as I'm concerned. I have all the women I need, real women. I'm not into baby snatching, if that's your worry.'

Somehow instead of being relieved, she was irritated. 'I am a real woman!'

'No, Connie, you aren't – take my word for it. You are a young girl with a burning ambition and with the ability to reach the top, but you have a lot to learn before you become a singer, and even more to learn before you are a real woman. Now I'm going to order. Have you got your appetite back?'

She grinned at him and said, 'Oh, yes. I could eat a horse now.'

'I think we can do better than that,' he said and called the waiter over.

As they ate, he said, 'Your father is going to be a problem, nevertheless. You are right, he has never looked beyond the Social Club as far as your abilities go, but I'll just have to talk him round.'

'He can be very stubborn, Mr Baxter.'

'So can I, Connie. Especially where business is concerned. You leave him to me.'

'What shall I say when he asks how today went?'

Les pondered this for a while. 'Just tell him the woman said you do have a good voice, nothing more. Nothing about lessons. Leave all that to me. Now I think we should have a glass of champagne to celebrate. Waiter, bring me your wine list!'

Chapter Four

It was almost seven o'clock when Les dropped Connie off at her home. He leaned out of the taxi window and said, 'Remember, don't tell them any more than we agreed.' And then he told the driver to move off.

With pounding heart, Connie opened the front door – waiting for the questions to begin. Her father was sitting reading the paper, listening to the wireless, her mother was doing the ironing but of Doreen, there was no sign.

'Hello, love,' said George as he turned the page. 'Have a good time?' he asked absently, his eyes still on the paper.

Freda glanced up and saw the look of abject disappointment on her daughter's face. 'How did you get on?' she asked. 'What did the teacher have to say about you?'

Taking off her coat, Connie said, 'She says I have a good voice. Good enough to be a professional.'

'That's nice,' muttered George, not really listening.

'She said I would be dead in six months!'

'Lovely,' said her father.

'George!' Freda remonstrated.

'What?' He looked up from the paper.

Connie blazed at him. 'A lot you care about me! I have been to London this afternoon and sung in front of a highly trained ex-opera singer who told me I was good enough to turn professional, and you couldn't give a tinker's curse! This is my life we're talking about here and all you are interested in are the runners at tomorrow's race meetings. Well, Dad, one day

27

you'll be sorry. Very, very, sorry!' She turned on her heel and ran up the stairs.

'George Ryan, you are such a fool at times!' said Freda angrily. 'You know how Connie feels about her singing, how much she wants to be a star.'

'All right, so I wasn't really listening. But let's face it, Freda; this is not going to go any further, is it? I mean, how can it? I don't know how you turn professional, but it's bound to cost money and we can't afford it – so what's all the fuss about? It was your idea anyway to let her go.'

'So, it's my fault!' She glared at him. 'Well, to be honest I didn't think she'd be told that. I thought she'd come home with her tail between her legs and we'd hear no more, so she must have something after all. You could have shown *some* enthusiasm. Congratulated her at least.' She put down the iron, unplugged it and went upstairs. She stopped outside the room Connie shared with her sister and knocked. There was no answer. She tried the handle but the door was locked. 'Connie, love, let me in.' But there was no response.

Connie didn't appear at suppertime. Her parents ate without conversation. The atmosphere between them was still tense and uncomfortable when Doreen came home from the cinema. She looked from one to the other and asked, 'Whatever is the matter?'

Freda, still fuming, said, 'Your sister has been told she is good enough to be a professional and your father hardly listened. Connie's been in her room for the last three hours.'

Doreen removed her coat, glowered at her father and walked slowly up the stairs. She tried the handle of the door, but it wouldn't give. 'Connie,' she called softly, 'please let me in. I want to hear what happened in London.'

Eventually she heard the key turn in the lock. Her sister's eyes were red with weeping. Doreen sat on the bed beside her and put her arm around her. 'What's wrong, Con?'

'I can be a star, Dor, if I want to be. You think that Dad

would be thrilled for me, wouldn't you? He's not bloody well interested. Don't you think that's criminal?'

'Never mind him. Wipe your eyes and give me a blow-by-blow description of what happened.' She hugged Connie. 'After all, it's not every day your sister is told she has talent!'

Slowly Connie began to describe her day and her visit to Madame Vicario. 'You should have seen her house, our Doreen. It was wonderful.'

'Tell me about it after. What did you have to do?'

Doreen was taken through every exercise, every note and given a demonstration of how Connie had to sing the scales. Then Connie told her that Irene had said with a six-month crash course of lessons she would be ready to sing as a professional. 'I'll have to continue with my lessons, of course.'

Doreen looked at her and asked, 'Where do you think the money is coming from for all this?'

'Les Baxter!' She put her hand over her mouth after she spoke. 'Oh dear, I'm not supposed to tell anyone that until he's spoken to Dad.'

Doreen looked perplexed. 'Well, I think you had better tell *me* everything. Why would he do such a thing? This is obviously going to cost a lot of money. Now I know he's got plenty but *why* is he doing this?'

'Because he's going to be my manager.'

Doreen looked sceptical. 'And what does he want in return?'

'Nothing, honest. I asked the same question – he said it was strictly business.'

'And you believe him!'

Connie met her gaze and said, 'Yes, I do. Absolutely.'

'God knows what Dad will have to say about it.'

'I don't give a pig's ear what he thinks. I'm going to train with Madame Vicario and I *will* turn professional. No one will stop me, Doreen. No one!' She looked at her sister. 'You won't tell Dad what I told you about Les Baxter, will you?'

'No, of course not.' But Doreen decided that she would

29

have a word with the bookie herself. No one paid out such a lot of money for nothing. Connie was so blinded with ambition that she could easily find herself in a situation beyond her control. Well, that wouldn't happen if she could help it.

'Come on,' she said, 'go and bathe your eyes or you will look like hell tomorrow.'

By the time the girls came downstairs the following morning, George had already left for work. Freda cast a sideways glance at Connie but said nothing as she made some toast and tea for the girls. Doreen looked across the table at her mother and shook her head, trying to stop her saying anything more at this time, but she could foresee great problems ahead. There was going to be an almighty row when Les Baxter approached her father, because she knew that George would turn down his offer and her sister wouldn't accept that. Connie could now see a chance of bringing her dream to fruition and her father wasn't going to stand in her way.

At work, Molly came rushing over to Connie. 'How did it go yesterday?' she asked.

'Fine,' Connie answered, dying to tell her friend everything, but knowing what Molly's response would be: very much like her sister's. No one would believe that the bookie wouldn't want something in return over and above a business deal. Les was well known for his womanising. He was a free man after all, but his reputation didn't help her case.

'Madame Vicario said I had a good voice and the talent to go professional, if I wanted to.'

Molly looked a trifle downcast. 'That's great, of course, and you must be pleased, but you must also be really disappointed that you can't do anything about it.'

'What do you mean?'

'Well, Connie, it takes money, doesn't it? You know, money for clothes, for places to appear.' She put her arm around her. 'Never mind,' she said, 'at least you know you were good enough.'

Connie knew her friend was trying to be kind, but she was incensed that everyone dismissed the idea that she could go forward. That this was it! Nobody really understood that she was driven to succeed, that it was her destiny. She had been sure of this since she was ten years old. Why did no one understand? How little faith they had in her. Well, she was going to show them. Les had faith in her abilities and so far he was the only one . . . apart from Madame. She would cling to this whilst everyone else wittered on. There was no greater revenge than success. All she had to do was wait for Les to talk to her father.

The bookie sought out George Ryan on Saturday evening at his Social Club. He was sitting alone as Freda had gone to the pictures with a neighbour and the girls were off dancing. Taking his glass of whiskey over to the table, Les sat down. 'Hello, George. I was hoping I would find you here.'

'I suppose you expect me to stand you a drink seeing how I won a few quid yesterday,' said Ryan with a grin.

'Not at all. I wanted to talk to you about Connie.'

'Oh, yes. Thanks for taking her to London. How much do I owe you?'

'Nothing. It was my suggestion, I'll pay. She told you, I expect, that the music teacher thought she was talented?'

Glancing around the room, George said indifferently, 'Yes, she mentioned it.'

Les could have shaken him. 'Do you realise what this means?'

Now he had the man's full attention. 'I don't follow.'

'Connie can turn professional, she has the ability. Doesn't that make you a proud man?' asked Les, trying to drum up some kind of enthusiasm.

'I'm proud of both my girls, and I know our Connie can sing. Haven't I let her perform here?'

'But now she can do much better. She can aspire to great things.'

George's mouth tightened. 'Aspiration is one thing, fruition is another! I don't have the money to spend on her *aspirations*. Connie will have to accept her limitations – and mine!'

Les Baxter was getting very irritated with the small mind of Connie's father. 'Why should she? Just because you have a comfortable little niche in life and are happy to continue to stay there, why should Connie be kept back, when she could go far?'

George was angry. 'Don't you understand? I can't afford to do anything for her.'

'No, but I can.'

Connie's father gave the bookie a startled look. 'And what exactly do you mean by that?'

'I think that Connie has the potential to be a big star and the singing teacher agrees. It means lessons for six months before she can begin to appear before the public, but once she does . . . the sky's the limit. One day she'll have her name in lights. I know it!'

'And you are prepared to foot the bill for all of this?'

'Yes, I am.'

'Why? Because she's a good-looking girl? Is that it? You think you can buy my daughter with a few lessons. A few promises! You've got a bloody nerve!'

'You misunderstand me, George, this would be strictly business. I'll be her manager, nothing more.'

'Yeah, and pigs might fly. You must take me for some kind of fool.'

It was Les who was angry now, and he was not a man to be crossed. 'Now you listen to me, Ryan.'

The menace in his voice brought George's rantings to a stop. 'You are a small-minded man who will never amount to anything. To me, Connie is a young girl with talent, nothing more. Once in a lifetime this kind of thing comes along and I am willing to give her a chance. It is purely business. I'll make money and so will she, but most important of all, she'll be able to rise above her humble beginnings, to really make something of herself. Ask yourself this – are you being fair to her by denying her the right to use her God-given gift to better herself? You know how much she wants to get to the top.' He picked up his drink. 'You deny her this chance, she'll hate you for the rest of your life!'

The truth of what Les was saying was not lost on George Ryan, but the fact that he couldn't be the one to provide for his daughter when the opportunity was there dented his masculine ego. *He* couldn't, but the man sitting with him could. A man whose reputation was dodgy to say the least. A man who was respected and feared at the same time. A man who was telling him to his face how to provide for his family. It was just too much!

'Maybe you are doing this from a business point of view only, but to think you have the gall to sit here and tell me how to run my own family. Who the bloody hell do you think you are?'

Les Baxter looked straight at George and said, 'I'm the man who is going to make your daughter a star, whether you like it or not!' He got to his feet and, leaning over the table, he said softly, 'You have absolutely no idea just how driven your Connie is. She will do exactly as she wants to get to the top because she's got the guts to do it. If you try to stop her, you'll lose your daughter and that would be a pity.'

George sat mulling over the proposition that had been offered, but he was deeply offended by it. He had been a good provider for his family. He had never been out of work in his life. There had always been food on the table, clothes for the kids. All right there hadn't been holidays as such – a caravan for a few days at Highcliffe before the war when the children were small. During the war he'd worked in a munitions factory instead of going into the forces, due to his perforated eardrum, and after VE Day, he'd returned to his job at Oakley and Watling. Humble beginnings? What a bloody nerve! Working-class he might be, and proud of it, but his family had never had to do without. Never! He got up from the table and went to the bar for another pint. Sitting down once again, Les Baxter's words still hit a raw nerve. Well, maybe he hadn't quite appreciated just how good a voice his Connie had, but as for being a star, where would that get her in the end? She would think she was better than she was. No it was better all round if she stopped stuffing her head full of dreams. He was going to put his foot down about all this once and for all.

Freda was already in bed when the girls came home from the dance, but George was sitting by the fire, waiting for them.

'Hello, Dad,' said Doreen.

'Have a good time, did you?'

'Yes, we went to the Metronome for a change – it was Gil Hume and his band. Do you want some cocoa? I'm making some for Connie and me.'

'Yes, thanks.' He waited until they were sitting down at the table before he said, 'I saw Les Baxter tonight at the Social Club.'

The two girls exchanged looks.

He stared over at Connie. 'He was telling me how he was prepared to finance you to take singing lessons and become a professional.'

Connie visibly brightened. 'Yes, he is, isn't it wonderful?'

'Wonderful? How do you think I felt with another man telling me I'm unable to find the money for your lessons, but that he could, thank you very much?'

'It would be a business deal, Dad. Mr Baxter will be my manager. When I start earning, he'll deduct the money he invested, then he'll earn a percentage of my wages.'

'Yes, he said you would both be making money. Well, there would have to be *something* in it for him, wouldn't there? Are you sure, Connie, that's *all* he wants?'

Connie was furious. 'Of course! What sort of a girl do you think I am, Dad?'

'To be quite honest I'm really not sure. Did you know he was going to approach me about this?'

'Well, yes I did,' she reluctantly admitted. 'He asked me to wait and let him talk to you.'

'Embarrass me more like! Now you get this straight, my girl. No other man finances any member of my family ever. If I can't afford to pay, then it doesn't happen. Understand?'

Connie pushed her chair back and stood glaring at her father. 'I understand one thing and that is you are prepared to ruin the only chance I'm ever going to have to become a singer. Now *you* understand something . . . I *will* do it. I *will* accept Les Baxter's offer and you won't stop me!'

George rose from his chair. 'The hell you will.'

'Quite right, Dad. The hell *I will*!' And she rushed upstairs to her room.

Her father went to follow, but Doreen barred his way. 'Sit down, Dad, please. This won't get you anywhere.'

Sulkily he returned to his chair by the fire.

Doreen said calmly, 'If you don't let her do this, she'll never forgive you. Can you live with that?'

'I'm saving her a lot of unhappiness. I'm really looking after her interests.'

'No, you're not! You are nursing your wounded pride!'

He glared angrily at her. 'How dare you say that to me?'

'Because it's true.' Her voice softened. 'Listen to me, you are a good father, we have never gone without, but this is one thing you can't do for Connie. What you can do is give her the chance to find out if she can make it. You can't deny her that can you?'

He didn't answer.

Doreen picked up her handbag and walking over to George bent and kissed his forehead. 'Think seriously about this, Dad. If you make the wrong decision, the repercussions could be disastrous.'

Chapter Five

Connie was striding up and down her bedroom, rage such as she had never experienced before coursing through her. How dare her father deny her this chance? How could he sit there in his chair and pompously tell her that if *he* couldn't afford things, they wouldn't happen? Well he could say what the bloody hell he liked, but she *was* going to accept Les Baxter's offer and *nothing* her father could do would stop her. She sat on the edge of her bed and tried to calm down. It wasn't easy. Her heart was pounding, she felt as if she couldn't breathe. Remembering how she had to take deep breaths in the singing teacher's music room she stood up, placed her hand on her abdomen and breathed in, then slowly let her breath escape. She did this several times, and found to her great relief that she began to relax.

In a calmer frame of mind, she started to scheme. What would she do if her father stuck by his guns? She would have to leave home, but where would she live? She would have to rent a room somewhere, but if she was having two lessons a week, she would no longer be able to work full time. Would a part-time job be enough to keep her? She didn't think so. She pondered on this problem for a long time without finding a solution. Well, Les Baxter would have to sort it out! He was the one who caused this situation and, as he seemed so eager for her to continue, he would have to be responsible for her. Yes, that was the answer.

A small smile lifted the corners of her mouth. It didn't

occur to her for a moment that she would be using him. She was so blinded by her ambition that all she could think of was the six months she would have to train before she could sing in front of an audience, and a small thing like parental consent and her own lack of funds was not going to stop her.

When Doreen entered the room she expected to see Connie distraught and was more than surprised to see her sister sitting curled up on her bed, staring into space with a satisfied smile on her face.

'Well, you look pleased with yourself I must say, under the circumstances!'

'What circumstances?' Seeing the shocked expression on Doreen's face she added, 'Oh, you mean Dad.' She shrugged. 'Makes no difference to me, whatever he says. If he agrees to let me go, fine. If he doesn't, I'll just have to leave home, that's all.'

'Leave home?' Doreen was horrified. 'You can't do that!'

Connie flared up immediately. 'Now don't *you* start to tell me what I can and can't do.'

'But if you left home, where would you go?'

'I have no idea. Les Baxter will have to arrange something.'

'Les Baxter?'

'Yes. He's my manager so he'll have to manage me, won't he? That means taking care of my well being.'

'Are you completely out of your mind?'

The smile was replaced with a grim, determined look. 'I have never been more sane in all my life. I know exactly what I'm doing. I'm grabbing the only chance I'll probably ever get, with both hands.' She glared at her sister. 'Don't you try and stop me, our Doreen, because you'll be wasting your time.'

'But if you do leave home, you'll be completely at the mercy of Baxter. Is that wise?'

'How many times do I have to tell you that he isn't interested in me other than as an investment.' She saw the worried frown on her sibling's brow. 'Come on, Dor, you know I'd never be an old man's darling! Besides, I've got my career to think about, I haven't time for men, young or old.'

Doreen sank down on her bed. 'I don't know where all this will end,' she said. 'Whichever way Dad decides, it'll upset him.'

'There you go!' Connie exploded with anger. 'Nobody cares a damn about how *I* feel if Dad has his way! I think it's so unfair. I'm the one with the voice! I'm the one with the talent! Dad and Mum live in a narrow little world. Well, I want to spread my wings, I want to be a success—'

'It's all you, isn't it?' said Doreen quietly. 'To be honest I don't know which of you and Dad are the most selfish. You can only think of your name in lights and Dad is nursing his male ego. It's pathetic!'

But Connie was not to be deterred. 'And what about you, Doreen? Which side of the fence are you on?'

Her sister stood up and looking at Connie said, 'I'm not at all sure I want to be part of this at all. I can understand your burning ambition, but is it to be achieved at any price?'

Connie met her gaze. 'Frankly? Yes.'

'I see. All I can say to you then is I hope that success turns out to be all you expect, and more, I really do because I know how much you want it. But remember this, if it all falls down around your ears – *you* chose the life, *you* made the decision, and *you'll* just have to live with the consequences.' And she quietly left Connie and went into the bathroom.

Downstairs, George was fighting his own battle. He was having to accept that Connie's ability was indeed better than he'd ever envisaged. It must be, to be told by a professional that she had talent. In his own way he was proud of this, but the consequences of such a statement scared him. He had been secure in his world until now. He was working, his family was taken care of, he had his friends, and the biggest thrill in his life was when he got a winner on some racetrack or other. Was it so very wrong to be happy with so little? He was content with his world, or had been until Les Baxter intervened.

His jaw tightened as he thought of the bookie. It was not his policy to be beholden to anyone, but if he accepted Baxter's offer to finance Connie until she started earning, he would be beholden to a man like that, and that certainly stuck in his craw. Besides, he wasn't at all sure if he wanted his Connie mixed up with a man like Baxter. He was totally confused. He knew that Connie had always been going on about being a star but he thought it was just childlike and that she'd grow out of it. In truth he'd paid scant attention to her dreams and now he felt guilty about it. Had it been any other man but Baxter he might have given the offer some serious consideration, but as it wasn't someone else! He couldn't give his consent, he just couldn't. He told himself he was looking after Connie's welfare – protecting her. She wouldn't like it! He grimaced when he thought of how she'd take it when he told her his decision, but she'd get over it, given time.

Having at last solved his dilemma, he turned out the lights and went to bed.

In the morning, Connie rose early enough to catch her father before he left for work. Putting on her dressing gown she went downstairs to the kitchen. George was sitting at the table eating his scrambled egg on toast.

Connie didn't mince her words. 'Have you made a decision about my taking singing lessons?' she asked.

George looked up at her and said, 'Yes, I have. I'm sorry, Connie, but I can't let Les Baxter finance you this way. I'm sorry, love.'

'Fine,' said Connie and went back upstairs.

George Ryan let out a sigh of relief. Well, she took that much better than he thought she would, and now they could forget about it and get on with their lives. He sipped his tea and finished his breakfast.

On her way to work, Connie stopped at a telephone box, picked up the telephone directory and thumbed through it looking to see if Les was on the telephone. She knew he lived in the Polygon area. She ran her finger down the lines of Baxter until she found the Ls and saw an address in Newcombe Road. That was in the Polygon. Putting her pennies in the box, she dialled the number and waited, her heart pounding.

'Hello.'

With a sigh of relief as she recognised the voice, she pressed button A and heard the coins drop. 'Mr Baxter?'

'Yes, who's that?'

'It's Connie Ryan.'

'Connie, what can I do for you?'

'Could we possibly meet during my lunch hour, I need to talk to you.'

'Yes, I can manage that. What time?'

'One o'clock and could you meet me outside the shop?'

'Yes, Connie. I'll be there.' He replaced the receiver and thought, What now? He imagined there had been some altercation at home. It would be interesting to find out what had been going on.

Les was waiting as Connie left Sands' sharp at one. He ushered her over the road to a café where they could have some coffee and a sandwich

'What did you want to see me about?' he asked.

Connie sat upright and said, 'My father won't accept your offer, but I will. This means I will have to leave home and I don't think I can afford to do that, so what are you going to do about it?'

He was highly amused at her arrogance, but managed to keep a straight face. My God, this kid had guts and gall, he thought. Well, he liked that. Nothing was going to deter her from the path she had chosen. This would stand her in good stead for the future because he knew that show business was a tough business and this young Connie Ryan must be able to stand her corner.

'What do you think I should do?'

'The problem is, you see, if I need lessons twice a week, I

can only work part time, and that won't give me enough money to pay for a room and to live. As my manager, you could help me financially and take it out of my earnings in the future.'

'You do realise that it will take some time to pay me back, don't you?'

'Of course, but after all, we are talking about a long and eventually successful career, aren't we?'

He looked at her in amazement. 'Are you sure you are only eighteen?'

'Yes, of course! What a silly question.'

He shook his head. 'Eighteen going on forty I would say. All right, but what is your father going to say to all this – you leaving home, I mean?'

'I suppose some of it would depend on where I was to live.'

He thought about this for a moment. 'If you were to stay with my mother, do you think he would object to that?'

'Do you live there too?' she asked quickly.

Les burst out laughing. 'Good God, no! I have a house of my own. Mother lives alone in Wilton Avenue, she's a widow. Well, you met her in the shop, do you think you could get on with her?'

Connie beamed. 'Oh, yes. I thought she was a lovely old dear.' She paused. 'I thought of asking my boss if I could go part time, what do you think?'

'It's a good idea. As far as I can tell, you are good at your job and hopefully he would want to keep you on. Ask him and see what he says. Meantime I'll tell my mother she will have a lodger. I'll meet you again at lunchtime in two days' time. And Connie, keep all this under your hat for the time being. All right?'

'All right.'

'And another thing, don't get arsey with your father meantime. Act as normal, otherwise he'll catch on and may be even more difficult.'

'All right, Mr Baxter, and thanks.'

'Off you go then or you'll be late. I'm going to have another coffee.'

He sat there mildly bemused by his protégée. What a girl she was. My God, I'm glad she isn't my daughter, he thought. George Ryan would no doubt turn very awkward when Connie informed him she was leaving home. Well, he spent half his life dealing with awkward customers, so it wasn't too much of a problem. He would sort it when it happened. He rose from the chair, left some money on the table and went out into the street. He'd better go and see his mother.

Back in the hat shop, Molly looked at Connie and asked, 'What have you been up to?'

Looking startled for a moment, she said, 'Whatever do you mean?'

'I mean that you look like the cat who's had the cream. You've been scheming, I can tell.'

Walking towards a customer who had just entered the shop, Connie said airily, 'I don't know what you're talking about.'

But Molly knew her friend very well and was concerned, especially as Les Baxter seemed to be in the middle of things. He was a dangerous man, but Connie was blind to things that she didn't like, that didn't suit her plans. Well, she hoped her stubbornness wouldn't lead her into trouble.

Connie on the other hand was delighted with the way things were going. Surely her father couldn't object to her staying with Mrs Baxter. She was an old lady, smart, harmless, well liked *and* respected. She would have a chaperone. It wasn't as if she'd be in a room somewhere with strangers, so she felt that was one argument that wouldn't hold water. The rest? It didn't matter – apart from locking her in her room, what could stop her? Nevertheless, she didn't look forward to the inevitable confrontation with her parents.

Two days later Les and Connie met again. She was happy to

be able to tell him that her boss was going to let her work part time: four days a week instead of five and a half. 'On my days off, I'll be able to visit Madame Vicario for lessons.'

'Good. My mother says she would be glad of the company,' he told her, 'but you will have to look after yourself. Keep your room clean, do your own washing and cooking. After all, Ma is in her sixties, I won't have her waiting on you. You do understand that, don't you?'

'Of course.' She frowned. 'I don't know what my dad is going to say when I tell him.'

'You won't have to, I will.'

At her look of surprise he said, 'It will be better if I come to your house to collect you and let your parents know exactly what is happening. After all, we must keep them in the picture, show them that everything is above board.'

Connie was relieved. With Les there, she would have some moral support.

'I'll come round on Sunday afternoon, is your father usually home then?'

Connie nodded. 'We have our lunch at two o'clock, then Dad usually has a snooze in his chair while Mum reads the paper.'

'Very well, in the morning you pack your clothes. Have you got a suitcase?'

'No.'

'I'll buy one and bring it into the shop later today. Try not to let anyone see you take it into the house, or questions may be asked. All right?'

'Yes, fine.'

Les got to his feet, picked up the bill and said, 'Right, I'll be round at three o'clock on Sunday.'

As she walked back to her workplace, Connie suddenly realised the big step she was taking, and for a moment was panic-stricken. She had never defied her father over anything important before, and until this moment hadn't considered her mother at all. What would Freda say? How would she react?

But she took a deep breath and thought, This is my future here and I'm not going to jeopardise that for anyone. When she was a success, her family would realise she had made the right decision. All she had to do was prove herself.

Chapter Six

Connie had successfully sneaked her new suitcase into her room and pushed it under her bed. She had furtively started packing her things when Doreen was out of the house, leaving enough clothes hanging in the wardrobe they both shared to allay any suspicions on her sister's part, but as Sunday crept even nearer, she was overcome with nerves. Her father was going to have a fit and God knows what her mother and Doreen were going to say. Yet she couldn't help being excited too. She was about to embark on a new way of life – one that couldn't be more different, and despite all her fears about the confrontation that was now imminent, she couldn't wait to begin this exciting journey into the unknown.

Sunday morning dawned and Connie had barely slept a wink. Whilst Doreen was taking a bath, she hurriedly packed her remaining clothes, emptying the wardrobe, after seeing her sister had laid out the clothes she would be wearing that day. She only just managed to push the suitcase out of sight as Doreen opened the bathroom door and called to her father that the room was now vacant.

Connie heard him whistling as he shaved, a particular habit of his, and it struck her that she wouldn't be hearing it again after she had left the house with Les Baxter. The thought curbed her excitement for a moment, but she told herself that it wouldn't be for ever. Once she was a success, she could come back, then she paused. If she *was* a success then of course she

47

would be able to afford her own place, so she probably would never live with her parents again. And that did give her a strange empty feeling inside.

At lunchtime, they all sat down to their roast chicken, roast potatoes and a mixture of vegetables from George's allotment. And to follow, stewed rhubarb and custard. Connie forced herself to eat, but every mouthful was a battle.

'What's the matter with you, our Connie?' asked Freda. 'Something wrong with the meal?'

Her head shot up with surprise as she looked at her mother. 'No, it's lovely, why?'

'Well, usually you are the first to clear your plate, but look at you!'

And it was true, the others had long finished theirs but her dessert had hardly been touched. Putting down her spoon, Connie said, 'Sorry, Mum, but I'm just too full. I can't eat any more.'

Freda cleared the plates wearing a thunderous expression. She hated to see food wasted.

Connie glanced nervously at her watch. It was two thirty. Les Baxter should be arriving within the next half-hour. She took the rest of the dishes out to the kitchen and prepared to wash up. Freda looked at her with surprise.

'You sick or something?'

This comment brought a flush of guilt to her daughter's cheeks. 'No, I'll wash up, you go and sit down.'

The opportunity to hand over the washing up to Connie didn't present itself often so Freda didn't waste a moment in doing just that. She settled in a chair opposite George on the other side of the fireplace to read the papers, while Doreen dried the dishes that Connie washed.

'Have you turned over a new leaf?' asked Doreen. 'Only to get you to do this without asking is so unusual, I'll have to make a note of it in my diary!'

Connie didn't answer, but continued with her chores. This in itself was also unheard of, as she always was ready with a sharp retort at all times, and Doreen looked quizzically at her. 'Are you all right, Con?'

'Yes, I'm fine. Good God, you would think I never did anything to help!'

This was so near the truth that Doreen started to laugh, but she didn't say any more, as at that moment there was a knock on the door. Connie dropped a plate, which smashed on the stone floor of the kitchen.

'Shit!' she cursed and got a dustpan and brush out of the cupboard to pick up the pieces. Her hands started to shake as she heard the voice of Les Baxter.

George ushered the bookie into the living room. 'Would you like a drop of beer?' he asked.

'No, thanks, George. This isn't really a social call.'

George looked decidedly puzzled. Baxter had never before visited him at home and he couldn't think why on earth he was here now 'If this isn't a social call on a Sunday afternoon, then what is it?'

Doreen was standing in the kitchen doorway looking at the visitor, but Connie was gripping the edge of the kitchen sink so tightly that the knuckles of her hands were white, as she waited to hear what Les was going to say.

'I suppose in some ways it's a business call.'

'Business! What business? I don't owe you any money, I pay for my bets up front!'

Les gave a little smile. 'No, it's nothing to do with book-making, I've come to talk to you about Connie.'

George glared at him. 'Now look here,' he began, 'I've already told you I'm not interested in you financing my daughter and this fancy of hers.'

Les's tone changed. Quietly but firmly he said, 'I know what you said, but you see Connie wants me to, and as I told you not so very long ago, I'm going to make her a star.'

'Connie!' George's angry voice rang out.

Taking a deep breath, Connie wiped her hands on a tea towel and walked past Doreen who was looking askance at her, and said, 'Yes. I'm here.' She looked across at the bookie who winked at her, trying to give her courage for what was to follow.

Her father was blazing with anger. 'What's all this nonsense about you wanting to take up this man's offer?'

Very coolly, although inside she was all of a tremor, she said, 'Yes, that's right. Mr Baxter and I have come to an agreement.'

'An agreement! What sort of bloody agreement?'

'He is going to be my manager, he will finance my training and take care of my career. I'll be moving in with his mother, today.'

'You what!' Both George and Freda spoke simultaneously.

Turning to her mother, Connie said, 'I have already arranged to work part time at Sands', so I can take my two lessons a week, and, knowing that Dad doesn't believe in my talent and will put everything in my way, I thought I'd better find another place to stay.'

Les Baxter intervened. 'She'll be quite safe with my mother; she has a nice house in Wilton Avenue. She lives alone so will be a good chaperone for your daughter. I wouldn't dream of putting her anywhere else and I hoped that knowing this you will readily accept she will be safe and cared for.'

Freda and George Ryan were floored by all this. George sat down suddenly in his chair. He looked across the room at Connie with such a hurt expression it was as if someone had put a knife in her.

'How could you be so devious? I would never have thought a daughter of mine could be so two-faced. You've known about this for some time, yet you said nothing. Nothing!' His voice rose.

But Connie stared straight back at him. 'It's because you are as you are that I had to go behind your back. You never gave *my* wishes a second thought. Most parents would make any sacrifice to give a child of theirs a chance of success – and *you* don't have to make *any* sacrifice. All you had to do was give me your blessing.' She stopped her tirade and asked quietly, 'Was that asking *too* much, Dad? Was it?'

At this juncture it was Doreen who stepped forward. 'You may as well face it, Mum and Dad; whatever you say will make no difference at all. Connie has made up her mind and Mr Baxter has the wherewithal to help her. You can't prevent her doing what she wants.'

Connie turned to thank her sister but the cold glare that Doreen gave her stopped her.

'It's not as if you won't be seeing Connie,' said Baxter. 'She will still be able to come and visit you, after all she's still going to be living in Southampton.

George glared at Connie and said, 'If you proceed with this against my wishes you won't ever step inside this house again. Do I make myself clear?'

Connie looked across at her mother but Freda stared coldly at her. Connie glanced at Les, but he said nothing – and she knew this was the moment when she had to decide her future.

'Very well! If that's the way you want it, I'll get my case.' And she walked upstairs, put on her coat, looked around the room for the last time and smoothed the eiderdown on her bed. Then, picking up her suitcase, walked downstairs.

'Can I have my ration book, Mum? Only I'll need it now.'

Freda crossed to the sideboard, opened a drawer, removed the book and thrust it at her daughter. 'Here! Take the damned thing.'

Connie looked at Les Baxter and said, 'Ready?'

'When you are.'

She went to the front door, opened it and, without a backward glance, walked into the street.

'I'll never forgive you for this, Baxter!' yelled George Ryan as the front door closed.

Outside Les took Connie's case and said, 'I've got a taxi at the end of the street, come on.'

'Well that's that then!' George got to his feet, picked a packet of Gold Flake cigarettes off the mantelpiece, took one out and lit it. 'She's made her bed and now she can lie on it!'

'You didn't mean what you said about her never coming back here, did you?' asked Freda.

'Bloody right, I did!' he puffed angrily on his cigarette. Turning to his wife he said, 'I've never heard anything like this in my whole life, a daughter defying her father like this. Leaving home and all. Who the hell does she think she is?'

Doreen sat down at the table and said, 'She's a young girl with ambition. Neither of you have ever realised just how much she meant what she said. Had you done so, this may not have happened.'

'So, it's my fault, is that what you're saying?'

Letting out a deep sigh she said, 'Not exactly, but you just dismissed her, Dad. You could at least have talked to her about her singing.'

'What was the point? I couldn't afford to pay for lessons.'

'I know that, but,' she persisted, 'would it really have been such a bad thing to have agreed to let Les Baxter be her manager? If you had, our Connie would still be living at home!'

He looked at his wife for some support, but she just glared at him.

'Have you forgotten that man's reputation? Do you think I want a daughter of mine mixed up with the likes of him?'

'But she is, isn't she? At least if she was living at home, we could have kept an eye on her, but now how will we know what she's up to? What's happening to her?'

Throwing his cigarette end in the fire, her father took his coat from the peg and swept out of the room, slamming the front door in his wake.

'What are we going to do, our Dor?' Freda asked, as she dabbed a tear away. 'Connie's my baby, after all.'

Getting up from her chair, Doreen went over to her mother and held her. 'Don't you worry,' she said, 'I'll keep an eye on her. So, she can't come here but we can meet her outside. Both of us – we won't lose touch – as Les said, she's still going to be around. She hasn't moved very far away. Now come on, cheer up. I'll make us a nice cup of tea.' But as she filled the kettle, Doreen couldn't help but worry about her sister, knowing how impulsive she was. But at least she was lodging with Mrs Baxter, that was something to be grateful for.

Meanwhile, sitting in the back of the taxi, Connie was absolutely stunned by what she had done. She was barely aware of the taxi's passage until it stopped outside a house in Wilton Avenue.

Les paid the driver and taking the suitcase said, 'Come on, Mother's waiting for us.' He put a key in the lock and opened the door. 'Ma! Are you there?'

There was a long hallway, not unlike the one in Madame Vicario's, but this was covered in highly polished linoleum. There were doors leading off and Mrs Baxter appeared at one of them. She was neatly dressed in a skirt and jumper with a floral pinafore around her waist.

'Come in, my dear,' she said.

Connie followed her into a room at the side of the house. It wasn't very big, but it was cosy with a small slightly battered settee in a shiny material with brass studs around the edge, and a fire burning beside the black leaded stove which had been lovingly polished. On the mantelpiece sat two empty brass gun shells left over from the war. In the centre of the room there was a small square table with a ruby-coloured chenille cover, in the centre of which stood a vase of bronze chrysanthemums.

'Sit down, my dear.' She took the large kettle off the top of the stove and, taking it into the kitchen, said, 'I'll make us all a nice cup of tea, then we'll go to your room and you can unpack. Leslie – take the girl's coat. Don't stand around looking like a lemon!'

It seemed strange to Connie to hear the bookmaker spoken to like that by this small elderly lady and she glanced at him, half smiling at the situation.

He met her gaze and just raised his eyebrows, daring her to make any comment.

As she sat in the living room of the house in Wilton Avenue, Connie began to relax. There was such an air of peace in this house as opposed to the hostile environment she had just left, Connie felt as if she had entered a new world. She felt she could be happy here, but she couldn't help but wonder what was going on back home. The look on her father's face when she told him she was leaving home was indescribable and she thought of the hurt expression of her mother – the anger of her sister. She deeply regretted all that, but she had no choice. None at all.

'Come along, my dear,' said Mrs Baxter, later, 'I'll take you to your room. Leslie, the case!'

Connie followed the woman upstairs, aware that Les was behind her. The room was in the front of the house, overlooking the wide street. 'I sleep in the back,' she was told by her new landlady. 'I prefer it. There, put your clothes in the wardrobe, there are plenty of hangers.' She walked to the door. 'The bathroom is at the end and the toilet in the room beside it. I've put a couple of towels on your bed.'

'I'll meet you outside your shop when you close on Wednesday lunchtime,' Les told her when they were alone. 'I've booked a lesson for you at three thirty, so don't be late, and don't forget, I don't want Ma waiting on you hand and foot. Understand?'

'Yes, I understand, and I have already told you I'll look after myself.'

'Good,' he said and went down the stairs.

Connie stretched out on the double bed and thought, I've got a room to myself. What a luxury! She and Doreen had always had to share. Still, her sister could now say the same. But what else would she have to say when next they met, as Connie was certain they would? Doreen had always looked after her, played the big sister, and she didn't think for one moment she would stop. Well, now she would have to! She was her own boss. But that of course wasn't the case, she realised. Les Baxter called the tune now. She would have to do as she was told.

She slid off the bed, walked over to the window and smiled. Well, that would be fine whilst she was learning, but things would change when she became a professional. Then she would be the one to call the tune . . . She could wait.

Chapter Seven

Connie walked into her place of employment the following morning with a jaunty step, feeling grown up and independent for the first time in her life. In the staff room, without preamble, she declared to her bosom pal Molly, 'I've left home and I'm starting my singing lessons this week.'

For a moment her friend was speechless. 'Left home!' she said. 'Left home as in living somewhere else?'

'Yes,' beamed Connie. 'I am now residing in Wilton Avenue with Mrs Baxter, Les Baxter's mother. I have my own room and everything!'

'I'm surprised your dad agreed to that,' Molly retorted.

'Well, as a matter of fact, he didn't. Les came to the house on Sunday to talk to him about my training. There was a bit of a hoo-ha as you can imagine, but I had already packed my case and arranged with Mr Baxter to move out . . . so we left.'

Molly stood open mouthed. 'You what?'

'I walked out.'

'Are you mad?'

'What's mad about wanting to get on?' asked Connie defensively.

'Now let me get this straight. You are living with the bookmaker's mother, so I suppose he's paying the bills, right?'

'Right.'

'Is his room near yours by any chance?'

57

'He doesn't even live there! What on earth are you driving at?'

Molly opened the door leading into the shop and said, 'Well, he may say this is purely business at the moment, but you mark my words, Connie, one day he'll expect his pound of flesh. Those type of men always do.'

Connie followed her, arguing hotly, 'You are absolutely wrong there, this is strictly business. For Christ's sake, he is about the same age as my father!' She suddenly recalled seeing the bookie in the cinema with his arm around a young girl, a girl not that much older than she was, but she quickly dismissed such thoughts; after all, this was different. She was a sort of protégée: in his care, with the possibility of a great career ahead of her which would make both of them a lot of money if she became famous. He wouldn't jeopardise that – no, Molly was just being cynical.

The following Wednesday, Connie travelled up to London alone. Les Baxter had given her the train fare and money for the taxis, and the address of Madame Vicario.

'There is no need for both of us to go. Besides, it doubles the cost. Make sure you do everything she asks.'

'Do I have to pay her too?' asked Connie.

'No, I have a monthly account with her, so it's all taken care of. She is going to send me regular reports of your progress, so you'd better work hard. I want to make sure I get value for my investment in you,' he said sharply.

Connie glared at him. 'Look, Mr Baxter, I upset my family and left home for this, I'm not likely to waste the opportunity, am I? Too much is at stake here. I have just as much to lose as you have, perhaps you would kindly remember that!'

There was just a glint of admiration in his eyes as he looked at her and said, 'Quite a little firecracker, aren't you! Just as long as you know I won't settle for less than your best.'

'That makes two of us then,' she retorted.

58

Connie, coat collar turned up to keep out the cold November winds, felt very sophisticated travelling to Waterloo alone, and when she climbed into the taxi and airily gave the driver the address in Maida Vale, she felt quite the lady. It was only when she had to tip the driver, having reached her destination and realised she didn't know how much to give him, that she came down to earth.

Seeing her dilemma, the driver grinned and said, 'A couple of bob will be all right, miss, thanks.'

Irene Vicario smiled at her pupil when she opened the door. 'Connie! Please come in.'

Connie entered the room which had so fascinated her on her first visit and, looking round, she found it just as interesting as before.

Madame asked her to sit for a moment. She looked at Connie and said, 'I am actually very sorry to see you here, my dear.'

'But why? Have you changed your mind about me?' Connie asked anxiously.

'Not at all, I had hoped that when you returned home, *you* might have changed your mind about turning professional, that's all.'

Removing her gloves, Connie said, 'I thought about what you said, Madame, but singing is the only life that I want, nothing else holds any interest for me.' She looked defiantly at her teacher and said, 'I am prepared to face any consequences of that decision.'

'I see that you are driven – and in as much as you have decided to stick with this, that is just as well, because only those who have that driving ambition will succeed, as long as they have the voice, of course, and you have.' She rose from her chair. 'Very well, let's get started. We have a great deal of work to do in the next six months.'

Connie didn't realise that learning voice exercises and to breathe properly could be so exhausting. She went up and down the scales a million times, it seemed to her.

'Take a rest,' said Madame after a while. 'Sit down for a minute.' And whilst Connie took her breather, the teacher played a piece of music. It was melodic and relaxing. Debussy's 'Clair de Lune', she was told.

'It's a great pity that you can't read music,' said Irene. 'Perhaps later Mr Baxter will allow you to learn the basics, it would help a great deal.'

'For heaven's sake, don't mention that yet,' exclaimed Connie. 'He's already paying for enough. Mind you,' she added, 'it will all be repaid when I start to earn some money.'

The teacher studied the girl sitting opposite her and wondered just what the relationship was between her and her benefactor. She didn't think it was a physical one, but neither did she think they were related, so why was he doing this? What was his motive? If it was because he wanted to give someone with talent a chance, that was commendable, but he certainly didn't seem the type to do anything without some return. There was a ruthlessness about him that worried her. She would have a word with Jeremy Taylor; he was the one who gave her address to this person. For some unknown reason, she felt protective towards her new pupil. In her she could see just how she used to be at her age, and alas, she knew the pitfalls that were ahead of her.

'Right,' she said, bringing her thoughts back to the task in hand, 'let's carry on. Take a deep breath and hold this note for as long as you can and let's see what happens, and then I will give you the exercises I want you to do at home.'

At the conclusion of the lesson, Irene gave Connie her instructions. 'I want you to practise twice a day for half an hour each time . . . no longer, do you understand?'

Connie nodded. 'Yes.'

Putting her hand on her pupil's arm Irene said sternly, 'Now when I tell you half an hour at a time for the moment, I'm doing so for a purpose. Your voice is your most valuable asset, one you must protect as if it were a child. If you think to yourself, Oh, I'll do a bit more, you will be on the road to destruction – and I will know, I can assure you. If this happens, our lessons will be terminated.'

Connie smiled at her and said, 'I promise to do exactly as you tell me.'

'Good. Now I understand that Monday afternoons is your other free time, is that correct?'

'Yes.'

'Then that is when I will see you next, at the same time as today.' She kissed Connie on both cheeks. 'I look forward to it, my little nightingale.'

It was a couple of days later that Madame Vicario sat in a small exclusive restaurant in the West End opposite Jeremy Taylor, the theatrical agent. She lifted her glass of wine and said, '*Santé*. It is lovely to see you again.'

Jeremy joined her in the toast and said, 'My darling Irene, it has been far too long, so I was delighted to get your call. Let's order and then you can tell me what this is all about.'

As they started on their hors d'œuvres, she said, 'Tell me about that man Baxter. The man to whom you gave my address.'

He looked surprised. 'Did he get in touch with you then?'

'Yes, he brought a young lady to see me and asked for my professional opinion.'

Jeremy raised his eyebrows in surprise. 'Really? I wasn't at all sure that he was serious. What was the girl like? Was she any good?'

Irene looked at him with some amusement and said, 'Tell me first about the man.'

'I've known Les Baxter for a number of years. He's a very successful bookmaker, worth a small fortune.'

'All from bookmaking?'

Jeremy laughed. 'Good Lord, no! He made a packet in the war. He was into every black-market scam you could think of and probably still is, and yes, his business is worth a great deal.' He frowned. 'He's a hard man though, Irene. If you were

61

in business with him, you wouldn't want to upset him.'

'Is he philanthropic?'

He roared with laughter. 'Not at all! Everything has a price with him – except for his mother – he is good to her. Now tell me about the girl. Does she have talent?'

Irene's eyes shone. 'She is going to be very big, if she follows my instructions.' She sipped her wine and said thoughtfully, 'It isn't often these days that I find someone who excites me, but this girl does. Not only does she have a superb voice and perfect pitch, although I doubt she would even know what that was, but also she has that certain wonderful quality about her. She sings from the soul.'

Jeremy Taylor became very interested. 'Could I come along and hear her?'

Irene shook her head. 'No, it's much too soon. I am giving her a crash course of six months to begin with. At the end of that you can call.'

He looked thoughtful. 'Mmm. If she is as good as you say, and you have never been wrong, I could do a lot for her. Perhaps I'd better sign her up.'

With a chuckle the teacher said, 'I don't think Mr Baxter will let you get near her. It is my guess he sees himself as her Svengali.'

'But he has never been interested in theatrical things before.'

'Well, perhaps before he hasn't needed to be, but he has discovered this girl. He won't let her go, I'd bet money on it. My guess is he can see the financial benefits, having been acquainted with you.'

'I can always wait,' said Jeremy slyly. 'There will come a time, there always does. Just keep me in touch with her progress. After all, I introduced her to you, so I also had a hand in her discovery.'

Irene laughed at her friend. 'You are a sly old bird,' she said.

'Not so much of the *old*, darling, *if* you don't mind!'

She looked fondly at him as he ordered their main course. Apart from being a very shrewd businessman, he was a true gentleman, a man of breeding which showed in his every gesture and word. He always dressed exquisitely and correctly for each occasion, and for Irene and others, he was a perfect companion with his broad knowledge and witty repartee – unlike Les Baxter, she thought. He dressed well, his suits made for him, that was obvious, but he lacked class and breeding. He was a rough diamond and Irene couldn't help but wish it were Jeremy Taylor and not Baxter who was behind Connie Ryan and her blossoming career.

Back in Southampton at the Ryan family home, the atmosphere was still unsettled with each member suffering the loss of Connie in different ways. Freda was simmering with anger and resentment against her husband for not giving his blessing to Les Baxter's offer, therefore keeping Connie at home; Doreen was beside herself with worry about the safety of her sister at the hands of the bookie, and George was still fuming that his youngest daughter had defied him and left home. How was he going to explain that to his workmates?

Doreen made a point of going to Les's local pub one evening shortly after Connie's departure, knowing that the bookmaker was usually there about seven o'clock most evenings. She pushed open the door of the Lounge Bar and saw Baxter standing at the bar talking to the landlord. She walked up to him and said firmly, 'Could I have a word with you, please?'

Recognising her and seeing the interested expression on the face of the landlord, he said, 'You, of course. Let's sit over here – can I get you a drink?'

'No, thanks.' As soon as they were seated, Doreen wasted no time in coming to the point. 'I want to know just what you have in mind for my sister?'

Les was amused at the hostility in her tone. 'I'm not planning to deflower her, if that's what you mean.'

'Then exactly what are your intentions? She's only just eighteen.'

'I'm well aware of that, young lady. I am seeing to her training, her lessons, the fact she has a roof over her head in a safe place, and, when the time comes, I will see that she gets bookings at the right places, and meet the right people.'

'In other words, you are going to run her life!'

'Yes.' He stared at Doreen as if daring her to comment, but she was made of sterner stuff.

'You certainly are not!'

'What do you mean?'

'I mean that you may be in charge of her singing career as her so-called manager, benefactor, whatever you like to call yourself, but don't think you will ever run our Connie's life. She won't let you and neither will I.' She glared angrily at him. 'I'm not scared of you, Mr Baxter, and if I think you are endangering my sister in any way, I'll be there, you can count on it!'

He watched the flashing of her eyes as she blazed at him in defence of her sibling and thought what a pity she didn't have a voice like Connie too, they certainly made a feisty couple. He admired her spirit and wondered if Connie, selfish, self-centred girl that she was, so driven with ambition, really deserved such loyalty. He doubted that she did.

'Have no fear, Miss Ryan, your sister will be safe with me, I promise.'

She rose to her feet. 'Good. I'll be keeping an eye on her to see that she is.'

Les watched her walk out of the bar with an amused expression. My, but the Ryan women were full of fire. He'd heard the mother put her husband in his place once or twice at the Social Club in the past. A pity the old man wasn't made of the same stuff. George was all right, but he had reached the zenith of his ambition and was content. It wouldn't do for us all to be the same, he mused as he finished his drink, and went on to his next port of call, the Social Club.

As he sat at the bar of the club and watched a darts match in progress, he saw George Ryan talking to a couple of mates and overheard one ask, 'When is that lovely daughter of yours going to sing for us again?'

The animated expression died as George murmured some reply and put his glass to his lips. As he did so, he saw Les sitting watching him. A look of fury crossed his features and he downed what was left of his beer and walked out of the club.

Chapter Eight

Although Connie had been really excited about leading her own life, after two weeks of travelling to London, practising her lessons and working in the hat shop, she found she was pining for the old family life she'd been used to. Mrs Baxter was a delightful woman, but at her age, she had a set routine, which Connie learned to her cost she did not like disturbed.

'Now, Connie my dear,' Mrs Baxter began one evening when they were both in the kitchen trying to prepare food for themselves, 'two women can never share a kitchen at the same time, so I'm afraid you'll have to wait every evening until I'm finished.' Seeing the look of horror on the young girl's face, she added, 'If you think that will be too late for you, I suggest you buy some snack or other on the way home, to tide you over.'

'Yes, Mrs Baxter,' her lodger agreed, remembering wistfully how her mother always used to have a meal ready for her on the table when she'd finished a day's work. It was great to have a room entirely to herself, but she missed Doreen more than she thought was possible, and although she was still resentful towards her father, she missed him too. So it was with some delight that she greeted her sister when she came into the shop the next day.

Doreen, a shorthand typist at a nearby office, was clutching some letters to post. 'I'll meet you at five o'clock, our Connie. All right?'

Connie readily agreed. 'I'll wait outside,' she said.

Molly sidled over. 'What's this then?' she asked. 'A happy family reunion?'

Connie was joyously enthusiastic. 'God, Molly, you have no idea how much I've missed being home. I didn't realise just how much Mum did for us, you know?'

'Well, don't forget to tell her,' gibed her friend. 'Mothers get a poor deal I think. Take her some flowers, why don't you?'

With a frown Connie said, 'I can't. My father forbade me ever to enter the house again if I left with Mr Baxter.'

'Then you'll have to arrange to meet her somewhere else.'

And this indeed became the pattern for the women of the Ryan family during Connie's six-month training period. Once a week, they would try and go to the pictures together, or meet in a quiet pub and have a drink and a meal at some nearby cheap café, but the winter of 1946 was so bad, that interfered with the best-laid plans.

It was a bitterly cold Christmas, which Connie spent with Mrs Baxter, missing the usual family gathering on Christmas Day. Freda and Doreen called to see her on Boxing Day bearing gifts, but it made her realise even more how much she missed them.

Early February brought chaos with heavy snowfalls, affecting light and heating and, to Connie's horror, the normal running of the trains, and, in consequence, she missed some of her lessons.

When things returned to normal, and the three of them met, Connie would regale them with tales of her trips to London, of Madame Vicario and her lessons. 'You wouldn't believe the change in my voice,' Connie confided. 'It's clearer, it's gone up another octave and I can sing in an even deeper tone if I want to. And now, I can really hold a note. Madame is marvellous! And what do you think? She has even taught me a bit of opera.'

'Opera?' Freda looked amazed. 'Go on!'

They were walking through the park, Connie to get a tram and the others making their way home. Connie stopped and suddenly, standing on a nearby bench, launched in to an aria from Bizet's *Carmen*.

Both Freda and Doreen were astonished as they stood and listened. Connie sang as always from the soul with the actions making her leap from the bench and strut around acting out the words, the French language adding to the drama.

Others stopped and listened, and when she'd finished, there was a burst of applause, to the surprise of her sister and mother who had been so mesmerised that they hadn't noticed the small gathering.

Connie smiled and curtsied her thanks and, as everyone moved on, Freda gazed at her with a new understanding and a little awe. 'Blimey, our Connie, I had no idea you could sing things like that. *And* in a different language!'

'Neither did I, Mum, until Madame Vicario taught me. I never knew much about opera, except I thought it was something posh people listened to and went to see, but the music and the words are wonderful. It is so full of drama . . . I can't really speak French of course, I learned that parrot fashion.'

'Are you taking up opera then?' asked Doreen, with some wonderment.

With a deep chuckle, her sister dismissed the notion. 'Good God, no! You have to train for years and years to be that good. No, I'll stick with popular music . . . but it is nice to try these things.' She suddenly grinned broadly and said, 'They would have a bit of a shock if I sang that at the Social Club!' Her happy smile faded as she asked, 'How is Dad these days?'

'Fine,' Freda told her.

'He never changes, Con. You know that,' added Doreen, but in fact neither of the women were telling the truth. George had become something of a bitter man since Connie had left home. It still stuck in his craw that another man was financing his daughter's career. What's more, as soon as people became aware that she was no longer living at home, questions were asked, and, not wanting anyone to know the truth, George had fabricated various excuses until in the end no one asked. Instead people made up their own minds about the reason, giving rise to many rumours which, in turn, led to angry words between Freda and her husband.

It was Doreen who put an end to all the speculation when she overheard one of the women at the Social Club suggest that, of course, the girl was probably pregnant! She marched over to the table and glared at the woman. In a clear voice which could be heard by all, she said, 'I'm sorry to disappoint you ladies who seem to enjoy gossip so much. My sister Connie is certainly *not* pregnant. She is training to be a singer, and one day you'll all have to *pay* if you want to hear her.' She leaned towards the woman who had been spouting off her opinions and said, 'You are a wicked old bitch and should watch your tongue before it gets you into trouble!'

As she sat down again at her own table, her father, red with embarrassment, made to leave. Doreen caught him by his sleeve and held him down. 'You damned well sit here!' she demanded. 'It's your stupid fault that all this speculation is going on in the first place. You should have been honest with people. Now your lies have made a mountain out of a mole-hill.'

Of course it became common knowledge shortly after that Les Baxter was funding Miss Connie Ryan, and that led to even more lurid gossip. But those who whispered about that fact made sure that Doreen Ryan wasn't around when they discussed it.

It was now the month of May and the six months' training were almost over. There were just another couple of weeks to go and Jeremy Taylor was on the telephone to Irene Vicario.

'What can I do for you, Jeremy?' she asked. But she already knew the answer.

'Can I come and listen to your star pupil, darling? Don't you think it's time that we met?'

70

Smiling softly to herself, Irene said, 'Yes, I do. Come along next Wednesday afternoon at four thirty. Not a minute before, Jeremy!'

'I'll be there . . . on time!'

Irene wanted to be sure that Connie's lesson would not be disturbed but afterwards she wanted to hear Jeremy's opinion of her pupil, knowing how he had a feel for talent. She had already chosen a couple of songs for Connie to sing to him. Now her anticipation was tinged with excitement.

During the final weeks, Irene had put together a programme she felt would be suitable for Connie to sing when she gave her first performance. It was nicely balanced, giving the audience the benefit of the range of Connie's voice, which had of course increased considerably. She had even included the aria from *Carmen*.

Connie had looked very uncertain about it. 'Don't you think it might put the audience off?' she asked.

Irene shook her head. 'No, darling, the customers will be so surprised, it will be a delight. Trust me!'

Towards the end of the lesson, Irene said, 'We'll take a short break here and have a cup of tea, then I want you to sing these two songs.' She handed Connie the music. 'And by the way, a friend of mine will be here any moment and he can be your audience!'

'Who is this man?' Connie enquired. 'Is this a secret admirer, Madame? One you haven't told me about perhaps?'

Seeing the teasing smile on the face of her pupil, Irene told her, 'No, he's not a lover, just an old friend. Whilst I make the tea, you practise.'

Jeremy was on time, as Irene knew he would be. She greeted him with a kiss on both cheeks.

'Is she here?' her visitor enquired.

Irene put a finger to her lips and as they both hushed, Connie could be heard practising in the music room.

Raising his eyebrows in anticipation, he followed Irene into

71

the kitchen. Espying the tray all set out he said, 'Where shall I take this?'

'Into the music room. Now no mention of your profession until after!' she insisted.

As Jeremy opened the door, all he could see was Connie's back. She was reading the music sheet as she sang, her concentration was such that she was unaware of the other person until her teacher bustled in and, turning, she saw the stranger.

'Oh! Hello. I didn't know you were there.'

Putting the tray down, Jeremy walked over to her and shaking her hand, introduced himself. 'Jeremy Taylor, old friend of Irene's. I do hope you don't mind my being here?'

Taking the cup of tea handed to her, Connie smiled and said, 'Not at all.'

As she sipped her tea, she observed the stranger as he and Madame exchanged small talk. She rather liked him, she thought. He seemed very sophisticated with his smart city suit, cultured voice and beautifully clean hands and nails. Not a man for manual work, she mused . . . and then they were ready for her.

The first number was 'Can't Help Loving That Man' from *Showboat*. As Connie began, Jeremy felt the short hairs at the back of his neck stand up. He applauded politely at the end of the number and waited for the next.

As she sang the opening lines of 'Long Ago And Far Away' the rich fruity voice rang out, full of poignancy. Jeremy was spellbound. During his many years in the business, he had never been quite so moved by a beginner and he knew, without a doubt, that Irene had been correct in her assessment that here was a girl who could go a very long way in the business . . . if she was handled correctly. And then he thought of Les Baxter. It would be an absolute sin to let him handle this girl! He didn't have the right contacts; he had no idea how to build her career whereas *he* could do so much for her – take her right to the top, but protecting her at the same time from the sharks in the business. He was frustrated beyond measure, but he rose to his feet, took Connie's hand in his and kissed it. 'My dear young lady, that was absolutely wonderful! I agree entirely with Madame Vicario, you do indeed have a special talent.'

Connie was thrilled. 'Thank you,' she said and glanced at Irene.

Irene left the piano and joined them. She smiled at her pupil and said, 'You should be very pleased to be told this by this gentleman, my child, because he is one of the most important theatrical agents in the business.'

Connie's eyes widened in surprise. 'You are? How marvellous that you like me.'

'And I would very much like to be *your* agent, Miss Ryan.'

'That's very nice of you, Mr Taylor, but you see Mr Baxter looks after me, he was kind enough to finance my future, so of course, I owe him everything, including my loyalty.'

'Yes, I know the gentleman of whom you speak and of course you are right, you have to stay with him, but . . . if ever in the future you feel like a change, come and see me. Here is my card.' He withdrew one from his wallet. 'If you are ever troubled at any time, please feel free to call me. I mean it.' Turning to Irene he said, 'I must go, I have an appointment. Goodbye, Connie, and good luck.'

As he walked to the front door he said to Irene, 'She shouldn't be in Baxter's hands, he has no experience in this line of business. Is she still going to have lessons with you?'

'Yes, for the foreseeable future.'

'Then keep an eye on her, and keep in touch I want to know how she gets on. All right?'

'Don't worry, I'll let you know.'

As he walked away, Jeremy frowned. He was extremely unhappy about Connie's future. Baxter wasn't without his own contacts, but to perform at the wrong type of venue at the start of her career could be critical, whereas he knew just where to place her, and which type of publicity to arrange. Damn it!

★ ★ ★

But Baxter wasn't quite the incompetent that Jeremy Taylor thought. Through gambling he had made many contacts, and there were quite a few that owed him a favour or two for various reasons, one of whom was a man who had been the manager at the Palace of Varieties in Southampton, a very popular venue for performers until the Blitz, which had destroyed that building and many others in the town centre. The man, Les knew, was still in the business running a place in Southsea, and he paid him a visit.

'I was surprised to get your call, my old friend,' said Bill Phillips, as the two of them sat at the bar of a local pub together. 'Now what can I do for you?'

'I've gone into the theatrical business,' said Les. 'I have a young singer with a great future and I wondered just where to start her off. I thought you would be the man to know.'

'With a new singer, it's not always easy to get her a spot on a variety bill. You could get her to try out as a singer with a band.'

But Les didn't like that idea at all. 'No, no, that won't do. This girl will always be a solo artist. I know a couple of night club owners, I'll have a word with them.' But when he got back to Southampton and bought a copy of the *Southern Daily Echo*, his problem was solved. There, on the inside page, he read: 'Talent Night. Two bands. 2000 seats. Entrance one shilling.' He would enter Connie for this and when she won – never did he doubt that she would – he would get all the free publicity he wanted to launch her career!

Strangely enough when he told Connie of his plans, she was less than happy. 'But that is for amateurs!' she exclaimed. 'I am a professional!'

'Not yet you aren't, young lady, and don't you forget it. You have been *taught* by a professional, but you are very much waiting to step *up* onto that bottom rung, so don't start getting big-headed now before you've done anything!'

'It's just not how I thought it would be,' she sulked.

'Huh! I suppose you thought you'd start at the top, did you? Well, it's time you learned that life's not like that!'

'Jeremy Taylor didn't say that.'

Les spun round. 'When did you see Jeremy Taylor?'

Connie knew she had made a grave error. 'He came to tea at Madame Vicario's when I had almost finished my lesson.'

His face was like thunder. 'Did he hear you sing?'

'Yes, he did. Two numbers.'

Glaring at her, Les asked, 'I suppose he asked to represent you?'

Connie answered hurriedly. 'Yes, but I told him you were my agent and my loyalty was to you.'

'It had bloody well better be!' he snapped. 'I have invested a great deal of money in you.'

'I know that, Mr Baxter, and I appreciate it.'

'It's not your appreciation that I want. I want work and success, and I will draw up a contract that you will sign as my client, do you understand?'

'Yes, yes, I do.' She would say anything to appease him at this moment, aware as she was of the temper that was smouldering behind her mentor's cold eyes.

'We need to get you a decent gown to wear for this talent show. One that will knock spots off everyone. Presentation is everything – remember that.'

'I will.'

'I'll go and put your name down for the show. It isn't for a couple of weeks, so when you go to London for your final lesson of this crash course, I'll give you some money and Madame Vicario will take you to a shop and choose something suitable, then she can decide which number would be the best for you to sing.'

'I don't have enough clothing coupons for an evening dress!' she exclaimed.

'Don't worry about that, I'll take care of it.' He paused. 'You will win this contest.'

Connie stared at him. 'You don't know that.'

'If you really have what it takes, you will.' His eyes narrowed. 'Of course, I've not had the pleasure of hearing you sing after your training – not like Mr Taylor – but I am expecting great things from you, Miss Connie Ryan, and you had better not disappoint me!'

Chapter Nine

Connie voiced her disappointment when she was with Madame Vicario the following week. 'I didn't expect to be entering an *amateur* contest as my first appearance in public!' she complained angrily. 'I expected to be on a stage with people coming to see *me* alone, and paying for the privilege! Jeremy Taylor wouldn't be doing this to me if he were my agent.'

Irene looked sternly at her. 'But he isn't! Now please . . . don't start your career by becoming a drama queen because it won't get you anywhere, my dear.'

Connie was nonplussed by her chastisement.

'Maybe you're right about Jeremy, but Mr Baxter doesn't have the same contacts, and he's doing the best that he can for you. Remember, Connie, without him you wouldn't have come to me in the first place! A little gratitude would not go amiss.'

Connie forgot her disappointment when she and her tutor went shopping for her gown. They went into Harrods' dress department, and when Connie saw the rails filled with glamorous gowns, it took her breath away.

She tried on several that were chosen by Irene, but they both agreed on a deep red satin dress which was strapless with a fitted waist and a full skirt. The top of the bodice was trimmed with roses made from the same material. With her dark hair, Connie looked stunning.

Looking at her reflection in the mirror, she could hardly

recognise the woman staring back at her. 'Oh, my God! Is that really me?'

Irene looked on with a smile of satisfaction. 'Now all you need is a decent haircut and style. Come along.' Two hours later, the transformation was complete. With expert cutting, the hairdresser brought out the natural movement of the hair, which followed the contour of Connie's head with the slightest fullness.

Looking at the finished result, she asked, 'How can I possibly keep it like this?'

The girl showed her how to pin curl and how to brush it out afterwards. 'You'll soon get used to it,' she said.

She made the journey home clutching the box which contained her gown and the sheet music to 'Can't Help Loving That Man'. As Madame had said, 'If you sing this as well as you did before Jeremy, you'll be doing just fine.' Kissing her, she wished her luck.

Connie was desperately nervous on the night of the talent contest, but Mrs Baxter was on hand to calm her. 'Just take lots of deep breaths,' she said kindly. 'I'm coming with you in the taxi, as Les has saved a seat for me. Now go upstairs and get ready.'

Connie did deep-breathing exercises and practised her scales as she changed. As soon as she stepped inside the dress, she felt calmer. She had to ask Mrs Baxter to fasten the zip up at the back, and when she stood in front of her landlady and saw the look of admiration in her eyes, she felt ready for anything.

'My dear girl, you look absolutely beautiful. Has my son seen you in this outfit?'

Connie shook her head. 'No, I wanted it to be a surprise,' she said.

'Well, it certainly will be that! Come along, I can hear the taxi tooting outside.'

Connie had told Doreen and her mother about the contest and

of course they were very excited. 'You are coming to see our Connie, aren't you?' Freda asked George.

'No, I've got to play in a darts match,' he snapped.

She looked angrily at him. 'You would prefer to do that than to support your own daughter?'

He looked somewhat uncomfortable at her accusation. 'It's all been arranged,' he said. 'My name is on the list of players.'

'And I suppose it didn't occur to you to ask them to play the reserve!'

'Now don't start,' he growled.

'Start! I haven't even begun!'

Doreen took hold of her mother's arm. 'Leave it, Mum. It's a matter of pride with him . . . his own! My Eric will take us.'

Freda turned on her husband. 'Well, George Ryan,' she cried, 'I won't forget this in a hurry, mark my words.'

When Connie arrived at the Guildhall, she was ushered into the Green Room with the other contestants. What Connie didn't know was that all of them had been through preliminary rounds where the judges had sorted the wheat from the chaff, therefore presenting a decent programme for the paying public, but Les knew the director of the Guildhall and when he assured him that Connie was as good as a professional and had been trained in London, he allowed Connie's name to go forward, therefore paying off a favour that was owed to the bookmaker.

Connie stood apart from the others, not wanting either to socialise with them, or to crease her gown. They were a mixed bunch: a ventriloquist, a couple of comedians, a magician, a group of tap dancers and several singers, both male and female. Listening to them chat, Connie realised that they had all auditioned before at different places around the country and so when another girl approached her and asked where she had auditioned, she was ready with a lie. 'London,' she said convincingly.

'And what do you do?'

'Sing,' answered Connie.

'So do I. I'm singing "Ave Maria". What about you?'

'I'm singing "Can't Help Loving That Man" from *Showboat*.'

'Well, good luck,' said the other contestant as she walked away.

Connie studied her closely. She was tall and angelic-looking, dressed in a simple blue gown with long blonde hair halfway down her back, which gave her an ethereal look. Connie guessed at once that this girl would be serious competition. She would really have to pull out all the stops to counteract the look of innocence this girl portrayed. She had the dress and she had the song and she knew she would have to portray a sensuous woman – the exact opposite to the other contestant. And she blessed the drama training that Madame Vicario had given her when she taught her to sing *Carmen*. This would be her weapon.

The evening began and Connie thought it would never end as she was drawn near the end of the programme; the blonde, two performers before her. She slowly sipped water to lubricate her throat, singing softly to keep her voice supple.

The blonde moved forward and Connie listened intently. From the Green Room she could just about hear the other girl sing. Her voice was pure and clear, and there was no doubt at all that the audience appreciated the performance, as the applause was loud and prolonged and far more enthusiastic than for other performers.

Eventually it was her turn.

In the audience, Connie's family and her pal, Molly, sat with bated breath as her name was announced. Les Baxter's nerves were wound tighter than a spring. But when Connie walked upon the stage and he saw his protégée, he was amazed at the transformation. Connie had always seemed to him just a bit of a kid, but standing before the microphone in front of the four-piece band with such an air of confidence was this alluring young woman, oozing sex appeal – and he was astonished.

Every man in the audience sat up and took notice. The women too, but for different reasons. As the band played the opening chords, there was absolute silence, and as Connie sang the poignant words about her deep love for this man, there was not a person watching who wasn't moved by the throaty rendition of this beautiful song.

The audience applauded loudly, Connie smiled, curtsied with great dignity for one so young, and walked off the stage. She knew her performance was the best she could give and she waited impatiently for the programme to finish. Then there was an interval whilst the judges made their final selection. Connie accepted the cup of coffee that was on offer in an effort to calm her nerves.

In the audience Doreen, Eric, Freda and Molly were beside themselves with excitement, and absolutely overwhelmed by Connie's performance. 'I couldn't believe that was my daughter up there,' said Freda with tears in her eyes. 'If only your father was here to see her. He would be so proud.'

Les Baxter was like a cat on hot bricks. He took himself to the gents during the interval and swilled his face with cold water. Now he fidgeted in his seat until his mother leaned over and said, 'For heaven's sake! Will you be still.'

The band struck up once again to settle the crowd before the final announcements were made. The Master of Ceremonies stepped forward at the end of the number and smiled at the audience.

'Ladies and gentlemen, I'm sure you will agree that we have all been well entertained this evening with so much raw talent presented to us.'

'For God's sake, get on with it!' muttered Les. His mother dug him sharply in the ribs.

'And here is the Mayor to give you the judges' results.'

The Mayor, resplendent in his gold chain, stepped up to the microphone. 'I will give the results in reverse order.'

The contestants, standing in the wings, held their breath.

'In third place, the ventriloquist, Peter Biggs.'

81

The young man, clutching his dummy, came on stage to be presented with a certificate and a handshake. He stood to one side of the stage, a broad grin on his face.

In the wings Connie waited, hardly daring to breathe.

'In second place . . . Bridget Palmer who sang "Ave Maria" for us so very beautifully.' The girl walked forward and accepted a kiss from the Mayor and her certificate with a smile.

'And finally, the winner . . . Miss Connie Ryan.'

There was wild applause and cheers from some of the young men in the audience as Connie walked towards the Mayor, smiling. She was presented with a silver cup and a bouquet of flowers.

Immediately several reporters stepped forward, cameras at the ready. 'Smile, Miss Ryan.' 'Look this way, Miss Ryan.' 'Connie . . . over here.'

She was in her element, accepting the plaudits of success as if this happened to her every day. Before she knew it, she was led off stage to where Les Baxter was waiting. She looked at him expecting his praise, but he caught her by the arm and said briskly, 'Come with me. I have lined up an interview with the *Southern Daily Echo*.'

In the Green Room, Les seated her opposite a man holding a notepad and pencil. 'Miss Ryan is my client,' began Baxter. 'We have great plans for the future because after tonight, she is turning professional.'

The reporter turned to Connie. 'How do you feel after winning tonight's contest?' he asked. But before she could answer, Les interrupted. 'She's thrilled, of course, but it just endorses the fact that she's ready for the professional stage.'

Connie glared at him. 'I believe the reporter addressed the question to me,' she snapped and, turning towards the young man, said, 'I'm thrilled, of course. I have only one ambition in life and that is to sing and do it well.' She looked at him with lowered lids and asked softly, 'Did *you* enjoy my performance?'

Completely smitten, he said, 'Oh yes, Miss Ryan. I thought you were wonderful.'

'Thank you,' she said. 'I do hope you'll put that in your article.'

'You can rely on it,' he said as he got to his feet. 'Good luck!'

As he left Les Baxter turned on her. 'Don't you *ever* do that to me again!'

She spun round and glared at him. 'And don't you ever give an interview on my behalf. When *I* am asked the questions, *I* will give the answers! You are my manager, but *I* am going to be the star!'

'Now don't you get above yourself, young lady! If it wasn't for me you wouldn't even be here tonight.'

She said coldly, 'I am well aware of that, but you can't say you didn't get your money's worth this evening.'

'You cheeky little bitch!'

She met his gaze unflinchingly. 'Not at all. I'm just stating a fact. Yes, you have invested in my talent, so we need one another. Without my voice and success, your investment means nothing!' She rose to her feet. 'I'm going to see my family. I'll get my own taxi home.' And she walked out of the Green Room leaving Les Baxter fuming and speechless.

In the Guildhall, Molly and her family greeted Connie ecstatically. Freda hugged her enthusiastically and said, 'Oh, Connie love, you were wonderful!'

Doreen kissed her and said, 'It was worth all the trouble after all, that's clear to see. You'll go far and I'm really proud of you.'

Eric looked admiringly at her. 'You're great, Connie.'

'Was Les Baxter pleased?' asked Freda.

'Absolutely,' lied Connie. 'He was full of praise.'

'I'm glad because you owe him a lot.'

'Let's go to the Polygon for a celebratory drink,' Connie suggested.

'The Polygon!' exclaimed Freda. 'That's a bit posh, isn't it?'

'No,' said Eric. 'It's absolutely the place to go after such a success.'

Connie beamed at him and, putting an arm around her mother's shoulders, said, 'I'm going to be a star, Mother, so you'd better get used to posh places, because when I'm earning lots of money I'm going to take you and Doreen to all of them. One day, to the Savoy in London, and that's a promise. Come on, Molly.'

Freda giggled. 'You are a one, our Connie. I'll happily settle for the Polygon.'

Chapter Ten

The following day, the *Southern Daily Echo* had a half-page coverage of the talent contest with a picture of Connie, smiling, clutching the silver cup and bouquet. The headline read, A STAR IN THE MAKING. The young reporter had kept his promise and whilst mentioning the others he gave a glowing account of Connie's performance. She and Molly read it together

'You did really well,' her friend said. 'It was hard to believe it was your first appearance. What happens now?'

Connie shrugged. 'I don't know, but I would expect that Mr Baxter should be able to book me in somewhere, after this!' She waved the paper in the air. 'And if he doesn't, I know someone who will.'

'What do you mean?' asked Molly.

'When I was in London having a lesson, a theatrical agent heard me and offered to be my manager, I told him I had one already, but he gave me his card in case I changed my mind.'

Molly was appalled. 'But you can't possibly – not after Les Baxter paid for your lessons!'

'Well, that's up to him, isn't it? After all, I haven't signed a contract with him. Not yet anyway.'

Although Molly was fond of Connie, she knew she could be selfish and self-centred, but this time she couldn't reconcile herself to such inconsideration. 'All I can say,' she said hotly, 'is if you treat this man this way, you won't be a friend of mine any longer.'

85

'You don't even like Les Baxter!'

'That's beside the point.'

'Oh, tosh! Look, Molly, in the entertainment world you have to look after number one.'

'Just listen to yourself . . . "in the entertainment world". Who the hell do you think you are? And what the hell do you know about it? You've sung a couple of times at the Social Club and won a talent competition! That's hardly the world of entertainment – if you don't mind!'

'You just don't understand,' said Connie dismissively. 'Before there was only Mr Baxter and of course I'm grateful to him, but the other man had so much class, and he's been in the business for years.' She looked at Molly, eager for her friend's approval. 'He's in the business and Les is just a bookmaker!'

'What do you mean, *just* a bookmaker? He was good enough for you to take his money! All I know is that you are a selfish bitch – and that I *do* understand.' With that she stormed off.

But Connie, flushed with her latest success, wasn't a bit upset. She would wait and see what happened in the aftermath of the publicity. Surely now Les could get her some bookings – she knew that really he was as anxious to start her professional career as she was, after all he wouldn't like to lose the money he had already spent on her. But, she thought, smiling slyly to herself, it was always nice to have an extra string to her bow in the shape of Jeremy Taylor. She really didn't see how she could lose!

In the Ryan household that evening, Freda was showing Doreen the write-up in the *Echo* when George walked in the door at the end of his working day.

'What's all the excitement about?' he asked.

Doreen thrust the newspaper at him, saying, 'Look, Dad. It's about our Connie.'

He took the paper from her and read the article, then looking at the picture he said, 'Well, she looks happy enough.

86

I hope she thinks all this was worth leaving home for!'

Freda glared at him. 'You gave her no choice, did you? But at least as a father you should be proud of her. After all, she's your own flesh and blood . . . or doesn't that mean anything to you any more?'

His cheeks flushed as he said, 'Of course it does. What sort of a man do you take me for?'

'To be honest, George, I don't know anymore. Ever since our Connie left home, you've changed and I'm not at all sure that I even like you any more!' And she stormed into the kitchen.

He looked at his older daughter and asked, 'What did I say?'

Doreen looked at him in despair. 'If you have to ask, Dad . . .' And she too left him, taking her coat upstairs to her room.

George looked again at the picture and reread the article. Bitter though he was about Les Baxter, he couldn't help a feeling of fatherly pride seep through his bones as he read the glowing account, wishing that things could be different. But Connie was on her way and this worried him. After all, she was only eighteen, barely a woman, and if she was going to be a success, would she be able to handle it? Would all this go to her head? He couldn't help but think that it would. Then what?

Les Baxter was still smarting about the way his young protégée had spoken to him after the contest. It was time that chit of a girl realised who was boss. He paid a visit to his solicitor and had a contract drawn up, then he called round at his mother's house that same evening and took Connie into the front room and closed the door.

'Sit down!' he demanded. When Connie was seated he took from his pocket the new contract and a pen and said, 'Sign this.'

She looked at him and asked, 'What is it?'

'A contract between you and me. It states that I am your

87

manager and that when all the money I have spent on your training has been returned, I will take ten per cent of your future earnings.' He pointed to the bottom of the last page and said, 'Put your signature there.'

Connie put down the pen and said, 'I'm not signing anything until I've read it.'

He gave a snort of anger. 'You don't understand the first thing about contracts.'

'You're quite right, but I can read! Anyway I had better get used to them, hadn't I? I'll read it this evening.'

Les leaned on the table, his face a few inches from her face, his voice full of menace. 'Now you listen to me. You are just a kid who I have given the chance of a lifetime to, and who was extremely grateful at the time as I recall, so now because you have won a talent competition, don't you start getting smart with me. I have destroyed people for far less.' He stood up. 'I'm off to the pub down the road; I'll be back in an hour. You had better have read and signed it by then or you will wonder what's hit you!'

Despite her arrogance, Connie looked into the cold expression in his eyes and knew that he meant every word and, for the first time since she'd met him, she realised that the stories she'd heard about him were true. It would be dangerous to cross this man. But she wouldn't show him she was worried.

'I'll make a cup of tea, then I'll read it.'

'One hour!' he said and left the room.

Sitting with her tea, Connie studied the three pages. She couldn't understand the legal jargon, but the rest was as he said about recovering his costs and his percentage of her future earnings. Then she read that she was tied to him for the next five years: if she signed this, she would sign away her freedom for some considerable time.

Searching through her handbag, she found the card Jeremy Taylor had given her and, slipping out of the front door, she walked along to the nearest telephone box and asked the operator for his London number, but when she was put through it was only to be told that Mr Taylor was abroad and would be away for some time.

She returned to the house. Now she had no choice, she would have to sign.

When Baxter returned an hour later, he held out his hand and said, 'Give me the contract.'

She did so without saying a word.

He glared at her and said, 'I have a couple of people to see about you appearing for them.'

Her fears fled at these words. 'Really? Where?'

'You do change with the wind, don't you, girl?' he said sarcastically. 'Now there's a *different* tone to your voice.' He held up the contract. 'You are *my* property for the next five years and you'd do well to remember that because I have your career in the palm of my hand. I can help you, or if you get too full of yourself, I can pull the rug from under you!'

She felt her bones chill. 'What do you mean?'

'It means that I can forget the money I've spent on you, and for the next five years, you can't appear anywhere if I don't want you to.'

The blood drained from her face. 'You wouldn't do that to me, would you?'

'That all depends on you. Stop playing the prima donna and you'll be fine, but any more nonsense . . . well, you know the consequences.' He turned and left the room.

Connie sat frozen to her seat, knowing now she would have to watch her Ps and Qs. Les Baxter had her just where he wanted her. Under his thumb!

Within a couple of days, Connie had some good news. She was to appear as a guest singer at the Guildhall on a Saturday night with Bert Osborne and his band, and then, the following week, she had a solo spot in a night club in Southampton.

She swapped one of her half days with Molly to allow her

to rehearse with the band on Saturday afternoon. She arrived feeling more than a little nervous. After all, this was a professional band and she had only ever sung with a pianist and the four-piece band at the talent competition. The leader gave her the sheet music to two numbers, and asked her if she knew them, which fortunately she did. It was to be his choice, she realised, not hers.

She smiled nervously at the musicians as she stood at the microphone waiting for the introduction and when Bert Osborne nodded to her she began to sing 'All of Me', an upbeat number. This was followed by 'Begin the Beguine', with a Latin rhythm.

They went through both numbers again at the bandleader's suggestion. 'You sing well, Connie,' he said, 'just relax a little more. I know this is the first time you've sung with a big band, but you'll be fine. Enjoy it!'

And she did.

In her enthusiasm she came in before the right beat once or twice and he stopped the musicians. 'Watch me, Connie, I'll let you know when to come in. Listen to the music, don't be over-eager.'

The rehearsal eventually went well and she returned home to get changed, feeling far more confident about the evening ahead. She had only the one dress to wear, but she felt lucky in it as it won her the talent competition. She was ready by the time Les called for her in a taxi.

'At the end of the evening, you'll come straight home with me,' he said. 'I've booked a cab. But you'll need another dress for the night club. You can't be seen in the same one there. We'll sort it out next week.'

'Will Madame Vicario be taking me shopping again?' she asked hopefully.

'No. I can't afford Harrods every time, not until you have made your mark. There are several gown shops in Southampton. I'll take you to one or two and see what they have.'

'You are going to take me?' She was shocked by the idea.

'Yes,' he said firmly. 'And I'll choose the gown.'

She knew better than to argue.

Later that evening, she waited in the wings whilst the band-leader made an announcement. 'Ladies and Gentlemen, last week there was a talent contest held in this very hall and this evening we have the winner here to sing with the band. Please give a warm welcome to . . . Miss Connie Ryan.'

Connie walked on to the stage with a broad smile and a bow to the applauding dancers, then the music began and she was in her own world – relaxed and in excellent voice. And at the end of the second number, the applause was loud and enthusiastic.

Bert Osborne stepped forward and kissed her cheek. 'Well done,' he whispered. 'And good luck in the future.'

She rushed off into the wings where she saw Les Baxter waiting. 'Was I all right?' she asked breathlessly.

'You were fine,' was all he said, before taking her out of the building and into the taxi.

'That was my very first professional appearance,' she said proudly. And then . . .'Did I get a fee?'

'Yes of course. But it goes against my expenses, naturally.'

He face fell. 'Naturally.'

He put his hand in his pocket and drew off a five-pound note from the wad in his hand. 'Here,' he said as he handed it to her. 'Just so you can tell all your mates you earned your first fee.'

She beamed at him. 'Thanks, Mr Baxter, I did, didn't I?'

'And after your night club appearance you can honestly feel you have put your foot onto that bottom rung of the ladder.' He paused. 'We'll have to sort out a programme for you.'

'Oh, but Madame Vicario has already done that and I've practised with her,' she stated firmly.

He was silent for a moment and then said, 'Right, then we'll stick with it as long as it fits in with the time allocated for your appearance.'

'I have several numbers in reserve if it doesn't,' Connie insisted. 'When do I continue with my lessons?' she asked with some hesitation. After their confrontation over the signing of the contract, she was a little hesitant to upset him again.

He didn't answer. 'We'll go along to the club and meet with the manager. He'll tell you how long your spot is, then you will have to confer with the bandleader when you rehearse. I'll come along and make sure everything is all right.'

'You don't need to,' she said quickly.

'I do, I'm your manager. It's part of my job.'

She didn't argue further, recognising the tone of his voice.

On her next afternoon off, when she would normally have been in London with Madame, she was escorted to the club by the bookmaker. In her arms she clutched the music for the numbers she and Madame Vicario had chosen for her programme.

As the taxi drew up, Connie looked at the building with some disappointment. Outside it looked very ordinary, apart from the name over the door: The Peacock Club. She wondered if the sign was lit up at night. Once inside, she didn't see anything much to cheer her either.

There was a long bar on one side. The rest of the room was filled with tables and chairs, apart from a small dance floor in the centre and at the end a small stage. The walls had murals of musicians painted on them. They were well done, but age had flaked the paint and there was an air of deterioration about the place. Connie's dream of working in a high-class club was shattered. But she determined to make the most of it.

A man stepped forward. 'Mr Baxter?'

'That's right. Are you Johnnie Bellingham?'

He came nearer and shook Les by the hand and, turning to Connie, said, 'And this is our little star, I take it?'

She smiled at him and said, 'How do you do? I have all my music here.'

He raised his eyebrows and said, 'Have you now? Well,

perhaps we had better sit down and look at what you've got.'
He leafed through the papers and pulled out four numbers.

'Is that *all* I'm going to be able to sing!' she asked aggressively.

Johnnie Bellingham grinned broadly. 'Yes, I'm afraid so. You will have two spots and each time you will have two numbers.'

'What if the audience want an encore?'

'Connie!' snapped Les.

Johnnie looked at him and laughed loudly. 'Quite a little spitfire your singer, isn't she?'

Not to be deterred, Connie shrugged and said, 'Well, it's surely best to be prepared, isn't it?'

He gave her a searching look and said, 'The people in the club come to talk, to drink and to dance, they don't really listen to the singer.'

'They'll listen to me, that I *can* promise you.'

Picking up a sheet of music he said, 'Here, bring this over to the piano, then when I've listened to you, I'll tell you whether they will or not!'

Bellingham had chosen two Cole Porter numbers which pleased Connie who loved his music. The first was 'Begin the Beguine', which she had sung with Bert Osborne's band. She waited for the introduction and then started to sing.

She could tell he was impressed by his expression and the change of the tone in his voice. She picked up the sheet music to 'Embraceable You' and said, 'Shall we run through this too?'

'Why not?' he said as his fingers picked out the opening bars on the piano.

She began singing and her sweet, deep, melodious voice caressed every word. At the end she looked at Johnnie Bellingham and asked, 'Well?'

He grinned broadly at her. 'Definitely an encore I would say.'

Whilst Les sat at a table and smoked one of his cigars, she

and Johnnie worked out her programme together and finally he said, 'That should just about do it. I would like you to come along a couple of hours before we open so you can do a quick run-through with the band, but I don't foresee any problems.'

They shook hands and Connie walked over to Les and said, 'Shall we go?'

'When I've had a word,' he said coldly. 'You have done your work, now I must do mine.'

It was her turn to sit and watch. She couldn't hear the conversation but Les seemed to be laying down the law and making a point, which eventually was agreed by Bellingham and the two men shook hands.

Les walked back to her wearing a satisfied smile. 'Come on!' he said and walked towards the door.

Outside Connie asked, 'What was all that about?'

'All what?'

'You seemed to be pushing a bit when you talked, that's all.'

He laughed. 'You're right there. After hearing you sing I asked for more money!'

'You did?'

'Damn right I did. I've been to this club and heard some of his singers. You were in a class of your own, and so I made him pay.'

It wasn't the fact that she'd been paid more that pleased Connie, it was the fact that Les spoke well of her performance.

'You thought I was all right then?' she asked, fishing for compliments.

'So you should be after six months' solid training,' was his only comment.

Chapter Eleven

Two days later, when Connie had another free afternoon, Les Baxter took her shopping, which she found deeply embarrassing. He marched into a gown shop in the town and told the assistant what he wanted. Then he searched through the evening dresses on a rack, picking out one or two, looking at them, handing some to the girl and returning the others, then he sent her off to find more.

'Right!' he said to Connie. 'Go into the dressing room and try these on.'

As she changed into the first one, she thought this was not nearly as enjoyable as when she went shopping with Madame Vicario. She hadn't mentioned the clothing coupons this time, but wondered how Les had procured his. Then she remembered that he had been — and probably still was — into the black market. Well, that was no concern of hers, she told herself.

The following hour was stressful for her. Les lacked finesse and his outspoken remarks made her curl up inside with embarrassment as she stepped out of the dressing room in one gown after another. He didn't like the ones she liked and she was worried that his choice would be something she would hate, knowing if she felt a mess, she wouldn't have the confidence to give a good performance.

The manageress of the establishment stepped forward and took charge, much to Connie's great relief, making suggestions, advising against one or two gowns which she deemed too old for such a young and beautiful girl. Eventually she brought out an emerald green dress that heightened the colour of Connie's eyes and showed off her small waist and rounded bosom to perfection.

The gown was strapless, close-fitting at the waist with a full skirt, and then she produced a chiffon scarf which matched perfectly and placed it loosely round Connie's neck in the front with the rest hanging down the back. It looked sensational.

As she paraded in front of the bookmaker, Connie held her breath.

Les studied her from every position making her turn left then right. 'We'll take it,' he said.

Connie couldn't believe her luck as she had seen the price on the label, but Les didn't query it at all. However, she heard him ask the manageress if she thought Connie should wear any jewellery with it.

'Just a simple pair of drop diamanté earrings,' she said. 'Keep it simple, the dress and the girl do the rest.'

He thanked her, paid the bill, handed over the required number of coupons and waited for her to pack the gown.

'Thank you, Mr Baxter,' said Connie. 'I really liked that dress.'

'Yes, you looked good in it. It should please the punters,' he said smugly.

As requested, Connie, already dressed in her finery, arrived early at The Peacock Club on the Saturday evening and was introduced to the band. They were a mixed bag, she thought. Several of them were in their late forties, and looked somewhat jaded. They gave her a cursory glance and began to tune their instruments, but the pianist winked and said, 'Hello, there. Welcome to the poor man's idea of nightclubbing!'

The run-through was without problems and while the members of the band left the stage, Ben Stanton, the pianist, invited Connie to a small shabby kitchen where he made them both a cup of coffee.

'It's only Camp coffee, I hope that's all right?'

She nodded her agreement.

'You sing well,' he remarked as he waited for the kettle to boil.

'Thanks. It's all I've ever wanted to do,' she told him. 'How about you?'

'The keyboard has been a part of my life since I was a boy. When I was in the army I was lucky, I played with a service band entertaining the troops. We were part of E.N.S.A. It was better than being in the fighting.' He made the coffee and handed her a mug.

'Sorry, it's a bit basic here. Be careful not to spill it on your gown.'

'I was a bit disappointed when I first walked into the club,' she confessed.

'We all have to start somewhere,' he said with a look of understanding. 'Is this your first professional appearance?'

'No. Last Saturday I sang with Bert Osborne at the Guildhall, and the week before I won a talent contest there.'

'Oh, yes, I saw your picture in the *Echo*; I thought your face was familiar. Well done.' He gave a sardonic grin. 'And now it's the big time, I suppose?'

'You can smile,' she retorted, 'but I am going to the top. I'm going to be famous one day. You'll see!'

He gazed at her admiringly. 'Well, Connie Ryan, I must say you look the part.'

'Do I really?'

'You have the looks and the voice, but this is a tough profession.'

'I'll do anything, go anywhere to make it,' she said defiantly.

'And you may have to,' he said with some bitterness.

'What do you mean?'

'Before I went into the army, I had a girl with a voice and an ambition like yours; by the time I came out of the services, she was doing very well. But then she would, she slept her way there!' He looked steadily at Connie and said, 'Fame and the need to be famous can change people. It can become an obsession, but there is always a price! My girl sold herself to achieve it. I'll never forgive her for that!'

Connie was about to protest that that wasn't her way of doing things, but before she could utter a word, she heard Les Baxter calling her name.

'Who's that?' asked Ben.

'Just my manager,' she said, annoyed at the interruption. She glanced towards the door as she heard his approaching footsteps.

The door flew open. 'There you are! I've been searching everywhere for you.' He glared at Ben then said to Connie, 'For goodness' sake, come out of this place. I didn't buy that gown for you to get it soiled in some dirty kitchen.'

She turned to speak to Ben but was silenced by the expression of disappointment as he looked coldly at her before turning away.

Following Les out of the room, Connie said angrily, 'That wasn't very polite. The pianist was only trying to make me feel welcome.'

'And had you spilt coffee down your gown that would have been just dandy. It would have looked bad on the stage and been a waste of my money! And for goodness sake don't sit down until after your numbers, otherwise it may crease.'

Johnnie Bellingham, the bandleader, showed Connie into a small ante-room and told her to leave the door open, then she would hear him announce her about an hour after the club opened. 'We'll be playing Glenn Miller's "American Patrol" just beforehand,' he said. 'When you hear that, come out and stand in the wings of the stage. OK?'

'Fine,' she said.

Noting the tension in her he said, 'Don't worry, you'll knock them dead!'

When she was alone, she wondered where Les was, but was pleased he wasn't around. She softly sang her scales and ran through her four numbers gently, saving her voice. She wished she could sit down and relax but, mindful of her dress, she walked about the room for a while, and then leaned against a wall, practising her deep breathing.

After what seemed an eternity, she heard the opening bars of 'American Patrol', and walked slowly to the side of the stage. From her vantage point, she could see the club members jiving to the music and when the number was finished, they walked to their tables. She noted the buzz of conversation as Johnnie made his announcement about their guest singer, and realised what he said about the members coming for a dance and a drink and a chat was true. They were certainly not listening to him at all.

She walked onto the stage to polite applause from a few. She looked at Johnnie and smiled. The opening bars of 'Begin the Beguine' brought several couples to their feet to dance.

The song was perfect for Connie's deep and rich tones and she noticed that slowly the members began to listen as they danced and the chatter in the background grew quieter. The applause at the end was more enthusiastic and as she began to sing 'Embraceable You', she knew she had them. The poignancy of the love song she brought out to perfection, and some of the dancers stopped in front of the band just to listen, swaying to the music. She smiled her thanks at the enthusiastic applause as she made her exit. She could hardly wait for her next call, and when she returned to the rostrum later, this time the audience settled down to listen – some at their tables, others on the dance floor, but not very many now ignored her presence.

She sang Cole Porter's 'Every Time We Say Goodbye' and followed it with 'You're Nobody Till Somebody Loves You'. This time, the applause was wild and as she took her bow, there were calls for 'More!' She turned to look at Johnnie who was grinning broadly. She raised her eyebrows and asked, 'An encore?'

He nodded and the band played the opening bars of the

song they had rehearsed. This time, no one danced. They all sat or stood, listening intently until she finished. As she sang the last note, she glanced over towards the piano where Ben was playing, a wayward lock of hair over his forehead as he studied the keys. He looked up and smiled at her, then he winked. For no apparent reason, this delighted her.

To her surprise, the band followed her off the stage and she found Ben beside her. 'It's our break,' he explained. 'They play records for fifteen minutes. You were great!' he said. 'Come on, I'll buy you a drink at the bar.'

They sat at the bar on high stools and Connie was grateful to be able to relax at last. 'What will you have?' asked Ben.

'I don't really drink,' she said, 'well, not very often.'

'But this is a special occasion,' he insisted, then turning to the barman he said, 'A glass of champagne for the lady and I'll have a whiskey and soda.'

Ben handed her her drink, lifted his own glass and said, 'A toast. To Connie Ryan and may all your wishes come true.'

She sipped the contents of the glass and wrinkled her nose as the bubbles burst. 'Thanks,' she said.

Ben looked past her and she turned to follow his gaze. Les Baxter was in deep conversation with Johnnie Bellingham. 'My manager is funding everything until I get established,' she explained, 'but it is strictly business.' She felt she really had to make this clear.

Ben smiled. 'I see. You aren't an old man's darling then!'

'No, I certainly am not!' she retorted.

He chuckled. 'I'm only teasing,' he said. 'Look, the club closes on a Monday, could we perhaps go out in the evening? Take in a film or a meal?'

Before she could answer, Les Baxter came breezing over. He pointedly ignored the pianist, looked at her glass and frowned. 'I've some good news,' he said. 'Johnnie wants you here every Saturday. You'll be the resident singer at the weekend.'

She was thrilled.

'That's great,' said Ben. 'Congratulations.'

Glaring at Ben, Les said, 'I need to talk to Connie. Do you mind?'

'Les!' she exclaimed, appalled by his rudeness.

Ben slid off the stool and smiled at her. 'I'll be seeing you,' he said, then he walked away.

Connie was livid. Ben had asked her for a date and she so wanted to go; now Les had ruined everything. 'You have no manners, Les Baxter,' she said angrily. 'Barging in on my conversation without a by your leave.'

'One thing you should learn from the very beginning, my girl, is not to get involved with musicians you perform with. Business and pleasure don't mix!'

'What I do in my own time is none of your bloody business!'

'Wrong! Everything you do from now on *is* my business. And by the way, you start your singing lessons with Madame Vicario on Monday afternoon, usual time. Come on, I've booked a taxi to take you home.'

'And what are you going to be doing?' she demanded.

'What I do has nothing to do with you!' he snapped. He glanced towards the entrance. 'There's the driver. Off you go. Here's the money for the fare.'

Connie had no choice. She fumed as she made her exit, but at least she would be seeing Ben next weekend, and maybe he would ask her out again. As she settled in the taxi she was pleased with her first appearance at the club. She had made the punters take notice of her, *and* she had a regular weekly booking. Not bad for someone with her foot on the bottom rung of the ladder. The club wasn't much to speak of, but at least she would see Ben again.

Connie was desperate to tell her family of her good fortune, but her father had forbidden her to enter the house again. Well, to hell with him, she thought, as she dressed the next morning. It's my home, my family. I have every right to visit if I wish, but she knew that what she really wanted was his approval. If he could now see she could make a success of her career, he might take her seriously.

With a thumping heart, she stood in front of the door of her parents' home, wondering whether to knock or walk in, knowing the door, as always, would be on the latch. I've never knocked before, she thought, so why start now? With gritted determination she turned the handle and stepped into the living room.

Her mother was sitting beside the table, peeling potatoes, and Doreen was drinking tea whilst reading the paper. They both looked up.

'Bloody hell!' said Freda.

'Hello, our Connie,' said her sister, seeming unfazed by her unexpected appearance. 'Come in and sit down. There's some tea left. It's a bit weak, though.'

Connie gazed across at her mother expectantly.

'Yes, come and sit down,' she said somewhat nervously. 'Your dad is down at the allotment collecting vegetables for lunch . . . he will be back soon,' she added.

It sounded like a warning, thought Connie. Was her mother expecting her to flee? 'Good,' she said, 'I haven't seen him for ages.'

She saw the worried expression on Freda's face. 'I've got a regular booking, every Saturday night,' she proudly declared.

Freda's face lit up. 'Have you? That's wonderful. Where?'

'The Peacock Club.' At the disappointment now mirrored in her mother's eyes she added, 'It's not a great place, but it is a start.'

'Well done!' said her sister.

At that moment she heard the latch on the kitchen door open, and George Ryan walked into the scullery. The chitchat stopped and there was a sudden air of tension as they all waited for him to enter the living room.

When he did, he was so surprised to see Connie sitting at the table he stood still. Speechless. Doreen took the initiative. 'Look, Dad, our Connie's come to call. She's got some good news to tell you.' She gave her sister a hard look and a nod. Connie took her directive.

'Hello, Dad. Yes, I've got a regular booking every weekend at The Peacock Club.'

George was battling with his thoughts. He was pleased to see his daughter, the place had been so quiet without her and he had missed her more than he would ever admit, but at the same time she had defied him. However, he was mindful of the cruel taunts thrown his way of late by his wife whom he adored and he knew this was an opportunity to get back into her good books. He took a deep breath.

'That's good news,' he said quietly.

Freda looked at him with surprise; Connie, with relief.

'And the other Saturday I sang with Bert Osborne and his band at the Guildhall. That was the week after I won the talent competition,' she added, hoping for some words of approval from him.

'Did you?' was all he said . . . but at least he didn't order her from the house. The tension eased just a little.

'What's the club like?' asked Doreen, trying to be helpful.

'Well, if I was honest I'd have to say it's a bit run down, but the band is good and it's busy. The pianist says it's the poor man's idea of nightclubbing.'

'Poor men can't go clubbing,' snapped her father.

'George!' said her mother sharply and glared at him. Her daughter was home and she was damned if she was going to let George drive her out again!

He said no more and picked up the Sunday papers, shaking the pages loudly.

Doreen pulled a face at her sister and grinned. Then the three women exchanged local gossip, much of which was new to Connie these days, and she realised just how much she missed being the centre of the family.

'I'll do a few more potatoes,' said Freda with a note of defiance in her voice. 'We have a couple of rabbits cooking, we can easily make it stretch to one more.'

George lowered his paper and looked at her, but she pointedly ignored him and as Connie made to refuse she caught the angry glare her mother gave her, defying her refusal.

'Thanks, Mum, that would be lovely.'

The meal was very tasty and they all tucked in, but the conversation was stilted and strained. As soon as she could, Connie made her departure. 'Thanks, Mum.' She hugged and kissed her.

Freda held her tightly as if she'd never let go. 'You come again, darlin'. This is your home.'

Doreen rose from her seat and did the same. She whispered in her ear, 'Lovely news, Con. He'll come round, you'll see. Just give him time.'

Connie walked to the door. 'Bye, Dad.'

He didn't look up but grunted something utterly unintelligible.

She smiled at the others and left, but as she walked down the road, tears ran down her cheeks. She felt an outsider, no longer part of the family . . . and couldn't her father have said something? Anything! If only sod off!

As she put the key in the door of Mrs Baxter's house in Wilton Avenue she thought how strange life was. Today she'd had lunch with her family, yet she felt completely alone in the world.

Chapter Twelve

Madame Vicario was delighted to see her star pupil again and hugged her warmly. 'Connie, my dear! How are you? Come in, come in.' She ushered her into the drawing room. 'Now tell me what has been happening to you?'

At last Connie was able to share her success with someone who appreciated her talent. She regaled her with details of the competition at the Guildhall, and told her of the virginal-looking girl who was on before her. 'I knew I would have to be as different to her as I could. Thank God for the acting lessons you gave me when you taught me to sing *Carmen*! I was as sultry as I could be!'

Irene clapped her hands together with delight. 'Wonderful! And you won?'

'Yes, I did. I was so thrilled. The sound of the applause was so exciting.' She looked across at her teacher and said, 'Applause is so satisfying, isn't it?'

Madame chuckled. 'Sometimes it is the only thing you live for . . . that affirmation from your audience is something that becomes vital to your very existence.'

'And now . . .' Connie could hardly contain her excitement, 'I have a regular Saturday booking at a local nightclub!'

'Oh, Connie, you have done well. Have you been keeping up your exercises?'

'Yes, Madame, just as you taught me.'

'Mr Baxter must be very pleased with you.'

Connie hesitated. 'Yes, I suppose so, he doesn't say a lot, but he did get me to sign a contract. I am tied to him for the next five years.'

Madame Vicario raised her eyebrows. 'Who can blame him? After all he has invested a lot of money in you, Connie. He must be allowed to recover his expenses and make a little on the side. That's business.'

'I did phone Jeremy Taylor before I signed, but he was away.'

'Why did you do that?'

'I didn't want to sign five years of my life away.'

'But what if Jeremy had offered you the same deal?'

Connie beamed, 'I would have accepted!'

'After all Mr Baxter has done for you?'

Connie felt her colour rise. 'Yes! Mr Taylor knows what he is doing. Les Baxter is a bookmaker!'

Irene frowned but made no further comment except to say, 'So tell me about the club.'

She was absolutely truthful. 'It's a bit shabby and run-down, but they are busy and the band is good.'

Seeing the sudden brightness in Connie's eyes Irene asked, 'So which musician is the good-looking one?'

Her pupil burst out laughing. 'How did you know?'

'All singers have a weakness for musicians. Well?'

'It's Ben Stanton, the pianist. He asked me out on a date but before I could say anything Les interrupted our conversation.' And then she added indignantly, 'Do you know what he told me?' Without waiting for a reply she continued, 'He told me not to mix business with pleasure, to keep away from all the musicians I sing with!'

'Much as you will hate me for this,' said Irene, 'I have to say he has a point. It doesn't always work. It can come between you and a good performance.'

'Nothing will ever do that!'

The teacher rose to her feet. What a lot about life this young girl had yet to learn. 'Come along, let's get down to work,' she said, and she walked through to the music room.

The following hour was bliss to Connie. She so enjoyed the discipline meted out to her during her lessons and she blossomed as a singer before her teacher. She took any reprimand without comment because she knew that this wonderful French woman could take her beyond her own expectations.

At the end of their time, Irene said, 'You have improved beyond all recognition. Your voice is deeper, richer, your enunciation is clearer and your breathing is better. Your timing?' She shrugged. 'It needs a little work. Your trouble, my girl, is you are too eager. Wait – and listen to the music.'

'Bert Osborne said the same thing when I sang with his band,' Connie admitted.

'There you are then!' Closing the piano lid she said, 'Let's go and have a cup of tea before you go.'

'There is one thing,' ventured Connie.

'And what's that?'

'I have only two gowns to wear on Saturdays.'

Madame Vicario spun round. 'Then you alternate them! Really, Connie, sometimes you amaze me! We are living in such difficult times – almost everything is rationed, haven't you heard of Make Do and Mend?'

'Of course, I have.'

'You are so lucky to have such gowns and I don't even want to *think* where Mr Baxter got the coupons for them. Just be grateful, my girl!'

Connie felt embarrassed by this unexpected outburst. 'Well, I am really,' she said. 'I just thought the customers might get bored by seeing the same thing, that's all,' she finished lamely.

'The men will hardly notice and the women will be envious. Anyway, you said the place was a bit run-down, so their customers probably won't be that interested.'

Connie now felt thoroughly deflated.

Seeing the look of dejection on the face of her pupil, Irene said, 'The only thing that really worries me is that you are so young and unworldly.' She paused to pour the tea. 'You have such a burning desire to succeed that sometimes you are very self-centred.'

'What on earth do you mean?' asked Connie with horror at such a remark.

'You expect too much too soon,' said Madame gently. 'I *totally* understand your ambition, but what concerns me is that you are *so* driven that you think only of yourself and where you want to go. You tend to forget those who help you along the way.'

'How could you say such a thing?'

'I say it because I am so fond of you. You were quite prepared to dump Mr Baxter for Jeremy Taylor. Now I think that is not only devious but ruthless, and frankly, unforgivable . . . and in one so young!' She shook her head. 'Remember this, Connie, my dear: never forget those who put themselves out for you – and the little people. You may need them in the future. If you stab them in the back, *they* may turn the knife on *you*, one day!'

Back in Southampton, Les Baxter was trying to sort out a major problem. A London syndicate was trying to muscle in on his territory and he wasn't having it! Several of his runners were coming to him telling tales of being threatened with violence by the strangers if they continued to give their bets to Baxter. One or two of the braver men had already been roughed up – as a lesson to the others, they were told.

Baxter was livid. Others had tried, unsuccessfully, in the past to do the same, but these people were far more of a threat. Baxter had heard of Kenny Pritchard, the son of a West End villain who had died recently in an accident. Kenny had taken over from his father. He was young and he was greedy, and he was finding his feet, trying to show he was as good as his old man. As far as Les Baxter was concerned he was a loose cannon and a dangerous one at that. But Les had been in the business far too long. He was wily, cunning and equally dangerous, especially when he was looking after something that he thought was his. He had built his business up over the years and no little whippersnapper was going to spoil things for him. It was quite obvious that young Kenny Pritchard needed teaching a lesson, and he was just the man to do so.

He gathered his strong-arm boys around him and told them to police the areas covered by his runners and to deal severely with any interlopers. 'No dead bodies,' he warned. 'Leave them breathing, but make sure they know they've been punished.'

The following weeks kept the Southampton Police Force on its toes. There were strong rumours of gang warfare. The emergency ward at the local hospital seemed suddenly inundated with broken arms, shattered kneecaps, broken ribs. But none of the victims would give any details except to say it was accidental – or a fight in a pub with someone whose name escaped them because they were drunk at the time. Then as soon as they were able, off they would go back to their homes, which all turned out to be fictitious addresses when the local force checked with the Metropolitan Police.

It was quiet for a time, but Les knew that young Kenny would try again, just to satisfy his ego and to prove himself. Well, he was ready for him.

Connie returned to work on Tuesday morning, full of her appearance at The Peacock Club. Molly was intrigued by it all. All thoughts of her argument with Connie on the day after the talent contest had long been forgotten. 'Weren't you nervous, Con?'

'Not once I stepped onto the stage. The waiting around was tedious, but I'll take a magazine on Saturday,' she said as she dusted a showcase. 'The pianist asked me for a date,' she added casually.

'Really?' Molly's eyes shone with excitement. 'What was he like? Did you go out with him?'

'His name is Ben, and he's really nice,' Connie confided, 'but we didn't get the chance to make arrangements because that Les Baxter interfered. Hopefully next weekend he'll ask again.'

'Oh, Connie! What an exciting life you do lead these days.'

But Connie didn't entirely agree with her friend's sentiments. Yes, she had a regular booking and went to London once a week for her lessons, but she was still living away from home. Residing with Mrs Baxter was boring and lonely. Connie had been practising her exercises and songs in her room and the old lady had asked her to stop as it interfered with her being able to listen to the radio. Connie had blown a fuse.

'Now look, Mrs Baxter, I can't cook my meal until you've finished in the kitchen, I don't have any say in which radio programmes we listen to . . . I have to practise. This is important and your son will be very cross if I don't and my voice suffers!' She could see the old girl wasn't impressed. 'If I don't and I can't sing well, Les will have lost a lot of money spent on my training and thanks to you, he'll never get it back because my voice will be ruined!'

At the mention of money, Mrs Baxter changed her tune. After all, if Les was out of pocket, she might not be as indulged, and she did enjoy the things and the money her son lavished on her.

'Very well,' she conceded grudgingly. 'But from seven o'clock until eight. One hour only!'

Connie cursed and pulled a face at the retreating back of her landlady and burst into song at the top of her voice, making Les's mother jump almost out of her skin.

She turned and glared at Connie, who just laughed and went into her room, slamming the door behind her.

The following Saturday evening, Connie arrived for her rehearsal at the club as before and ran through the numbers Johnnie Bellingham had chosen for her. She was disappointed that Ben remained on the stage going through a couple of musical arrangements with the band. He had said hello but had been busy discussing something with another of the musicians, so she didn't have chance to talk to him. At least Les Baxter didn't seem to be on the premises. She started to read her magazine, waiting for the number that was to be played before her entrance. Then, as she was announced and walked onto the stage for her first appearance, Ben smiled at her and played the opening chords of 'That Old Black Magic'.

The dancers appreciated the rhythm and once again the people who had heard her before listened intently and applauded, and again showed their enthusiasm when she finished a Sammy Cahn number, 'Saturday Night is the Loneliest Night of the Year'.

And later, after her second appearance, Ben walked off the stage behind her as the band took their break. 'Hello, Connie. You look great in that dress, and you sang like a dream.'

'Thank you,' she said, a little shyly now Ben was beside her.

'Is your watchdog with you tonight?' he asked with a grin.

Connie chuckled. 'I haven't seen him.'

'Good, then perhaps we can arrange that date. Will you let me take you out next Monday evening?'

'Yes, that would be lovely.'

'I'll meet you outside Tyrell and Greens at seven thirty. Will that be all right?'

'Yes, that's fine.' She quickly calculated that if she didn't linger behind at Madame Vicario's she would be back in time to change and get to the appointed meeting place.

'How about a drink?' he asked, and led her to the bar. 'What'll you have?'

'I'm very thirsty,' she said. 'Could I have a shandy?'

'You can have what you like when you're with me.' He ordered the drink and then excused himself saying, 'I just need to pop to the gents, I won't be long.'

A young man settled on the empty stool beside her a moment later. 'I'm sorry,' she said to the stranger, 'but that seat is taken.'

'Yes, I know, I saw him leave. I just wanted to say how much I enjoyed your singing.'

She beamed at him with delight. 'Oh, thank you.' She thought he was very good-looking in a raffish sort of way and wondered what he was doing here, as he was exceptionally well dressed.

She saw Ben coming towards her and so did the stranger. 'Here comes your friend, I'd better go for now, but I'll be seeing you again, of that you can be sure. By the way, my name is Kenny Pritchard,' he said.

As Ben sat beside her he raised his eyebrows. 'I don't know, I leave you for a second and another man makes a pass at you!'

'No, he didn't,' argued Connie, 'he just told me that he enjoyed my singing. Who is he?'

With a shrug Ben said, 'I've not seen him here before. From the cut of his suit I'd say he's from London, we probably won't see him again. I'd guess this place is a bit downmarket for him.' He gazed at Connie and said earnestly, 'You must be very careful in this game, young lady. Lots of men will try and make up to you. Be cautious, that's all.'

She pulled a face. 'You sound like my father.'

'Not at all, but you are so young, you're a beautiful girl and let's face it, Connie, you haven't been around much. It's easy for a man to turn a girl's head with flattery.'

'Is that what you're doing?' she asked with a smile.

He laughed. 'No! I'm different. Surely you can see that? Look at these hands, they do honest work.' His eyes twinkled as he added, 'And have you ever seen a more honest-looking face?'

Chuckling softly she said, 'No doubt as I'm seeing you next Monday I'll find out, and remember we'll be working together too.'

'I'm looking forward to that,' he said.

At that moment the barman said, 'A taxi has arrived for you, Miss Ryan. Mr Baxter said to tell you it's paid for.'

The smile faded from Ben's face. 'Your manager certainly sees to everything, doesn't he? Where are you going now?'

'Home.'

'And where is that?'

'Wilton Avenue. I stay with his mother.'

'Now that's convenient.'

'He doesn't live there!' Connie explained heatedly. 'Les Baxter lives in a house of his own.'

'Come on,' said Ben. 'At least I can walk you to the door, that way I can be sure that smart alec who spoke to you before doesn't accost you again.'

Outside he checked with the taxi driver that he was the driver for Miss Ryan, then turning to her he said, 'I'll see you on Monday, Connie.' He leaned forward and kissed her briefly on the mouth, opened the door of the vehicle and waited for her to be seated. 'You take care,' he said.

Connie sat back, her head in a whirl. Ben had kissed her. How wonderful! True, it was a friendly kind of kiss, but she wondered if he would do the same after their date on Monday, and her heart beat just that little bit faster at the thought.

Chapter Thirteen

Kenny Pritchard was keeping a low profile as he toured around Southampton, looking over the different areas covered by the runners working for Les Baxter. His information had been correct: the man was making a fortune! His network stretched across the town and his organisation was terrific. There were several places for the runners to drop off the daily takings and bets, and each day the location was changed. Very smart, he had to admit. No doubt Baxter had several of the police force taking kickbacks, but not all men could be bought, he knew that.

He liked Southampton after the dirt and smoke of London, he mused. Here, the air was clearer and it wasn't a bit like the crowded streets of the East End of London where he operated. He loved the tang of sea air, carried on the breeze. Yes, he'd quite like staying here now and again, and that's just what he'd do once he'd taken over from Baxter.

This town was ripe for the picking, with a steady flow of seafarers arriving with each liner, their pockets full of gratuities from grateful passengers, especially after a cruise.

He wondered what Baxter was like. He was reputed to be a hard man, but everyone had their weakness; if he could only discover Baxter's it would give him an edge. He knew about hard men, his father had been one, and although he was saddened by his death, it had almost been a relief in a way. Now he was free to do with the organisation as he wished, do things that his father had always decried.

'You're too full of yourself!' his father had told him. 'You come up with these harebrained schemes without thinking them through. If I let you have your way, you could cost me half my business!' Well, now he could do what he liked and he wanted Les Baxter's lucrative patch.

Never one to stint himself, he sat quietly in the residents' lounge of the Polygon Hotel where he'd stayed for the last few days, and suddenly thought of the young singer he'd seen at the crummy little club the previous night. Great voice, great body. Yes, he fancied a bit of that! Well, he'd be around now and again, setting up his plans to depose Baxter. She would be a delightful distraction. He downed his drink and made for the lift. He must get back to London in the morning.

On Monday, in the music room in Maida Vale, Connie was so excited about meeting Ben later that evening, she was finding it hard to concentrate and Madame Vicario was becoming increasingly irritated with her.

'For goodness' sake, whatever is the matter with you today?'

'I'm sorry.'

'So, what is it?' Irene asked. 'Your mind is on other things. Concentrate!'

Trying to appease her teacher, Connie confessed, 'I'm meeting Ben Stanton, the pianist, this evening and I'm so excited, I can't think.'

Madame placed both hands on her hips and declared, 'Mr Baxter was right, you should never become involved with people you work with. Already it is interfering. You need to make a choice – a career or a man! You want to make it to the top, you can't have both.'

'But I must be allowed a little fun, surely?'

Irene gazed at her steadily. 'Have I made a mistake? I thought I was teaching a girl who was dedicated, who would kill to succeed. Maybe, after all, I was wrong.'

'No, no. I do want it, I want it all! I'll concentrate, really I will.'

'Do you, Connie? It doesn't seem that way to me! If you want to get to the top, this is no time for romantic liaisons. Later, when you've become established, that is the time to decide whether love or a career is more important to you. Now you need to concentrate entirely on your singing!'

And so, at last, she got down to some real work and eventually Madame was happy with her.

Later that evening, Connie made her way to Tyrell and Greens and was relieved to see Ben was already there. It was strange to see him in a dark grey suit instead of evening dress. He walked towards her.

'Hello, Connie. How are you?'

'Fine,' she said. 'You look so different!'

'So do you, without all your finery, but you still look good enough to eat. Talking of which, what do you want to do, see a film or go for a meal?'

Thinking that she would rather talk to Ben than sit in a cinema for three hours, and if she went for a meal it would eke out her weekly rations, she chose the latter.

'Tell me about your time with E.N.S.A.,' she said, once they were settled in a corner of a small restaurant.

'It wasn't all fun,' he said, frowning. 'We visited the troops in some pretty dodgy situations. We went out to entertain Monty's army in Egypt, near El Alamein. The desert wasn't the most comfortable of places, but my God, those boys were pleased to see us.'

'Whose band were you with?'

'They were all organised by Geraldo.'

'Really!' She was impressed. He was one of the top bandleaders.

'Then why on earth are you at The Peacock Club? It's a bit of a comedown, isn't it?'

He found her bluntness amusing. 'Do you always come straight to the point like that?' he asked with a grin.

117

Realising what she'd said, she began to apologise, but he stopped her.

'No, it's all right. I prefer a woman who speaks her mind. As a matter of fact, when I came home and was demobbed, I found out about my girl sleeping her way to the top and I went a bit wild for a while – drinking more than was good for me – and I ended up in Southampton. One day, I saw an advert for a pianist and I've been here ever since.'

'And you're satisfied with second best, are you?' Connie couldn't understand his attitude at all.

'Musicians are a bit lazy; you'll find that out in time. As long as I can make a living, pay the bills . . . after all, I have no woman in my life to consider, I've only myself to please. I don't have your burning ambition.'

'I can't help it,' she said, 'ever since I was ten years old, I've wanted to be a star. It's my destiny, I know it.'

He gazed at her with admiration. 'I envy you your drive,' he said, 'but do take care, Connie, show business is full of sharks. As long as you are on your way up, that's fine, you'll be surrounded by people wanting to be your friend, bleeding you dry, especially if you're in the money. But they'll drop you like a stone if you start to slip from that top spot.'

'I'm not a fool!' she exclaimed. 'I'll make sure that doesn't happen to me. Anyway, Les Baxter will make sure it doesn't.'

'Ummm. The ever-present Mr Baxter. I'm not at all sure I trust that man. He looks too much like a predator for me! I've seen his type many times. Older man with money – finding young pretty girl.'

To her credit, Connie jumped to his defence. 'If it wasn't for him, I wouldn't be here talking to you now, because we would never have met. I would still be singing occasionally in my father's Social Club!'

'Now that *would* be a pity. It's just that you are such a good-looking girl that I can't imagine any man wanting just a business relationship with you. Are you absolutely certain that's all he wants?'

'For goodness' sake, he's almost as old as my father!'
'You think that makes a difference?'
'To me it does!'
He didn't look convinced. 'Just take care, that's all.'

The rest of the evening passed off pleasantly. They spent the entire time talking about music and songwriters, and he tried to explain to her different ways to phrase her lyrics, humming the melody of a song to her to demonstrate his point – much to the enjoyment of the diners who were sitting close by. Not that either of them were aware of this, so engrossed in their conversation were they.

As he walked her home, his arm around her shoulders, they sang together and to Connie's surprise, Ben had a good tenor voice.

'We could do a double act,' she joked.

He squeezed her shoulder. 'You are strictly a solo artist, my sweet. You don't need anyone else except a band to accompany you . . . or a good pianist!'

At the front door of her lodgings, he took her arm and held her close.

'Darling, Connie,' he murmured, 'I really don't think you're safe to be let out on your own, you could get into so much trouble.' He lowered his lips to hers and kissed her

Connie had been kissed by young men a few times, but never before by a man who was as experienced as Ben. Her senses reeled beneath his expertise. She melted into his arms and returned his kisses eagerly and was disappointed when he released her. He gazed deeply into her eyes and said, 'Yes, indeed, a lot of trouble. It's time I went home. I'll see you on Saturday.' He kissed her forehead and walked away.

Connie was thrilled when, on Saturday night, Eric and Doreen came to the club to watch her perform. Seated at a table, Doreen looked around and remarked disdainfully, 'Not much of a place, is it? What is that Les Baxter up to, I wonder?'

Eric tried to appease her. 'I'm sure this is just a starting point, darling. After all, we know Connie is a knockout, but she does have to make a name for herself before the public.'

Later that night, Doreen saw Baxter arrive and order a drink from the bar. She excused herself and marched over to him.

'Doreen!' he said when she tapped him on the shoulder.

Her eyes flashed with anger. 'Is this what you call looking after my sister?' she demanded. 'This is nothing short of a fleapit! I want to know what you're up to.'

He chuckled and said, 'Calm down. I am doing the best I can for the moment. She needed a place to make her mistakes. Here it wouldn't be noticeable that she's a beginner. Now she's learning how to handle an audience, and soon she'll be moving up the ladder – I promise.'

The explanation did make a lot of sense, so Doreen said, 'You had better keep that promise. Our Connie left home because of you and I haven't forgiven you for that yet!' She turned and walked quickly away.

The following weeks passed quickly for Connie. Summer was nearly over and soon the autumn would be upon them and she wondered how the time had flown so fast. She occasionally visited her family, but the atmosphere was still strained between her and her father, who couldn't find it within himself to forgive her for defying him. But as a performer, her confidence grew and her singing improved, as did her timing with the added help from Ben.

He would ask her out from time to time, but although he kissed her goodnight, she felt he was keeping her at arm's length. Nevertheless, they were good friends and she was so wrapped up in her music now, she was as interested in his teachings as his affection. He had also taken over writing the band arrangements of the numbers she was to sing, and she was both grateful and amazed at his artistry. What Connie was unaware of was the battle Ben was fighting with his feelings towards her. He knew that if he wasn't careful, he could become deeply emotionally involved here. He had been down this road once before and couldn't face the same result again. It wasn't easy because Connie was blossoming as a woman. A fact that hadn't escaped the notice of her manager.

To his own surprise, Les Baxter was jealous of the attention that Ben paid to his protégée. He realised the pianist, being the fine musician that he was, was able to educate Connie about music, which was to her advantage. And she was learning – that was apparent in her performance – but every weekend, Les resented the intrusion more and more, telling himself he was only protecting her.

He began to pay Connie compliments, which seemed to please her. Little did he realise that she was only delighted because she had done her best for him, mindful of her obligation – and her five-year contract – and until now, he'd never praised her. He even suggested that he buy her another dress, but she refused. Les gave her five pounds every Saturday, but she wanted to be in a position to earn real money.

'No, thanks. I'll never earn any money if you keep buying stuff. I'll be forever paying you off!' She was frustrated knowing she was working, but very aware that there must be a horrendous amount yet to repay.

'It'll be my treat,' he said. 'Not a ball gown, a little cocktail number, it'll be perfectly suitable. Just to show how pleased I am with you.'

This was too much of a temptation. 'Oh, well, that's different then,' she said, feeling that she deserved some reward for her hard work. She may well be growing up, but Connie was still, at heart, a self-centred girl.

When she told Ben about it, he scowled. 'What's he after?'

'He's not after anything. The other two gowns will come out of my earnings, this dress is a reward, he said.'

'I've seen the way he looks at you lately!'

'Don't be ridiculous!' she told him. 'He's only looking after his investment.' But when, after the Saturday performance was

121

over, Les invited her out to dinner the following Wednesday, she began to wonder.

Seeing the suspicious expression on Connie's face, he said, 'We need to talk over future plans for your career.'

This made sense to her, so she agreed.

'I'll come round to Ma's and collect you at half past seven. All right?'

'I'll be ready,' she said, but bearing Ben's remarks in mind she decided to be wary.

To her surprise, Les arrived at the house driving a new Riley RMA. As he opened the door of the vehicle, she admired the sleek lines of the chassis and the cream-coloured leather upholstery.

'I didn't know you could drive,' she said as she settled in the passenger seat. 'You always go everywhere by taxi.'

'I always had a car until the war,' he explained, 'then with the petrol rationing, it became too difficult.'

'But it's still rationed!'

He laughed at her. 'It's always possible to buy what you want if you know the right people, Connie.'

She remembered the rumours about him earning a fortune in the black market; well, that still continued. She'd only recently read of someone being sent to prison for selling black market goods. As far as she knew, Les had never been inside, so he'd been smart. But she wondered just what would happen if he was found out; after all he seemed to have a never-ending supply of clothing coupons. Her heart sank. If that ever happened . . . what would happen to her career?

He drove along the avenue and pulled into the car park of the Cowherds Hotel, on the edge of the Common. Once inside they were ushered to a table by a waiter who seemed to know him.

'This is your table, Mr Baxter. So nice to see you again.'

The landlord, Mr Trestrail, made his way over and shook Baxter by the hand. 'Everything all right?' he asked.

'Fine,' said Les. 'This is Miss Connie Ryan. She's a singer at

The Peacock Club. You should take a Saturday night off and see her perform. She'll be a big star one day.'

The landlord shook her hand. 'Have a nice evening,' he said, then turning to Les added, 'I've got some nice steak outside if you fancy it. I keep it for my special customers.' And he walked away to greet another diner.

Les grinned at Connie. 'See what I mean about knowing the right people?'

They started with hors d'œuvres and then the steak, which was tender and delicious. The waiter attentively poured the wine that Les ordered, but as yet he had made no comment about her career and she began to wonder if this invitation had been some sort of ploy after all.

It wasn't until they were drinking the coffee served after the dessert, that Les broached the subject. 'You have done really well at The Peacock Club and you've learned a lot with the help of Madame Vicario and your pianist, but soon it will be time to move on.'

Connie's heart sank. She did desperately want to move up the ladder, to perform in more salubrious places, but she felt secure where she was with Ben to guide her. The thought of a new venue without him completely threw her.

'Have you anywhere in mind?'

'Not at this moment, but I have a few feelers out and I'm expecting some replies soon.'

She breathed a sigh of relief. But when she was taken home later, she sat on her bed and thought of Madame Vicario's words about getting to the top without the encumbrance of a man. But what would Ben say? She decided that she would keep quiet until something definite had been arranged.

Chapter Fourteen

Les Baxter had indeed been looking around for places to move his blossoming star higher up the ladder. He could have found her bookings in similar places to The Peacock Club, but that wasn't what he wanted for Connie. Southampton was just a starting place, and he felt she was now ready for London, but here, he was out of his league. He didn't know anyone in the city in the entertainment business other than Jeremy Taylor. But who could be better? he thought with a sly smile. And that afternoon he called the theatrical agent at his office.

'Jeremy! How the devil are you?'

Recognising the voice, Jeremy answered. 'Good Lord – Les Baxter of all people! What can I do for you?'

Never one to beat about the bush, Baxter said, 'Remember that young singer I was asking you about earlier in the year?'

Jeremy immediately caught on but casually said, 'The one for whom I gave you the address of the singing teacher?'

'Yes. She's been working Saturday nights locally in a club, but now she's ready for better things. I thought you might know someone.'

Now Jeremy Taylor was a very astute businessman and he was not about to give something away for nothing, especially as he'd heard the girl sing and knew her potential. 'And what's in it for me if I help you?' he asked.

Les winced. He had hoped to keep Connie to himself, but he was wise enough to admit he needed help at the moment and that to get it he'd have to give away a little piece of the action, as he called it. 'I'm sure we can come to some arrangement,' he conceded, reluctantly.

'I should bloody well think so! But first I need to come down to Southampton and hear your girl perform.'

'You've already heard her sing at Madame Vicario's,' said Les, wanting the other man to realise he knew about his visit.

'This is true, but that was hardly a performance, old chap. She sang a couple of songs, that's all. I want to see her with an audience. I'll come down this Saturday evening. What time is she on, and where is the place?'

Les gave him the necessary details and arranged to meet him there. After he put down the receiver, he sat and thought carefully. He needed Jeremy Taylor's help but he wasn't about to give away too much of Connie, not unless it was really going to be worth it. He decided to keep the agent's visit to himself as he didn't want Connie to be nervous before she went on. Then – it would be negotiations! Taylor was well known for his skill of procuring the best deals for himself and his clients – this was why he was so wealthy. But Les too was no fool. If Taylor wanted a piece of Connie, it would be because he thought she was good and with the hope of getting her contract for himself. Les grinned. Well, he had that all signed and sealed for the next five years and by then, he planned to be well in with the right people. Taylor would be the man to put him on that road. Dangling Connie and her talent before him was like a sprat to catch a mackerel!

On Saturday evening, Les watched as Connie rehearsed with the band. The new arrangements by Ben Stanton were excellent and although Les was no musician, he could appreciate the fact.

Connie was wearing the new cocktail dress he'd bought for her in a shot silk shaded in dark blue with lighter hues in the material. It had a wide neck and was figure-hugging at the waist, slightly fuller over the hips. The skirt was mid calf, just like Christian Dior's New Look, and the dark blue satin shoes

he'd purchased from a man he knew set off the dress and
Connie's shapely limbs. He was more than pleased with the
effect. But he wasn't pleased as he watched Connie leaning
over the piano singing to the pianist in a very friendly manner.
Smiling as she did so. He listened to the words of 'It Had to
Be You'.

He watched Ben Stanton smiling back at Connie. And he
didn't like it at all.

Two hours later, Les was sitting at the bar when Jeremy
Taylor arrived. Taylor looked around the club dismissively.
'Couldn't you have done better than this for the girl?' he asked
as he approached the bar.

Baxter looked uncomfortable. 'It was the best offer in town
and she had to start somewhere. After all, she's unknown, but
now she does have a small following,' he protested.

Taylor shrugged. 'It's not London though, is it, Les?'

'No, It's not London.'

At that moment, Johnnie Bellingham announced the arrival
of their regular singer and Connie walked onto the stage
amidst enthusiastic applause.

Baxter cast a glance in Jeremy's direction but he gave
nothing away by his expression, but as Connie started to sing,
Jeremy felt the hairs on his neck stand up again, just as they
did when Connie sang in Maida Vale.

He applauded politely with the others at the end of the
number but made no comment; however he listened carefully
as she sang a number from the new show, *Annie Get Your Gun*,
the poignant, 'They Say That It's Wonderful', and knew she
had that indefinable magic that makes a star.

As Connie left the stage after her first stint, the two men
moved to a table with their drinks, enabling them to talk
without being overheard.

'Well, what do you think of her?' asked Les impatiently.

With a nod of his head, Jeremy said, 'She's come along very
well, my boy. Now, she has stage presence. The crowd love her,
but who does the arrangements for her?'

Baxter didn't look pleased. 'The pianist, Ben Stanton. Why?'

'Because they're great! He should work with Connie permanently.'

'I don't see that is at all necessary!'

With great patience, Jeremy explained. 'Most good singers have their own pianist and this one arranges the music to the advantage of the singer. She needs him! Especially at this stage of her career.'

Les tried to argue further, but Jeremy was adamant. 'If you want me to help Connie, the pianist comes too. And think about it, Les, she needs someone who knows what's going on. He could help *and* protect her. You know what show business is like!' He looked at the bookie. 'Of course, I forgot, you don't, do you?' he made his point in a brutal manner. One to which Les had no answer.

'So, do you think you can help Connie?' Les asked.

'Oh, yes, there is no question about that. The only question is, will you make it worth my while to do so? I want part of this girl if I'm to help her.' He smiled disarmingly. 'After all, that's only fair, old chap.'

Les's heart sank. He wanted to keep a hundred per cent control over Connie, but he really didn't have a choice. And so they began to haggle.

'I'm prepared to give you twenty per cent of her,' said Les magnanimously.

Jeremy looked lazily at him and said, 'You jest, my friend, of course! I can take your girl to the top. *You* will never get her there. With a bit of luck you may find some insignificant little club and no one but the clients will ever hear of her. I can make her a huge star, in time. A huge star!'

'How much time?'

Jeremy shrugged. 'It depends how much interest I am given. There is big money to be made here for all of us – eventually.' He took a cigar from his pocket, slipped off the band, slowly pierced the tip, and waited.

Les was battling within himself. He knew he had a potential success on his hands but he was wise enough to know he couldn't possibly take her to the top alone, even with his underworld connections. He took a deep breath and made another offer.

When the band took their break, Ben and Connie headed for the bar as was their habit now, and as she sat talking to the pianist, she looked around and spotted Les with a man who looked familiar. Could it be . . .? 'My God!' she exclaimed.

'What is it?' asked Ben.

'My manager's talking to Jeremy Taylor.'

'The theatrical agent?' asked Ben in surprise.

'You know him?'

'Good Lord, no, but everyone in the business has heard of him. He's about the best there is. What on earth is he doing here?'

Unable to smother the opportunity to impress him, Connie casually said, 'He offered to take me on earlier this year.'

Ben looked at her with open mouth. 'Good God!'

'He heard me singing when I was having a lesson, but I refused him.'

'You what!'

'What else could I do? Les had paid for my lessons and everything.'

Ben covered his eyes with his hand. 'I don't believe this. You, just starting out, turned down Jeremy Taylor.' He shook his head in disbelief. Then he said quickly, 'They're coming over.'

Jeremy smiled at Connie when he reached the bar. 'Hello, my dear girl. How are you?' He extended his hand and when Connie took it he kissed hers. 'You have come a long way since I heard you at Irene's. I will make sure to tell her when I see her.' Turning to Ben, he held out his hand again. 'Congratulations on those arrangements, young man. They were excellent.'

Ben beamed. 'Thank you, sir.'

With an expression of thunder, Les looked at Ben and asked, 'How would you like to work for me?'

'Us!' interjected Jeremy, firmly.

'I don't understand,' said Ben very slowly.

Jeremy took control of the conversation. 'Mr Baxter and I are in a sort of partnership with the management of this young lady and I want you to be her pianist—'

'Just a minute,' interrupted Connie. 'What do you mean a sort of partnership with my management?'

Les made to speak but Jeremy took Connie's hand in his and said, 'I'm going to help to get you established in London, my dear.'

With wide eyes she said, 'You are?' And she turned to look questioningly at Les.

'Yes, that's right!' he said abruptly, still unhappy about the arrangement he'd been forced to make.

'I have forty per cent of you, dear Connie!' Jeremy's eyes twinkled as he looked at her.

'You do?' She looked absolutely delighted which didn't please Les Baxter at all.

'But I have the controlling interest, Connie. Be very sure to remember that,' the manager said forcefully.

'Yes, of course,' she said. She looked back at Jeremy who gave her a conspiratorial wink and then continued his conversation with Ben.

'I am going to set about getting decent engagements in London for this young lady, which may take a few weeks, but when I do I want you as her pianist and arranger. What do you say?'

Connie held her breath.

'I'm very interested,' he said, 'but of course it depends on the deal you are prepared to offer.'

'In that case I think we men ought to go and talk about it.' He glanced at Les. 'Baxter?'

Les said, 'Right.' Turning to Connie he said, 'Wait here for me.'

130

She didn't need to be told, she wasn't going anywhere until she learned the outcome! She watched anxiously as the three of them sat down. She saw that Les looked grim, whereas Jeremy and Ben seemed quite amicable, although it was evident that Ben was bargaining quite earnestly. Eventually the three men shook hands and rose from the table, then walked back to her.

'That's all settled then,' said Jeremy. 'Ben has agreed to be your arranger and pianist. We'll have a contract drawn up for him to sign.' Then looking at Les he said, 'And you and I need one between us. I'll get my lawyer to send it to you.'

Les looked at Connie and Ben and said, 'Now, not a word to Bellingham until we have a definite booking for you. Then you can give your notice. Ben hasn't a written contract so he can leave in a week if necessary.'

Jeremy Taylor looked at his watch and said, 'I must make tracks.' Smiling at Connie he said, 'We're going places, young lady. This time next year, we should have your name in lights.'

'Big lights, I hope?'

He laughed loudly. 'Oh, Connie, you are incorrigible. Big lights, I promise. I'll be in touch,' he said before he and the bookie walked to the door, still deep in conversation.

Connie looked expectantly at Ben and asked, 'Are you pleased we'll be working together permanently?'

'Yes, Connie, I am. Taylor knows what he's doing and he'll make good his promise as you have the talent, and I'll be very interested to be part of it.'

Eyes bright with anticipation, Connie sat up and spreading her arms said, 'I'm going to be a star! I wonder what my father will have to say for himself then!'

'You'll have to work very hard, Connie. I hope you realise that. It's one thing to have Jeremy Taylor behind you, that will open many doors, but if you don't come up to expectations, his or anyone who books you, you'll be back in Southampton in a flash!'

She was furious. 'Do you think I'd throw it all away just

when everything is within my grasp? I'll work my socks off. No one, but no one, will stand in my way!'

'Mr Baxter didn't seem all that thrilled about sharing you with Taylor.'

Flicking back her hair she retorted, 'I don't give a hoot about what he thinks, the most important thing is that I have a top agent!'

'He still has the controlling interest, Connie. He can veto anything he doesn't like, and then where will you be?'

She smiled slowly. 'Then I'll have to keep him sweet until my five-year contract is up.'

'And then?'

'And then I'll be free!'

He gripped her arm. 'You be very careful how you handle Baxter. He's trouble and he's not a man I would like to get on the wrong side of.'

At that moment Les Baxter returned. 'Come along,' he demanded, 'I've got the car outside, I'll drive you home.'

Connie was about to say she'd like to stay a little longer but she saw the cold expression in his eyes as he waited and decided it would be unwise, tonight of all nights. She slipped off the stool and said to Ben, 'I'll see you next week, and I'm delighted we'll be working together.'

Ben sat alone at the bar. Well, he thought. What a turn up! He was now on the books of Jeremy Taylor, and Ben knew enough about the business to realise that if Taylor said he would take Connie to the top – he would. But if he was to be working with Connie permanently this became a dilemma, because he knew he could easily fall in love with her. She was getting beneath his skin every single day.

He shook his head. This wouldn't do at all. If he wanted to work with her, the only way was to keep it on a professional basis. This way no one would get hurt, it had taken too long to recover the last time. Besides, he was still uncertain about the hold Baxter had over Connie. To him, it wasn't a healthy one.

★ ★ ★

Once they were in the car, Les turned to Connie before he started the engine and said, 'Now you listen to me, young lady. Don't get any wrong ideas now that Taylor is in. I still run the show and one thing I insist on is your relationship with that pianist.'

'You mean Ben Stanton,' she said sharply. 'He has a name, you know!'

'And he works for me! I don't want you seeing him other than when you have to work together – is that clear?'

'You can't tell me how to run my life!'

He stared into her eyes. 'Oh, yes, I can. You do as I say or I'll fire him!' He turned on the ignition and started the engine. 'It's up to you whether he stays or goes.'

They drove home in silence.

Chapter Fifteen

There were mixed emotions in the Ryan household when Connie told Freda about Jeremy Taylor and his plans for her. Her mother was deeply concerned.

'I don't like the idea of you living in London on your own – and where *will* you be living, by the way.'

'I don't know, Mum,' Connie snapped. 'That hasn't been talked about yet. After all, Jeremy needs time to find the right place for me.'

'And who is this *Jeremy*? What sort of a name is that anyway!'

Connie was livid. Here she was, euphoric about her good fortune, and all her mother was doing was trying to find fault with everything and everyone, instead of being thrilled . . . and impressed. What Connie really wanted was to be feted by her family. She wanted them to look at her with new eyes, as a person of standing – a girl who was going to do great things.

'Jeremy Taylor is a gentleman, Mother! He speaks beautifully and has the most wonderful manners. He's a real toff!'

'Humph! It's only their money as makes them so.'

Connie laughed derisively. 'What do you know about such people? Only what you read in the papers. Well, I'll be mixing with the likes of them once I'm a success!'

'Oh, Miss la de da! They'll soon discover your roots, my girl, don't you worry. My God! The first time you sit down in a posh restaurant you'll understand what I mean. You won't know which knife and fork to use. They live a very different lifestyle.'

Freda wasn't at all sure how to approach George about Connie moving to London. Her husband had not been himself the previous week, complaining of feeling unwell, but she couldn't let Connie's news pass by without his knowledge. She waited until he'd eaten his supper before she broached the subject.

When she'd finished, George just said, 'What do you want me to do about it? Connie doesn't listen to a word I say any more.' He frowned and rubbed his forehead. 'Got any aspirin, love? I've got a splitting headache.'

Freda's words gave Connie something to think about over the next few days. She wanted to fit into the world of Jeremy Taylor and if she was to be the success he predicted, she needed to know how to behave. Connie was no fool. She knew their worlds were wide apart, you only had to listen to him to know that, but she wanted to be a part of it too.

She had dreamed so often of living the high life, dressed in furs, dining at the Ritz, after she'd seen a picture of it in a magazine. The elegance, sumptuous furnishings, the chandeliers. Oh, yes, she wanted to swan through the doors of such places . . . and belong!

She voiced her concerns to Madame Vicario when she had her next lesson. Irene was very supportive.

'After your lesson, I'll lay the table and we will sit down. Then I'll explain which knife and fork is for what, and then when you do visit such a place, you'll know. After all, are you not my pupil? Do you think I don't want to be proud of you? I consider it my duty to prepare you for such things.'

Connie threw her arms about her. 'Oh, Madame, what would I do without you? My mother didn't help me one bit! All she did was to pick everything to pieces.'

Irene placed her hand gently on Connie's arm. 'Now then, darling, don't talk about your mama like that. She does the best she can. She's worried about you, as only a good mother would be. She doesn't want you to be embarrassed by ignorance, that's all. You should love her for her concern.'

'I *do* love her – and my father, but they live such dull lives and think that I should too. Our Doreen is more understanding, but even she doesn't understand just how far my dreams stretch.'

'We must all have a dream, Connie, but never lose sight of reality. The theatre, show business, is such a different life. Much of it is pretence, it's full on insincerity, of people who pay you lavish compliments to your face and talk about you behind your back. You'll meet a lot of this, I'm sad to say. It's always best to keep your own council.'

'Yes, Ben has already told me about this.' She looked up at her teacher. 'Les Baxter has forbidden me to meet Ben other than when we work together. What do you think of that then? He says he'll fire him if I do!'

Irene raised her eyebrows. 'Did he say why?'

'No. But he meant it.'

'Then you *must* respect his wishes. Ben Stanton will be a great help to you. From what you've told me, he's a fine musician and he knows his way around, but leave it at that.'

Connie pondered over Irene's words and realised the wisdom of them.

Irene smiled. 'Besides, Jeremy has great plans for you, my dear. But do listen to him. Do as he says – in all things.'

'But what if Les doesn't agree with him? He is still my boss.'

'Leave everything to Mr Taylor, he'll handle Baxter in his own way.' She picked up some new sheets of music. 'He asked me to run through these numbers with you.'

After the music lesson, Madame Vicario set about teaching her pupil the mysteries of etiquette. 'If the menu is in French—'

'I can't speak French!' exclaimed Connie in horror.

'I know, but in time you will become familiar with it the more you move in these circles. When you don't understand something you have two choices, firstly you could ask your escort to order for you, the other is to ask the waiter what he would recommend. *Never* pretend you know when you don't because that's the best way to be caught out!'

Connie sat down at the table and glanced at the array of cutlery in confusion. 'At home we just have a knife and fork and a spoon for pudding.'

'Dessert,' Irene corrected her. 'If the dish is called a something pudding then fine, otherwise it is dessert.'

'Oh, Madame, there is so much to learn!'

'Yes there is, but you pick up things very quickly, my dear. Now let's begin.'

All of this training, Connie passed on to her friend Molly during their working hours.

'Whenever am I going to be eating lobster? Honestly, Connie, behave!'

'You will be eating it with me! When I'm in the money, I'll take you to a posh restaurant . . . when I'm ready,' she added wistfully. 'Oh, Molly, I don't know if I'm coming or going. One moment I can't wait to move to London, the next I'm so scared I feel sick!'

'Is this Connie Ryan saying this to me? The same Connie who defied her father and left home to get her own way? I just don't believe it.'

For once, Connie put her fears into words. 'I want success so badly I can taste it, but I'm terrified I'll fail.' She covered her face with her hands. When she looked up at her friend her eyes were filled with tears. 'I couldn't bear to fail, Molly. I just couldn't. Imagine having to come home with my tail between my legs. Dad would *really* enjoy that!'

Her friend caught her by the shoulders and shook her. 'Stop it! I have seen you perform when you won the talent competition. My God, Connie, you don't realise what you do to an audience. You won't fail – I promise.'

Connie hugged her and said, 'Thanks, I really needed that.'

And she picked up a very extravagant hat from the display and placed it on her head, then proceeded to walk up and down the shop pretending to be a grand lady, only to be reprimanded by her boss.

As she returned the hat to its position she winked at Molly and said, 'I'll be leaving soon anyway, and who knows, I might just buy it before I go!'

It was a further three weeks before Jeremy got in touch. Les Baxter had a call from him asking him to meet him in London at his office, as there were papers to sign and business to discuss.

Les replaced the receiver and wondered if Taylor had found a booking for Connie, as he was getting restless waiting. Apart from which he'd heard rumours that young Kenny Pritchard had been sniffing round again, although his runners hadn't been approached, but it made him watchful and edgy.

When he reached Waterloo the following day, Les took a taxi to Wardour Street where 'Taylor Incorporated' was situated. He took the lift to the first floor and entered the office of the man who now was his partner. The receptionist smiled at him.

'Good morning, sir. Do you have an appointment?'

As he looked around at the well-furnished waiting room with its glossy magazines and the latest copy of *The Stage* on a fine mahogany side table, he felt a surge of envy. Connie could give him this kind of setting once she was established and a success. By then he would have learned the ropes of the theatrical world and could set up an agency for himself, leaving his trusted few to run the bookmaking business. He would like to move up in the world. He had the money, although he knew he was not as well educated as Jeremy, that didn't bother him. The racing world brought him into contact with all classes and he had yet to find anything or anyone who could not be bought for the right price. 'Yes, Mr Taylor is expecting me,' he said sharply. 'Baxter is the name.'

'Please take a seat and I'll tell him you're here. He's with a client at the moment.'

Les sat down. Five minutes later the office door opened and Jeremy escorted his client to the door. He shook hands with him and saw him out of the room, then turning to the bookmaker he said, 'Come in, Les.'

The inner office was spacious, with comfortable leather chairs on one side of an enormous desk and a large leather swivel chair on the other. Jeremy, elegant in a Savile Row suit, picked up some papers and handed them to Les.

'Read through those, old chap, while I send for some coffee. It's the contract between you and me for the future of Connie Ryan.' He pressed the intercom and requested a pot of coffee and biscuits for them both. Then sat back on his chair and waited.

Baxter read every word carefully. It was straightforward enough. It stipulated Taylor's forty per cent interest in Connie Ryan and the fact that he bought into the contract by paying forty per cent of the outgoings up to now. But there was a clause in it that surprised Les which said that the salary to be paid to Miss Connie Ryan would rise in proportion with her income as she climbed the ladder of success.

'What's this all about?'

Jeremy had omitted to inform his new partner that he'd had a call from Connie querying the amount of money that would be paid to her, and decrying the fact she only got five pounds a week at the moment, when she was the one earning the money.

'You can't expect your star to work hard without seeing something for the effort,' he said. 'Above all, we have to keep her happy. Give her some encouragement.'

'For God's sake! She's just a kid. Right, she has a voice, but she does as she's told!'

The agent sat back in his chair and shook his head. 'You will never get anywhere with that attitude, my friend.'

'What do you mean?'

'Ask yourself, Baxter, why are the two of us here?'

'To work out a contract between us.'

'Correct. But only because of Connie and her stupendous talent. All right, you discovered her, but without her we would not be here this very day. In this world of the theatre and show business, she and people like her are our bread and butter.'

'In your case, caviar and champagne!'

Taylor burst out laughing. 'Right!' He leaned forward. 'But I earned that money by getting the best for my clients and nursing every bloody one of them. If you want her to succeed and be happy – and believe me if she isn't she won't perform at the top of her ability – you have to nurse her too.' He paused. 'That man who left just now, you didn't recognise him, did you?'

'I didn't take much notice,' Les admitted.

'He's one of our best Shakespearian actors. Virtually unknown when I took him on. I have just fixed a contract for him to appear in a film in the States. The salary is enormous. But to get him there, I had almost to powder his bottom, he was so uncertain of his capabilities in the beginning. Now his ego is what I have to keep in check.'

'Yes,' argued Les, 'but you don't know Connie Ryan. She's wilful, stubborn and filled with such a burning ambition that she needs to be kept under control.'

'I accept that, but does it have to be with an iron fist?'

Les shrugged.

Leaning forward again, the agent said, 'Yes, Connie has ambition and that's great, she'll need that to survive in this business, but she also has a dream. Fortunately she has the talent and between us we can fulfil that dream. But you can't destroy her in the process. If she's nurtured and encouraged, she'll blossom.'

'But she has to work to do so,' declared Les. 'Have you found a booking for her?'

Jeremy smiled. 'You are as impatient as Connie.' He lit a cigar as his secretary brought in the coffee. 'Leave it there, we'll manage,' he said. Then he poured two cups of coffee and handed one to Baxter.

'Yes, I have found the very place for her.'

Les sat up and looked expectantly across the desk. 'Well – where?'

'It's in the Palm Court Club in Mayfair,' he said. 'Very upper class. Lots of the aristocracy go quite often.'

Les looked suitably impressed. 'How did you manage that?'

'Wheels within wheels, old chap. It's not always what you know but who you know and I have the contacts, which is why you came to me for help, isn't it?'

Although this was the truth, the bookmaker found the fact hard to admit, but after all, this was why he had been forced to hand forty per cent of Connie's contract over to this man.

'I'd like to take a look at the place,' he said, trying to take back some of the high ground he felt was his as the holder of the greater half of his client.

'That won't be possible, I'm afraid,' said Jeremy casually. 'It is a strictly members-only club.'

'And no doubt you are a member.'

'Exactly! You will have to trust me on this. I'll take you as my guest one night.'

'One night! What the bloody hell do you mean? I am her agent – I should be there! They can't refuse me.'

Jeremy just smiled at him. 'I too am her agent, and they could, but as I have the membership, it won't be necessary. Don't worry, old man; I have both our interests at heart. Trust me.'

'Where will Connie live? We haven't discussed that. I don't want a young girl left on her own in London. Her parents wouldn't like it, neither would I.'

'No, of course not. I wouldn't dream of such a thing. My son is at university; she can use his room for the time being. My wife is at home, she won't mind. I have done this many times in the past. Besides, Connie is bound to be nervous. From what I've heard, she hasn't been around much, so she needs taking care of. Much as you did for her when you moved her in with your mother.'

There was no way Les Baxter could argue with the arrangements. 'But I don't want her going off with that pianist chap. I've told her, her relationship with him is strictly business!'

To his surprise, Taylor agreed.

'Quite right. At eighteen and in a strange city she is vulnerable. Ben Stanton will give her confidence on the stage and my wife and I will give her a home until she finds her feet. Now her first booking is in November. She appears nightly for a month. How's she fixed for gowns?'

'She has two gowns and a cocktail dress.'

'Then we will hire others for her. She has to look stunning at every performance. We are talking class here, Les. It will be a great place to start. Look.' He pushed a contract towards him. 'This is her salary for the month.'

Baxter struggled not to show his surprise at the figure. 'Yes, a good start,' he conceded.

Jeremy Taylor rose to his feet and walked to the window. 'Couldn't be better. The right people will hear her sing and I will be taking her out in the evenings to the places where she will meet more of them. I will be selling her talent at these times, making people who can help curious about this young lady. By the end of the month, they'll be clamouring to take her on all over London.' He turned. 'Don't forget to sign that contract between us before you go, there's a good chap.'

Les took a pen from his pocket and signed. 'What about Stanton?'

'I've already got his signature.'

As Les shot him a look he said, 'It's a contract in both our names, have no fear.'

As Les made his way out of the building, he felt thrilled with the morning's work. He wasn't so pleased that Connie would be in such close proximity to Jeremy. Although he couldn't fault the other man for the arrangements he felt that if he wasn't careful the London agent could quietly push him out of the picture. Well, he could try, but he wouldn't bloody

143

well succeed. He'd see to that. Maybe he didn't mix with the same crowd but he was not without influence in other directions. He smirked to himself as he made his plans.

He hailed a taxi and gave them an address in the East End of London.

Chapter Sixteen

It was now the month of October and things had been moving very quickly. Connie had given in her notice at The Peacock Club and Sands' hat shop, promising Molly she would keep in touch, and was now in the midst of packing to move to London. She was relieved to be staying with Jeremy and his wife as the thought of being in the city alone terrified her. It was enough to be starting her career proper (as she viewed it) in a classy club, without the added pressure of London itself.

Jeremy had been down to Southampton to reassure her that he would personally be introducing her to this new life. 'I know this is all a great deal for a young girl to cope with, but don't worry, my dear, I'll be there to hold your hand.'

'And where will Les be in all this?' she asked with some trepidation. Jeremy fitted beautifully into the London lifestyle, but Les Baxter . . .? She didn't want him to let her down with his sometimes uncouth ways.

'Don't you worry about Baxter,' she was told. 'London is my territory not his and he knows it, that's why he came to me in the first place.'

'He's not going to like it!' Connie stated sharply.

Jeremy smiled softly. 'No, he won't, but he doesn't have a lot of choice.'

Studying him closely Connie said, 'I'm beginning to think you're not quite the gentleman you appear to be.'

This highly amused him and he laughed loudly. 'You are too smart for your young years, my dear – and you are absolutely

145

correct. In this business it's dog eat dog and I have been around for a very long time.' He paused. 'Fortunately, you have the attitude you need to succeed, as well as the talent.'

'What do you mean by that?'

'I'm a very good judge of character, Connie, and I know that you will tread on anyone who gets in your way. Am I not right?'

She blushed at his shrewdness, but glared back defiantly saying, 'Yes, you're absolutely right! I mean to get to the top and no one is going to stop me.' Then she smiled disarmingly at him. 'You can get me there, I know you can.'

He was no longer being jocular when he said, 'Yes, I can, because I believe in you, but you had better know this now: if you fail to live up to my expectations, I'll drop you!'

Connie was shocked by his bluntness, but at the same time she appreciated his honesty. 'Believe me, I'll work like mad to be the best and I will do it, you'll see!'

Later that day as the agent sat in the first-class carriage of the train taking him back to London, he thought about his conversation with young Connie Ryan and he could see what Baxter meant about her being headstrong and needing to be kept under control. He felt certain that as she climbed the ladder of success, she could well become a prima donna, unless she was held in check. Well, he thought, she's only a kid, but his better judgement told him he could have a load of trouble on his hands if he wasn't careful.

Meanwhile, Les Baxter had been making his own plans. His visit to his underworld friends in London's East End had paid off in many ways, which pleased him. He had also spent time doing a bit of digging into Kenny Pritchard's life. It appeared the young blade was pretty full of himself since the death of his father and was throwing his weight about, much to the dismay of the men who had worked for the old man through the years – there were rumblings of discontent in the camp.

The older men felt he could ruin a very lucrative business

that had run so smoothly for so long, but there was a younger element, some of whom Kenny had recruited himself, who were more than enthusiastic about his ideas, and who were not averse to using violence to achieve their aims, perhaps more than was necessary. All this, Les thought, he could use to his great advantage. He had yet to catch sight of his quarry or see a picture of him, but from what he heard he was a flash young man who enjoyed the best of everything, whatever the cost. In that, he mused, Kenny was not unlike himself. For a long time now, he'd enjoyed the very best because he could afford it, but he hoped he wasn't flash. He had good clothes sense, an excellent tailor, but he was aware, more so recently due to his partnership with Jeremy Taylor, that he did lack a certain *savoir-faire*, but it really didn't bother him too much. He had the money and that alone could take him to most places. A hefty tip to a maître d' always got him a table wherever he wanted. He stayed at the best hotels, where he always made a point of overtipping the bell boy or hotel porter, knowing that word would get around the rest of the staff who always then gave him the best of service. Yes, money paved the way just about everywhere. When he couldn't achieve his aims himself, he paid someone to do it for him!

Connie was spending her last evening in Southampton with her family. Freda had insisted she come to dinner before she went to London, and now they were sitting around the table tucking into Lancashire hot pot with the meat her mother had managed to charm out of the butcher.

'I told him it was for a special occasion,' she said proudly as she spooned the portions onto the plates. 'I'll put your father's meal to one side, then I can put it in the oven to warm for when he comes back from playing darts.'

'Is it a competition tonight, then?' asked Connie, disappointed that her father wasn't there to share her moment of glory.

'Yes,' Freda lied.

Doreen looked at her. 'Don't cover up for him, Mum,' she snapped. To Connie she said, 'He didn't want to be here, he made an excuse.'

Connie was furious. 'What is it with him? He should be proud of me!' She ruminated over this for a moment and then said angrily. 'When my name's in lights I bet he'll brag to all his mates about me then!'

'You're probably right,' agreed Doreen.

'Never mind, love. Dor and me, we're real proud of you,' said Freda.

'Thanks, Mum,' she murmured, but inside she was deeply hurt and vowed to herself that when she was a big name, her father could go and whistle Dixie before she would let him benefit. If he couldn't support her now, later would be too late. But tonight, she'd enjoy being with her mother and sister, because she knew once she'd moved away from Southampton, she would really miss them.

Doreen walked with her to the bus stop. 'I really hope it all works out for you in London,' she said, 'because I know how much you want this.'

Linking her arm through her sister's, Connie said, 'Thanks, Dor. But how about you and Eric? I've not had a chance to ask.'

There was a look of contentment on Doreen's face as she said, 'My Eric's lovely! We're saving to get married next year.'

'How wonderful!' exclaimed Connie.

'I'll keep working as a typist until we can afford to have a family. Eric hopes to get promotion. He's looking to become foreman at the factory.'

'You've got it all worked out . . . that's great!'

'It's all I've ever wanted. A home, a husband, children. Just as well. One star in the Ryan household is enough!'

The following morning, Connie bade goodbye to Mrs Baxter, thanking her for giving her a home. Despite the old girl's difficult ways, Connie had become fond of her.

'Take care, Connie,' she said. 'In my opinion you're too young to be setting out, but you have a good head on your shoulders, and my Les thinks you're going to the top. So good luck, dear.'

Connie gave her a hug, and climbed into the taxi, which was taking her to the station.

On her arrival at Waterloo, she saw Jeremy Taylor waiting at the barrier for her and let out a sigh of relief. He made her feel comfortable and secure, and she *was* nervous. She knew that Ben was going to the club ahead of her with the arrangements for the band, so they would be prepared for her rehearsal, but she could feel the butterflies in her stomach at the thought of what was ahead. Although she badly wanted this booking, she was understandably agitated.

The taxi Jeremy had hailed took them to St John's Wood, an élite part of London, which Connie admired from the cab window, and when they stopped in front of a large imposing double-fronted house, she was immediately impressed.

'So *this* is gracious living,' she remarked wryly.

Her companion chuckled. '*This* is what I work damned hard for!' he retorted. 'And this is what one day you'll be able to afford, if you keep your nose clean and your voice clear.'

Annabel Taylor walked forward to greet them as Jeremy opened the front door. Connie gazed at the slim, well-dressed woman before her with admiration and certain awe. She looked as if she'd stepped out of a fashion magazine.

'Darling, this is Connie Ryan – my new star.'

Annabel put out a well-manicured hand and shook Connie's. 'Welcome to my home,' she said quietly, but even though her hostess was smiling, Connie noticed the emphasis on *my* home, and the fact that the welcoming smile didn't reach the eyes which were studying her closely – and without enthusiasm.

Connie straightened her back and with a steely smile replied, 'How kind of you to take me in. I know it's not very convenient, but I hope it won't be for very long. I'm planning to be in a position to house myself very soon.'

'I'll show you to your room,' said Annabel.

'And don't unpack,' called Jeremy after them, 'we have to go to the club to rehearse. I've kept the taxi waiting.'

Mrs Taylor opened the door to a sumptuous bedroom which quite took Connie's breath away, but she put down her suitcase and, quickly glancing round, said casually, 'Very nice, but I'd better go.' She looked straight at Annabel and said, 'Thank you,' turned on her heel and ran down the stairs and out of the front door, thinking to herself, condescending bitch!

It was a day of revelations. The Palm Court couldn't have been more different from The Peacock Club. Its very opulence spelled money as they entered the swing doors. There was no peeling wallpaper here! The windows were draped in velvet curtains the colour of port wine, the long bar was stocked with bottle after bottle on the various shelves, there were several optics and glasses so well polished that they shone in the light, and the dining room was much bigger than Connie had ever envisaged. There was a dance floor too, and above, a stage where the band was already rehearsing. Ben, sitting at the piano, looked across at her and winked.

When they came to the end of the number, Jeremy approached the bandleader. 'Hello, Jack. How the devil are you?'

Connie watched the tall svelte man who walked towards them. His jacket was slung over his shoulder and his tie slightly undone as if he'd been too hot to bear it. He held out his hand to the agent.

'Jeremy! I must say the arrangements for the band are excellent!' He smiled at Connie and said, 'This must be Miss Ryan.'

She stepped forward and said, 'Yes, that's right. How nice to meet you.' They shook hands.

'You didn't tell me she was such a looker, Jeremy,' he said, with an admiring glance in Connie's direction.'

'You wait until you hear her sing!' retorted the agent.

'Then let's start,' he said to Connie. 'Your pianist and I have the running order. He has a list for you on the piano.' He threw his jacket over the back of a chair.

She walked over to Ben and said, 'Hello. Well, here we are.' She glanced down at the paper he handed her and seeing the first number on the list, said, 'Right! Let's set the place alight!'

He grinned broadly. 'Why not!'

She turned towards the members of the band who were eyeing her with some curiosity and said, 'Good morning, gentlemen. I'm Connie Ryan.'

There was a murmur in response and the musicians picked up their instruments and waited for the bandleader to raise his baton. He looked at Connie and asked, 'Ready?'

She nodded and winked at Jeremy, who had seated himself at a nearby table.

After the introduction she began to sing 'You're Nobody Till Somebody Loves You'. It was a lively upbeat number and Connie gave it all she had, enjoying every moment, glancing occasionally across at Ben who smiled at her, instilling her with confidence.

At the end of the number the musicians tapped their instruments, their way of applauding. She turned towards the bandleader.

He came over to her and said, 'I think we can safely say you'll be a success here if you sing the rest of your programme as well.'

'And I certainly will,' she said. She glanced over her shoulder at the musicians and said, 'Great band!'

Jeremy Taylor sat and watched the rest of the rehearsal and noted how Connie gradually got to know the musicians, exchanging quips with them, winning them over. For one so young, it might have been brash, but she had charm, and that made a difference.

They went through the whole of her programme, pausing now and again as Ben made a few changes, allowing her to take a break and drink a glass of water here and there.

Finally, they were all through.

Jack Granger walked over to Jeremy and said quietly, 'Now I know why you were so excited about this kid! She sings with a maturity beyond her years. And that voice! She can really sell a lyric because she gives it soul. The men will adore her.'

'And the women?'

Jack shrugged. 'Who cares! Her opening night is Saturday. In two days' time, we'll have a new star. If she keeps this up, I can see her being the toast of London.'

'That's the general idea,' said Jeremy a mite smugly, he was so delighted with Connie's performance. 'Come along, my dear,' he called, 'we have a lot to do.'

'What are *you* going to do?' Connie asked Ben.

'Work,' he said. 'I'll see you on Saturday and we'll knock them dead.'

Once outside the club, Connie looked at Jeremy and asked, 'What did you think? Did I do all right?'

He beamed at her. 'You were terrific, but now we have to go to the costumiers and hire some gowns for you. Then I want to make an appointment for you at the hairdressers. You must look your absolute best on opening night.'

'Will Les be here?'

'No,' said the agent as he hailed a taxi. 'He isn't a member, but I am and as I am also your agent it doesn't need both of us here.'

Connie was relieved, but knowing the man as she did, she remarked, 'I'm surprised he let you get away with that!'

Jeremy just chuckled, opened the door of the taxi which had stopped and said, 'Get in.'

Chapter Seventeen

The rest of the day was spent in a whirl of activity, which left Connie breathless with excitement. Jeremy took her to a famous costumiers, where they selected several wonderful gowns, covered in sequins and glitter, and as Connie tried each one, she grew in confidence. How could she fail, clad in such finery? She would be as well dressed as any of the wealthy patrons who came through the doors of the club.

Jeremy also chose several garments to be worn through the day. Smart couturier costumes with designer labels Connie had only read about in fashion magazines. Also several cocktail dresses and matching shoes.

'I will hate to return all of these,' she said wistfully.

'The evening gowns we can exchange for others, the rest of the stuff I've bought. Those you may keep.'

'What?' She was speechless.

'Society women soon get tired of wearing the same things, especially with so few clothing coupons to allow them to buy new clothes, so they exchange them, this arrangement suits them all. It's happening all over the country, a kind of exchange market, but this exclusive outlet is known only to a select few.'

'But what happens if someone sees something that once was theirs being worn by someone else?'

'They're certainly not going to admit it, are they? So, you see, pride is saved all round. After wearing them for a while, you can do the same.'

'What a splendid idea.'

'It's just an upmarket way of Make Do and Mend!' He selected a smart costume from his purchases, and a pair of shoes and said, 'I want you to change into this – we are going to the Café Royal to lunch.'

'A café . . . dressed in all this posh stuff?'

He hid a smile. 'The Café Royal, Connie dear, is a very smart restaurant where you will get to meet the best people. It is part of the overall plan.'

'I do like the way your mind works,' she said.

He gave her a knowing look. 'Yes, I thought you might.'

Dressed in her smart apparel and a matching hat with a fetching eye veil, Connie entered the doors of the Café Royal and immediately saw what Jeremy meant. It was thickly carpeted, the chandeliers were huge and the table linen pristine. The agent greeted a few people as they were led to their table by the head waiter. He didn't linger beside anyone, but as he sat down and casually glanced around, he said quietly, 'You are already the subject of curiosity among many, but don't look round, just study the menu as if you are used to coming here.'

She did as she was bid and smiled to herself as she saw it was in French. Closing the menu she looked at Jeremy and said, 'Why don't you order for me?' Madame Vicario would be proud of her.

Her host said, 'Certainly.' He questioned her about her likes and dislikes, then, when the waiter approached, he ordered their meal.

Whilst he was doing so, Connie studied the cutlery beside her and thanked God for the tuition on social etiquette that Irene had insisted on.

During the meal, several people stopped by their table to exchange a word with Jeremy, and he introduced her. 'Connie, this gentleman is Lord Hartford. Lord Hartford, Miss Connie Ryan.'

The well-spoken middle-aged gent held her hand and kissed it. 'A pleasure, my dear,' he said, and took his leave.

Connie was quite overcome. 'Was he a real live Lord?'

'Well, he looked as if he was breathing to me.'

She frowned. 'If I ever see him again, how do I address him?'

'My Lord. Then he'll tell you to call him Freddy.' He grinned across the table. 'He has an eye for the ladies, but he's harmless enough.'

Later he introduced her to Rudolph Davenport, who apparently was responsible for the running of many of the West End theatres.

Jeremy said to him, 'Rudy, you must come to Connie's opening night at the Palm Court Club on Saturday. I'll save you a place at my table.'

Mr Davenport smiled at Connie and said, 'I wouldn't miss it for the world, my dear.'

As the man walked away, Jeremy winked at her. 'He was the main reason we came here today – he has a table booked every Thursday. He knows I have the best list of performers in London, whom he hires to fill his theatres, so we need each other.'

'You are a schemer!' she accused.

'No, Connie, I'm a businessman, and this, very often, is how I do my business.'

'Do you do it in the evening as well?'

He looked puzzled. 'Yes, frequently . . . why?'

'Doesn't your wife mind?'

'She knows it's part of my work. Sometimes she comes too, but often she has other things that occupy her. She understands. I have a vital part to play if my clients are to succeed and there are no office hours in my job. Annabel likes the good things in life and the nice things that I can afford to buy for her, but this way of doing business is part of the price she has to pay.'

Thinking of how well, and how expensively, Annabel was

dressed that morning, Connie was certain the price of her upkeep was pretty costly, but she wondered if Mr and Mrs Taylor were happy in their marriage.

On Friday afternoon, Connie was taken to a hairdressing salon where she had her hair styled and her nails manicured before being taken back to the Taylor residence where she was told to wear a cocktail dress, as they would be going out later that evening. Jeremy instructed her, 'Be ready for seven o'clock.'

Mrs Taylor was not to be seen.

That evening Connie was taken to one smart place after another. Jeremy ordered a soft drink for her every time saying, 'You need a clear mind and you need to take care of your voice, so if the atmosphere becomes too smoky for goodness' sake say so,' and once or twice she did. But by then she'd been introduced to half of London's élite, or that's how it felt to her. There were so many introductions, her head spun.

'I'll never remember everyone,' she complained.

'You don't have to, the important thing is that they remember you.'

Eventually, in the early hours of Saturday morning, they were taken home by taxi.

As they entered the house Jeremy said, 'Now rest most of the day. When you do wake up, press that bell in the wall and the maid will bring you up some breakfast. Rest as much as you can, because you'll have a long night ahead of you. I'll leave instructions that you are to have a light lunch because you can't perform on a full stomach. I'll be back to collect you at seven o'clock and at five, the hairdresser will be here to comb your hair and re-dress it if necessary.'

She looked at him and said, 'All this must be costing a fortune!'

'Of course it is! Presentation in all things is vitally important. How the public first see you will stay in their minds, after that it's your singing. Don't you worry, Connie, both Les Baxter and I will see a return on our investment, and it will be sooner rather than later, I can promise you that.'

Later that evening, fed and watered, Connie was dressed and ready, her hair beautifully coiffured. She opened the wardrobe door and looked in the long mirror and couldn't believe the reflection! Before her was a beautiful girl dressed in a gown of ruby red in a soft flowing material, with a deep neck line which showed the soft rise of her breasts, the shapely waist, and soft roundness of her hips. Across the neckline, red and black sequins and bugle beads sparkled in the light. Her dark hair shone. Her shoes, which were satin and dyed to match her gown, peeped below the skirt as she moved. She turned this way and that, admiring herself from every angle.

'Hello, Connie Ryan, if it really is you?' she said softly. 'Your father would have a fit if he could see you now!'

Just before seven o'clock there was a knock on her door. 'Come in,' she called.

Annabel Taylor entered. She too was in evening dress. 'Jeremy wants you to wear this,' she said, holding out a pale mink cape.

Taking it from her, Connie stroked the soft fur and said, 'It's beautiful. Thank you. Is it one of yours?'

'Of course not,' said Annabel shortly. 'It's hired, like everything else you have.'

Connie's hackles rose. 'You don't like me, Mrs Taylor, you make that very obvious . . . well, the feeling's mutual! However, there will come a time when everything on my back will have been paid for by my own talent and hard work. I wonder if you can say the same?'

Annabel flushed with anger, turned on her heel and swept out of the room, leaving the door wide open.

'I'll close the door, shall I?' called Connie after her. Then with a broad grin she did so. She primped her hair in front of the mirror on the dressing table and muttered, 'No one treats me like that and gets away with it.' Then she wondered if the woman would be joining her husband at the club. If so, it should make for an interesting evening.

There was a strained atmosphere in the taxi, which took Connie and the Taylors to the Palm Court Club, but if Jeremy noticed anything, he made no comment, chattering away to Connie and telling her about the forthcoming event.

'The club should be packed,' he said. 'I have twelve at my table alone. You will be announced as the cabaret act around ten o'clock. Meantime, get in the right frame of mind, exercise your voice. I've put some magazines in your dressing room . . .'

Dressing room! Connie was thrilled. She wouldn't have to hang about like she did in Southampton.

'. . . and some sultanas for you to nibble on,' he continued.

'Sultanas?'

'Yes, I'm told they lubricate the throat and stave off any pangs of hunger. After the show, you'll join us, then you can eat.'

She felt Annabel stiffen beside her.

'That'll be lovely,' she said.

When they arrived at the club, the maître d' hurried forth. 'Take Mrs Taylor to our table,' Jeremy instructed the man, 'whilst I take Miss Ryan to her dressing room.'

'Good luck, Miss Ryan,' the man said, and then to Annabel, 'This way, Madam.'

The fact that Jeremy's wife ignored her didn't bother Connie one bit. At least the woman wasn't a hypocrite, wishing her luck and not meaning it.

To Connie's absolute joy, the dressing room had a gold star on it and her name beneath. She looked at Jeremy and beamed. 'Look! I'm a star!'

He opened the door for her and said, 'Indeed you will be, Connie my dear.'

She stepped inside and gasped.

In front of her was a dressing table with a large square mirror surrounded by lights. On the dressing table were various jars, cotton wool, paper tissues and make-up and before it was a comfortable chair. There was an easy chair in the corner, and opposite was a wide ornate screen for her to dress behind, but apart from all this, the room was full of flowers.

'My God!' she exclaimed. 'It's like a funeral parlour, there are so many flowers.'

Jeremy laughed. 'Good Lord, I hope it looks a bit more comfortable than that!'

Turning quickly she said, 'I didn't mean to be rude, but I have never seen so many. Where did they all come from?'

'Why don't you read the cards?' he suggested.

One magnificent display in a tall basket standing on the floor was the first one she made for. Taking the small envelope from the handle of the basket she read, *To Connie. A star in the making. Jeremy*.

'Oh, thank you,' she said.

He just smiled, enjoying the sight of someone new to the business thrilled to the core, and thinking to himself, They all start this way, but somewhere down the line, it all changes. He wondered if it would for Connie.

There was a bouquet from her family. The card read *From Dad and Mum and Doreen*. She knew her father probably didn't even know about the flowers, but as she moved to another impressive arrangement she was determined that nothing would spoil this moment. She removed the card and was very surprised to read, *To Connie, I always knew you could do it. Now show me how! Les Baxter*.

She was suddenly filled with sadness that he wasn't here to share in her triumph, after all, but for him she would still be in Southampton, and she felt ashamed that with all the excitement of these past few days, she'd hardly given him a thought.

At that moment, Ben knocked on the open door and walked in. Looking around he said, 'My goodness, Connie, what does it feel like to be the centre of so much attention?'

She flung her arms wide and said, 'Wonderful.' Then she walked over to him and hugged him. 'Your arrangements played a great part in this, remember.'

Jeremy interrupted. 'Look I have to go.' He kissed her forehead. 'Break a leg,' he said.

'Break a leg! What a strange thing to say.'

'It's what they say in show business, Connie. It means good luck. You're going to be great, so no nerves. I expect to see a star on that stage tonight!'

'Believe me, Jeremy, that's exactly what you'll get. Won't he, Ben?'

'Indeed he will.'

When they were alone Ben asked, 'Are you nervous?'

'No. I'm excited, of course I am – but nervous? I have waited for this moment since I was ten years old. I told you, this is my destiny. I was meant for this.'

He shook his head. 'I've never met any girl quite like you, Miss Connie Ryan! I have to get back. Someone will come for you when it's time. Just relax . . . if you can!'

Connie spent the interim time wandering around her dressing room. She discovered a door behind which was her own toilet. She glanced through the various magazines and paced the floor doing her voice exercises in an effort to pass the time, anxious to start work. She couldn't wait to face her audience.

At last there was a knock on her door. 'Are you ready, Miss Ryan?'

She opened it to see a fresh-faced young man waiting. 'I am,' she said and followed him to the wings. As she waited she heard the bandleader announce her.

'Ladies and gentlemen, tonight you are in a privileged position to see the birth of a new star. Never in all my years in this business have I heard such a voice from one so young. And I am certain she's going to take this town by storm. Ladies and Gentlemen, I give you . . . Miss Connie Ryan!'

Taking a deep breath, Connie walked on stage.

Just at that moment, the waiter appeared by the side of Jeremy Taylor and whispered, 'Excuse me, sir, this gentleman said I was to make room on your table for him.'

Jeremy looked up to see Les Baxter, in evening dress, smiling at him.

'What the devil are you doing here?'

Still smiling, Les said, 'I'm a member.' Turning to the waiter he said, 'Get another chair, there's a good man.'

The waiter looked at Jeremy, who nodded.

As Les sat beside him Jeremy whispered, 'Did you say you were a member?'

'Shh,' said Baxter, putting a finger to his mouth. 'Our girl is going to sing!'

Chapter Eighteen

Connie faced her audience, smiled confidently and began to sing, 'You're Nobody Till Somebody Loves You', then went immediately into 'The Sunny Side of the Street'. The applause was enthusiastic, and she waited until there was silence and said, 'Thank you, Ladies and Gentlemen. I am so thrilled to be here tonight, and now I would like to sing for you a favourite of mine by Cole Porter.' There was a hush as she began, 'Every Time We Say Goodbye'.

Jeremy Taylor rubbed the back of his neck as he listened and he glanced around the room. The diners were enthralled by the change of pace of the song and the heartfelt rendition. He looked at Les Baxter sitting beside him and was surprised at the intensity of his gaze. He could see by the bookmaker's expression that, for him, there was no one else in the room at that moment but young Connie Ryan – and it disturbed him.

With each number, Connie relaxed, and between songs she would say a few words about the composer whom she admired. She complimented the band, which endeared her to the musicians, and she made Ben take a bow as her arranger. She was as accomplished as anyone who was established in the business. Her love for her music and the lyrics, and her joy of singing shone through, and the patrons of the Palm Court Club took her to their hearts . . . she became an overnight star and the diners rose to their feet to applaud at the end of her performance.

Ben walked with her to her dressing room, as the normal

pianist took his place. Once inside the room, Connie flung herself into his arms. 'Oh, Ben, wasn't it wonderful?'

'You were absolutely terrific, and I was so proud of you,' he said.

The door opened and both Les and Jeremy stopped when they saw them in each other's arms. In her excitement, Connie was not in the least embarrassed. She put her arms around Les and kissed his cheek.

'How can I ever thank you?' she said and moved on to Jeremy. 'And you,' she kissed him too.

'Congratulations!' said Jeremy, who was beaming. 'They'll be banging on my door wanting to book you for future engagements. Rudy was very impressed!'

'Was he really?' She turned to Les Baxter and explained, 'Rudy controls many of the theatres in London, you know.'

'Does he now? I'll have to talk to him.'

Jeremy took her arm. 'Come along, young lady, I'm sure you're starving. We've all waited so we can eat together, so let's go.' He led her out of the room with Les and Ben following in his wake. Looking over his shoulder he said to Ben, 'You must join us too.' He saw Baxter frown.

The atmosphere around the table was very festive. There were guests of Jeremy's that Connie didn't know but she recognised Rudy Davenport who smiled at her, and she was thrilled to see Irene Vicario sitting opposite. Her teacher blew her a kiss. 'Well done,' she mouthed above the noise. Champagne bottles were opened one after another and they toasted Connie. She noted that Annabel too raised a glass to her, even if her enthusiasm was somewhat muted. Connie's cheeks were flushed and her eyes shone with the excitement of it all as she sat between her two agents.

Jeremy leaned forward and asked Les, 'Did you say earlier you were a member, or didn't I hear correctly?'

With a slow smile, Les answered, 'There's nothing wrong with your hearing.' He gave Jeremy a hard stare and added, 'You didn't really think you could freeze me out, did you?'

'My dear chap, that wasn't my intention at all.'

'Like hell!' was Baxter's riposte. 'By the way, tomorrow Connie will be moving out of your place.'

'What?'

'Madame Vicario will be giving her a room. Now, more than ever, she needs the professionalism that Irene can give her.' He paused. 'I'm sure you'll agree!'

'Yes, yes, of course. Good idea.' He glanced across the table but Irene was engrossed in conversation with another guest.

Les picked up his glass of champagne, held it up and said to Jeremy, 'To our girl.'

Jeremy Taylor thought to himself, You clever bugger. Not that he doubted the intelligence of Baxter for one moment. He'd seen him often enough, wheeling and dealing on various racecourses over the years, but he was intrigued as to how he'd wangled a membership. But then Les had contacts in many places, some of them not particularly choice, and there had been rumours that some of the financing of the Palm Court Club came from the underworld. If that were true, it would explain everything. He grudgingly admitted to himself that he had to admire the man.

Across the other side of the room, Kenny Pritchard and his small party were about to leave. As he passed the table, he stopped beside Connie.

'Congratulations, Miss Ryan. You've come a long way since I saw you sing in The Peacock Club in Southampton.'

She looked up and vaguely remembered the young man. 'Thank you,' she said.

He smiled and walked away, saying, 'I'll be seeing you.'

'Who was that?' asked Les.

'I met him briefly in the club in Southampton. He did tell me his name but for the life of me I can't remember what it was.'

With a smile Les said, 'You did very well tonight, Connie. I was really proud of you.'

Such praise was so unusual that she was thrilled. 'Thank you,' she said. 'Do you remember at Dad's Social Club I told

165

you how much I wanted to be a success?'

'I remember it well. I was impressed by your determination then, that's why I was willing to help you. By the way, the club is closed tomorrow, so after you've had a good sleep, I want you to pack all your things and—'

'Why?' Connie interrupted.

'Because I'm moving you to Irene Vicario's house. You are to stay with her for a while.'

Connie was greatly relieved. She loved Irene, felt at ease with her, felt able to confide in her, and she wondered just how long she could bear to be near Annabel Taylor. 'That's wonderful!'

Les was pleased by her reaction. 'You don't mind then?'

She leaned towards him and in a very low voice confided, 'No, not at all. Mrs Taylor is a first-class bitch! I don't know what Jeremy sees in her.'

'Really?'

'I've already crossed swords with her.'

Trying to hide his amusement Les asked, 'Why, what happened?'

When she told him he burst out laughing. 'Oh, Connie, you are too much!'

She looked at Les, sitting relaxed and laughing and thought how smart he looked and, for an older man, quite attractive. He had been so dominating to begin with and for the first time she saw the charm of the man and was really pleased he had been here on this important occasion.

'I am so happy I could burst,' she confided.

'Well, Connie, you deserve it. You have worked hard, you have the dedication and you have the talent, but now you must work even harder.'

'Irene will see to that,' she laughed.

'No, I don't mean with your lessons so much, although they are really important, I mean in your behaviour. You will be the centre of attention now, so you will be under scrutiny. Especially by the press.'

Her eyes widened.

'There were a lot of reporters here tonight, I arranged some and Jeremy was sure to do so. They will be watching you closely.'

'So I mustn't pick my nose in public,' she joked.

'Don't treat this lightly,' he cautioned. 'You were a big hit tonight and there will be lots of offers coming in. You have a natural charm, don't lose it.'

'What do you mean?'

'I mean, don't let this go to your head. Don't get carried away with "I am a star!" It won't wash with the people who matter.'

She frowned. 'Yes, Ben warned me about that and also to be watchful for jealousy within the business.'

'Exactly! You are no longer in Southampton. Now you are in the real world.'

'Have you seen my father?' she asked suddenly

He shook his head. 'He still places his bets, but he keeps out of my way. I'm sorry about that, Connie.'

She shrugged his concerns aside. 'Doesn't matter.' She paused. 'Can I ask a favour of you?'

'It depends.'

'I would love Mum, Doreen and Molly to come to the club one evening, could it be arranged?'

'Leave it to me,' he promised.

Connie was far too excited to sleep that night. She kept going over every moment of the evening, every word, every note, every compliment. She sat up in bed and hugged her knees. Tonight had been the fulfilment of her dreams. How she wished Molly could have been there, she would never believe what had happened these past few days. The shopping, the gowns, the posh places she had been with Jeremy . . . and she had met a Lord! She would write and tell her all about it. She pulled out a pen and pad from her drawer and started to write.

★ ★ ★

The following lunchtime, Connie had a telephone message to be ready to leave the house at one o'clock as Les Baxter would be collecting her, and Irene would be giving them lunch.

She had spent time with Jeremy in his study, where he told her he had already been approached by several people, but would be sorting through the offers with Les Baxter that afternoon, planning the following months, after her time at the club was finished.

'You need to keep fit and concentrate on your lessons,' he advised. 'I've already spoken with Irene, so she knows what is needed.'

'Before I go I would like to thank your wife for her hospitality,' she said, thinking how much pleasure saying goodbye to Annabel would give her.

'I'm sorry my dear, but she's gone away to stay with friends. She left early this morning. I'll pass on your message though,' he said.

And so, later that day, Les delivered Connie, with her bag and baggage, at Irene's house.

'My darling!' Irene greeted her. Hugging Connie, she said, 'I was so proud of you last night and now you are here to stay a while. We have a lot of work ahead of us, but today – you rest. Come in, come in.'

Connie felt as if she was coming home.

Les stayed only for a short time, refusing lunch, as he said, 'I have to meet with Jeremy, but I'll be in touch. Take care,' he said to Connie and, to her surprise, he kissed her on the cheek.

'So, darling,' said Irene as they sat in her drawing room after their meal, sipping coffee, 'how was it for you last night in front of all of those people?'

'Wonderful!' Connie looked a little sheepish and said, 'I felt as if I belonged there . . . does that sound big-headed?'

'No,' said Irene quietly. 'I felt the same when I sang my first opera. It was as if I had arrived at my destination after a long journey. I loved every minute.'

'I knew you'd understand. I didn't want to stop. I could have sung all night long!'

'That wouldn't have done your voice much good!' she chided, but in fun. 'Jeremy is thrilled with you.'

'But not his wife!'

'Poor Annabel,' Irene laughed.

'Poor nothing. She was so condescending, I wanted to punch her in the mouth!'

'Connie! That is not lady-like talk.'

She giggled. 'I know . . . but I did.'

'Ah, well you see, my dear, this happens to Annabel so often, Jeremy lands her with his latest protégée, and sometimes it doesn't end there.'

'What do you mean?'

Irene shrugged. 'He's a man, what can I tell you?'

'He didn't make a pass at me.'

'But you are such a baby. Anyway, don't you worry, Annabel isn't without her *admirers*, shall we call them.'

'Really?'

'I will say no more, I have been indiscreet enough. Let's go for a walk to blow away the cobwebs of last night. Fill our lungs with good fresh air, ready for the morning.' As they were going out of the door, she gave Connie a woollen scarf. 'Wrap this around your throat,' she instructed. 'We don't want you to catch a cold on the threshold of your career. Never go out without it in the cold weather.'

They walked together in companionable silence, both lost in their own thoughts. Irene was delighted to have Connie staying with her, looking forward to watching her grow, anxious that she care for her voice, improve her capabilities, and pleased with the company. She was really fond of this young girl, but at the same time, knowing the pitfalls ahead in the unstable world of entertainment, she was more than a little concerned as to how Connie would handle them. Not that she thought her pupil couldn't stand up for herself, but how to temper this without upsetting the wrong people.

Connie was planning for her future, for the day she could afford her own place, have her mother and sister to stay, Molly too. Wondering just how soon it would be before her name was in lights as Jeremy had promised, and what sort of bookings were to follow. Thinking of the press who would be writing about her. Maybe her picture would be in the national press like it was in the local paper when she won the talent competition. Soon perhaps she wouldn't be able to walk down a street without getting recognised, and how exciting that would be, being famous! She was thrilled by the whole idea.

Chapter Nineteen

On Sunday morning, there were reviews about Connie in the entertainment section of several national papers, and she and Irene excitedly pored over them together.

'Listen to this,' said her teacher, and began to read. *'Last night at the Palm Court Club in the West End of London, a new star was born. Connie Ryan made her debut in grand style with her deep rich voice which seemed to caress the lyrics of every song. I predict a bright future for this young lady.'*

'Here's another,' said Connie. *'How refreshing to sit and listen to a singer who understands a lyric. Connie Ryan is appearing at the Palm Court Club. Don't miss her!'* Wreathed in smiles she said, 'Isn't it wonderful?'

'Only what you deserve, my dear. Congratulations! Now you need to work even harder as your audience will expect even more from you.'

In bed with her lover, Annabel Taylor was reading the same reviews, whilst sipping a cup of coffee. 'So the little bitch made the headlines,' she said in a bored voice. The hand of her companion slipped under the bedclothes and stroked her flat stomach.

Rudy Davenport continued his exploratory caresses and murmured, 'She's the hottest thing in show business at the moment. And as soon as I can arrange a free theatre, she'll appear on the bill.'

'Arrogant, that's what she is.' Annabel was still smarting

from Connie's spirited attitude towards her. 'She really needs taking down a peg or two, and I want to be there when it happens!' She put down the paper, spread her legs to allow Rudy's fingers easier access to her most intimate parts, and said, 'Let's get on with it, shall we?'

He chuckled. 'That's what I love about you, Annabel, your romantic side.'

As she turned and climbed on top of him she said, 'There's no romance between us, darling, you know that, but the sex is great, so let's enjoy it!'

The following week seemed to pass in a flash. Connie, happy at Irene's and driven by the flattering reviews, concentrated on her lessons. She ran through her programme with Ben who would come to Madame Vicario's daily and use her music room when it was free, introducing new songs for the benefit of those patrons who came to the club frequently.

'You must have a varied programme,' he explained. 'If it's the same old thing the regulars will become blasé and stop listening.'

'Same old thing! Do you mind?' she laughed.

'Well, you know what I mean.'

Ben taught her so much. She began to be able to understand the musical score under his tuition. They would sit side by side on the long piano stool and he would say, 'Listen to this chord, then come in immediately afterwards.' Then he would point out the notes on the music sheet in front of him. Connie told herself that she wasn't breaking Les's rule about seeing Ben other than through business.

Connie sat with her arm casually around his shoulders as she followed the score and sang the opening lines of 'Embraceable You'. Her gaze wandered to Ben's face, and watched the concentration as he played. She loved the way his hair grew in the back of his neck, the slight twist in the nape, and without thinking she ran her fingers across it.

The touch of her fingers on his skin caught Ben unawares

and he stiffened. How easy it would be, he thought, to let his feelings for Connie overcome his good sense! How trite that seemed. The nearness of her was driving him crazy and he realised how difficult it was going to be for him to hide behind a professional façade. But he had to. He moved away from her and said, somewhat abruptly, 'Shall we get on?'

Stung by his dismissal of her, Connie rose from the stool and stood by the piano. 'Yes, let's,' she snapped. 'We wouldn't like anything to get in the way, would we?' she challenged.

He ignored her barbed comment and began to play.

Two nights later, Les Baxter kept his promise and brought Freda, Doreen and her friend Molly to the club to see her perform. As she sang, she glanced over to their table and was thrilled to see the expressions of wonderment on all their faces.

Les insisted that he treat them all to a meal, which was met with great appreciation.

During the main course Freda leaned towards Connie and said quietly, 'Les seems quite nice. I am surprised.'

'What did you expect, Mum? A devil with two horns?'

Looking down her nose at her daughter she retorted, 'There's no need to be so sarcastic!'

Connie just laughed and asked, 'Are you enjoying yourself?'

Freda gazed about her and said, 'Of course I am. Such a posh place and they pay to hear you sing – *my* baby! We are all so proud of you.'

At the end of the meal as they were about to leave, Molly hugged her and said, 'You were terrific, Connie. It's a far cry from the hat shop, isn't it? Just look at the gown you're wearing!'

With a chuckle Connie said, 'Don't get carried away, it's only on hire. Thanks for coming. I do miss you, Molly, I'll keep in touch.' Turning to Les she said, 'Thanks. It was really good of you to arrange all this.'

He brushed her words aside. 'My pleasure. We must go now, Connie. I'll see you soon.'

★ ★ ★

It was the second Saturday, a week after her opening night. Connie, waiting in her dressing room until it was time for her appearance, answered a knock on her door. 'Come in!' she called.

Kenny Pritchard, resplendent in evening dress, entered. 'Good evening, Miss Ryan,' he said. 'I brought this for you,' and handed her a spray of orchids.

'They're beautiful,' said Connie as she looked at the exquisite white blooms with deep purple markings. 'Thank you.'

'Roses didn't seem appropriate, you are much too exotic for them, I thought.'

She was delighted. No one had ever called her exotic before.

'I wondered if you would like to come out to dinner after your performance?' he said. 'I thought I'd better ask quickly before you have a long queue of admirers outside, wanting your attention.'

She laughed and said, 'I don't think that's very likely.'

'Don't you believe it. If it hasn't happened already, it will after another week here at the club. You made quite a hit, you know.'

'I did?'

'Now then don't be coy. You know you went down well. You had a standing ovation on your opening night!'

'I did, didn't I!' she grinned mischievously. 'Well, I worked hard enough for it.'

'You are a person after my own heart,' he said. 'You have ambition. I like that in a woman.'

'You do?' she said. 'And why is that?'

'Because I like a woman with spirit, and you have plenty. Now what about it, will you dine with me?'

Connie thought, Why not? Neither Jeremy nor Les were going to be there that evening, both had other commitments and it would seem a bit flat after the success of the previous week, just to go home. Ben was obviously no longer interested in her, other than professionally, so why shouldn't she have a good time? After all, she was free to please herself, and she liked this somewhat brash young man. He might be fun to be with for a couple of hours and all she'd done for the whole week was work.

'Yes, I would like that . . . I'm really sorry,' she added, 'but I've forgotten your name.'

'Kenny. I'll come here after you've finished and collect you.' Looking very pleased with himself, he left.

Shortly after, Ben knocked on the door to check that she was all right. 'Would you like me to see you home after the show?' he asked.

'No, it's fine, I'm going out to dinner.'

'I didn't think Les or Jeremy were in this evening.'

'No, I'm going out with a customer. He was in the club in Southampton and was here on my opening night. I'm going with him.'

'I see.' He turned on his heel and over his shoulder he said, 'I'll see you on stage.'

The hurt expression as he turned away made her feel guilty. But she had given the situation between them some considerable thought – she really didn't have time for a serious relationship right now. Madame Vicario had said it wasn't wise to get too friendly with the musicians with whom you worked, and work would always be her priority.

Her audience once more enjoyed her performance, and when she sang the final number, 'Embraceable You', she glanced across at Ben, but he kept his eyes on the keyboard, which disappointed her. She wanted him to look at her the way he had before, when they were rehearsing. She knew she was being capricious, but it was a great feeling to know that she was that attractive to a man, and one who had been around. And now another was to take her to dinner. She wondered if this was what happened when you were a star . . . men vied for your attention. How exciting!

Kenny took her to a dinner club where he insisted they had

champagne cocktails before eating. He teased her, flattered her and made her laugh. It was just what she needed to unwind after her performance. He also intrigued her, as he wasn't forthcoming about his business. When she asked him what he did for a living, he fobbed her off.

'I'm a busy man,' he said. 'I have my finger in a few pies. I make plenty of money, enough to take you to the best places. Places a girl like you should be seen in,' he said, staring at her with twinkling eyes.

There was something about his demeanour that reminded her of Les Baxter but she just couldn't put her finger on what it was. He was well dressed, but there was a rough edge about him, a frisson of danger, perhaps that was it. She had seen the menacing side of the bookmaker as well as his charm and she wondered if Kenny too had such a side to *his* character.

She began to feel tired and said, 'I've had a lovely evening and the meal was great, but I'm sorry, my bed calls. It's been a long night,' she added, stifling a yawn.

He paid the bill and called a taxi.

When the vehicle pulled up outside Irene's house, he looked at it as he helped her out of the car and said, 'Mm, very nice. When can I see you again?'

'I'm really not sure,' she said. 'I'm busy every night as you know.'

He didn't try to persuade her. 'I'll be in the club again. I'll join the queue!' He laughed. Then he kissed her lightly on the lips and got back into the taxi.

The club was closed on Sundays, which gave Connie a welcome break from all forms of work. She was sitting in her dressing gown in the kitchen eating her breakfast when the ring of the front-door bell startled her. She was very surprised when Les Baxter came bursting into the room in a state of great excitement.

'Next Sunday you are to appear at a charity concert at the Palladium!' he announced.

176

'The Palladium?'

'Yes, and that's not all, it will be attended by Princess Elizabeth and the Duke of Edinburgh!'

She covered her open mouth with both hands. 'Oh, my God!'

'And of course at the end of the concert, you'll be presented to them.'

Connie was speechless.

'The publicity will be enormous. It will be a great boost to your career.'

'How on earth did this happen?' she asked.

With some reluctance he told her. 'Jeremy arranged it.'

Irene, who had been listening, said, 'We must practise your curtsy.'

'Oh, my God,' Connie repeated. 'The princess – that's royalty. I'll be too nervous to sing.'

'You'll sing your bloody heart out or I'll want to know the reason why!' Les exclaimed. 'You've got one number, that's all.' He sat beside her. 'From such an appearance, stars have been made. For you, this could be a short cut. The exposure will be tremendous.'

'Whatever will I wear?' she asked, now carried away by the excitement.

'Something new . . . and fabulous. I want to see your picture in all the papers!'

'Oh, Les, isn't it wonderful?' And she hugged him, and then turning to Irene she asked, 'What song do you think I should sing?'

'Something that shows your unique voice. Something sexy and smouldering. I'll go and look through my music.'

The rest of the day passed in a sort of hysterical haze. Connie dressed quickly and she and Irene sat in the music room going through various songs before deciding on Jerome Kern's 'You Go To My Head'. And as she tried it, Connie knew the choice was perfect.

★ ★ ★

Being so young and ambitious, Connie let the fact she was to sing before royalty inflate her ego, and the following nights at the club she became imperious and full of herself. She began to pick faults in the arrangement of a particular song she was rehearsing with Ben. He put up with her tantrum for just a little while and then he slammed his hands on the keys, making a dreadful discord, which stopped her carping.

He glared at her. 'Enough of this,' he said angrily. 'So you are going to sing in a charity concert, that doesn't give you the right to dictate to me about my work. I know what I'm doing, you are still learning, so come off that bloody high horse of yours before you fall.'

'How dare you speak to me like that!'

'Someone has to before you become completely insufferable. This kind of attitude doesn't wash with me or anyone else. It's only because of Jeremy Taylor's influence that you are on the bloody show.'

This enraged her. 'I'm there because I have a great voice!'

'You sing very well, and because of Jeremy pulling a few strings you have been given a chance, but make no mistake, Connie, there are a million people out there who can sing as well if not better. You can be replaced! Never forget that – especially in this business. If you become difficult to deal with you'll be out on that lovely arse of yours before you can blink.'

He rose from the piano, picked up his music and strode out of the room.

Connie slumped onto the piano stool, completely deflated. The idea that she could be replaced had never occurred to her, so carried away with success was she. And the awful thing was, she knew that Ben was right. She had been behaving badly. She was doing exactly what Madame Vicario had warned her against: being a prima donna. Well, she couldn't help it! Everything had happened so quickly. From being a nobody she was suddenly on her way, and this concert was the pinnacle, so far. She mulled over everything in her mind.

Maybe she could be replaced. But she'd make damned sure

no one would want to do that to her! Ben, though she was so angry with him a moment ago, had done her a favour, really, and she should be grateful she supposed, but her pride was still dented, nevertheless. She went off to her dressing room in a huff to change for the evening performance.

Ben's harsh words still rankled and they barely acknowledged each other as she began her performance later that night, and the fact that a small party sitting at a table near the stage were noisy didn't please her either. One young lady in particular was very vocal in her conversation and Connie heard her say loudly, 'This isn't my kind of music. I only listen to opera. That takes a real singer!'

At the end of the number, Connie held up her hand towards the bandleader who was about to start the next song and asked him to wait. Then to his surprise, she took the microphone off the stand and walked over to the edge of the stage just above the table where the young lady who had offended her was sitting and said, 'Madam, if you would prefer to hear opera, I will be only too happy to oblige.' And without music, she began to sing the aria from *Carmen* that Irene had taught her.

Ben quickly came in on the piano to accompany her, and the room hushed.

Connie gave it her all, with the actions adding to the drama, just as she had been taught. At the same time she saw the flush of embarrassment on the woman's face as her friends teased her. At the end, there was a stunned silence, and then enthusiastic applause.

Connie looked down at the woman and smiling, curtsied deeply, and walked back to the centre of the stage. She replaced the mike and nodded to the bandleader, who continued with the scheduled programme.

Back in her dressing room, feeling very pleased with herself, Connie was taken aback when the owner of the club knocked on her door and entered without waiting for an invitation.

'What the hell did you think you were doing out there?' he demanded.

'Giving the patrons what they wanted!' she retorted. 'That bloody woman said she preferred opera, because that took a real singer.'

'Do you have any idea who she was?'

'No.'

The owner snapped, 'Lady Victoria Danvers.'

Connie shrugged. 'So?'

'Her father is one of the most influential men in London. He sends a lot of business my way and you tried to humiliate his precious daughter. Do anything like that again and you're out!' He slammed the door behind him as he left.

Almost immediately Ben arrived. He didn't even bother to knock. He stood before Connie who was sitting sulking at her reprimand. 'See what I mean?' he said quietly.

'You heard?'

He just raised his eyebrows. 'You can't just do as you like, you know.'

'So it would seem!' she said. 'Yet I have to put up with the likes of that woman spoiling my performance and do nothing!'

'Until you are a big star, yes, you do. When you are at the top, then that sort of thing won't happen. Come on, get changed and I'll take you home.'

When they arrived at the house, Connie turned to Ben and said, 'I'm sorry about tonight.'

'Forget it,' he said. 'See you tomorrow.'

As she put the key in the lock to open the door she thought she *was* sorry she and Ben had exchanged cross words but she wasn't a bit sorry about the young woman.

She had thoroughly enjoyed that moment, even if she had been roasted for it! She relished the memory of the woman's discomfort – and walked into the house grinning broadly.

Chapter Twenty

During the next few days, Connie's nerves were shredded by the excitement of appearing before royalty. Les had taken her to one of London's finest stores and purchased a gown for her in midnight blue. It was a classic style, sleeveless, with a fitted bodice and full skirt. The simplicity of it was to be offset by a magnificent sapphire and diamond necklace and matching earrings that Jeremy would borrow from a famous jeweller he knew through his many connections.

'I'll collect them on the day,' he told her, 'then immediately after the final curtain and the presentation, I'll take them back. They cost a small fortune, so for God's sake don't break them!'

Connie couldn't believe what was happening to her. One minute she was ecstatic, the next a bundle of nerves. Jeremy saw this and asked Les, 'Do you think she'll be all right on the night? It's a lot to expect from her; after all she's still a child really. At eighteen it's a lot to handle.'

'She'll be absolutely fine,' he assured his partner. 'You don't know Connie as well as I do. When it comes down to the bottom line, she'd walk into a den of lions to perform if she thought it would help her career!'

'I hope you're right.'

At the Palm Court Club that night, after Connie had finished her performance, Les sat with her in her dressing room and talked to his protégée. As usual he didn't mince his words. 'Now you listen to me,' he began. 'You fought tooth and nail to get where you are, even defying your father, now you really have the chance of a lifetime. You make a balls-up of it – then you're finished!'

'What do you mean?'

'Your boss here is still angry with you upsetting the daughter of his best client—'

'Oh, you heard about that?'

'Yes, I did, and although I might have wanted to do the same, I would have had more sense. But now . . . he's made up with you being picked for the Palladium. Do well and you are laughing.'

'And if I don't?'

'You are out of a job, you'll be a failure, no one will be interested in you. Your popularity that is building will have disappeared and not only that, who else will employ you? Your career will be over, just as it's starting.'

She looked at the earnest expression on his face and realised the validity of his remarks. 'You don't need to worry about me,' she said haughtily, 'I'll be fine! I want this as much as you do.'

He rose from his seat and said, 'I'm glad to hear it. I'll pick you up in a taxi on Sunday; I'll let you know what time later. They have to run through the programme during the afternoon. As yet we don't know which spot is yours.' He broke into a smile and, cupping her chin in his hand, he said softly, 'Wherever it is in the programme, there's one thing I do know – they won't forget you.' And he kissed her gently on the lips and walked to the door. 'I'll be at the bar, when you're ready, I'll see you home.'

As he closed the door, a young man approached and paused in front of him. 'Yes?' said Les. 'Did you want something?'

'I am going to see Miss Ryan.'

'You are?' said Les, standing squarely in front of the door. 'And what do you want to see her about?'

'That is none of your business,' he said, looking straight at Les.

'Indeed it is, my young friend. I am Miss Ryan's agent and manager. She's very tired and I will be taking her home very shortly. Is there a message?'

'No, thanks,' said Kenny Pritchard. 'I always deliver my messages myself. I'll catch her another time.' He turned on his heel and walked jauntily away, whistling to himself.

Cheeky young bugger, thought Les. It was just as well he was there. He would have to get someone to stand by Connie's door each night. He didn't want her bothered by young Lotharios. He had to protect her from predatory young men. It was his duty to look out for her, after all.

Later, in a taxi on the way home, he casually asked, 'Do you get bothered by people asking you out after your performance when I'm not around?'

There was something possessive about his tone that made her lie. 'No. In any case at the end of the night I'm too tired to go anywhere.'

'Good,' he said. 'You need your rest, and I can't be here every night to look after you.'

Connie wondered what he would say if he knew she'd been out to dinner with Kenny. She didn't think he would be at all pleased, and if she did it again, she'd best keep it to herself; after all, she was entitled to *some* fun.

Sunday morning dawned. After Connie had had a bath she sat at the table in the living room whilst Irene combed out her hair, which had been dressed the day before at the hairdresser's. Connie listened to Irene's advice as her teacher stood behind her.

'You'll probably find that backstage today will be mayhem. Try not to get involved with it – keep yourself to yourself. Do your breathing exercises, and do your scales. Ben will be around, so talk to him and when you are waiting in the wings to go on, take deep breaths, it will keep you calm. Tell yourself you are there because you have talent. They like to give a beginner a chance on these occasions, but only if they're any good – and you deserve that place.'

'Oh, Madame, what would I do without you?'

'This sort of occasion is the thing that memories are made of, darling. Enjoy it!'

'You are the first person to tell me that. All Les and Jeremy keep telling me is don't fail.'

'Pshaw! That's men for you. You take a deep breath and walk on that stage as if you own it, because it's yours alone for just a few minutes. Have fun with it.'

These wise words calmed the butterflies in Connie's stomach until it was time to leave.

Irene was right; backstage at the Palladium was mayhem. Stagehands rushed around moving scenery. Artists were being taken to various dressing rooms, which some had to share with others. Connie recognised many famous people as they passed by and could hardly believe she would be sharing the bill with such stars as Anna Neagle, who was walking towards her, carrying a pink floating ensemble of net, with Michael Wilding in her wake. Connie stood open-mouthed as they walked past and was thrilled to the core when Wilding winked at her.

From her small box-like dressing room, the orchestra could be heard tuning their instruments, and, amidst all this, Ben knocked on the door and walked in. He saw her dress hanging on a rail and let out a whistle of approval.

Connie was pleased the artists were allowed to rehearse in their everyday clothes; it was more comfortable as one could relax more. When it was her turn to go on she was surprised to see that Tommy Trinder was the compère, but she walked on stage without a qualm, smiled at the musicians and shook hands with the leader of the orchestra.

Her song went without a hitch and she walked off stage with Ben, who grinned at her and said, 'That was just great. Come on, I'll buy you a coffee,' and they slipped out of the stage door to a small café and sat, giving themselves a break from the fraught atmosphere of the theatre.

'Is it always like this?' Connie asked.

Laughing, Ben said, 'Pretty much. You get used to it in time.'

Shaking her head, Connie said, 'I doubt I ever will. It's like a madhouse!'

Time seemed to fly and before she knew it, Connie was made up and in her dress, wearing the sumptuous diamond and sapphire necklace and earrings that Jeremy had delivered – he'd insisted she wear them immediately in case they were stolen. 'Don't you dare take them off until I see you after the presentation,' he said. 'If you put them down somewhere, they could be lost or taken. They're very valuable, so for God's sake be careful. Break a leg!' he said as he left.

Connie was listed to close the first half of the show. The tension backstage was almost palpable, although it was quiet of course as the show had begun. The callboy came to her dressing room and told her she had five minutes and, taking a deep breath, she made her way to the wings where to her relief she saw Ben waiting.

The audience seemed to be enjoying the balancing act that was on before them and as they took their bow, Ben looked at Connie . . . Her face was as white as a sheet. He turned her so she was facing him.

'Look at me!' he demanded. There was sheer terror in the eyes that stared at him.

'Connie,' he said softly, 'you are beautiful and you have the voice of an angel and they are going to love you – as much as I do.' He kissed her softly. 'Come on, darling, let's go and knock their socks off!'

The expression changed slowly, and she smiled at him. She took a deep breath and let it out slowly just as Tommy Trinder announced her name. '*We are delighted to introduce you to a fresh new talent. Miss Connie Ryan – you lucky people!*'

Standing tall, she walked on stage, stood in front of the

microphone, and quickly glanced across at Ben who winked at her. 'Good evening, ladies and gentlemen,' she said clearly, then waited as the orchestra began to play the introduction to Jerome Kern's 'You Go To My Head', her jewels glittering in the lights.

She forgot about the audience, concentrating on the lyrics, and lost herself in the love song, singing from the soul, her deep voice caressing every note and word. At the end of her performance, the applause was deafening. Connie's smile lit up her face with glee and she curtsied to the audience with great dignity, turned towards the royal box as she had been instructed by the stage manager, curtsied again, then walked slowly off the stage. In the wings, Ben lifted her in his arms and swung her round. 'Congratulations, you were great.'

The stage manager hurried over and pushed Connie back onto the stage. 'Take another bow!' he told her, and she did, amazed at the prolonged applause. She smiled at the audience, curtsied again and blew them a kiss before returning to the wings.

During the interval, Jeremy and Les rushed around backstage to Connie's dressing room with a bottle of champagne and glasses. 'You were sensational, darling,' said Jeremy effusively.

Les looked at her and taking her hands in his, said quietly, 'Tonight you were something very special, my dear Connie. I have never seen you more confident, more professional . . . and more beautiful.'

His words moved her deeply, but the expression in his eyes was something new. There was admiration . . . yet something more. Could it be desire? Was she dreaming? She'd seen this look in other men and recognised it but she was more than a little shaken to see it in Les Baxter's eyes, whilst he was looking at *her*.

With a slow smile she said, 'Thank you,' and held his gaze, wondering if, for the first time, she had seen admiration in his expression.

Ben, observing the exchange, misinterpreted her gaze and, thinking there was some kind of chemistry between Connie and Les, deepened his resolve to keep Connie at arm's length. He wasn't going to let another woman treat him badly, ever again!

'I shouldn't have too much of the bubbly,' he said quietly. 'There is the finale and then the presentation. You need a clear head, Connie.'

But she didn't want the magic moment of her success spoilt. 'Oh, for goodness' sake! I know what I'm doing,' she snapped as she picked up a glass.

'I certainly hope so,' he said with great deliberation.

She cast a quick glance in his direction, but he made no further comment.

'Ben is right,' agreed Les. 'There is still the second half to go, and time will drag. I'll get some sandwiches sent in for you. Tonight you need all your wits about you, Connie.'

Looking at him she knew this was good advice. 'I know.'

'After the show we'll all go somewhere and celebrate,' said Jeremy. 'Then you can let your hair down and relax. Well done, Connie. I was so proud of you. Come on, Les, let's leave her now or we'll be late returning to our seats. We'll only upset some old dowager if we are.'

Suddenly she was alone with Ben.

'You were sensational out there tonight,' he said quietly.

She grinned broadly at him. 'I was, wasn't I?'

'Les Baxter certainly seemed to think so!'

'What do you mean?'

'I think you know what I mean. What was going on between you?'

'I don't know what you're talking about.'

'Don't lie to me, Connie, but let me give you a word of warning. Baxter thinks he owns you, despite having to sell part of you to Jeremy Taylor. As far as he's concerned, you are his property and now he sees you growing into a very desirable woman, before long he'll expect even more from you.'

'What are you suggesting?' she demanded angrily. 'He's old enough to be my father!'

'You didn't think that tonight, did you? I saw the look in your eyes. He excited you and that's dangerous. *He's* dangerous.'

'You're jealous!' she said teasingly.

'Don't play with people's feelings, Connie,' he warned, 'it can lead to all sorts of trouble.'

'When we were together in Southampton, you were different,' she accused.

'That was then – this is now!'

At that moment there was a knock on the door and a young man delivered a platter of sandwiches and some coffee.

Ben took them and said to Connie, 'Come on, I'm starving and I expect you are too.'

Eventually it was time for the finale. The artistes took their places on the stage one after another in the order of their appearance. Connie found herself between Patricia Roc and Diana Dors, and was thrilled.

Connie's heart was beating so fast she thought she'd pass out. She watched as Princess Elizabeth, followed by the Duke of Edinburgh, came down the line. She was glad to be wearing jewellery that was expensive as she saw the sparkling jewels of the princess from her tiara to the necklace and earrings, which glittered in their magnificence.

She curtsied deeply as the princess was introduced and held the gloved hand for a moment. 'Your Royal Highness,' she said softly.

The princess nodded, smiled and said, 'Very nice,' and moved on. Then, before she knew it, the Duke of Edinburgh was in front of her. She curtsied and took the outstretched hand. The grip was surprisingly firm, after his fiancée's. She looked up at the smiling face of the handsome young man and was astonished when he said, 'I enjoyed your singing.'

Beaming from ear to ear she said, 'Thank you, sir.'

★ ★ ★

Back in the dressing room, euphoric at being presented, and praised by the Duke, Connie was beside herself as Les and Jeremy entered.

'The Duke liked my singing!' she exclaimed.

'Lovely, my dear,' said Jeremy, 'but let me please have your jewellery!'

At a small select restaurant in London, they celebrated. To her surprise, Rudy and Annabel were among the party.

'Well done, Connie!' Rudy said. 'You really made an impression on that stage tonight.'

'Thank you,' she said.

Annabel ignored her, which amused Connie. She was far too euphoric to have her evening spoilt by this woman. After all, she'd been a success and the snooty Annabel couldn't take that away from her. She was surprised however by the attention Rudy paid to Jeremy's wife as the night wore on and the intake of liquor increased. They danced together several times and as Rudy held his partner tighter than Connie thought was necessary, she glanced across the table at Jeremy to see if he had noticed, but he was deep in conversation with Les. As Connie watched she got the distinct impression that there was something between the two. Not that they were indiscreet, but the odd intimate glance, the whisper in the ear, the soft smile . . . then she remembered Irene's remark about Annabel having her own admirers. Well, Miss Hoity Toity, she laughed to herself Who'd have thought it!

189

Chapter Twenty-One

Travelling back to Southampton by train on Monday morning, Les Baxter sat back in the seat, grateful that the first-class carriage was empty, as he was suffering from a terrific hangover. Despite his throbbing head, he gave a half smile as he recalled the previous night's celebration and Connie's excitement. She had been more impressed with meeting the royal couple than with her success, and according to today's papers it had been a resounding one.

Picking up the *Daily Mail* from the pile beside him he turned to the inside page and read the report of the show, looked at the pictures of Princess Elizabeth and the Duke of Edinburgh arriving, then at another picture of Connie curtsying to the Duke. A NEW STAR IS BORN, was the headline. *Young singer steals the limelight.* Well, at least this side of his business was working out. Back in Southampton, things were happening that he didn't like one little bit.

Over the past three weeks, some unusually heavy bets had been laid with several of his runners, both on the horses and on the dogs, and what's more, they were winning. Someone somewhere had inside information and Les's finances were suffering. The whole thing smelt fishy and now he would have to spend time getting to the bottom of it. Time he should have spent before, instead of being in London quite so much.

At least he knew that Connie was safe with Irene Vicario, and Ben Stanton wasn't a threat with Connie knowing the pianist's job was on the line if she defied him. He closed his eyes and pictured her standing in the middle of the stage at the Palladium. My God, she'd looked magnificent, and the way she sang that song, he doubted there wasn't a man sitting watching who hadn't desired her. The dress, the jewels, her interpretation of the lyrics. She might be only eighteen but she looked very much a woman. And she was his! His to nurture, for the next five years. Oh, he had great plans. Plans he kept to himself at this stage, knowing she would be climbing the ladder to success until he was able to . . . he rubbed his eyes. But now he must think about the task in hand. In his gut he felt that Kenny Pritchard was behind the betting scam, but he would have to step carefully until he knew for sure, then the little bleeder would get a lesson he wouldn't forget in a hurry.

Back on his own turf, he went round all the runners asking questions. Who laid the bets? Did you know any of the men? As he thought, they were strangers, mostly with London accents. Well, his time in London hadn't entirely been wasted; he'd been doing the rounds during the day there as well. He'd spoken to several of the men who'd worked for old man Pritchard and they were sick to the teeth with the arrogant son who tried to run roughshod over them. Rebellion was in the air, and that suited him very well.

Not satisfied with bookmaking, young Kenny Pritchard was spreading his wings. He was looking into buying a couple of clubs, with hostesses, which was a polite way of hiding prostitution, stepping on a few toes in the process.

'He'll have the Old Bill sniffing around,' grumbled one of the runners, 'and before you can say Jack Robinson, they'll be all over the bookmaking as well! The old man would never have let that happen.'

'He's wandering into other people's patches too,' said another. 'There are one or two villains that won't put up with him, that's for sure, strutting around like a fucking peacock!'

Les thought of this conversation and grinned to himself. The kid was walking on dangerous ground but was so arrogant he didn't even know it. But first he would have to make sure it was him that was behind this little scam. That wouldn't be a problem; some of his men would tail the punters next time and see who received their winnings. He'd lose a bit more into the bargain, but he'd gain in other ways. He could afford to indulge the little bastard one more time, especially if he laid off some of the bets with other bookmakers. He called his men together and told them his plans.

In the Ryan household that evening, Freda and Doreen were poring over the paper, almost hysterical with excitement over the picture of their Connie curtsying to royalty. Freda took great satisfaction in shoving the paper under George's nose as he sat down to eat his dinner.

'Look at our Connie! And *that* is the Duke of Edinburgh!'

He studied the picture for the umpteenth time that day. All his workmates had produced several different newspapers that carried an account of the show with a similar picture. He of course had bathed in her glory, taking a lot of the credit for her success himself. 'I always knew she had it in her,' he told them. But now, faced with his own family who knew how he'd tried to block her advance, he felt uncomfortable.

'I've already seen it,' he said.

'Well, don't overdo the excitement, will you, Dad!' said Doreen, her voice full of scorn. 'After all, if you'd had your way she would still be singing occasionally at the Social Club, earning you free drinks!'

'There's no need to be like that,' he retorted.

'She's your daughter, you should be proud of her.' Freda was furious. 'Yet not once have I ever heard you say so.'

'Of course I'm proud of her,' he replied.

'It would be really nice if you sent her some flowers and a card of congratulations,' suggested Doreen, anxious to heal the divide between her sister and father.

'I might just do that!'

'Yes, and pigs might fly!' murmured his wife.

She was wrong, however, because George was secretly

delighted at Connie's success which gave him a certain kudos with his mates, and so the following morning he placed an order for a bouquet to be sent to the house in Maida Vale.

In London, Connie opened the door to the florist, who asked, 'Are you Miss Connie Ryan?' When she said she was, he handed over the flowers.

Rushing into the living room, she excitedly opened the small envelope. The contents came as a great surprise. *Congratulations. With love, Dad.*

Madame Vicario entered the room as she read it. 'What beautiful flowers!' she exclaimed.

Looking up, Connie said coldly, 'I bet that broke his heart!'

'Whose heart?'

'My bloody father, that's who! I suppose he saw my picture in the paper.'

'Then why the anger, Connie?'

'Because it's too bloody late, that's why!' she said, casting the card aside. 'He can take his damned flowers and—'

'Connie!'

'I don't care! If he had his way I'd still be in Southampton, he forced me to leave my home, my family, because of his stubborn pride. He never ever considered what *I* wanted. He was more bothered about what his mates would think of him if they knew that someone else was going to finance me.' She picked up the bouquet and placed them in Irene's arms. 'Here,' she said. 'I don't want them, as far as I'm concerned they can go in the dustbin!' and she walked out of the room.

Later in the day when a reporter called at the house asking for an interview, the rising star, still seething, was able to get her revenge. She was alone in the house and invited him in.

'And what do your family have to say about your success?' he asked, once they were settled in the living room.

'My mother and my sister are thrilled,' she said, smiling at the young man, 'my father would have preferred it if I was a failure.'

Sensing a story, the reporter asked, 'And why is that, Miss Ryan?'

'When Les Baxter, who is my manager now, first heard me sing, he thought I had talent and told my father, but he didn't want to know and then, when Mr Baxter offered to pay for my tuition with a singing teacher and to finance me until I got started, my father refused.'

'Why would he do that?'

'His pride got in the way, it didn't matter to him that he was throwing away *my* chance. He just thought it wouldn't look good that he wasn't in a position to pay himself.'

'So how did you overcome this problem?'

'I left home.'

'Where did you go?'

'I stayed with Mr Baxter's mother.'

'Did Mr Baxter live there too?'

Suddenly Connie realised that her anger had made her indiscreet. 'Certainly not! He has his own place.'

'Quite a Svengali, this manager of yours, isn't he?'

The atmosphere had changed and Connie knew it. Thinking quickly she said, 'You do realise that Mr Baxter is now in partnership with Jeremy Taylor, the famous London agent? They *both* take care of me.'

Irene put her key in the front door and opened it. She was loaded down with shopping bags. As she entered the living room she was surprised to see a young man rising to his feet, she also noted the flushed look of embarrassment on the face of her pupil.

'Who are you?' she demanded, standing in front of the visitor.

'Press,' he said, sidestepping her and heading for the front door. 'Thank you, Miss Ryan, you've been very helpful,' he said as he opened the door and made good his escape.

'Connie?' Irene waited.

Twisting her hands together anxiously she said, 'I think I've just been very stupid.'

Putting down her shopping, Irene removed her gloves and hat and said, 'You had better tell me why.'

Connie related her interview word for word. When she had finished Irene shook her head in despair and said angrily, 'Why do you never listen to a word I say? How many times have I told you that when you are in this business you have to be so careful?' She ran her fingers through her hair, patting it in place. 'You have just given that reporter a story which, by the time he's finished with it, will no doubt be sensational and not at all flattering! You are indeed a very stupid girl. You are so headstrong you don't stop to think. When *will* you learn?'

'I was angry with my father!'

'And so you became spiteful – how very childish! How do you think your father will feel when he reads about it?'

But Connie wasn't all contrite. 'It will serve him right.'

'And what do you think Jeremy will think? He has worked so hard to get you where you are and you do this. Well, I can tell you he will not be pleased when I tell him.'

'Does he have to know?'

'Have you completely lost your common sense? Do you want it to come as a surprise when he reads the paper? Of course I must tell him, he must be prepared for the onslaught from other papers when this becomes news.' She walked up and down the room. 'I can't imagine what they will make of it but it won't be good. I must call Jeremy now,' and she picked up the telephone.

Connie could hear his angry voice bellowing over the line.

Eventually Irene said, 'You're right, we'll just have to wait and see.' Replacing the receiver she glared at her pupil and said, 'I'm sure you could hear. Now we have to wait until the morning paper.' She picked up the bags of shopping and left the room.

Connie sat with her hands to her head. She didn't care a toss about her father, but she may have harmed her career and that she did care about. Surely what she'd said in the interview couldn't hurt Les? She'd said how he financed her, and Jeremy

196

surely couldn't be angry, as she'd said nothing untoward about him. Oh, well, there was nothing to be done now. The morning may bring nothing to worry about after all, she told herself, but that night her anxiety stopped her from sleeping.

The next morning, Kenny Pritchard stopped at a news stand to buy a paper when a certain headline caught his eye. He paid for the paper, stood to one side of the stall and read, a slow smile spreading across his features. So Les Baxter was the manager of the gorgeous Connie Ryan. How very interesting.

Chapter Twenty-Two

RISING YOUNG STAR LEAVES HOME FOR MAN-AGER, was the headline spread across the front page of the newspaper – and Connie knew she was in trouble. Irene wasn't speaking to her except in monosyllables, Jeremy would go spare and she didn't dare think of Les's reaction. Taking a deep breath Connie read on.

18 year-old Connie Ryan, who caused a sensation when she performed at Sunday's charity performance, admitted yesterday that her father didn't want her to be a professional, but when 39-year-old Les Baxter offered to finance her career, she left home to be with him.

Connie closed the pages, unable to read further scurrilous lies.

There was a loud ringing of the front door bell and Irene hurried to answer it, calling to Connie, 'I'll get it, you stay out of sight.'

Connie crossed to the window and behind the net curtains, saw Jeremy Taylor waiting on the doorstep. To her surprise, at the gate were several reporters with cameras at the ready, snapping away, hurling questions at the agent who remained silent.

He came bursting into the living room, his face puce with anger. He stood in front of Connie and glared at her. 'What on earth do you think you were doing talking to the press without my permission?' he demanded.

'I'm sorry, I just didn't think.'

'No, that's your trouble, my girl.' He took off his gloves and his Homburg hat, undid his overcoat and turning to Irene he asked, 'Could I have a cup of coffee, do you think?'

'Of course,' she said, taking his coat.

Connie waited with some trepidation and was grateful when the telephone rang, but when Irene handed the receiver to her she was mortified, as Les Baxter raged at her. 'You stupid little bitch! I've got reporters all over me here, delving into my life story. Next I'll have the police breathing down my neck. Have you any idea of the trouble you've caused?'

'I'm sorry, Les.'

'A bloody lot of good that is.'

'Jeremy's here,' she told him, anxious to get off the line and away from his tirade.

'Put him on,' she was told, and gladly handed the receiver over.

'I know, I know,' Jeremy was saying, then silence as he listened. 'Just leave it with me, Baxter, I'll handle everything. I'll get back to you,' he said and replaced the receiver. Turning to Connie he said, 'He is not a happy man but I'm sure he told you that.'

She nodded and was silent.

Picking up his cup of coffee, which Irene had brought in, he sipped it slowly, and was quiet as he thought out his strategy. 'Right!' he said. 'Well, you can't hide away or the press will think there is something to the story. Get your glad rags on, we're going out.'

'What'll I say if they question me?'

'If they ask you about your relationship with Baxter, say he's just your agent. Anything else is ridiculous.'

Connie went upstairs and dressed in a deep purple velvet costume and black fur Cossack-style hat, and put a fox fur over her shoulders, smoothing the double tails down the front. She looked in the mirror and murmured, 'This is the performance of your life, Connie Ryan, and it had better be good.'

Jeremy looked approvingly at her when she entered the

room. 'Right,' he said. 'Once through the front door, you behave as if all this publicity doesn't bother you because it is preposterous. You smile and you charm every one of those buggers. Do I make myself clear?'

'Crystal!'

At the front door he asked, 'Ready?'

'Yes, I'm ready,' and she smiled as she stepped outside.

The flash of bulbs from the cameras caught her by surprise, but she posed on the top of the steps and listened to the shouted comments.

'What do you think of the report in the paper this morning?'

'The whole idea is preposterous.'

'Les Baxter isn't your sugar daddy then?' asked another.

Connie picked out the man who asked the question, and fluttered her eyelashes at him. She glanced around at the others and said, 'Gentlemen. With so many handsome young men around, why would I want to be an old man's darling? Really!'

Jeremy eased her down the steps to his waiting taxi.

'What about your father?' asked another as she sat in the back of the vehicle.

'Well, at least I know who my father is . . . do you know yours?' she asked as she closed the car door.

As the taxi drew away she let out a deep breath.

Jeremy said acidly, 'You did very well. What a pity you couldn't have been so sharp before!'

'Will this harm my career?' she asked anxiously.

He shrugged. 'It can work either way. This has thrust you into the limelight, in a way that could be detrimental, but if you watch your step and your tongue, it may work in your favour. It might be a seven-day wonder. Fortunately the wedding of Princess Elizabeth in two weeks' time will be the main feature in all the papers. You'll just have to keep your nose clean until then. This notoriety may step up the attendance at the club, but on the other hand it could have the adverse effect.

We had better hope for the best, especially as Ciro's the night club were wanting to book you for three weeks immediately after your contract with the Palm Court Club finishes.'

'Ciro's!' She was delighted. It was one of the most popular and selective nightclubs in London.

'I'll have to go along there later and test the water,' Jeremy said. 'They may be having second thoughts. I may have to do a bit of persuading.'

'Oh, Jeremy, I'm so sorry.'

'You will be if you are as stupid again.' The taxi stopped outside the Café Royal. 'Come along,' he said, 'we may as well face the music.'

As they made their way to a table, one or two people from the theatrical world made some comment as they passed, but Connie just smiled at them, and when one wag said loudly, 'She likes older men so you'll be all right, Jeremy,' she stopped and walked back to the table where the man sat with his friends.

Staring straight at him she said, 'Never believe what you read in the papers. For your information, I like intelligent men – so that lets you out.'

The man looked embarrassed as his dinner companions teased him.

'Very waspish, my dear,' said Jeremy as they sat down.

'How dare the paper print these lies?' she said angrily. 'Les Baxter isn't interested in me that way.'

'Are you sure about that?'

With a startled look, Connie asked, 'Whatever do you mean?'

Lowering his voice Jeremy said, 'You may not be aware of it, my dear, but Baxter would like to be more than your manager.'

'Don't be ridiculous!'

'I've seen the way he looks at you. Surely you've noticed how possessive he is?'

She immediately thought about Ben and how Les forbade

her to see him outside of performing on stage together, but she also remembered the way in which he had gazed at her at the charity concert – and she knew that Jeremy was right.

The following day, Les arrived at Irene's house. He had been hassled by the police before leaving Southampton and was in a foul temper, which was not improved as he glanced through the open door of the music room. Ben was seated at the piano with Connie standing behind him, leaning over his shoulder, her arm around him. To Les, this seemed far too cosy and intimate. It enraged him. He burst into the music room.

'What the bloody hell is going on here?' he demanded.

Ben casually looked round, unperturbed by the outburst but Connie, remembering Jeremy's remarks, jumped down his throat. 'Working! What does it look like?'

'How long has this been going on?'

'We need to rehearse if you want Connie to do her best,' said Ben quietly. 'What better place to do so than here in Irene's music room?'

Irene, hearing the raised voices, came in and caught the tail end of the conversation. 'Come along, Les,' she said, 'let them get on with their rehearsal, we'll go into the living room and I'll make some tea.' She put her arm through his so the bookmaker had no choice. He glared at Connie as he left.

She was fuming. 'That bloody man!' she cursed. 'Why doesn't he leave me alone?'

'Never mind him, let's work,' Ben said. 'That's why we're here. He's lucky there are no reporters around. Think what they would have made of his visit!'

But at that moment there was a ring on the door bell. Connie went to answer it saying, 'Irene's got her hands full at the moment so I'll answer the door. I won't be long.' When she did so, she was surprised to see Kenny Pritchard standing there, one arm behind his back.

'Hello, princess!' He grinned broadly. 'I read the papers and thought it was time for you to be seen with a young man!

Come on, I'm taking you out. How do you fancy the Savoy Grill? Enough people will see us there.'

She was sorely tempted knowing that after he'd had his tea, Les would be on to her about the newspaper article. She knew she'd made a grave error and, after the telling-off she'd had from Jeremy, the thought of facing Les's anger was almost too much. In a temper he could be frightening. Drawing the front door behind her so that it was almost closed, she admitted, 'I could do with escaping right now, but if I go back for my coat and handbag, they'll know I'm going out.'

He took his hand from behind his back and held out a full-length silver fox fur coat and held it out to her. 'Put this on, darling. It's just your size.'

Connie gasped as she felt the softness of the pelts and slipped her arms through the sleeves. It fitted perfectly. Quietly closing the door she whispered, 'Let's go!'

Ben stood at the window and watched Connie, clad in a fur coat, climb into the sports car and smile at the young man who carefully closed the door for her before he drove away. He frowned as he walked back to the piano. What on earth was she up to now? He was so angry that he wanted to take her by the shoulders and shake some sense into her. He began to gather up his music, certain that Connie would not be returning and furious that she'd walked out, leaving her rehearsals for another man.

At that moment, Les came in and, looking round, asked, 'Where's Connie?'

'Gone out.'

'What do you mean gone out? Out where?'

'I've no idea. Someone came to the door and she drove off with him.'

'Why didn't you stop her?'

Ben stood in front of the bookmaker and in measured tones said, 'I don't have her on a leash like a dog. She's free to do what she likes.'

'The hell she is! She should be working.'

'You've changed your tune. Earlier you were furious to find her here with me. You think I'm some kind of threat because Connie and I have grown closer through our working together, you can't stand that – and let's be honest – you want her for yourself.'

'That's a lie!'

'Oh, come on, Baxter, I'm a man for God's sake. I've seen the way you look at her, the way you want to control her every moment. You can't bear to see her with anyone, because you lust after her.'

'You're fired!'

Walking towards the door, Ben smiled. 'No, I'm not. You should read my contract more closely. Taylor has tied up my position very tightly as Connie's arranger. Without me, Jeremy Taylor doesn't want Connie. We come as a pair. Without Taylor there will be no lucrative bookings. You'll be left high and dry!' Picking up his music case, he left.

Les Baxter sat on the piano stool fuming. Everything was going wrong. He had heard on the underworld grapevine that it was Kenny Pritchard who was behind the betting scam and he was up in London to meet with some of the disgruntled men from his organisation. His Southampton business had been suffering badly ever since the newspaper article. The press and the police were watching him carefully so now, if all things worked out, he would be moving his operation to London. There were enough men working for Kenny who would be only too happy to work for someone else, someone who knew the ropes and who was reliable. Then when the heat had cooled down in Southampton, he could take up the reins again. In the meantime, young Connie Ryan needed to be taught a lesson. It was time she learned who was boss and to do as she was told.

Chapter Twenty-Three

As she entered the swing doors of the Savoy Hotel, Connie was both excited and full of trepidation. Les would be furious with her, as would Ben and Irene – walking out of the house like that, forfeiting the rehearsal. But she felt she had to get away. The pressure had been awful after the newspaper report and with Les breathing fire . . . It was more than she could take. She would face the consequences on her return, but meantime she would have a little fun to ease the tension.

Once settled in the dining room, Kenny Pritchard was enjoying himself, sitting opposite the protégée of Les Baxter, the man he was going to try and overthrow. Perhaps he would take Connie too! Apart from that she was very newsworthy at the moment and he wouldn't mind seeing his picture in the paper. It would give him a certain kudos, he thought. He smiled as he remembered her delight when he handed her the fur coat. Women! How easily they could be bought with a few luxuries and a lot of flattery. Glancing around the dining room, he was pleased to see that they were under a certain amount of scrutiny and the subject of gossip from the other diners.

Whilst they ate, Kenny entertained Connie with his ready wit, teasing her about her notoriety. 'You should be seen more often with me, princess,' he said. 'That would put a stop to all this gossip about you and your manager.'

'Perhaps you're right,' she agreed. 'How could anyone think I'd be attracted by someone so much older than me?'

'It happens, you know. Lots of wealthy men have young and beautiful women on their arms when they go out. Wealth can buy many things.'

'I'm not for sale!' she retorted.

'Everyone has their price, Connie.'

She looked uncertain. 'Not if you have any principles at all.'

He smiled knowingly. 'If the devil came to you and said, "Connie Ryan, I can give you fame and fortune, but there is a price to pay," I bet you'd ask what the price was!'

'Well, wouldn't anyone?'

He laughed. 'There you are then, you've just proved my point.'

At the end of a very enjoyable meal, Connie reluctantly said, 'Kenny, I really have to get back, but thanks for such a good time, I really enjoyed myself.'

'My pleasure, princess.'

He paid the bill and walked her to the entrance. Outside, a photographer suddenly appeared, aimed his camera lens at Connie and took a photograph.

'Damn!' she muttered.

'Don't worry,' said Kenny. 'You are with a handsome young man, what harm can that do?'

'I don't know, all I do know is that I don't trust the press any more. Come on, let's go before any more show up.'

Once they arrived at the house, Kenny opened the passenger door of the vehicle for Connie and walked up the steps of the house with her.

'Thank you for the use of the coat,' she said, and went to remove it.

He stopped her and, pulling the front halves together, said, 'Keep it, darling, I bought it for you.'

'Oh, Kenny!' She snuggled into the fur collar. 'It's beautiful. That's very generous of you.'

'My great pleasure, Connie. I'll be seeing you very soon.' And he pulled her gently into his arms and kissed her.

As he climbed into his car and started the engine, the front door opened.

'Where the hell have you been?' Les's angry voice rang in Connie's ears. He looked past her at the car that was pulling away from the pavement and caught a glimpse of the smiling face of the young man driving the vehicle. 'Who is that?' he demanded.

'A friend,' she snapped as she walked past him into the hallway.

'And where did you get this?' he asked, catching hold of the sleeve of her coat.

'I hired it!' she lied. 'Like a lot of my evening gowns. It's what we women do in these hard times. Not even *you* have an endless supply of clothing coupons.' She glared defiantly at him and walked into the living room, taking off her coat as she did so and tossing it carelessly over a chair.

'Well, go on then!' she dared him. 'You came here to have a go at me, so let's get it over with!'

His voice was low and menacing. 'Don't talk to me like that, Connie, unless you want to feel the back of my hand. Through your stupidity, you have all but ruined my bookmaking business in Southampton, for the time being. The police are keeping a close watch on me at the moment, all because you let your mouth and your spite run away with you.'

'I've already said I was sorry.'

'You think that makes a difference?'

'What else can I do?'

'As you are told. You forget, I own you lock, stock and barrel.'

'No one owns me. My father found that out!'

'But your father didn't hold your career in the palm of his hand. I do.'

She suddenly became afraid. 'What do you mean?'

'I've told you this once already but ever since Jeremy Taylor came on the scene you seem to have forgotten. I own the largest percentage of your contract. If I say you are not free to

209

accept any more offers, there is nothing he can do about it.'

'That would be cutting off your nose to spite your face!' she declared. 'Just now, when I am getting known. I have success within my grasp and you know it!'

He smiled benignly. 'That's quite true. How sad it would be for you to be so near . . . but so far. To nearly make it but to miss the chance of stardom through your own foolishness. It would certainly cheese Jeremy Taylor off too. He wouldn't lift a finger to help you again!'

She was beaten and she knew it. 'So what do you want from me?'

'Your complete obedience. You go to work, you practise, you go out with only Jeremy or me, either together or alone.'

'You can't be serious? Am I to have no fun at all? No life of my own?'

His tone softened. 'Come now, Connie my dear. Jeremy is good company. You will be invited to many showbiz occasions, and I am not exactly an ogre, am I? You and I can have good times together, you'll see.'

'But if we are seen together the papers will have a field day.'

'With the royal wedding you will be long forgotten, by then no one will care.' His steady gaze held hers. 'I can give you anything and probably more than any young man you may meet.' He kissed her forehead.

Connie felt a shiver run down her spine.

Picking up his hat and coat from the chair he said, 'I have some business to attend to, but I'll be at the club tonight to run you home.' And he walked out of the room.

All Connie could think of were the words that Kenny had said earlier in the day. *Everyone has their price.* If she wanted to succeed, was Les Baxter the price she would have to pay? If it were so – did she really have a choice?

When she arrived at the club that night, Ben glared at her and said, 'So you have stopped playing games long enough to remember you have a job to do!'

'I don't expect you to understand,' she said defiantly, 'but I had to get away.'

'I understand one thing,' he retorted. 'I made a great mistake.'

'What do you mean?'

'I thought you had grown up, but you are still a child, a spoilt, indulged and selfish child!'

'I don't understand?'

He said quietly, 'I thought you had grown into a woman. You are such a disappointment to me, Connie, but at least you can still sing so you had better go and get ready for tonight's performance.'

She watched him walk away, tears brimming her eyes. Of all people, she wanted Ben to think well of her, and his words were so cutting. Well, she'd show him! Tonight she'd give the performance of her life.

The publicity had not had any effect on the clientele of the Palm Court Club at all and, on this particular night, all the tables were full. Connie's performance, fuelled by defiance, had a certain edge to it, a charisma of its own, and when she sang the final song, 'Someone To Watch Over Me', she glanced across at the piano several times, catching Ben's eye once or twice, leaving him in no doubt that she was alluding to him.

This fact did not escape the attention of her mentor when he arrived, just in time to catch the last number. He felt the anger inside him rise. What game was she playing? Hadn't she got the message that she belonged to him?

At the end of her performance, Connie walked off the stage with Ben amidst enthusiastic applause. Turning to the pianist she said, 'It went well tonight, didn't you think?'

'Oh, yes, it did. You played your part very well,' he said with a disparaging tone. 'Apart from your singing, everything else is one long bloody game! Well, my dear, you can't treat people like that and if you carry on like it you will come unstuck.'

'What do you mean?'

'I mean that Les Baxter doesn't play games. He plays for real.' And he left her outside her dressing room and stormed off.

Connie sat on the chair in front of her dressing-table mirror and gazed at her reflection. She sighed. Life should be marvellous! Here she was doing what she had dreamed of most of her life and suddenly it was a mess and she only had herself to blame, she conceded. If she hadn't wanted to hit back at her father, none of this would have happened, and for the first time she wondered what he had thought of the newspapers and their lies. What would he think of her now? She supposed he would think he was proved right, that she was too young to leave home.

Her dressing-room door opened and Les walked in.

'Would you mind knocking next time!' she said angrily. 'I could have been changing.'

He ignored her. Standing behind her he gripped her shoulders firmly and asked, 'What is there between you and Stanton?'

She shook off her hold. 'Absolutely nothing.'

'That's not what it looked like tonight, you singing to him that way. Do you think I'm some kind of fool?'

'For goodness' sake, it was only acting. Another time I might sing to a client.' She glared at him. 'I might even sing to you, so you see it doesn't mean anything!'

'Get your coat,' he said, 'we're going home.'

Connie didn't argue. She just wanted to get away from everyone – including Les – and when the taxi stopped outside Irene's she opened the door and got out before he could say anything, slamming the door behind her.

Hearing the front door open, Irene walked out of the living room in her dressing gown, her hair loose and brushed. She took one look at Connie and said, 'Whatever is the matter, my dear?'

Connie burst into tears.

A while later, she had told Irene everything. About her feeling of spite against her father, about Ben, and finally – about Les saying he could give her everything a young man could.

Irene was aghast. '*Zut alors!* You must nip this in the bud. Now!'

'But he can ruin my career!'

'He's using this as emotional blackmail. Why would he do that, just as you are beginning to make a name for yourself, which in time means a name for him too, as a successful agent? No!' She clapped her hands together. 'Mr Baxter wants to succeed in the theatrical world, wants eventually to do so without the help of Jeremy Taylor. He needs you to flourish so that he can too.' She sat and shook her head. 'Men can be so devious.'

'How can I keep him at arm's length?'

With a chuckle Irene said, 'By being devious too. Darling, women have ways and means of getting what they want, they always have since the Garden of Eden.'

'What can I do?'

'Firstly try and make sure you are not alone with him.'

'He just walked into my dressing room tonight.'

'Lock the door!'

'And if he wants to come in?'

'Oh, for goodness' sake, Connie, use your imagination say you are changing, then, when you are ready to leave, unlock it and walk out into the corridor.'

'And if he tries to kiss me again but on the mouth?'

'Turn your cheek to him, move away. You can do it, many women have kept the wolf from the door this way. A man can be like putty in a woman's hands if she is clever.'

'And what can I do about Ben? I really care about him.'

'Nothing. Just treat him as a friend. It will make life much easier . . . for both of you.'

Connie gazed at Irene and said, 'I didn't realise there would be so many complications when I left home.'

With a shrug Irene said, 'Anything in this life that is worth anything at all is never easy. You have to decide where your priorities lie, that's all. Come along, darling. Go to bed, you look all in. We'll talk some more in the morning.'

'I can't imagine what my father thinks of all this,' said Connie as she rose from the chair.

George Ryan had read the newspaper reports with growing anger. How could Connie do this to her family, disgrace them in this way? He had come in for some ribbing from his peers about Les Baxter and Connie, which hadn't improved things at all. He had told Freda it was all her fault for talking him into letting Connie go to London to see the music teacher in the first place which had caused a huge family row with Freda and Doreen accusing him in turn.

Nevertheless, as her father, he was concerned. He had never trusted Baxter from the first and he wondered just how much truth was in the rumours. He couldn't bear to think of Connie consorting with this man and wondered just what he could do about it. But knowing Connie's burning ambition, he doubted that anything he could say or do would make the slightest difference.

Chapter Twenty-Four

As it happened, Les Baxter was too busy putting his plans into operation to be of any great threat to Connie. His meeting in London with several members of Kenny Pritchard's organisation had proved very advantageous, and he had set up a new bookmaking business with a team of runners, putting some of his own men in charge. He wasn't foolish enough to trust the new boys. Not yet anyway.

They planned to filter the incoming bets away from Pritchard with some stealth so as not to alert him to the situation, until it was too late. Young Kenny was too busy buying a couple of hostess clubs, so he wasn't paying too much attention to the bookmaking side, and as his accountant was now in the pay of Baxter, everything should move smoothly.

Les had also returned to Southampton for a few days. As he seemed no longer to be of interest to the press, the police were not being so vigilant. After all, he had all but stopped trading, except for the Turf Accountant's office where telephone bets were legal, so there was nothing for the police to report, and the manpower employed was eventually needed for other things.

In London, Connie was coming to the end of her month at the Palm Court Club and was looking forward to a three weeks' appearance at Ciro's, which Jeremy had managed to secure for her.

Ben and she worked together as usual, but there was a certain reticence on his part, which made Connie unhappy.

She wanted that old closeness back, but Ben did not reciprocate her overtures of friendliness. The one bright spark in her life at the moment was Kenny Pritchard.

Connie ignored Les Baxter's orders about her escorts. She was damned if she was going to be kept a prisoner! After talking to Irene, she had decided that if she handled Les carefully and obeyed his rules when he was around, she could relax in her own way when he was in Southampton. Besides, Kenny was fun, but more than that, he was ambitious, which she understood and empathised with. He'd taken her out on her nineteenth birthday and bought her an expensive watch, which delighted her. He told her he was buying two clubs and promised that she would be certain to entertain there, which of course delighted her even more.

'You will be my star attraction,' he told her. 'My clients will be people with a great deal of money and, as you know, Connie, money is powerful. My friends are powerful.' He paused. 'I'm powerful.' He gazed at her, wondering what her reaction would be.

But Connie was learning fast. After all, during the time she had been in London, she'd mixed with the wealthy, seen powerful men at work and was not so easily impressed by this brash young man. 'Really?'

This was not the reaction Kenny expected and he felt the need to press his point home. 'I took over my father's business when he died,' he said. 'He made a packet and when I've finished, I'll have made even more.'

'Doing what?'

'Dealing in finance.'

She liked Kenny, enjoyed their outings to restaurants or night clubs. She did have to fight off his amorous embraces when he kissed her goodnight, but he made her laugh, and if he was able to offer her work, that was a bonus. But when he arrived one evening in her final week at the Palm Court Club, she became slightly wary of him as his companions were somewhat menacing.

Four men accompanied Kenny that evening and after her performance, she was invited to join them at the table. Whereas Kenny was light and funny, his companions seemed to be looking around, studying the other customers and glowering most of the time. But there was more to it than that. Although dressed in smart suits but of a lesser quality than their host, there was a definite roughness about their features and manners, a certain cruel expression in the eyes, a hardness that Connie found very disconcerting.

'Who are these men?' she whispered in Kenny's ear.

He smiled and said, 'They work for me.'

'In the finance business?' she asked with surprise.

'Of course, princess,' and he turned away to order more drinks.

Connie glanced at all of them in turn, concluding that the only finance business they would be involved with was debt collecting, and she felt they would be somewhat brutal in their dealings. When one of them said to her, 'I believe that Les Baxter is your manager?' and was quickly hushed by Kenny, she began to wonder just what was going on.

'Do you know him?' she asked the man.

There was a strange expression on his face as he said, 'Not yet.'

Kenny glared at the man and immediately changed the subject. 'I'm hoping to settle my deal on the two clubs I'm buying fairly soon, Connie,' he said. 'Then we'll have to make arrangements for you to appear there.'

'You'd best discuss this with Jeremy Taylor,' she said.

The man she'd spoken to before asked, 'Who's he?'

'My other manager,' she replied. 'I have two. They're in partnership,' she explained, then she excused herself, not wanting to be with Kenny's companions any longer.

There was a knock on her dressing-room door a few minutes later and when she called out 'Who's there?' it was Kenny who answered, so unlocking the door, she let him in.

217

'Why the sudden disappearing act?' he asked.

'I don't like your friends,' she told him bluntly.

He laughed. 'They're not my friends, Connie, they work for me, that's all.'

'They look like a bunch of criminals to me!' she retorted.

He seemed to find that very amusing. 'I've come to take you to dinner,' he said, but she declined. Suddenly the idea of being with him didn't seem so inviting. It was as if seeing Kenny with those men had made her aware of another side to him, a somewhat frightening side, and she decided to gradually bow out of their relationship. If these people were the type to work for Kenny, just what would his clubs be like? Not perhaps the type of place she would want to be seen in. Much as Kenny was an entertaining companion, he was not important to her and after tonight she thought it wise to bring the friendship to a close, especially as her career was on the way up. A wrong move at this time would be a disaster. Besides, the only man she was really interested in was Ben, but he was keeping her at arm's length.

It had taken a while for her to realise her true feelings, but the distance between them seemed to be getting wider each day, just as she was beginning to understand how much she needed him – wanted him. Southampton had been fun, but now she wanted him much more. If only Ben would let her get close to him again, but now it seemed as if she had lost him for ever. Was it all too late? They would, however, have to spend time putting together a programme for the new venue and she hoped, then, to improve their relationship.

At midday the following Sunday, Ben arrived at Irene's, arms full of sheet music, and they retired to the music room to work. He didn't waste time on chit-chat but said, 'With the royal wedding, songs from *Annie Get Your Gun* are popular. Rumour has it that the young couple have a favourite song from the show, "They Say It's Wonderful", so we certainly should include that as it is so topical.'

She looked at him despairingly. He seemed so cold and

businesslike and she longed to recapture their easy friendship. Walking over to him she sat beside him on the stool. 'Please don't shut me out, Ben,' she pleaded softly.

'I don't know what you're talking about,' he said as he leaned forward and shuffled the pages of the sheet music.

Her frustration boiled over and she beat him on the back with her clenched fists. 'Don't do this to me . . . you know what I mean. Don't do this – I need you!' And she dissolved into tears.

Between her sobs she felt Ben put his arms around her, shushing her, patting her back like a baby. 'Now come along,' he coaxed, 'there's no need to get upset. Here.' He took a handkerchief from his pocket and handed it to her. 'Now that's enough or I'll have Irene rushing in here breathing fire, thinking I'm beating you within an inch of your life!'

She had to smile at the thought. Looking up into Ben's eyes she said, 'Please don't hate me.'

'Oh, Connie, if only I could hate you, life would be so simple.'

'What do you mean?'

'I'm crazy about you, you silly girl.'

'You are?'

'Unfortunately, yes. You are headstrong, thoughtless and so young, but it makes no difference.'

'I'm nineteen now,' she retorted.

'And when you appear on the stage you are much older in your understanding of an audience, but in normal relationships . . . you haven't a clue!'

'But I can learn,' she quickly replied.

He wiped a stray tear away. 'What am I going to do with you?'

She suddenly looked stricken. 'Absolutely nothing. Les will fire you if you do!' She flung her arms around Ben and clung on tightly to him. 'What am I going to do?'

'Baxter can't fire me! Jeremy Taylor has all that tied up in my contract. That's an empty threat, but we can't let Les see that there is anything between us or he'll put you through hell. Are you any good at keeping secrets, darling?'

'Oh, yes,' she said, remembering how deviously she had plotted to leave home. 'I'm very good at it.'

Kissing the tip of her nose, he murmured, 'If only you knew how hard I tried not to love you.'

'But why?'

'I was worried that you would go down the same path as my ex-girlfriend.' He kissed her softly. 'But you know I didn't stand much of a chance with you. This time my love was even stronger. It wasn't your fault that Les wants you. I believe in you, Connie. I know you won't betray my trust.'

She clung to him in desperation. 'I won't! I won't! I promise I'll never leave you – why would I want to?'

He nuzzled her neck and said quietly, 'You will have to make a choice one day.' He held her away from him and looking into her eyes he said, 'I wonder what it will be?'

'I'll never be his!'

'What if the choice is him or your career? What then, Connie?'

'Are you trying to test me, Ben?'

'No, of course not.'

She looked appealingly at the pianist and whispered, 'Just kiss me and then stop asking questions.'

Slowly and deliberately he tilted her chin upwards and lowered his mouth to hers.

Connie felt her senses swim as Ben moved his lips sensuously across hers, exploring, demanding, his hold on her tightening until she thought she'd pass out from sheer ecstasy.

'Come on, darling,' he said as he released his hold, 'we have work to do. Ciro's is a very swish joint, and we need to be on our toes to satisfy their clientele.'

Bursting with happiness now that she knew Ben's true feelings, Connie was ready to work and the next few hours were well spent choosing and rehearsing the numbers for the show.

'We need a really good finale,' he said. 'Something big to

finish with. After all, you have a whole hour as the cabaret act. We've varied the type of songs and the tempo, but we need something at the end that will knock their socks off. I'll have to give this some thought before opening night.'

When they had finished, he rose from the piano stool and taking Connie into his arms asked, 'When does the watchdog return?'

'I'm not sure, but he said he'd be away for a few days.'

'Then let me take you out to lunch tomorrow. I want to spend time with you, away from work, just the two of us.'

She wound her arms around his neck. 'That would be lovely,' she said as she kissed him ardently.

'I'll pick you up at noon.'

She waved him goodbye and, singing softly to herself, she went in search of Irene.

Her teacher looked up from the kitchen stove as Connie walked in. 'My word, what a change. What has happened that has brought that glow to your cheeks . . . or do I need to ask?'

Connie spun round in a circle, arms outstretched. 'Ben Stanton loves me and I love him!'

'Are you certain of this or is it just infatuation?'

Sitting on a stool she told Irene, 'No, I really do love him. Since we became estranged I realised my true feelings. If Ben wasn't around, I don't know what I would do.'

'Then for God's sake don't show your feelings in front of Mr Baxter!'

'Do you think I'm mad? Of course I won't!'

'That's easily said but difficult to do,' warned Irene. 'A look can give you away. When you sing a love song, keep your eyes on the audience, not the pianist!'

Knowing the truth of the warning, Connie chuckled and said, 'Yes, I'll be very careful about that.'

'You're playing a dangerous game, Connie.'

She looked back at her teacher and, with a defiant shake of her head, said, 'I don't care! I can have fame and a love life, surely?'

'I'm not sure Mr Baxter will agree and if he ever finds out about you and Ben . . .'

'He won't, I'll make sure of that.'

Ben took Connie to a quiet French restaurant the following day. Now their feelings for each other were out in the open, it was a joyous occasion. They laughed, teased one another, argued about various things, but in a light-hearted manner. Ben stretched across the table and took Connie's hand in his.

'You are beautiful, talented, unpredictable, wilful . . . and I love you.'

'Oh, Ben. I love you too and I'm deliriously happy.'

'What about this Kenny chap you've been seeing?'

'He was just for fun and anyway I won't be going out with him any more.'

'Good,' he said.

'I have to go to the costumiers to hire some gowns for Ciro's. Will you come with me and help me choose?' she asked.

'I'd be delighted. We need something very special because I have a feeling after your appearance, you'll be going straight to the top.'

Her eyes lit up with delight. 'Do you really think so?'

He laughed. 'Darling Connie, you are such a child. It's as if I told you Father Christmas would be calling.'

'Don't ever leave me, Ben. I do need you so much.'

He squeezed her hand. 'I promise.'

Chapter Twenty-Five

Les Baxter was seething. One of the London mob had sent him a page out of a paper several days old showing Connie coming out of the Savoy with a young man. The accompanying note said, *What is your protégée doing with Kenny Pritchard? This could cause problems.* Looking at the date on the top of the page he realised it was the day that Connie had done her disappearing act.

So this was Kenny Pritchard! He also recognised him as the same person who had come round to Connie's dressing room and he had told to go away. It also looked very much like the driver of the car that he caught a glance of as he drove away from the house . . . leaving Connie, wearing a fur coat – which she said she'd hired. A likely story!

Les paced up and down, his anger mounting with every step. How long had this been going on? And more to the point – had Pritchard touched her? The more he thought about it the more the pictures in his head tormented him. Well, he'd had enough! He thought he'd settled the problem of the piano player and he was damned if he was going to let her continue any friendship with another man, especially the one who was his arch rival. That was really pushing things too far! He picked up his car keys and walked out of the door.

It was the penultimate night of Connie's stint at the Palm Court Club and her audience had been very appreciative. She was sitting in her dressing room after the performance, removing her make-up, when the door burst open. With Les in Southampton Connie hadn't felt the need to lock it. Baxter slammed the door behind him and thrust the newspaper cutting in front of her on the dressing table.

Glancing at the picture Connie's heart sank. Looking at Les in the mirror she was suddenly very frightened. She had never seen him so angry.

'I warned you!' he began, shaking his finger at her.

At that moment there was a tap on the door and Jeremy Taylor popped his head in. 'Can I come in?'

'Yes, please do,' said Connie hastily.

'Well, Connie my dear, all ready for Ciro's next week?'

Before she could answer, Les said, 'She may not be appearing!'

'What?' Jeremy looked shocked – and Connie's face paled.

'Just give me a little while with my client,' said Les with great deliberation. 'I'll come and find you in the bar.'

'Now just a minute, old man,' began Taylor.

Les took him by the arm and walked him to the doorway. 'The bar . . . later!' he said, and firmly pushed him into the corridor.

Connie didn't move a muscle but sat, hardly daring to breathe. Were all her dreams to come to an end? Would she be returning to Southampton, her tail between her legs? She waited.

Pacing up and down, Les ranted at her. His rage pouring out of him like a man possessed. 'You don't listen to a word I say, do you? You just go on your merry little way and do as you bloody well please! This time you've pushed me too far. Well Miss Dolly Daydream, you will *never* see your name in lights, you will *never* appear in another club – or at the Palladium as top of the bill!'

'Palladium? What are you talking about?'

He stood still and with a sardonic smile said, 'Jeremy was going to tell you tonight, Rudolph Davenport has booked you to appear there after your stint at Ciro's. He will be disappointed.'

Connie shot to her feet. 'You can't do this to me! You *can't* turn down this opportunity, it's everything that I've worked for, dreamed of – wanted more than anything in the world. You *can't*, you just can't!'

Seeing her anguish pleased him and he sat in the easy chair and took out a cigar, then slowly lighting it he puffed on it, smiled at her and said, 'Oh, but I can – and I will.'

Connie crossed the floor and knelt before him, pleading. 'Please, Les, don't do this to me. I'm sorry I was so stupid, I'll do exactly as you say from now on, I promise.'

His steely eyes glared at her. 'That's not enough I'm afraid, Connie my dear. Not nearly enough.'

'What more do you want? I'll do anything, only don't take this chance away from me, I beg you.'

His smile was as cruel as the expression in his eyes. 'No longer the arrogant, wilful Connie Ryan, are you?'

She didn't know what to say to him – how to appeal to his better nature, although at this moment there was no softness about him. Before her was the hard ruthless person she'd been warned about and she deeply regretted breaking his rules. Her whole career was in jeopardy and she didn't know what to do.

'What do you want from me?' she asked helplessly.

He caught hold of her face with one hand in a grip of iron that made her wince. 'That's better,' he said. Retaining his hold he peered into her eyes and said, 'You are mine. You belong to me and no one else . . . do you understand?'

She nodded.

'I have great plans for our future and I won't have them ruined by your silly games, do you understand that?'

'Yes,' she murmured with difficulty.

'You and I are a team, at the moment we need Jeremy but our future is together, and when Jeremy has done enough there will be just the two of us. DO YOU UNDERSTAND?' he shouted into her face.

'I do, I do,' she whispered.

'Good.' He stared into her eyes and softly said, 'If only you behave yourself, stardom will be yours, and we will have a great life together. I can give you everything you have ever desired, because I have the financial backing to do so. Is that what you want, Connie? The decision is yours.'

She could hear Kenny's voice saying, 'Everyone has their price, Connie.' And she now knew what he meant as she looked back at Les Baxter and said, 'Yes. That's what I want.'

'Good,' he said. Then he leaned forward and kissed her hard on the mouth.

Connie shut her eyes as she felt his lips on hers – trying to shut out the truth. For the price of stardom, she had sold herself to the devil!

Les released her and she put her hands to her bruised face where his grip had held her, and slowly got to her feet. Sitting in front of her dressing table she looked at her reflection. The face before her was white, apart from the finger marks either side of her jaw.

Walking over to her, Les placed his hands on her shoulders and said, 'Freshen your make-up and meet me in the bar. I'll give Jeremy the good news, and by the way, remember one more thing.'

'What's that?' she asked fearfully.

'Your pianist can't play if his fingers are broken!' Then he walked out of the room.

Her eyes filled with tears as she thought of Ben. Darling Ben, whom she loved and who loved her. But she realised how dangerous Baxter was. He didn't have the power to fire Ben, but he was capable of much more. She couldn't bear to think of the pianist with broken fingers. She couldn't be the cause of such destruction. But what on earth was she going to say to him? Just as they had found each other . . . She couldn't put him in danger, but it would be so awful to be with him so much and not be able to touch him, kiss him.

She could walk away from all this and go home, but she knew she couldn't give up singing, she'd worked too hard and now she was on the brink of stardom. She had to stay.

★ ★ ★

Meantime in the bar, Les had joined Jeremy Taylor. 'Let's have a drink,' he said.

Taylor looked sharply at his partner and said, 'Not until you tell me exactly what the devil is going on!'

Baxter just laughed and said, 'Nothing, absolutely nothing. Connie will be appearing at Ciro's and I hope you don't mind but I've already told her about the Palladium, and she was thrilled.'

There was a deep furrow on Jeremy Taylor's brow as he looked at Baxter. His eyes narrowed as he observed the satisfied smile of the bookmaker. 'You are up to something, you devious bastard,' he said.

Les just laughed and ordered two brandies, as Ben walked over to join them.

Jeremy told him the good news about the Palladium and asked if the programme for the nightclub had been sorted.

'Yes,' said Ben, 'and we have a great finish.'

'Oh, and what is it?' asked Les.

Ben looked at him and said, 'We want it to be a surprise.'

There was an expression of anger on Baxter's face but Jeremy interrupted.

'Good, we'll look forward to it, but now you must work on something for the Palladium. This appearance will take Connie to the top. After that, there will be no stopping her. She'll have her name in lights as *I* promised.' He glared at his partner as he said it but Les was looking past him. Jeremy turned and saw Connie walking towards them.

Les stepped forward and took her by the arm. 'What would you like to drink?'

Jeremy was shocked by Connie's pale face and set expression. She looked as if she'd been crying. He also observed the stricken look on Ben's face as he looked at her.

'I'll have a large gin and tonic,' she said quietly.

Les told the barman to bring their drinks to a table and led Connie over to it. He put his arm around the back of her chair in a possessive manner and smiled like a Cheshire cat.

Jeremy saw the tightening of Ben's jaw as he sat opposite. He was staring hard at Connie, but she wouldn't meet his gaze. Trying to lighten the atmosphere, Jeremy said, 'Great news about old Rudy booking you at the Palladium, young lady. I promised you your name in lights, didn't I?'

She summoned a smile. 'Yes, Jeremy, you did. It's wonderful. Thank you.'

Les moved one hand to Connie's shoulder. 'You're thrilled, aren't you, my dear?'

Jeremy noticed the grip tighten as she hesitated.

'Yes, I'm absolutely thrilled. I can hardly wait.'

Connie lifted her glass and seemed to peer into the depths of it as if looking for something before she took a sip. As she looked across at Jeremy he saw the tears glisten in her eyes.

'If you need any advice about your appearance,' he said, 'I'll be back to have a chat about it, or I'll see you on the opening night at Ciro's.' He felt the need to throw her a lifeline but he didn't quite know why.

'Drink up, Connie,' said Baxter. 'You must be tired and tomorrow is your final performance here so you want to look your best.'

She downed the contents of her glass, rose to her feet and kissing Jeremy on the cheek, whispered, 'Thanks,' and walked towards the door.

Ben rose and, quickly crossing to Connie, asked anxiously, 'Are you all right?'

'Leave me alone!' she cried, and walked quickly towards the exit.

Les shook hands with Jeremy and said, 'See you tomorrow night.'

Once he was alone, Jeremy lit a cigar and mulled over the final part of the evening. Something major had changed here. He didn't know what the devil had happened but he was determined to get to the bottom of it.

Chapter Twenty-Six

Les drove his Riley deftly through the London streets to Maida Vale, talking about Connie's forthcoming appearance at the Palladium with great enthusiasm. 'The publicity that Jeremy will organise should certainly fill the house,' he said. 'After all, people will be curious to see the girl that took the royal charity concert by storm.' He glanced across at her and added, 'Who knows, the Princess and the Duke may come to see you again, they do go to concerts other than those on their official list, you know.'

But Connie wasn't listening, she was thinking about the hurt look on Ben's face as Les had put his arms around her. She was going to have to face the man she loved tomorrow evening, and what was she to say? What words could she find to explain she had no choice but to meet the demands that Baxter had made, and then most frightening of all – would Ben leave her? She couldn't bear the thought. What on earth could she do? Then she remembered Jeremy saying he would be at the opening night at Cho's – but that would be too late! She would call him in the morning. He would help her. Ben *must* stay with her, even though they couldn't continue to be more than business associates. If he left it would break her heart, and it would be unbearable for her to see another man sitting at the piano when she worked.

'Connie!'

Les's sharp voice brought her back to the present.

'You haven't been listening to a word I've said!'

'Sorry, but I'm tired. It has been quite a night, one way and another,' she snapped, furious with herself for being in this invidious position.

His voice softened as he said, 'Yes, of course it has, but you'll see . . .' He placed a hand on her knee and patted it. 'We'll have such good times together.'

'And what about the press?' she said, clutching at straws. 'They'll have a field day if they see us together.'

'Don't worry about the press, I'll tell them we plan to get married later.'

'What!'

'Oh, yes, didn't I say. It's part of the overall plan for the future. You will keep your own name for the stage of course.'

Connie spun round in her seat to face him. 'I didn't agree to that!' she yelled at him. 'I will *never* marry you!'

He smiled benignly at her. 'Of course you will, but not yet, a little later, next year sometime. But we'll keep this to ourselves for now, we don't want any other publicity to overshadow your Palladium appearance, so in the meantime, we'll be careful.'

Connie was speechless. This was far more than she'd bargained for and she was absolutely determined that she would never become Mrs Les Baxter. She'd rather die first!

Whilst Connie was coping with her dilemma, Ben was slowly drowning his sorrows at the bar of a jazz club in Soho. As he ordered his third large Scotch, the barman placed the glass in front of him asking, 'Woman trouble?'

Ben looked up with a puzzled expression. 'What?'

'When a customer downs his drinks as quickly as you it's usually through some woman or other, a wife, a girlfriend – or a mistress.'

With a wry smile Ben said, 'Yes, you're right. I'll never understand them as long as I live.'

'My advice to you, sir, is to give up trying, it's wasted effort as far as I can see,' and he walked to the other end of the bar to serve another customer.

Ben was both angry and puzzled. Something had changed tonight – and Les Baxter was behind it. What had transpired in Connie's dressing room to make her look so distressed – and – to make Baxter look so very satisfied? It was obvious to him that Connie had been crying, but why? Her performance had been excellent and as far as he knew Baxter hadn't even been there to see it – so what was it all about? He finished the contents of his glass and climbed down from the bar stool. He needed to sleep. Tomorrow morning he would go round to Irene's house, see Connie and find out for himself.

When Les arrived at their destination, he drew the car to a halt and switched off the engine. 'Have a good rest,' he told Connie. 'You need to be on top form for your final night at the Palm Court. Leave the punters wanting more.'

'They are not *punters*,' she said derisively, 'that's the language you use for your racing cronies!'

He laughed at her indignation. 'They're all punters, my dear, one way and another.' He pulled her towards him and made to kiss her but she turned her cheek.

'You'll get used to me in time, Connie,' he said with a grin. 'I can wait . . . but not for too long!'

She got out of the car as quickly as she could to get away from him, wiping her cheek where he'd kissed her, filled with distaste that this man should have such a hold over her. She couldn't keep him at arm's length for five years! She desperately needed to be free of him and that was impossible – but to be an old man's darling! Never! She put her key in the door and rushed up to her room. She needed time to think.

After a sleepless night, Connie rang Jeremy Taylor and begged him to come and see her. 'I have a problem,' she said.

'I thought you might have,' he said. 'Give me an hour.'

When he arrived Connie opened the door. She was conveniently alone in the house as Irene had an early dental appointment. She ushered him into the drawing room.

Jeremy took off his coat and, coming straight to the point, asked, 'What's going on, Connie?'

She told him what had transpired the previous evening in her dressing room.

He was outraged. 'The man's mad! How dare he make these indecent demands on you? My God! It's a form of procuring – and blackmail.' He rose from his chair and paced the room.

'But he can stop me working, Jeremy, and he knows it.'

The agent scratched his head and said, 'Yes, my dear, I'm afraid he can, after all he holds sixty per cent of your contract. He has the final say and I'm helpless to interfere if he does pull the rug from under you, and of course you are signed to him for quite a time.'

'Five long years . . . I'll never marry him!' she declared angrily. 'They could chain me to the altar steps but I would never take the vows.'

Jeremy sat down beside her on the settee. 'You do have a choice, Connie. You could tell him to go to hell.'

She looked at him with an anguished expression. 'And lose everything I've ever dreamed about.' She shook her head slowly. 'No, I'm damned if I'll do that. I'll handle him as best as I can, keep him at arm's length as long as I can, but there is another thing. It's Ben.'

'The boy's in love with you,' Jeremy remarked.

'And I love him too,' she said. 'How am I going to handle that situation?'

The agent took out a cigar and lit it. 'Oh, Connie, you do get yourself into deep trouble.'

'I don't want to lose him.'

'My God, girl! You can't expect him to stand by and watch Baxter take his place!'

She held out her hands in a helpless gesture. 'I don't want to lose him as my pianist either.'

'Well, as far as that's concerned he has a contract, but musicians are a strange lot, he's liable to up sticks and take off – contract or no contract. Oh, Connie, what a bloody mess.'

'He threatened to break Ben's hands too,' she said quietly.
'What?'

'He has already forbidden me to see Ben, apart from working with him and we are careful when he's around, but I suppose he wanted to make sure there was nothing between us.'

'That's threatening behaviour. You could take him to court!'

'And a lot of good that would do. He'd deny everything, after all there are no witnesses,' she said grimly, 'and that would only harm my career, after the other publicity.'

'Yes, I'm afraid you're right. I feel so helpless!' he stormed. 'I should be able to do something, but my hands are tied.'

'It's all right, honestly. It was just good to get it all off my chest. But tonight, when I close at the Palm Court, would you be there, in case he is?'

'That I can do, and I'll insist on running you home.'

'Thanks. That will be a great help. I don't want to be alone with him if I can help it.'

Jeremy rose from the settee. 'If you think of anything I *can* do, you let me know, but, Connie,' he took her hands in his, 'are you sure you want to go through with this?'

Her eyes shone with anger and determination. 'No one, least of all bloody Les Baxter, is going to stop me reaching the top.'

The agent let out a deep sigh. 'I only hope the price isn't too high. I'll see you tonight.' He bent forward and kissed her on the cheek. 'Take care. I'll let myself out.'

Connie made her way to the kitchen to make a cup of tea and just as she was pouring it from the pot, the front door bell rang. When she opened the door, she was horrified to see Ben Stanton waiting.

'Hello, Connie,' he said. 'I think you and I need to talk.'

Chapter Twenty-Seven

As soon as Connie saw Ben she knew she couldn't tell him the truth. He would never understand, no man would, and there was no way she was going to take the chance of him walking out of her life. Stepping back she said, 'Come in.'

They walked into the drawing room where she casually asked, 'Would you like a cup of coffee?'

He grabbed her by the arms and glared at her 'No, I bloody well wouldn't! I want to know what was going on at the club last night between you and Baxter!'

'I don't know what you mean,' she said, playing for time. She tried to think, but her heart was pounding and her mind seemed a complete blank.

He released her and said, 'Don't lie to me, Connie. What did he say to you to make you cry? And don't deny it, it was obvious to us all that you were upset.'

'He told me I was putting on weight,' she said desperately, 'and that I'd better do something about it.'

He looked at her in astonishment. 'What? Is that all?'

'Well, you know Les, he's never ever satisfied with my performance and picked me to pieces, as he does. I was tired and I just burst into tears.'

He collapsed onto the settee utterly confused, then he stared at her and asked, 'Are you telling me the truth, Connie?'

She quickly sat beside him. 'Of course I am. I'm sorry if I worried you.'

His eyes narrowed when he said, 'He seemed to be a bit

familiar with you, putting his arm around you. He doesn't usually do that!'

'Well, he was feeling pleased with himself, he'd just told me about appearing for Rudy at the Palladium.' Stroking his cheek she said, 'Stop being so grumpy and kiss me.'

Gazing into eyes that held no guile, he was at last convinced and putting his arms around her, kissed her passionately. 'You have no idea the thoughts that have been racing round inside my head.'

'And I don't want to know,' she whispered as she nuzzled his neck, breathing a sigh of relief that the crisis seemed to have passed . . . for the moment.

'We will have to be doubly careful though when Les is around,' she said with some hesitation, not knowing what Ben's reaction would be.

'Oh, to hell with Baxter!' he exclaimed. 'Let's just be honest and tell him we're in love. As long as we continue to work for him, what's the harm? Let's get things out into the open. It would certainly stop any rumours in the press about you and him.'

Connie nearly had apoplexy! But on the surface, she remained calm. 'No, that wouldn't do at all; you know how he feels about two people working together. He likes to keep it strictly business. Let's not upset him, you know how he goes off on a tangent – besides I love a secret, don't you?'

At last he smiled. 'You are a conniving little devil,' he said as he pushed his fingers through her hair. 'No wonder you drive me crazy, I never know where the hell I am with you.'

'That's exactly what a woman thrives on,' she teased. At that moment, the sound of a key in the front door lock announced Irene's return.

Rising to her feet Connie said, 'You'd better go, I have a lesson with Irene this morning and then I've things to do in preparation for tonight's performance.'

Ben stood up and taking her into his arms kissed her longingly. 'See you later,' he said and walked to the door, passing Irene on the way.

She came into the room and, looking at Connie, said, 'It's somewhat early for Ben, isn't it?'

'He just popped in,' she explained, 'it was just a query about a number for tonight. Nothing serious.'

'I'll just put my things away and we'll start,' Irene said. 'Then I want you to rest your voice.'

Connie sat down once again on the settee and, placing her hand where Ben had sat, lovingly smoothed the cushion, thankful that her meeting with him had passed as smoothly as it had. So, she had lied through her teeth, but what else could she do? With a deep sigh, she wandered off to the music room. At least here she was safe and she started to hum the melody of her final number for tonight's performance.

The Palm Court Club was packed that night, and as Connie sat in her dressing room preparing, she felt the rush of adrenalin surge through her as it always did before a performance. God! She loved this life. There was nothing more satisfying than the acclamation from the audience that you had performed well, and she thrived on the applause from her faithful following, which was growing every week.

As she put the finishing touches to her make-up, she thought she would die if this were all taken away from her. She was where she ought to be, before an audience, singing for them.

There was a knock on her door. 'Who is it?' she called.

'It's me, Les,' came the reply and the handle turned, but this time the door was locked. 'Let me in, Connie,' he demanded.

She sat there, looking at the key in the lock, and slowly smiled. 'I'm not dressed,' she called, 'I'll see you after the show.' She could hear Baxter's voice as he muttered to himself, cursing softly, before he eventually walked away.

There was a definite sense of occasion in the club that night and Connie didn't disappoint her audience. She sang for an hour with a selection of Gershwin songs, others by Cole

Porter and Irving Berlin. At the end, the audience shouted for more as she left the stage. The bandleader stepped forward and said, 'Connie Ryan will be back with an encore – just give her a minute.' They cheered.

In the wings, Connie was frantically changing her gown as the band played the final passage from her last number, to give her time. When she was ready, she nodded to the bandleader and there was a roll of drums. The audience looked up expectantly. Connie strode onto the stage dressed in a gypsy costume, her red full skirt swirling as she walked barefoot, towards the microphone, the white peasant blouse slightly off her shoulders, her hair loose and big gold hoop earrings swaying from her ears. The band started to play an aria from *Carmen*.

There was complete silence as her audience wondered what was happening. Connie's deep, throaty voice rang out as she stood mid-stage, then she slowly walked through the audience with the mike, flirting with all the men just as Carmen had done in this scene from the opera, where in a square in Seville she flirted madly with the soldiers and townsmen. It was an electric performance, which she finished back on the stage with a flounce of her skirt – showing her shapely legs.

The place erupted! People stood to applaud. Men put their fingers in their mouths and whistled. For several minutes, it was pandemonium. Connie was overwhelmed by the reaction and looked at Ben who was grinning broadly and applauding – as were the band. It was an absolute triumph.

Jeremy Taylor, sitting at his table, was speechless. He looked across at Les Baxter who was staring at Connie as if he had never seen her before – then he too started to clap. Looking across at Jeremy he called out loudly so as to be heard, 'Bloody hell! I didn't know she could sing like that.'

Jeremy thought, There's a lot you don't know about Connie Ryan! But he kept his thoughts to himself. As Baxter made to leave the table, Jeremy asked, 'Where are you off to?'

'To see Connie of course.'

Jeremy stopped him. 'Give her time to get her breather, for God's sake! Come on, I'll buy you a drink.' He called the waiter over, so Baxter had no choice but to stay.

Back in her dressing room, Connie was clasped in Ben's arms. 'They loved it, didn't they?' she asked, her face flushed with excitement.

'It was a *tour de force*,' he said proudly. 'You were absolutely brilliant. Your rendition was marvellous. Oh Connie, I do love you.' And he kissed her.

Connie didn't know when she'd been more happy and only wished her family could have been here, remembering when she sang the same aria to them whilst walking through the park in Southampton. They would have been even more impressed tonight. Even Les couldn't possibly fault her.

Oh, my God! she thought. He was bound to be round soon. She moved away from Ben and said, 'I must get changed. Jeremy and Les are out there and they'll be calling.' She hesitated and said, 'Look, why don't you come to the house tomorrow and I'll cook you breakfast? Then we can be alone.'

'Hardly. Irene will be there.'

'No, she won't,' she said quietly. 'She is spending the weekend with a friend. She left this evening.'

He stared intently at her and then he said, 'That could be very dangerous.'

With beating heart she asked, 'Why?'

'I'm not sure I can trust myself to be a gentleman in such circumstances.'

'I'm not sure I would want you to be.'

'Be very sure you know what you are saying, Connie darling.'

She put her arms around him and whispered, 'I know exactly what I'm saying,' and she covered his lips with hers, kissing him with a passion that couldn't be misconstrued.

'I'd better go,' Ben said, 'before this gets out of hand here and now. We wouldn't like Les and Jeremy to walk in at the wrong moment.' He picked up his sheets of music and said, 'I'll see you in the morning.'

A few moments later, the two men arrived, both effusive with their praise.

'Come along,' demanded Baxter. 'You were sensational, and I'm taking you out to dinner to celebrate.'

'That's really kind,' Connie answered quickly, 'but I'm so tired. I just want to go home, have a bath and go to bed.'

Jeremy rapidly intervened. 'I'll drive you,' he said, 'I have to drop some papers in to Irene so I can kill two birds with one stone.' Picking up her coat he helped Connie into it and looking at Les said, 'It's probably just as well. Connie must be fresh for Monday. Ciro's is so important to us all,' and he ushered her out of the room.

'Goodnight,' Connie called over her shoulder as she hurried down the corridor with her saviour.

Baxter was left standing, and was not too happy about it. He had been strangely moved by Connie's performance this evening. He wasn't interested in opera, he didn't understand it, but Connie's rendition had been extraordinary, and he realised the depth of her talent. He also realised the great heights she could achieve in her field, given a few lucky breaks, and Jeremy behind her, and he wondered if when she reached the pinnacle of her career, he would still be able to control her. It was a distinctly disconcerting thought.

Meantime, in the back of a taxi, Connie and Jeremy were shaking with laughter.

'You really are something, Jeremy Taylor,' she said. 'Les didn't know what hit him. We were out of there before he could blink.' She caught hold of his hand and squeezed it. 'Thank you so much. I really didn't want to be in his company tonight.'

'My pleasure, darling,' he said. Then, with a wicked grin, he added, 'I enjoyed every minute. I love to get one over on that bastard. He thinks he's so smart!'

'He's no dumbbell, you know.'

Jeremy frowned. 'I know, that's what makes him so dangerous. I never know which way he's going to jump. Never mind, tonight you were unforgettable. I was so very proud of you.'

These words meant a lot to Connie, knowing Jeremy's reputation in the business. 'Thank you,' she said.

'When they arrived at their destination, Connie said, 'Irene's away, so can I give her a message.'

'No, darling. I don't have to see her – that was just an excuse.' He leaned forward and kissed her on the cheek. 'See you at Ciro's. You have a rest. Goodnight.'

Later, as she lay in her bed, Connie mulled over the night's events. It had been so wonderful, the reaction of the audience and the feeling that she had performed really well. Singing Carmen had been a milestone, and now she had the morning and Ben's visit to look forward to. That would be another milestone. One for which she could hardly wait.

Chapter Twenty-Eight

When Connie opened the door to Ben the following morning, she was still in her dressing gown. 'I slept in,' she explained.

Closing the door behind him, he held her close saying, 'I don't mind at all.' As he caressed her he asked, 'Have you anything on under here?'

Suddenly shy as well as nervous, she broke away from his embrace and said, 'Come into the kitchen, I'll give you a cup of tea whilst I cook.'

Sensing her mood, he followed, making polite conversation. 'I bought the papers,' he told her.

'Would you like to go into the living room and read them?'

Ben smiled and said, 'For goodness' sake, relax will you. Nothing is going to happen this morning unless you want it to. Here, let me help you.' He removed his jacket and picking up a floral pinny of Irene's, he tied it around his waist. 'Now what can I do?'

When Connie saw what he was wearing she burst out laughing, and the tension of the moment was broken. They pottered around the kitchen together preparing a meal, then sat at the table. 'Shall I be mother and pour?' he asked, putting the tea cosy on his head.

She chuckled. 'You are a fool.'

They sat and chatted, read the headlines and after the meal, washed up the dishes.

'You're quite domesticated,' she remarked.

'Well, for goodness' sake, Connie, I've been living alone for years. I was not going to starve and live in clutter. I was brought up nicely by a good mother.'

She wiped her hands and encircling him in her arms said, 'I can see that. You are certainly house trained.'

There was silence as they stood and gazed at one another. Ben undid the belt around her silk dressing gown and opened it. He then slipped it from her shoulders.

Connie let it fall to the ground and stood naked before him. He stroked her smooth skin. 'My God, you're beautiful.'

'Take me to bed,' she said.

'Are you sure that's what you want?'

'Oh, yes, it's exactly what I want.'

Picking her up in his arms he asked, 'Where is the bedroom?'

He lay her down on the bed covers, leaned forward and kissed her softly. She undid his tie and the buttons of his shirt, slipping her warm hands inside to stroke his broad chest. 'You have too many clothes on,' she said.

With a raised eyebrow he said, 'You are a forward hussy, do you know that?'

'I am?' Then she added, 'I do hope you won't be disappointed.'

As he stepped out of his trousers, he said, 'You could never disappoint me, darling,' and gathered her to him. 'Just relax,' he said as he kissed her.

Never in her wildest dreams did Connie think she could feel this way. To be loved and desired was still so new to her, and here in the arms of the man she loved in return, she felt wonderful. Slowly and tenderly, Ben initiated her into the ways of making love.

He was gentle and unhurried. Caressing her, coaxing her, tempting her – teasing her, until she was ready for him.

'You don't have to do this,' he said.

'Oh, but I do – and I want to. I want to belong to you, absolutely and completely.'

'My darling Connie, I don't think any man will ever feel that you belong to him entirely, you are much too independent for that, but I'll happily accept as much as you are prepared to give me, because I love you.'

'Then for heaven's sake show me, you selfish brute, instead of talking about it!'

He chuckled to himself as he rolled on top of her. 'You seem in a mighty hurry to lose your virginity.'

'I am, Ben darling, I am!'

And she did as he made love to her, slowly and deliberately, and with great skill, until she lay back on her pillow, sated and satisfied. She caressed his head as he lay on her. 'Oh, Ben, that was one of your best arrangements ever!'

He was convulsed with laughter, as he lay beside her. 'You're crazy, you know that, don't you?'

She looked at him and asked, 'Do you give an encore?'

'Are you trying to kill me! Later perhaps,' he added as he leaned over and kissed her.

'I can hardly wait,' she murmured as she closed her eyes.

He lay looking at her. Her hair, spread across the pillow; her face devoid of make-up was clear and soft. Her dark eyelashes curled and her breasts rose and fell as she breathed, and he knew he'd never loved anyone else the way he loved her. He stayed like this for a time, like a sentinel, watching over something of value, until his eyes closed and they both slept.

They spent the rest of the day together. Ben lit a fire to keep out the cold December chills. They raided the fridge and made a meal in the late afternoon, which they ate sitting on the settee in front of the cheering fire. They read the papers – snuggled up together – and talked. Discussed each other's thoughts, likes and dislikes, teased one another, kissed one another and made love on the rug. And when it was time for bed, they lay in each other's arms.

'This has been a wonderful day,' said Connie, as she cuddled up to him and felt his strong arms about her. 'Here with you at this moment, I feel safe.'

'I'll always take care of you,' he said, 'as long as I live.'

But Connie knew that was not going to be easy. Today she could forget about Les Baxter, and had he knocked on the door, she wouldn't have answered, but come the morning, her dilemma with the bookmaker would still have to be faced, and she knew that Ben could not save her from that situation.

By the time Irene returned, the house was empty as Ben and Connie had a rehearsal with the resident band at Ciro's. Ben had already taken the band parts to them a few days before, so when it came for Connie to join them, they were familiar with the arrangements.

As was her habit, she chatted with the musicians, showing them how much she appreciated their work, and got on with the job in hand. As she stood upon the stage she could see how much more select this place was by the fittings alone and she wondered if any famous people would ever visit the club during her time there.

She knew that Jeremy had booked a table for her opening night and wondered how she would cope with Les, who was bound to come along. But she forgot about him as the rehearsal continued.

As it happened, Les Baxter was busy. All hell had broken loose in London because Kenny Pritchard had at last discovered that his business was being sucked away from him.

The accountant had handed in the monthly figures and Kenny had a fit when he saw the drop in takings. 'What the bloody hell is going on?' he asked.

The accountant looked puzzled. 'Beats me,' he said, denying any knowledge of the situation, 'but the figures have been dropping slowly since the beginning of the month. Perhaps the punters are getting wise.'

'Don't be ridiculous! Men will always gamble. I can't afford to lose this amount, not on a regular basis. Not now I've bought those two houses.'

The other man shrugged. 'I did warn you about making such a purchase. I told you the business couldn't stand such a big outlay.'

'Don't give me I told you so! That's not what I need right now.'

'Your dad would never have gone into that kind of business,' the man added for good measure, knowing how much Kenny hated to be compared with his successful father.

The young man's face reddened with anger. 'Well, I'm going to find out what's causing this, 'cause I don't like the feel of it. Something's wrong here and I intend to get to the bottom of it,' he said as he swept out of the office.

The accountant smirked to himself, picked up the telephone receiver and made several calls.

Les Baxter was the recipient of one of them. Listening to his caller he said, 'Fine. I understand. The men know what to do.'

Kenny marched into the Stag's Head, a pub in the East End of London where he knew that several of the senior men in his organisation always met for a drink after all the bets had been gathered for the daily racing, and found them sitting together at a table. He pulled up a chair and said, 'All right, is someone going to explain why the month's takings are down so much?'

One tough-looking individual spoke for all of them. 'We don't work for you no more, my son.'

'What?' Kenny's face was ashen. These were his best men.

'No, laddie,' said another, with a thick Glaswegian accent. 'We was happy with the way your old man ran things, but we don't like your way of thinking, so we're getting out. We have another boss now, who runs things the old way.'

'And who might that be?'

'As a matter of fact these men work for me now.'

Kenny turned and saw the man standing behind his chair.

'What's your bloody game, Baxter?'

Les sat in the chair next to the young Londoner. 'It's like this, my boy: when you start getting greedy and come to Southampton to try and interfere with my patch, it's like declaring war. You fired the first shell and I had no choice but to retaliate. You have just lost your first battle.'

'You bastard! I'll get you for this! I'll put the Old Bill onto you.'

Very quietly Les said, 'Now don't be silly. If you do that I'll have to tell them about the two brothels you're about to open. I have all the names and addresses of the girls you have employed as escorts. No, you leave me alone and I'll do the same for you, otherwise you'll be left with nothing – and knowing your extravagant tastes, you'll be skint in a couple of months!'

'You've only yourself to blame, son,' said one of the men. 'If you had stuck to your father's way, none of this would have happened.'

Kenny pushed back his chair, sending it crashing, and glaring at Baxter said, 'I'm not through yet!' He left the bar with the sound of laughter from the others ringing in his ears.

He drove down to Limehouse and sat in his car, overlooking the River Thames, where he lit a cigarette and tried to calm down. That clever bastard, he thought. He's pulled the bloody rug from under my feet – and he bitterly regretted trying to move in on Baxter. But it was too late for regrets. He had to do something to get his business back, he badly needed that income. The bookmaker had been right, he had spent a lot of his father's money and the purchase of the two houses in the East End had eaten into what was left. Baxter had said he'd leave that business alone as long as he, Kenny, didn't try to interfere by calling the police, and he believed him there. What would be the point of them both suffering? So at least he would have an income from that and thankfully both houses were to open this weekend. He needed time to think of a plan. Baxter was too clever by far, and any plan he came up with would have to be watertight against such a man. He drove away, deep in thought.

The opening night at Ciro's went well, but all the time she was singing, Connie was aware of Les Baxter sitting watching her every move. What's more, he didn't look very happy. Kenny Pritchard wasn't there, for which she was grateful, but he had sent her an extravagant bouquet of flowers. She had quickly removed the card before Les could see it, as she didn't want to give him any reason to be difficult.

She had been most careful not to glance in Ben's direction when she was singing. It had been so hard to do. He had visited her in her dressing room before the show when they had spent a few minutes together, but, mindful of the threats from Baxter, she was fearful of his discovery.

At the end of the evening, dear Jeremy had offered to take her home, but Les had immediately stepped in.

'No, that's fine,' he said firmly. 'I want to talk to Connie, so we'll have a drink and then I'll take her to Maida Vale.'

'Well, if you're sure.'

'I am.'

Jeremy looked at Connie and raised his eyebrows as if to say, I tried.

Ben came over and said, 'I'm off then. See you tomorrow night.'

'Right,' said Connie, longing to leave with him. 'Thanks for tonight – it went well.'

'Of course it did. We make a great team.'

She saw Baxter stiffen and she was grateful that Ben left without lingering.

'Is something wrong?' she asked when they were alone.

Baxter's jaw tightened. 'Your poncy boyfriend Kenny Pritchard tried to muscle in on my business,' he said coldly, 'but I taught him a lesson.'

Connie felt her spine chill. 'What on earth do you mean?'

'He took over his father's bookmaking business and—'

'Bookmaking!' she interrupted. 'He told me he was in finance.'

With a sardonic grin, he said, 'Well, it's not too far removed from the truth, but he got greedy. He tried to move in on me in my own territory. Cheeky bugger!'

'So what did you do?'

A satisfied look crept across his features. 'I took over his London connection.'

'You did what?'

He fixed his gaze upon her. 'No one puts anything over on me and gets away with it, Connie. You would do well to remember that, and if that little bastard comes sniffing round, you had better send him packing or I want to know the reason why. Understand?'

'Don't try threatening me!' she retorted. 'I might just tell you what to do with your contract!'

His laughter was filled with derision. 'Don't give me that! Your need to reach stardom is part of who you are. That will never change.'

She looked away. He was right, of course, but there had to be a point in everyone's life when enough was enough. Just how far would she let him push her until that point was reached? She didn't want to think about it.

'Take me home,' she said. 'I'm tired.'

They drove in silence and when he stopped the car outside Irene's house, he caught hold of her arm before she could escape, and pulled her to him.

'I'll be busy for the next couple of days, but I'll be in touch. Just keep out of trouble and don't cause me any problems, I have enough to cope with at the moment, I wouldn't be pleased to have any more.'

She glared at him defiantly. 'What time do I have to do so?'

'That hasn't stopped you in the past as I recall!'

She opened the car door with her free hand. 'Go home, Les,' she snapped.

Before she realised his intention he'd caught hold of her head pulled her close and kissed her hard on the mouth as if stamping his authority on her.

'I'll see you in a couple of days.'

As she opened the front door she thought, At least I have a couple of days of freedom . . . but she felt his net closing about her, even as he drove away.

Chapter Twenty-Nine

George Ryan was sitting in his doctor's waiting room in Southampton feeling more than a little anxious. He had been suffering from headaches for some time, but as they grew more severe, he had been forced to visit his physician and today he was there to get the result of an X-ray taken a week previously. The door to the surgery opened.

'Come in, Mr Ryan,' said Dr Mills. 'How are you feeling?' he enquired, once they were settled.

'To be honest, no better. The pains in my head are as bad, and now I keep feeling sick.'

'Have you been vomiting?'

'Yes, every now and again . . . I feel really rough.'

The doctor leaned forward. 'Hold out your hand so I can take your pulse please, Mr Ryan.'

George watched the expression on the physician's face and saw him frown. Sitting back in his chair, Dr Mills said, 'I have the result of your X-ray here. It's not good news, I'm afraid.'

Feeling his heart beat faster, George was filled with dread. 'What do you mean?'

'The result of the X-ray shows the reason for your severe headaches and now the sickness you're suffering is just another symptom, as is your slow pulse rate. There's no easy way to tell you this, Mr Ryan – but I'm afraid you have a brain tumour.'

'What? Oh, my God!' He took a handkerchief from his pocket to wipe his brow, which was suddenly damp with perspiration. He felt dizzy and was told to put his head between his knees.

The doctor rose from his chair and crossed to the washbasin where he poured some cold water into a glass. Handing it to his patient he said, 'Here, drink this.'

Sipping the water, George Ryan tried hard to gather his thoughts. A brain tumour. Surely not! He just needed new glasses, that was all – when he read the paper, the newsprint had become a little blurred on occasion. No, that was all – new glasses. 'I really should go to the optician's and have my eyes tested,' he said stubbornly.

Dr Mills eyed him sympathetically. 'I'm afraid this is more serious than that, George. I realise that this has been a great shock to you, and it will certainly take some time to understand what I'm telling you – are there any questions you would like to ask me?'

His face drawn and white, the patient enquired, 'What can you do about it? Can it be cured? Can I have an operation?'

'I'm afraid it's too advanced for surgery, but I will try and keep you as comfortable as I can with medication.'

In a voice barely audible George asked, 'Are you telling me I'm going to die?'

'I'm sorry, but this *is* terminal.'

'How long?' asked George in a choked voice.

'It's very difficult to tell – a few months.'

'Christ, Doctor, I've got a family. What about my job?'

'It would be inadvisable to continue working. Do you pay into life insurance?'

It was that question that destroyed George Ryan. He did have insurance on his life, but never ever did he think it would be paid out. It was something people did if they could scrape the payment together. He thought it would safeguard his family if he had an accident at work, but now . . . he broke down and sobbed.

Leaving the surgery a little later, George Ryan walked as if in a dream towards the pier, turning up the collar of his coat against the chill wind. The shop windows were full of Christmas gifts. Brightly decorated Christmas trees sparkled with lights and baubles and he realised this would probably be the last festive occasion he would live to see. He stumbled as tears filled his eyes. He stopped in a doorway and lit a cigarette. Sheltering from the wind he wondered just how he was going to tell Freda and Doreen . . . and Connie. He couldn't keep this to himself because according to the doctor, his symptoms would worsen in time and he would eventually need nursing.

With tear-stained cheeks he walked along the esplanade. He was a young man, for Christ's sake! Forty-five was no age. He kicked out angrily at stones beside the water. Why? Why did this have to happen to him? He'd led a good life, hadn't done harm to anyone – loved his family, had taken good care of them. He wasn't a waster like some husbands he knew who boozed away most of their wages every week. And even worse, he wouldn't be there when the girls were married. The opportunity to lead his daughters, resplendent in their bridal gowns, down the aisle of some church, was to be denied him. It all seemed so unreal, he just couldn't get his head around the things he'd been told by the doctor, in fact most of it he couldn't recall, he'd been so dazed by the news. He did remember the doctor telling him to go back and bring his wife . . . Eventually, mentally drained and physically exhausted, he made his way home.

Freda Ryan was singing away to herself in the kitchen as she prepared the vegetables for supper that night. The fire in the grate was burning brightly and a pile of newly ironed clothes were stacked on a chair waiting to be put away upstairs. In the corner stood a small Christmas tree that George had brought home from Oakley and Watling a few days before and which they had decorated along with the paper chains, which crisscrossed the room, weaving in and out of the paper lanterns suspended from the ceiling.

She enjoyed Christmas – loved all the excitement of shopping for presents, preparing the turkey and all the trimmings – the whole occasion, and she was hoping that Connie would come home to make the family complete. She would write to her this week and ask. She turned as she heard the front door open, wondering who on earth it could be. Both Doreen and George were at work . . . and when George walked in the room, she was so shocked by the white, stricken look on his face, she stopped singing.

'Whatever is the matter?' she asked.

He just stood in the doorway, unable to take another step. 'I've got a brain tumour, Freda, love.'

She dropped the cup she was holding. 'What *are* you talking about?'

'Those headaches I've been having . . . the doctor sent me for an X-ray a week ago. Today he got the results.'

'X-ray? Doctor?' She rushed over to him as he seemed on the point of collapse, and helped him to the chair by the fire. 'I didn't know you'd even been to the doctor.' She knelt beside him and held his hands. 'Now start at the beginning, George.'

He told her about his visit, the trip to the hospital for an X-ray and the results that were given to him today.

'You never told me any of this.'

'I didn't want to worry you,' he said quietly.

She put her arms around him, trying to fight her tears. 'Can they operate?'

'No, Freda, it's too late for that.' He looked at her and said, 'I'm going to die. I have only a few months left.'

She let out a cry of anguish and covered her mouth with both hands, trying to smother the sound of the sobs which wracked her body. 'Oh, my God!' she wailed. 'Oh, my God!'

They clung together in desperation.

Freda was the first to recover her equilibrium. Hastily wiping her eyes, she said, 'Right. Now you listen to me, George Ryan. You and I are going to fight this thing together . . . I'm not ready to be a widow yet! I want to see Doctor Mills myself and see what he has to say.'

Looking at her with admiration mixed with a certain sadness, he said, 'He asked me to go back in a couple of days with you to have a talk.'

'Two days, my arse! We'll go tomorrow. As soon as we know what's before us, we'll know how to fight it.' She cupped his face in her hands and said, 'Don't you dare give up yet, you understand?'

'Oh, Freda, what would I do without you?'

'Come along, dear, I think you should go up to bed and rest. You look exhausted. I'll bring you up a nice cup of tea in a while. Now go along.'

He rose from the chair, kissed her forehead and said, 'I do feel weary. Don't let me sleep too long.'

When she was alone, Freda sat in the chair, rocking back and forth, arms clasped across her chest, tears streaming down her face, staring vacantly into the fire, and that was how Doreen found her when she came home.

'Mum? Whatever is the matter?'

Freda just shook her head, unable to find the words.

Kneeling beside her mother, Doreen enfolded her in her arms and just held her until Freda said, 'It's your father . . .' And then she told her the tragic news.

Doreen looked stunned. 'Could they have made some mistake?' she asked, desperately seeking a solution.

Shaking her head, Freda said, 'It seems the tumour showed up on the X-ray.' With an expression of despair she said, 'What are we going to do?'

Lowering herself to the floor beside her mother whose hand she now clasped, she said, 'I don't know. This is like a bad dream. Poor Dad . . . Where is he?'

'In bed. He looked shattered. I thought it was the best place for him.'

'I'll pop up and see if he's asleep,' said Doreen getting to her knees, 'then I'll make a strong cup of tea. No, bugger that, we'll open that half bottle of brandy we bought for Christmas. I reckon we both need it.'

The door of her parents' bedroom was slightly ajar and she carefully pushed it open. George was sleeping, the blankets drawn up to his chin. She crept across the wooden floor and stood on the mat beside the bed, gazing at the sleeping figure. He looked so peaceful lying there that it was hard to conceive that his time with them was limited. She slowly shook her head in despair, still unable to believe what her mother had told her. Creeping out of the room, she pulled the door to and went downstairs.

Crossing to the sideboard she took out the brandy and poured two measures into a couple of glasses and handed one to Freda. 'Here, drink this.'

They both sat in silence, sipping their drinks. 'We'll have to tell Connie,' Doreen said.

'This is not the kind of thing you can say over the telephone,' said her mother.

'No, of course not. I'll go up to London on Sunday. She doesn't work then so she should be at home.'

'I'm going to make an appointment to see Doctor Mills with your father tomorrow sometime,' said Freda, thinking aloud. 'Dad can't work any more, so we'll have to let Oakley and Watling know.' Still staring into the fire she added, 'We have some savings to tide us over, and the money you give me. We'll manage somehow.' She looked up and said, 'I thought your father and I would grow old together. Funny how you take such things for granted, isn't it?' And she burst into tears.

Chapter Thirty

The following Sunday, Connie woke at eleven thirty and ran a bath. She lay in the hot water, relaxing after a strenuous night. The Saturday show had gone well and she had sung several encores before escaping her enthusiastic audience, but it had been the early hours of the morning when she'd crept between the sheets. She was humming softly to herself, then stopped and listened, thinking she'd heard someone at the front door. There was a muffled sound of voices, then footsteps on the stairs, followed by a tap on the door of the bathroom.

'Are you there, Connie?' Irene called.

'Yes, what is it?'

'You have a visitor.'

'All right, give me a minute or two,' she said and got out of the bath, quickly drying herself, thinking it was probably Ben who had arrived early. Putting on her dressing gown, she ventured downstairs to the drawing room.

'Doreen! What on earth are you doing here?'

'Hello, Con.' She crossed the room and embraced her sister. 'I'm sorry to disturb you.'

'Don't be an idiot,' Connie interrupted, 'it's a wonderful surprise, isn't it, Irene?' But when she turned towards her teacher and saw the look on her face, she hastily turned back. 'Is something the matter? Is it Mum? Is she ill or something?'

Irene took her by the arm saying, 'Sit down, Connie. Your sister has some bad news, I'm afraid. I'll go and make us some coffee,' and she left the girls alone.

With a sick feeling in the pit of her stomach, Connie asked, 'What is it, our Dor? For God's sake, tell me.'

'It's Dad.'

'Dad?'

'Yes. He's been having bad headaches, and they became even worse so he went to the doctor who sent him for an X-ray . . .'

Connie felt a sudden chill, which started at the top of her head and travelled down the length of her body. 'Go on,' she said quietly.

Doreen's voice caught in her throat and tears brimmed her eyes. 'Oh, Con! He's got a brain tumour and he's going to die!'

'Going to die? Don't be ridiculous!'

'It's true. He's only got a short time left. A matter of months, but not much longer.'

'Can't they do anything for him? Operate or something?'

'No, the tumour is too far advanced.'

Connie felt as if her head was going to burst. She covered her eyes with her hand and was overcome with guilt, remembering the awful row she'd had with her father when she left home. The flowers he'd sent her, which she had dismissed so readily. She looked up to see Doreen weeping silently. She crossed to the settee and held her sister tightly.

'That poor bugger! Is he in a lot of pain?'

Blowing her nose into her handkerchief, Doreen said, 'I haven't seen him when he's had a bad head, or at least he hasn't said anything, but he can't work, Connie. He's at home and Mum is looking after him. He has been pottering on the allotment off and on the last couple of days. It gives him something to do.'

'How is Mum?'

'Shattered, as you can imagine, but you know her, she puts on a brave front.'

'If he's not working then he's not earning, is he?'

Doreen shook her head.

'Well, at least I can take care of that situation.' She stood up. 'I'll get dressed and then I'll come back to Southampton with you.' As Irene walked in the room with a tray, she said to her, 'Give Doreen some coffee whilst I get ready, will you? I'm going home. I'll be back for my performance on Monday night. Tell Ben for me when he comes, will you?'

'Of course I will,' said Irene. 'You go along, I'll look after Doreen.'

Alone in her room, Connie let go the emotions she'd managed to control in front of her sister. As she dressed she shed her tears for the father she'd always loved but with whom she'd so often crossed swords, whom she'd defied to enable her to follow her destiny, and whom she'd shamed by that damning report in the paper. She closed her eyes to shut out the memory of the words, which must have been so hard for such a proud man to stomach. But she told herself at least that by leaving home, she was now in a position to help her family financially – so that was indeed a godsend. She was earning good money, thanks to her arrangement with Jeremy Taylor, and she was able to support them all. She frowned as she took her coat out of the wardrobe. George wouldn't like that idea, she was certain, but he had little choice. She would just have to be diplomatic with her arrangements.

Connie ordered a taxi and they caught a train from Waterloo station. She bought first-class tickets, feeling they needed to be on their own, and when they stepped into the carriage, Doreen smiled at her saying, 'My Lord, Connie, this is travelling in style.'

With a broad grin she confessed, 'I've never done this before, so let's enjoy it.'

Trying to get away from the tragic circumstances, which had brought them together, Doreen questioned Connie about her life and told her about her boyfriend Eric, and for the first part of their journey the conversation was almost lighthearted. But as they neared their destination, the mood in the carriage became sombre.

Connie caught hold of Doreen's hand and said, 'Please try

not to worry too much, love. Financially, you and Mum will have no worries, I can see to that. We just have to get through these next months somehow.'

'I know. I know.' Her gaze was full of sadness as the older girl looked at her sibling. 'How on earth are we going to do it?'

'One day at a time, that's the only way. We have to be strong for both Mum and Dad. It's not going to be easy, but come on, Dor. We're the Ryan girls!'

With a wan smile Doreen said, 'Indeed, we are.'

When they arrived at the house and Doreen pushed open the front door, Connie took a deep breath, then followed her in. Freda came out of the kitchen and when she saw her youngest daughter, she flew into her arms.

Connie held her tightly and said, 'It's all right, Mum, I'm here. Come and sit down,' and led her to a chair. 'Where's Dad?' she asked.

'He went to have a lie-down after lunch,' she said. 'He asked me to take him up a cup of tea about four o'clock. I've just put the kettle on.'

Taking hold of her mother's two hands in hers, Connie looked at her and said, 'I can't tell you how shocked I am by the news, but I want you to know one thing, you'll have no money worries, because I'm in a position to look after you. Anything Dad wants you get. I'll leave a cheque and Doreen can open up a bank account for you in the morning. Every month I'll put a sum of money in it to cover the rent, food etc.'

'George won't hear of it,' protested Freda.

'Dad won't know because we won't tell him. Let him think it's all out of your savings. OK?'

Freda smiled warmly at her. 'Just look at you – my baby. Doing so well, looking so smart and successful. I'm so proud of you, Connie.' And she hugged her.

Connie felt a lump rising in her throat. 'How about that cup of tea? We'll all have one together than I'll take one up to

Dad.' At Freda's look of uncertainty she said, 'It'll be all right, don't worry.'

A while later she walked up the stairs, her heart pounding, telling herself she *had* to be strong. The last thing her father needed was a woman weeping all over him. She knocked on the door, and walked in.

George Ryan stirred, opened his eyes and saw Connie standing beside him. 'Hello, love. What are you doing here?'

Connie was filled with relief. She wondered how he would greet her after the newspaper report. She smiled, put the cup of tea down on the bedside table, sat on his bed and took his hand.

'Hello, Dad. I don't know, I can't leave you for five minutes but you get into trouble. How are you feeling today?'

'You know, then?'

'Yes, Doreen came up to London to tell me and of course I came back with her.' She gently squeezed his hand. 'I owe you an apology, Dad. I'm so sorry about the newspaper report, if I could take it all back I would.'

He raised an eyebrow. 'Really? That's not like you at all!'

But Connie saw the corners of his mouth twitch and knew he wasn't really scolding her.

'What's done is done and, after all, in the scale of things now, it isn't important,' he said.

'The important thing, Dad, is for you to try and get better.'

He patted her hand. 'You know that's not going to happen, Connie.'

She looked down at his hand holding hers and in a choked voice said, 'I know, but I don't want to believe it.'

'Help me up, girl, so I can drink my tea. You and I need to talk whilst we are alone.'

She did so and handing him his cup she waited.

'Now at the moment, I'm able to get about most of the time when my head's not too bad, but it won't always be the case.'

'How can you sit there and talk about this so calmly?'

'Because I've done a lot of thinking these past few days. I

don't have much time left so I don't want to spend it whining about what's going to happen. That will only make it unbearable for your mother.'

'Oh, Dad.'

'Now don't go all tearful on me, Con. You've got a lot of guts and I'm going to need you to be strong . . . for all of us.'

'I'll cancel my appearance at Ciro's,' she said.

'You'll do no such thing! You have been through a lot to get where you are and I'm real proud of you. You know that, don't you?'

'No, I didn't, but I hoped you would be.'

'I'm your father, why wouldn't I be?'

Shaking her head, she said, 'I don't deserve this after what I put you through.'

'Now then, you had the courage of your convictions.' He smiled at her. 'I never had a quarter of your ambition and I admire you for it.' He paused. 'That Les Baxter treating you right?'

'Yes, Dad,' she lied. 'And Jeremy Taylor, my other manager, is great, and I have a terrific pianist called Ben. He's a really nice chap.'

'Something special, is he?'

'Why do you ask that?'

'It was the way you said his name. It might surprise you to know that I have been in love myself . . . I married the girl.'

Connie gazed at him with deep affection. 'Why have we never talked before like this?'

He chuckled. 'Because you lived in a world of your own, my dear.'

'We've wasted so much time,' she murmured.

'But we didn't leave it too late, that's the important thing. I want you to continue in your chosen field. Be the star you wanted to be . . . do it for me.'

It was then that Connie broke down. 'Oh, Dad, I don't think I can bear it.'

'Come along now,' he said, wiping the tears away with his

hand. 'You could take on the world if you had a mind to.'

'I'll take on the family,' she said. Taking a chance on his response, but wanting to alleviate any worries he may have about his family's future, she added, 'I earn good money. That much I *can* do for you.'

'Good. I'll go to my maker a lot easier knowing that. Now off you go downstairs and let me get into my trousers. I feel like a sandwich, tell your mother.'

As Connie got off the bed she said, 'I'll be down every Sunday to see you.'

'You don't need to.'

'Yes, I do,' she replied firmly as she left the room.

In the living room, Connie quickly told her mother that George was aware of the financial situation. 'So now there will be no reason to lie about it,' she said.

Freda looked at her in amazement. 'I'm surprised he agreed.'

'Me too, but Dad has been doing a lot of thinking it seems, and he's accepted what's going to happen,' she paused as the words stuck in her throat, 'which is more than I can do at the moment.'

'I know what you mean, love,' said Freda. 'It seems all so unreal. On the days he feels good, you can't believe this tumour business, but of course, it won't always be that way.'

Unable to say anything to comfort her mother without breaking down, Connie said brightly, 'By the way, Dad said he would like a sandwich. He's getting dressed.'

Freda escaped into the kitchen to be alone and to prepare to feed her husband.

George came down the stairs and settled by the fire. 'Tell me what you're up to then, our Connie. Where are you appearing now?'

The atmosphere lifted as she regaled him about her life, and the forthcoming engagement at the London Palladium. He sat and listened intently, smiling at her stories.

★ ★ ★

Connie spent the evening by the fire, listening to the radio with her family. She noticed her father quietly taking his pills at one point, but said nothing. Being back in the heart of her family without any tension, despite the circumstances, soothed her soul, and she realised just how much she missed them.

Then the following morning she strolled to the allotment with her father. At this time of year the earth was bare as the winter frosts lay upon the ground. 'I hope I'm still around to see the crocuses bloom,' he said quietly. 'Spring is my favourite time of the year, when the first blossom opens on the cherry trees. It always looks so pretty.'

Connie was unable to speak, but she tucked her arm through his and they walked slowly home.

Later that afternoon she caught a train back to London wondering just how she was going to perform that night, but then she remembered George's words ... *Do it for me*. And she knew that she couldn't fail him.

Chapter Thirty-One

Ben was hovering around her dressing-room door when Connie arrived at the club that night. He looked anxiously at her and asked, 'Are you all right, darling?'

She shook her head and entered the room. Putting down her handbag she took off her coat and said, 'No, I'm not. I don't know whether I'm coming or going, to be honest.'

He gathered her in his arms and held her tight. 'I was so worried about you when Irene told me the news. How is your father?'

'Being immensely brave, which makes me feel an absolute pig after the way I treated him.' She sat down at the dressing table and started her make-up. With a sad smile she said, 'We had a long chat, probably the longest and most serious that I can ever remember – we sorted out a lot of things.' Looking up at him, she said, 'I feel that I've aged ten years over the last two days.'

'I'm sure this is the last place you want to be tonight.'

'You'd think so, wouldn't you? But to be honest if I didn't have a show to do, I think I'd fall apart.'

Looking at her strained expression, Ben could believe it. 'Are you going to be all right?' he asked.

'I'll be fine as long as you hang around. You won't leave me, will you?'

The plaintive note in her voice reminded him of a lost child. Kneeling beside her he kissed her cheek. 'I'm never going to be far away, ever. I love you, Connie; your worries are my worries.

When are you going to Southampton again?'

'Next Sunday. I told Dad I would come every weekend.'

'Would you like me to come with you?'

She gazed at him, tears brimming her eyes. 'Oh, would you?'

'Of course. We'll talk about it later. You get ready, I'll go and get you a cup of hot coffee.' Kissing her briefly he left.

Jeremy Taylor dropped by to say how very sorry he was to hear about her father: Irene had called him and told him the sad news. 'Is there anything I can do for you, my dear?'

She thanked him for his kindness and said, 'No, really. I'll go home every weekend of course. Ben said he'd come with me next time.'

'Take care, Connie, if Les gets to hear about Ben, he might make trouble.'

'What trouble could he make that would be worse than my father dying?'

He placed a hand on her shoulder. 'I know, but nevertheless, take care. I have to go, I'm afraid, as I have an appointment. Are you going to be all right?'

'Yes. Anyway, Ben will look after me and I've thought of a way to protect him from Les, so don't worry.'

'Right. I'll come again in a day or two, but call me if there is anything I can do.' He kissed her forehead. 'You're a gutsy girl, Connie, and I'm afraid you are going to need to be even more so in the future.'

Connie had no idea how she managed to get through her performance that night, but once she was on the stage beneath the lights, the band behind her and her beloved Ben at the piano, she was the true professional, giving her all, as she did at every show, but she was absolutely exhausted at the end. And it was the same every night that week, as she wished the days away until she could see her father again.

Ben was always solicitous, taking her home, making sure she ate, walking her in the park to try and stop her thinking of what lay ahead for the Ryan family. He sent flowers to Freda in the hope that it would lift her spirits; and he bought silly little gifts for Connie, hoping to do the same.

As she opened yet another small parcel and found a minute, framed cartoon picture of a fraught pianist, coat tails and hair flying wildly as he played, she laughed. 'Is this meant to be you?'

'Damned right it is!' he exclaimed. 'You have no idea how hard I work!'

She cuddled into him and said, 'You're quite wrong. I do know, especially this week when you were *not* at the piano. I don't know what I would have done without you.' Putting her arms around his neck she kissed him. 'I do love you, Ben Stanton.'

'And I absolutely adore you, Connie Ryan.'

Just as she started to sing the final session of songs on the Saturday night show, Connie saw Les Baxter arrive at the club, order a drink and stand at the bar, watching her perform. She was filled with an absolute rage when she saw him. He was the very last person she needed around her at this moment and when at the end of the show he came to her dressing room, she was ready for him, leaving her door unlocked.

He tapped on it and walked in, went over to her and made to kiss her. She pushed him away.

'Get off me!'

He looked at first astonished and then angry. 'I think you have forgotten our little arrangement,' he said.

'You can do what you like with your arrangement!' she cried. 'I don't want you anywhere near me. My father has a tumour and is dying; do you think I care about you and your demands? You want to stop me performing . . . then go ahead!' And she stormed out of the room and called a taxi.

Les was still trying to recover from the shock of Connie's behaviour and her news when Ben came along.

'Where's Connie?' he asked.

'She's gone. She said her father was dying from a brain tumour . . . what did she mean?'

Ben explained what had happened.

'I'd better go after her,' said Baxter.

'You'll do no such thing! God! What sort of a man are you? Can't you see she's facing a crisis? She's been performing magnificently every night and it must be killing her. She has more than enough to cope with – leave her alone!' And he walked away.

Les Baxter had been in London's East End all week, dealing with his new business, which was doing really well and therefore had not heard about George Ryan. He walked back to the bar and sat having a drink. Poor bugger, he thought. He had no liking for the man, thinking him small-minded and parochial, but he couldn't help feeling sorry for him . . . and he wondered how it would affect his rising star. He thought he had her nicely under his thumb, but tonight's outburst unsettled him, because for the first time, Connie had put something else before her ambition. She really *didn't* care if he stopped her performing. In fact, he got the impression she may have welcomed it, and that was dangerous. Then he would have no hold on her whatsoever.

Ben took a taxi to Maida Vale and, asking the driver to wait, he knocked on the door. When Connie opened it he said, 'Are you OK?'

'Yes. I'm sorry I left like that but I couldn't stand being near Les Baxter tonight, I just needed to get away.'

'You look tired, darling. What time do you want me to pick you up in the morning?'

'I'll be ready by eleven thirty. I must get some sleep or I'll be no company for Dad.'

'Right. I'll see you then. Try and get a good night's rest.'

The next morning saw the two of them on the train from Waterloo to Connie's home. She was tired and a little tense and sat silently clutching Ben's hand.

As he sat beside her, he wondered just how much she could take, and indeed the rest of the family. It must be dreadful for Mrs Ryan and Connie's sister, but they didn't have to perform in front of an audience every night and pretend that all was well. The added strain on Connie would begin to tell in time and that worried him.

They eventually arrived and took a taxi to the house, where they were ushered in by Doreen.

Connie hastily introduced her to Ben then asked, 'How's Dad?'

'He's not too bad this morning, but he has been sick a few times over the past few days, which apparently is part of his illness. He's sitting by the fire reading the papers.' She placed her hand on Connie's arm and smiled. 'He's been asking what time you were arriving, Con, so he's looking forward to seeing you.'

Outside the living-room door, Connie gave Ben's hand a squeeze then entered. 'Hello, Dad. I've brought Ben to meet you.'

He was a godsend that day. He sat with George, drinking tea, talking about his time in the army when he was part of E.N.S.A., entertaining the troops. Telling him of the places he'd seen, the soldiers he'd met, the difficulties he'd encountered being in a war zone . . . men's talk. The women sat back and listened, prepared a meal, washed up and chatted among themselves. They would have their time after lunch when George went for a rest, but now they were content to do little, leaving the men to themselves.

When eventually George excused himself to go to his room for a rest, Connie hugged Ben. 'Thank you so much,' she said. 'Dad really enjoyed talking to you.'

Freda looked over and smiled her thanks. 'It was good of you to come.'

'Not at all, I wanted to meet Connie's family. Thank you for a lovely lunch. I don't remember the last time I sat at a table as

271

a family. It was very comforting in a strange way. How are you two coping?' he asked.

Doreen said, 'We manage. I take over from Mum when I come home from work. We try to keep everything as normal as we can. It's the only way.'

'I'm sure you're right.'

'When are you going back?' asked Freda, 'If you are staying overnight, I can only offer Ben the settee.'

He looked at Connie and said, 'I've slept on worse when I was in the desert!'

'Are you sure? Only I want to spend as much time here as I can.'

'Of course you do.'

And so it was settled.

During the evening when they were all gathered around the fire listening to the radio, there was a female singer on and George looked at Connie. 'You can sing better than she can! How about giving us a song?'

She feigned shock. 'You want me to perform without a band and my pianist?'

'I've got a comb,' said Ben with a broad grin, 'all I need is some paper!'

It was a special time, Connie going through her repertoire accompanied by Ben with his comb and paper and her father playing the spoons. There was a lot of laughter and joshing about the musicians and when it was time for bed, the atmosphere was light and happy.

George kissed the girls goodnight and said to Connie, 'I really enjoyed that. My God, I don't remember when I last played the spoons.' Turning to Ben he said, 'Goodnight, son. The settee's quite comfortable, I've spent a few nights on it in the past when Freda and I fell out.'

'George Ryan!' his wife admonished. 'How can you say such a thing?'

He chuckled softly. 'It's true, but the making up was better.'

Freda blushed and hustled him off to bed, with a 'Really! What a thing to say.'

Connie and Doreen cleared away and collected sheets and a pillow with a couple of blankets for Ben to use.

'Leave that,' he told Doreen as she attempted to make up a bed for him, 'I'll manage.'

'I'll get off too then,' she said. 'Thanks, Ben, for being so understanding and kind.' She gave Connie a peck on the cheek and left them alone. They snuggled up together in the glow of the firelight.

'That was such a good evening,' she murmured, 'one I'll always remember.'

'It makes you wonder why people go out to nightclubs, doesn't it?'

'It's just as well they do,' she teased, 'otherwise we'd be out of a job.'

After breakfast the following morning, George suggested that Ben walk with him to the paper shop at the end of the road, to everyone's surprise.

'I'd be glad to, I need to stretch my legs,' Ben said as he put on his coat.

'Well, don't stretch them too quickly,' joked his host, 'only I don't walk so fast these days,' and they set off.

On the way George came straight to the point. 'You love my Connie, don't you, son?'

'I do, sir, very much.'

'Good. She needs someone to keep her in check. Connie is a lovely girl, but she can be stubborn and headstrong. You look as if you've got the measure of her.'

Ben grinned 'As much as any man when it comes to a woman!'

With a laugh George said, 'I know what you mean. But I don't trust that Les Baxter, and it worries me.'

Ben's jaw tightened as he said, 'Don't you worry about him, he won't bother Connie, I'll see to that.'

'Good, that's all I wanted to hear.' By then they had arrived at the corner shop where they bought a daily paper, and walked back in companionable silence.

Whilst Connie had been visiting her parents, Southampton had another visitor from the metropolis. Kenny Pritchard knocked on the door of the house in Wilton Avenue and waited. When the door opened, he smiled, raised his hat and said, 'Mrs Baxter?'

'Yes, who wants to know?'

'Your son Les has sent me to see you. I've come with a message from London.'

'Oh, well, you'd better come in, young man.'

Chapter Thirty-Two

It was two days later that Les Baxter returned to his home town. With Christmas rapidly approaching, he had promised to take his mother shopping and at noon he let himself into the house. He picked up two pints of milk from the doorstep, and wondered why they were still there.

'Ma!' he called, looking down at the letters on the mat. He frowned as he picked those up too and began to feel anxious. 'Ma, where are you?' He walked into the kitchen which was tidy except for a dirty cup and saucer on the side. Now he was getting worried, Mrs Baxter was a meticulous housewife.

He leapt the stairs two at a time, calling her name loudly. The bathroom was empty. The bedroom was empty – as were the other two. He ran downstairs again to see if there was a note in the living room . . . there was nothing.

He went to the next-door neighbours and asked if they had seen his mother. They hadn't, neither had the lady on the other side. He was frantic. Where on earth could she be?

The telephone he'd had installed began to ring. It was a moment before the sound registered with him, then he snatched up the receiver. 'Ma?'

'Les?'

He breathed a sigh of relief. 'Where the hell are you? I've been worried to death.'

There was a nervous note in the voice of the elderly woman as she said, 'When are you going to fetch me? The young man told me it would be soon . . . I want to come home, Les.'

'Come home? What are you talking about?'

'Hello, Les, how are you doing? It's Kenny Pritchard.'

Baxter was shocked to hear his voice – then enraged. 'What have you done with my mother, you bastard?'

There was the sound of laughter down the phone. 'Language, Les, your old mother might hear you.'

'If you harm her in any way so help me I'll kill you!'

'What happens to her is entirely up to you, my friend.'

Les Baxter was seething but he was wise enough to control his anger. 'I'm listening.'

'I want my patch back – the one you stole from me, that's all. Not too much to ask I don't think.' The younger man was holding all the cards and he knew it – and so did Les.

'If I agree, what then?'

'Then you get your dear old mum back, but naturally I will hold on to her until I see a result of your handover – my men returning to me, yours going back down to your own territory, the money coming in – to me, of course. But you won't tell the men about your mother. That will be strictly between us.'

'But that will take time and what if your men don't want to come back, even if I pull out? They weren't too happy about the way you were running things.'

'That wouldn't be a good idea. Now I am sure you can be persuasive, after all you talked them into leaving. All you have to do is talk them back, then you and I can carry on as if nothing happened. An armistice if you like.'

The bookmaker knew he had no choice. 'All right, I'll get a train back to the Smoke right away, but you had better take good care of my mother, you little shit, or I'll bloody well have you! Put her on the phone.'

There was silence on the other end for what seemed a lifetime, then his mother spoke, 'Les?'

'Look, love, I've got a bit of business to see to but I'll pick you up in a couple of days. Are they looking after you all right?'

'Yes, but they won't let me go out and I don't know where I am . . . I want to come home.'

'All right, dear, you just stay calm and I'll see you soon. All right?' The phone went dead.

As he replaced the receiver, he gave vent to his feelings, filling the air with expletives, stomping up and down, ranting and raving as he did so . . . then when eventually he was calm enough, he rang a taxi to take him to the station.

During the train journey, Baxter was racking his brains as to how he was going to approach the men who had quite happily decided to quit Pritchard's organisation and work for him. He could easily come up with a reason to quit, but to get them to work for the young thug again was another matter. These were hardened men who had been living beyond the law most of their lives; a few of them had served time for various felonious reasons, they wouldn't easily be pushed around. He had on his hands a problem of immense proportions if he was to secure the safety of his mother.

His poor old mum . . . she had sounded so fragile and frightened. He balled his hands into fists as he thought about Kenny Pritchard taking her from her familiar surroundings and hiding her away. His mind was filled with murderous thoughts of what he would do to the young man once his mother was safely at home. He wouldn't let him get away with this. His business, that he wanted back so badly, was small potatoes in comparison. He would have far more to worry about in the future.

By the time he reached Waterloo station, Baxter had made up his mind as to how to approach his men and he made his way to the Stag's Head, ordered a beer and waited for them to arrive at the end of the day, as was their habit.

When eventually they were all together, Les listened to them talking of how well things were going, how good it was to work for someone who knew how to handle things and not a young fool who wanted to run before he could walk and who would have got them all put behind bars had they stuck with him and his wild schemes.

The bookie waited until they had all finished, then he bought them a drink and said, 'I have something to discuss with you which is of the utmost importance to me and I'm hoping to get your full cooperation.'

There was an immediate air of expectation – but also, suspicion.

Les didn't beat about the bush; neither did he hide the truth of the matter in hand as Kenny had asked of him.

'That little shit Pritchard has got my mother.'

The suspicion changed to one of anger. 'You mean he's lifted her?'

Les nodded. 'Yes, she wasn't at home this morning, two days' milk was on the doorstep and the mail still on the mat.'

'How did you find out where she was?' asked one.

'Kenny rang and told me.'

'That kid has more front than the bloody palace,' snorted another. 'So what's he after, money?'

'In a manner of speaking. He wants his London patch back.'

'Over my dead body!' remarked another.

'*Or my mother's!*' Les looked at the expression on their faces. 'Now, gentlemen, this is my situation and this is the way I intend to play it . . .' and he began to explain.

At the end of the next day's racing, the accountant rang Kenny at a given number as directed and told him, 'The money is coming in and it was a good day.'

Kenny smiled with satisfaction. 'And the men?'

'They are a bit quiet, none of them saying anything, but the main thing is they are handing over the dosh.'

'Excellent. Call me again tomorrow and every day as the cash arrives. I want a daily total, understand?'

'Yeah, Kenny. I understand.'

He looked across the room to where Mrs Baxter was sitting dejectedly, listening to the radio. 'It looks as if you'll be going home soon, Ma.'

She glowered at him. 'Mrs Baxter to you, young man!'

Whilst all this was going on, Connie, of course, was left in peace. Baxter wasn't around to upset her and her affair with Ben Stanton was progressing under Irene's watchful eye. Knowing Baxter's possessiveness, Irene was concerned as she watched the two lovers together, but by now she realised that Ben's feelings towards Connie were genuine and at this moment in her life, Connie really needed a man like him around to comfort and support her. She wondered, however, what would happen when Baxter showed up again. Would these two be able to hide their feelings?

Connie herself wasn't a bit concerned. She had too much on her mind and the only thing that was holding her together was her contract at Ciro's and Ben. After one tiring performance she was at her lowest ebb and he felt she needed some real peace and quiet away from everyone, so he suggested after the show they return to his small flat where he would cook something light and then she could stay the night.

'We'll just cuddle up and sleep,' he explained.

'It sounds wonderful,' she said. 'Can you cook?'

'I can and have done so often, in the past. How do you fancy an omelette? It won't be too heavy so late at night.'

As Connie removed her make-up and changed, she said, 'It sounds wonderful.'

The flat was small, with a minute kitchen, sitting room and bedroom, and tiny bathroom. As she looked around Connie said, 'Good heavens! How tidy you are.'

'When there is so little space, you have to be,' he said, then he grinned broadly 'My army training comes in useful. Now sit on the settee, put your feet up, and I'll go into the kitchen.'

Connie curled up on the slightly worn but comfortable settee and fell asleep.

Ben put on the kettle to make a cup of tea, cracked the eggs into a bowl and beat them in readiness, then popped his head around the door to speak to Connie. She was sleeping. He crossed over to her, gazing at her, an expression of love in his eyes. She was never going to be able to eat, he decided. He turned back the bedclothes and carefully picking her up so as not to disturb her, he carried her into the bedroom, where he slipped the shoes, stockings and dress off the sleeping form and tucked her into bed. After turning off the lights, he undressed and slipped in between the sheets beside her, cradling her in his arms. And this was how Connie awakened the next morning.

As she stirred it woke Ben, who looked at her and said, 'Good morning, darling. Sleep well?'

Rubbing her eyes she asked softly, 'What time is it?'

'Ten thirty.'

'I don't remember coming to bed.'

'I carried you in,' he said. 'You fell asleep on the settee.'

Putting an arm around him under the clothes she said, 'Sorry, and you were going to make omelettes.'

'We can have them for breakfast.'

'I suppose we can,' she murmured, 'but not yet . . . later.'

'I like the sound of that,' he said as he kissed her and caressed her soft breast.

They made slow, tender, lingering love. It was just what Connie needed to chase away her anxieties, her weariness, the burden she was carrying whilst trying to fulfil her contractual obligations to the management of Ciro's.

She lay back in Ben's arms and said, 'You are so good for me.'

He chuckled. 'Well, I'm very glad to hear it, I would hate all that effort to have been for nothing!'

She started laughing. 'That didn't sound at all romantic!'

Holding her close he said, 'Romance isn't just candlelight

and roses, darling. Real romance is being with someone because you want to be, whatever the situation.'

Thinking of Les Baxter, she said, 'That can also be because you are possessive.'

'No, it's different. To possess something is to own it, romance is about cosseting something precious. It's totally different.'

'I do like your lyrics,' she said, teasing them. 'I just wish life could be that simple.'

'The trouble with you, my darling, is you want once-upon-a-time stuff, and that's not realistic. That's not life.'

'Sadly, it isn't.' She paused and said, 'About Christmas, I don't know what to buy Dad, under the circumstances.'

'You forget the circumstances, Connie. Treat it as you would if things were different. It's the only way.'

'Yes, you're absolutely right. Will you come down and spend it with us?'

He kissed the tip of her nose. 'Try and stop me.'

It was two days before Christmas Eve and Les Baxter was in the foyer of the Ritz awaiting the arrival of his mother. Kenny Pritchard was convinced that all was now well with his organisation and had arranged for Mrs Baxter to be delivered back to the safekeeping of her son.

Les was pacing up and down, constantly looking at his watch, when at last the doorman stepped forward to help a woman who had arrived. Les rushed forward.

'Ma! I am so pleased to see you!'

She looked coldly at him. 'What sort of game are you playing? You send someone to take me to London shopping and then I'm kept shut away for days and you don't come for me.'

He was in a dilemma. He couldn't possibly let her know that her position had been fraught with danger, but quick-witted as always, he said, 'I'm really sorry, there was a mix-up with appointments which I had to keep, but come on, to make up for it we'll have tea here. You'll love it – all the posh people come here – and then we'll go shopping. You can buy just whatever you like. Money no object.'

Somewhat ungraciously she agreed and Les gave a sigh of relief. It seemed that she hadn't been treated badly during her incarceration and for that he was grateful, but nevertheless, no one got away with treating his mother disrespectfully. No one.

Chapter Thirty-Three

Ciro's night club was crowded on Christmas Eve and there was a great air of festivity about the place, with the interior tastefully decorated with swathes of holly and ivy around balustrades and banisters. The tables laid for dinner had large gold-coloured expensive crackers beside each setting, ready for the pulling.

Connie was sitting in her dressing room, the door slightly ajar, going over final preparations for the evening's performance with Ben, when Les Baxter walked in. He was wearing evening dress and an overcoat, which he removed and threw over the back of a chair.

When they had finished their conversation, Ben looked at Connie and raised his eyebrows. 'Do you want me to stay?' he asked quietly.

She shook her head, and he reluctantly left the room.

'Did you want something?' she asked the bookie.

He stood behind her as she started to do her make-up. 'Don't use that tone of voice with me, young lady. Remember, without me you wouldn't be here in the first place.'

'I'm well aware of that, after all, you're constantly reminding me.'

He grabbed a handful of her hair and roughly yanked her head back. 'I'm sick of people trying to play me for a fool,' he snapped. 'Your gangster boyfriend thinks he's put one over me, but he'll learn and so will you if you don't pull your socks up.'

Connie managed to break free from his grasp. 'How dare you! My performance is better than ever, despite the family crisis I'm facing. You're getting your money's worth.'

'It's not your singing I'm referring to, it's your attitude to me.'

She looked at him in the mirror and continued with her make-up. 'The only person who interests me at the moment is my father. I don't have time for anyone else.'

'So what was Stanton doing in here?'

'We decided to change the final number, that's all.' She turned and faced him, her eyes flashing with anger. 'And please don't threaten him again. You harm him in any way . . . You won't have to hold out on my contract, because if you hurt my pianist I swear I'll never sing another note, for you or anyone! You can take your contract and shove it if anything happens to him!'

'Why the concern for a pianist?'

'My concern, Les, is your threatening ways. I just won't put up with them any more. Knowing my father is going to die has made me realise the important things in life and being bullied and threatened by you is intolerable. I'll work, and I'll get to the top if you behave in a decent manner.' A sly smile crept across her countenance as she added, 'After all, you want to make a name for yourself as a theatrical agent and I am the one who can do that for you, so it all boils down to who has the greater ambition.' She laughed. 'Strange, isn't it? It was mine that started this whole business, and now I don't care that much. I'm going to lose my father, and believe me, that's much more important than you or any kind of stardom!'

'All right! I understand the strain you're under and I'm sorry, but just you bear this in mind, Connie, I always get what I want in the end.'

'Leave me alone, Les. I have to prepare for a show. I need some quiet time to myself if I'm going to be able to do that well.'

He walked towards the door. 'All right, I'll go, but this isn't the end of this conversation. I'll be back.'

When she was alone, Connie let out a sigh of relief. She had meant what she said about harming Ben, although she needed to continue to work to be able to look after her family – but she didn't want Baxter to know that, he would use it to his advantage. She also knew that she had only bought herself time; Baxter was not to be put off so easily.

Les, already in a bad mood, was even more annoyed when he saw that Kenny Pritchard was sitting at a table near the stage, accompanied by two young men, who were members of his gang, and three women. Kenny happened to glance over and see Baxter. He raised his glass at him and smiled before turning away. Rage coursed through the older man. Young hoodlum! he thought. Well, let him enjoy this evening before he paid the penalty of kidnapping his mother. After all, he mused, Christmas was the time for goodwill to all men! And then he started laughing quietly. Armistice indeed!

Jeremy Taylor arrived with a party shortly afterwards, among them his wife Annabel and Rudy Davenport. They settled at a table with the other guests and ordered champagne.

'You'll be surprised when you see how much Connie has progressed,' Jeremy told Rudy. 'She'll be a great success at the Palladium, you'll see.'

'I'm banking on it,' replied Rudy.

'She's a jumped-up little bitch!' muttered Annabel spitefully.

'Actually she isn't!' Jeremy snapped, overhearing the remark. 'She's a talented, gutsy young woman. She has more character in her little finger than you have in the whole of your shapely body.'

There was an angry flush in her cheeks as she snapped back, 'I'm surprised you haven't bedded her in that case!'

He smiled benignly. 'I take to bed those who are good-looking and whose only talent is between the sheets – and in one crazy moment, I married one of them!'

Rudy laughed. 'So there you have it! Now be a good girl and let us enjoy the evening, after all, we've invested a lot in this girl, but just to wipe that sour look off your face, here's your Christmas present.' He handed her a long black jeweller's case.

Annabel opened it and smiled at the diamond bracelet nestling inside. 'Thank you, Rudy,' she said sweetly, and flashed the contents of the box in front of her husband.

He cast a quick glance at the bracelet and said, 'I'm sure you earned every stone!' Then he turned to the companion on the other side of him and started chatting.

At the bar, Les watched the guests at Jeremy's table. He knew who Davenport was of course and Annabel, but the others were strangers and he wondered if they had anything to do with the field of entertainment. Any other time he would not have hesitated to join them, even as an uninvited guest, but tonight he wanted to remain on his own to observe Connie's performance and to keep an eye on Pritchard. He certainly wasn't going to allow him to get within ten yards of Connie ever again. He was having enough trouble with her as it was.

As it happened, he needn't have worried. Kenny and his guests stayed together, watching the show, applauding enthusiastically, leaving when it was over. He walked past Baxter on his way out and with a broad grin said, 'Give my regards to your mother.'

It took all Les Baxter's self-control to stop him punching Kenny in the mouth, but this was neither the time nor the place. 'And a merry Christmas to you too,' was all he said.

At that moment he saw Connie leaving the club with Ben. It was so crowded that by the time he was able to make his way through the throng and to the door, he saw a taxi halfway down the road with the two of them in the back. He cursed loudly to himself. He had a present for Connie, but on reflection perhaps this was not the time to give it to her. He took a small square box out of his pocket and opened it. The square diamond solitaire glistened beneath the street lights. He snapped the lid shut and once again entered the club.

Ben and Connie arrived in Southampton at noon on Christmas Day, laden with gifts. As they walked in the door, the air was filled with a delicious aroma. Connie turned to Ben and said, 'You can't beat the smell of home cooking. Merry Christmas, everyone,' she called out as she made her way to the living room.

George was sitting by the fire whilst Freda was buzzing around in and out of the kitchen. Connie went over to her father and kissed him, then her sister and mother. She put down a bottle of champagne on the table.

'Get the glasses out, Mum, and let's celebrate.'

Freda, flushed with the excitement and the heat in the kitchen, looked flummoxed. 'I don't have any champagne glasses!'

'That doesn't matter, use tumblers, we don't mind, do we, Ben?'

'Absolutely not!'

'It's lovely to have you home for Christmas, our Con,' said Doreen.

'Yes indeed,' agreed George. 'I imagine you worked last night, so you must be tired.'

'Only because I couldn't sleep with excitement,' she said. 'What time are we eating, Mum?'

'After the King's speech, like always.'

'Right, we'll open our presents after the meal, shall we?' Connie asked. And they all agreed.

'Where's Eric?' Connie asked her sister.

'Spending the day with his parents. I'll see him tomorrow.'

Ben and George were soon in deep conversation, Ben making his host laugh about something or other. The women left them to it and gathered in the kitchen.

'How's Dad?' Connie asked her mother.

'Not too bad. The medication the doctor gave him helps with the pain and sickness, but it's all he can do to walk to the corner shop some days. Others he's not so bad.' Looking at her daughter she said, 'He doesn't complain.'

Connie put her arms around her and gave her a hug. 'And neither do you, I'll bet.'

After the King's speech, they settled round the table and enjoyed the traditional turkey with all the trimmings. Despite everything, it was a joyful time. Everyone determined to behave as usual, and the fact that George was well enough to enjoy it all helped. They pulled crackers, wore paper hats, read out the mottos inside and laughed. Then, after clearing the dishes away, they opened their presents.

'Here you are, Mum,' said Connie as she handed over a couple of small packages. Freda gave a cry of delight when she saw several pairs of silk stockings and a small bottle of Chanel perfume.

'I'll wear this when I go to the butcher,' she proclaimed. 'Perhaps it will tempt him to give me some extra meat!'

There were stockings for Doreen too, and an angora sweater in pale mauve.

'Oh, Connie! It's beautiful. You shouldn't have used your precious coupons on me.'

'I didn't but don't ask questions,' she laughed.

For her father there was a long woollen scarf and matching gloves and two pairs of socks. 'This will keep you warm,' she said.

He put the scarf around his neck and then donned the gloves. 'They'll be great when I walk to the allotment,' he said.

Connie unwrapped bath salts, talcum powder, soap and hair slides from Freda, a bottle of Coty's L'Aimant perfume from Doreen and a narrow silver bracelet from her father with her name engraved on it.

She was thrilled and thanked them all. She put the bracelet on and turning to George said, 'I'll never take it off.'

Ben gave them a bottle of port and sherry with a couple of

cigars for George. 'Every man should have a good cigar at Christmas,' he said, producing one for himself.

'Quite right,' agreed George and lit his.

Connie handed a package to Ben. 'And this is for you.'

Inside an expensive-looking box from Harrods he found a gents' white silk evening scarf. Putting it around his neck he said, 'It's lovely, darling. Thank you. I'll get a silver cane and then I'll be just like Fred Astaire!'

He handed her a small wrapped box.

With great excitement she removed the paper. Inside the box was a brooch. It was a peacock; the resplendent tail dotted with small emeralds and sapphires, with diamond chips for the eyes. It was exquisite.

'Just to remind you of where we met,' he said.

'Oh, Ben, it's beautiful. Thank you.' She kissed him without embarrassment. Freda and Doreen looked at each other and smiled.

Elsewhere, Christmas was not so enjoyable. Les Baxter had taken his mother to stay over the holidays with her younger sister and her family at Romsey, whilst he spent it alone, booked in at the Polygon Hotel where he could be waited on and fed without any effort on his part. This was an annual event for him, but whereas before he'd enjoyed the solitude, this year he felt lonely. He supposed that Connie was with her family, but much as he longed to see her, he knew he wouldn't be welcome.

In the Taylor household, Jeremy, as was his habit, had a house full of guests. He enjoyed being surrounded by people who shared his business interests and his way of life. Everything was cooked and served by professionals. The wine and champagne flowed all day which always proved to be interesting, he thought. People behaved so differently when their inhibitions were loosened by alcohol. Not least of all, his wife.

There were various entertainers present among the guests from stage and screen, as Jeremy's parties were legendary in the business, so the earlier part of the day – after the Christmas fare – was spent with someone playing the piano, accompanying a singer. Stage gossip was always interesting if not bitchy, but as the day wore on it was time for party games. Simple childish games – but always with forfeits – which became more bizarre as the hours passed.

It was Annabel who was next to pay a forfeit. Jeremy noted the brightness of her eyes as she waited to be told what to do.

'Right!' said the wag who was giving out the forfeits. 'You are going for an audition.'

'But I can't sing!' she exclaimed.

'We all know that, darling!' another called out and everybody laughed. She just pulled a face.

'No, you don't need to sing. You are being interviewed to perform in a strip club. You have to show your act to the producer. Just a minute, we'll decide on the music.' Two of them went in a huddle.

'Right.' The pianist walked over to the piano and started to play 'You're Nobody Till Somebody Loves You', which brought forth gusts of laughter, then Annabel started to divest herself of her clothes, keeping in time to the music.

Jeremy watched her, thinking to himself, she would have made a great Gypsy Rose Lee; after all, she'd stripped enough times for one lover or another. But he had long given up caring. She was a good-looking woman and when he needed her on his arm at an official function she was there. She knew how to play the perfect hostess and entertain any business guests. That was the arrangement *and* that she was discreet about her affairs.

He became bored with the whole thing and retired to his study. He thought of Connie. She was one of the few real things in his world at the moment, and he had a lot of time for her. He wondered how she was getting on at home. She had told him of her plans and he knew that it would be a difficult time for them all, but he hoped it worked out for them. He also wondered just how big a problem Les Baxter was going to be for her. He sighed. Life could really be a bitch!

Chapter Thirty-Four

On Boxing Day morning, George stayed in bed as he was feeling unwell. Connie could hear him in the bathroom, retching, and it broke her heart. 'Does this happen often?' she asked her mother.

'More frequently lately,' she admitted, 'but according to the doctor it's quite usual with his complaint. He said not to be surprised if he starts getting fits.'

'Fits! Oh, my God, how much more does he have to suffer?'

'Hopefully not that much more,' said Freda stoically, although her bottom lip trembled as she spoke.

'I should be *here* with *you*!' cried Connie.

Freda put an arm around her. 'No, Con, it wouldn't do any good. Your father wants you to continue with your career, he said he told you so.'

'Yes, he did, but I feel it's so wrong of me.'

'What would be wrong, love, is if you didn't fulfil his wishes.'

Eric arrived bearing gifts for everybody and as Connie saw the look of happiness on the face of her sister, she was delighted that Doreen had someone to care for her and support her through these difficult days, because she knew, without Ben beside her, she wouldn't have coped.

George got up later that morning and sat by the fire. He beckoned Connie over and asked, 'When do you open at the Palladium?'

'Next week, why?'

'I'd like to be there on your opening night.'

She felt the tears well in her eyes. It was the first time he had wanted to see her perform since she had become a professional. Swallowing quickly, she asked, 'Do you think you could manage a trip to the theatre?'

'To see my girl being a star, of course.'

Her mind racing, Connie started to plan. 'I'll send a car for you, that'll be more comfortable than a train journey. I'll book you all in a nearby hotel so you can rest overnight before the drive home.' She gazed anxiously at her father. 'Do you think that's a good idea, Dad? Could you manage that?'

He caught hold of her hand. 'It would be grand.'

On the way back to London, Connie discussed this with Ben. 'I'm worried to death it will all be too much for him.'

'It's what he wants, darling. The sooner it happens the more able he'll be able to cope with it. We can have a doctor standing by, just in case – of course we don't need to tell him that.'

'I'll insist that they have a box, that'll give them more privacy and then if he's unwell, there won't be others around. Oh, my God, Ben, I'll be a bloody wreck all night long.'

Putting his arm around her he said, 'No, you won't, you'll give the performance of your life, because you'll be doing it for him.'

The following two days were taken up with rehearsals, so Connie didn't have much time on her hands to fret about her father's trip. There were dresses to be chosen, alterations to be done, hair appointments made, and before she knew where she was, opening night arrived. Ben and Jeremy had taken over all the arrangements for the family visit between them, so Connie didn't have that to worry about as well.

In her dressing room, she was fussing about, a million things on her mind, but thankfully Jeremy arrived to calm her down.

'For Christ's sake, relax!' he told her. 'Leave your family to me. I've set up the box with a few sandwiches, some champagne and beer for your father and water in case he would prefer that. I booked the car early to enable them to arrive at the hotel at lunchtime to allow Mr Ryan to have a rest and when I rang earlier, all was well. I have a doctor in the theatre, sitting in the next box and a car at the ready should the worst occur, and I will be in the box with them so you have nothing at all to worry about – except your performance. All right?'

She had to laugh. 'Yes, Jeremy, there's no need to get a cob on.'

'I have no idea what a cob on is.'

'It's a Hampshire expression for getting tetchy.'

'Darling girl, I promise I'm not tetchy. I just want you to realise that everything is in hand, all you have to do is knock 'em dead . . . oh dear – sorry. What a dreadful choice of words!'

They looked at each other and creased up with laughter.

'Oh, Jeremy, thank goodness for a sense of humour,' she gasped, wiping away the mascara that had run. 'And thanks for everything. Is Les about?' she asked as an afterthought.

'Not as far as I know, but I'll put a guard on at the stage door to repel all boarders if you like?'

'Would you? I don't want him near me tonight if it can be avoided.'

'Leave everything to me. By the way,' he said, 'here's a little something for you to mark this occasion,' and he produced a small box.

On opening it Connie gave a cry of delight. Inside were a pair of diamond drop earrings. She put them on and said, 'Thank you so much, they're beautiful.'

Leaning forward he kissed her cheek. 'You truly deserve them. Break a leg.'

Ben arrived moments later. 'All set?' he asked.

'Look what Jeremy gave me,' she said, and showed off her earrings.

'What a lovely gesture. He's not a bad chap,' he said, then added, 'Your family are settled in the box and are fine. I popped up and had a word and Jeremy just arrived as I left.'

'How's Dad?'

'Absolutely fine! He's rested and all kitted out in his best suit. Eric and your mother are there too and Doreen looks wonderful. They are all very excited.'

'Five minutes, Miss Ryan,' interrupted the callboy.

She and Ben made their way to the wings and waited, watching the opening number with the boys and girls of the chorus dancing and swirling around the stage in their colourful costumes.

'There's a full house,' said Ben.

'Good. That will please Dad.'

'Are you all right, darling?' he asked.

She smiled and said, 'I've never felt better. This is what we've worked for, I'm with the man I love . . . and my family are in the audience. What more could I ask?'

The opening bars of her first number started and as Ben sat at the piano, Connie walked with great pride and dignity to the centre of the stage where she glanced up at her family and smiled.

Les Baxter was furious. He'd been round to the stage door, intending to see Connie before she went on stage and had been refused admission. 'What do you mean I can't come in? I'm Miss Connie Ryan's agent!'

'I don't care if you're the bloody King of Siam, mate, I 'as me orders and no one is to be admitted,' said the doorman. And he shut the door.

Les stormed to himself. He was late as it was, and he was breathless with rushing, then when he made his way to the front of the Palladium and went through the doors, into the foyer, the attendant asked him to wait as the show had started.

'If you could just wait to take your seat until after this number, sir, then you won't disturb the others.' Seeing the disgruntled look on his face she said, 'You could stand at the back until you can be seated.'

And he had to be satisfied with that.

As he stood at the back of the theatre he was delighted to see that there didn't appear to be an empty seat anywhere and in the far distance he could see the figure of Connie, as she came to the final chorus of 'That Old Black Magic'. He waited for the applause before making his way to his seat near the front.

During the interval, Connie popped along to see the family. They were tucking into some sandwiches, washed down with champagne. Jeremy smiled at her and winked.

'Everything all right?' asked Connie taking a seat.

'Oh, Con,' said her mother, breathless with excitement, 'this is lovely, and you are marvellous!'

'Thanks, Mum.' She turned and asked, 'Dad?'

He held up a half-pint glass of beer and said, 'This beats the Social Club every time! You really are a star, Connie, and my goodness how you've come on. You deserve to get to the very top. I'm really proud of you.'

No accolade could have thrilled her more. She drew her sister aside and asked, 'Is everything all right, Doreen?'

'You are to stop worrying,' her sister scolded. 'We're having the time of our lives . . . and Dad is fine, honestly.' She hugged Connie and said, 'Crickey! I didn't realise how glamorous you were. That gown, those earrings, and you sing like an angel. I do love you, Con.'

'You were a knockout,' said Eric enthusiastically.

Knowing that all was well took the pressure off Connie and the second half of the show was even better. At the end of one number she spoke to the audience saying, 'This next song is dedicated to the man I love most in the world.' There was a quiet murmuring in the audience, wondering if they were to be treated to a bit of show-business gossip and they waited expectantly – as did Les Baxter.

But as Connie began to sing 'My Heart Belongs to Daddy', they smiled at the sentimentality of it, and at the end when Connie stood and looked up, and blew a kiss, every eye was turned in the direction of the box and the man who was waving.

Les Baxter was also looking and was amazed to see the Ryan family in situ. He didn't know anything about these arrangements! Not that he objected, but he did like to know what was going on. He bet Jeremy Taylor knew and as the next and final number started, he glanced up and saw his partner sitting behind George Ryan.

As the audience made its way out of the theatre, Les battled against the crowd to the staircase. After all it was mainly due to him that Connie had reached these heights and he felt it his right to go and see the family. After tonight's performance he was sure that any animosity between him and George Ryan would be over. But as he approached the box, he saw Connie coming from the opposite direction.

Walking up to him she asked, 'Where do you think you're going?'

'To pay my respects to your family!'

She firmly placed her hand against his chest to stop him. 'You will do no such thing. I will not have Dad upset, not tonight, not ever!'

'Why *should* he be upset. Not after seeing you perform.'

'I'm sorry but I can't take that chance. It's been a very long day for him and he's weary. Leave us alone, please.'

He was about to protest when Jeremy came out of the box. Taking Les's arm, he said, 'Les! Great show, wasn't it? Come along, old chum, let's go and have a drink to celebrate,' and walked him away.

Ben and Connie went back to the hotel with the family and ordered tea and sandwiches from room service.

Freda was overcome with it all. 'Just look at the furniture and the curtains,' she said in hushed tones. 'My God, if my house was set up like this, the neighbours would be green with envy!' Then she giggled like a schoolgirl. 'A box in the theatre and champagne . . . I could get used to this, our Connie!'

'I hope you're not expecting everything like this when we're married,' laughed Eric, looking at Doreen.

They discussed the show, the hotel and what fun it was to stay in one, but all the time Connie kept an eye on her father until she said, 'You look tired, Dad. Ben and I are leaving. I'll see you at the weekend.'

George held out his hand to her and when she took it he said, 'It was a lovely experience, Connie. Thank you so much.'

She kissed his cheek and turning to her mother said, 'Leave any time you like tomorrow, it doesn't matter when. Order breakfast from room service and when you want the car to drive you home, call reception and tell them. All right?'

Freda gave her a hug and said, 'Oh, it was all lovely. Wait until I tell my pals.'

With a grin, Connie said, 'Remember ages ago I promised you the Savoy? We'll leave that for another time.'

Doreen kissed her goodbye and said quietly, 'You have no idea just how important this trip was to Dad.'

'It was important for both of us,' she replied. 'I'll see you all on Sunday,' and she and Ben left.

In a taxi on the way home, he put an arm around her and said, 'You were terrific tonight – the critics seemed to enjoy it.'

'Was I? To be perfectly honest I wasn't thinking about them at all. If I was to be closed down tomorrow, I have given my most important performance tonight.' And she smiled. 'That doesn't sound like me at all, does it?'

'That sounds unlike the old Connie, but you have grown up a lot lately. You see things differently.'

She shrugged. 'Maybe. I still want to get to the top so I haven't changed that much, but it doesn't seem quite so important as it was.'

'It will, in time.' He kissed her gently. 'You made your father a happy man tonight, how about coming back to my place and doing the same for me?'

'Mr Stanton! Do you have designs on me?'

'I certainly do!'

'Wonderful. I thought you'd never ask!'

Chapter Thirty-Five

In London's East End, Kenny Pritchard was sauntering around one of his hostess clubs, feeling very pleased with himself. Business was good here and in the other 'Cat House', as he called it. The décor was a bit gaudy, but suitable, and anyway the clients were more interested in the whores and their deviations than the surroundings. The bar was doing a good trade too, with girls ordering champagne, yet being served ginger ale by the barman, a lucrative ploy. Yes, things were going well.

He sat on a stool at the bar sipping a large whiskey. The daily take from his bookmaking had been excellent and he was delighted to think that he'd got one over on Les Baxter – as hard a man as ever his father had been. Finding out how the other man doted on his mother had been a master stroke. He grinned to himself. Everyone had an Achilles' heel . . . except him. He had no such weaknesses, except perhaps his enjoyment of the good life. But in his mind, that was down to good taste.

Now that everything seemed settled, he would have the time to pursue Connie Ryan. He liked her and her rising stardom would give him a certain standing, which would be no bad thing. After all, he was rising in his world – or so he thought.

It was the early hours of the morning and the available rooms were full, with some of the girls and their punters involved in the specialist practices. Other clients waited in the bar area, where some were dancing to the three-piece band.

'You need a bigger place,' complained one punter to Kenny. 'I don't like this waiting around.'

'You'll have to come earlier then, mate.'

'I can't, this is the only time I can get away.'

'Wife asleep, is she?' asked Kenny, on his way to his office, laughing loudly at the look of embarrassment on the man's face. Once inside the small room, he started counting the night's takings. He always emptied the bar till hourly, *and* the takings on the door. Too much money hanging around too long was too much of a temptation for sticky fingers.

He had almost finished totting it all up, when he thought he smelt smoke. He looked in the wastepaper basket thinking he may have thrown a lit cigarette end there, but there was nothing. He got up and opened the door. At the end of the corridor, smoke was seeping under the door to a spare room used for storage. He walked along and opened it.

Flames shot out and he fell back, his jacket smouldering. He quickly took it off and threw it away. He touched his face and felt the stubble remains of his eyebrows, the front of his hair. The smell of singeing invaded his nostrils.

Christ! The place was on fire. He ran back to the office stuffing the notes and change into a bag, then fled to the bar.

'Fire! Fire!' he yelled. 'Call the fire brigade,' he told the barman. Then rushing upstairs he threw open doors, yelling, 'Get out! The place is on fire.'

Men and women in various stages of undress tumbled off beds, grabbing clothes, running downstairs, trying to dress as they did so, before rushing into the street to safety. Some of the staff tried to quell the flames with hand-held fire extinguishers, but it had too fierce a hold and they were forced to flee also.

Outside, police cars arrived suddenly, a Black Maria followed, and eventually the fire engine. Standing on the steps of the club, Kenny watched as his girls and their clients were hustled into the Black Maria until it was full, and another drew up.

He was pushed out of the way by firemen carrying hoses. 'Is there anyone inside?' one asked.

'I don't think so.' But he was puzzled as to how the police arrived so promptly – no one had called them. They were even there before the fire brigade . . . and he quickly realised he'd been set up.

'Bloody Les Baxter!' he exclaimed angrily, as a police officer led him to a waiting car.

'You're in deep trouble, my son,' he was told.

He was taken into an interview room where two detectives questioned him, not about keeping a house for immoral purposes, but as to how the fire started.

'I've no idea!' Then he explained how he had discovered the stockroom alight.

'Someone trying to settle a score?' asked one.

'How should I know? I just hope you find the bastard. People could have been killed there tonight!'

There was a knock on the door and a police constable entered and whispered something to one of the detectives, then left the room. Looking across the table he said to Kenny, 'Someone did die! The firemen found a charred body, hanging by the wrists from chains in the wall.' Shaking his head slowly he said, 'Well, that sad devil got more than he bargained for tonight – so now we're looking at a murder case.'

'Murder!' exclaimed Kenny. He sat mulling over the thought that if only there was evidence of Les Baxter being involved, he could be shut behind bars for a very long time . . . and he liked that idea. There was not one grain of sympathy for the punter who had been hopelessly trapped, left to die by some young prostitute who had panicked and fled.

But then again there was none either from the perpetrators of the crime, the men who had returned to work for Pritchard, to secure the release of Baxter's mother. This was the first step in

303

the punishment to be dished out by Les, who made sure he was in Southampton with friends at the time of the fire. Strangely when he was told the news, he did feel sorry for the unfortunate victim. Poor bugger, he thought. Oh well, there were always casualties during a war and that was what he had declared on Kenny Pritchard.

Everyone who had been taken from the club to the police station spent a night in the cells before appearing in court the next morning. The girls were charged with prostitution and fined, and Kenny Pritchard was charged with keeping a brothel and living off immoral earnings. He was bailed until his trial came up at a later date. Most of the clients had been let off with warnings.

When he returned to his home, Kenny realised that he would have to watch his back now. He was smart enough to know that Les Baxter was retaliating for taking his mother, and mused that he had been a tad foolish in thinking that would bring everything to a satisfactory conclusion. On reflection, young Kenny didn't think it safe to wait until evidence against Baxter could be found and proved. He was too wily for that. No, if he wanted peace of mind, he would have to do something himself to solve the problem. He called his own young boys together, not trusting the old brigade, as he called the others.

Whilst all this was going on, Connie was playing to packed houses every night at the Palladium, and Jeremy was setting up a recording contract for her, as well as guest appearances on radio.

'The next thing is a tour of the major cities,' he told her when she and Ben were having lunch with him at the Café Royal.

'That's great,' she said, 'but could you hold off those for a bit, only Dad isn't well, and . . . you know . . .'

'I understand,' he said. 'By the way, Baxter is coming up to town later today,' he warned her, 'only I need his signature on some papers.'

'I see,' said Connie. 'Well, forewarned is forearmed.'

Later that evening, Les walked like a man with a mission towards Connie's room. He was sorting out Pritchard and now he was determined to get things straight between him and Connie. He knocked on the door.

'Come in.'

Connie was sitting at her dressing table in a silk housecoat before changing to go home. Les noticed how the front of it was open slightly, showing the soft rise of her breasts encased in a lacy bra. His blood began to race, his heartbeat increased. He put his hand in his coat pocket and took out the small square box.

'It's time we got our situation sorted,' he said gruffly, as he stood beside her.

'Oh, not that old chestnut!' she snapped.

He gripped her shoulder and she winced.

'I've warned you before about your attitude, well, now that's all finished. Here, open this.'

When Connie looked at the box, she went cold. Continuing to wipe the stage make up from her face she said, 'What is it?'

'Your engagement ring.'

'Don't be ridiculous!'

'I'm not playing games, girl. It's time we made our relationship public.'

She turned on him, throwing the face tissue to one side. 'We only have one relationship, Les Baxter, and that is one of client and manager. There is nothing in my contract that says I have to marry you!'

'Nothing on paper, but it is part of my plan for us. I told you before, we were going to get married eventually.'

'Oh, yes, you told me, but if you recall I said nothing. I certainly didn't agree.'

'I don't understand you!' he said. 'I can give you everything.

305

A nice home, clothes, jewellery, security.'

She looked scornfully at him. 'I will soon be able to afford those myself. I already have nice clothes.'

'Like that fur coat that Pritchard gave you, I suppose!'

'For Christ's sake! I have others which I bought myself.' She laughed. 'I do believe you're jealous and the stupid thing is you haven't the right. You mean *nothing* to me – apart from business. How could you ever have thought otherwise?'

'The fact that you are not in love with me isn't important.'

She looked horrified. 'Well, it bloody well is important to me! I would *never* marry a man for any other reason, especially one old enough to be my father. I am *not* an old man's play thing, so you can take your ring and go.'

'No, I'll leave it for you. You'll soon come round to the idea. I told you, I always get what I want.'

There was a cold menace in his voice that scared Connie, but she would never let this man know that.

'Do what you like with it, I'm not even going to discuss it with you.'

'How's your father?' he asked, changing the subject.

'As if you care!'

'Of course I do. I know how much he means to you.'

Her anger exploded. 'You keep away from my father; I don't want you anywhere near him. He's a better man than you'll ever be!'

He dragged her from the chair and held her in his arms so tightly she was unable to move. His mouth covered hers despite her struggles as he kissed her. Devoid of affection, full of passion, his brutal assault seemed never-ending and when he'd finished he said, 'I won't disturb your father, but you *will* wear my ring, that much I promise you!' And he slammed the door shut behind him.

Connie sat, her body trembling uncontrollably. There had been something about Les tonight that really frightened her. He was determined, and she had no idea how to handle him. There was a knock on the door.

'Who is it?'

'Ben.'

Quickly shoving the box in the drawer, and trying to pull herself together, she called, 'Come in.'

'Sorry, I got delayed,' he said, kissing her quickly. 'How long will you be?'

'Twenty minutes.'

'I'll order a taxi then.' He paused. 'Are you all right, darling, you look very pale?'

Smiling she said, 'I'm fine, just a little tired.'

'Right, I'll come back for you. I love you, Connie,' he murmured as he kissed the lobe of her ear.

'And I love you too.'

Alone, she shut her eyes and worried what Ben would do if he knew of Les Baxter's plans for her. She had to keep working, had to keep Les happy some way, because if he called her bluff and withheld her services, she was in trouble. Too many people were relying on her now.

Chapter Thirty-Six

George Ryan was seriously ill. His condition had begun to deteriorate shortly after his return from London. The pains in his head were excruciating and he'd started having fits. It became so bad during the early hours of the morning that the doctor who had been called summoned an ambulance and had him removed to hospital.

'He now needs professional nursing,' he told Doreen and Freda, who were frantic by this time. 'In hospital they can monitor the amount of morphine he needs for the pain and they know what to do for him when he has a seizure.' He looked at her sympathetically. 'I'm so sorry, Mrs Ryan, but now it's out of our hands. I suggest you call your daughter in London, then pack a bag for your husband and take it to the hospital.'

Grateful that Connie had had a telephone installed for her, Freda said to Doreen, 'Ring Madame Vicario's number and hang on until someone answers. They'll all be asleep at this hour and may not hear it at first. I'll go and pack some things for your father.'

Irene, who was a light sleeper, heard the telephone ringing almost immediately and ran down the stairs. When she heard Doreen's voice, she wasn't surprised at the news. They had all been waiting and dreading the call. 'I'll wake Connie,' she said. 'She'll get down to Southampton as soon as she can. I am so sorry, my dear. You take care and give my love to your

309

mother.' Then she climbed the stairs to wake Connie and pass on the bad news.

Connie sprang out of bed as soon as Irene turned on the light. 'It's Dad, isn't it?'

Irene relayed the message.

'What time is it?'

'Half past two,' Irene told her. 'Let me call Jeremy, he'll drive you down.'

'Thanks, and would he pick up Ben on the way, do you think?' she asked, her face drawn with anxiety.

'I'm sure he will. Put on warm clothes, Connie, it's bitterly cold.' And she left quickly to make arrangements.

Half an hour later Jeremy arrived with Ben and they all climbed into the vehicle and took off, Connie telling them briefly what had happened.

'I'll stay in Southampton for a while, then I'll catch a train back to London,' said Jeremy. 'Ben can keep the car to drive you around. The petrol tank is pretty full.'

Connie didn't even wonder how he had managed that in these days of rationing, to her it was quite normal. She'd been so used to everyone around her being able to get anything they really wanted, one way or another. And she didn't care – all she wanted was the means to get back and forth.

The journey down was passed mostly in silence. Ben and Jeremy exchanged words occasionally but all Connie could think of was her family and she sat huddled in the back beneath a rug.

When they eventually arrived at the hospital Connie and Ben enquired about her father and were told which ward to go to. Then the sister on the ward led them to a small room where Freda and Doreen were sitting beside the bed, holding George's hands.

'Hello, Mum,' said Connie quietly. 'How is he?'

'He's sedated, so he's asleep at the moment,' she was told.

Ben went and found two more chairs for them.

The room was in darkness apart from the small light over the bed. It gave the place an eerie feeling, Connie thought, as she looked down at the pale face of her father. She noticed the deep frown lines on his forehead, caused more by pain than advancing years, his chest barely moved his breathing was so shallow. She touched his forehead, his skin felt clammy beneath her fingers.

'How did you get down so quickly?' asked Doreen.

'Jeremy drove us. He's outside in the car.'

'What a nice man,' said Freda vaguely as she gently caressed George's hand.

Another nurse appeared with four mugs of cocoa, saying, 'I thought you could all do with this.'

They thanked her, grateful for the interruption – for something else to do. Then the nurse returned and took George's pulse and checked his respiration.

When she left Freda told Connie, 'They keep doing that.'

'At least he's not in pain,' Connie remarked.

But when the nurse came again and went through her routine, she frowned and left, returning a few minutes later with a doctor. They all became tense, hardly daring to breathe, as he examined his patient. Connie held Ben's hand in a vice-like grip as she waited. The doctor put his stethoscope back around his neck.

'I'm sorry,' he said quietly, 'when Mr Ryan arrived he was semi-comatose, but now he's slipped into a coma. It won't be long now. I'll leave you for a few minutes alone with him.'

'I'll wait outside,' Ben said and left them

Connie stood behind her mother, her hands on her shoulders. No one spoke for a moment, then Freda gently stroked the face of her husband and whispered, 'I've always loved you.' Moments passed and she said quietly, 'I think he's gone.'

The doctor returned, and felt for a pulse, then looking up he said, 'I'm sorry.'

The three women clung together, united in their grief. One by one they kissed George goodbye and left the room.

★ ★ ★

The next few hours seemed to pass in a haze. Jeremy drove them home, where Ben made them all strong tea and toast, which he insisted they eat to sustain them. There were papers to be signed, a death certificate to be collected, arrangements to be made with a funeral director. Connie did all this with Ben driving her from one place to another, whilst Doreen stayed with her mother. Jeremy had taken a train back to London, leaving the car behind as promised.

As he drove her back to the house, Ben glanced anxiously across at the set expression on the woman he loved and asked, 'Are you all right, darling?'

'Yes,' she said. 'I have to be. The family are my responsibility. I'm now the man of the house; I'll do my grieving when I have the time. Dad would understand.'

Ben didn't know when he had loved or admired her more than at this moment. And by keeping her emotions in check, she made it easier for the others.

Over a cup of tea, Connie said briskly, 'It's Saturday, so after the show tonight, I'll have a sleep and Ben and I will be down in the morning, then we'll go through Dad's clothes and get them out of the house. On Monday I'll go to the office of the *Southern Daily Echo* and put an announcement in the obituary column, when I get the time and date for the funeral. Have I forgotten anything?'

'No, love,' said her mother. 'You've been great. We don't know what we'd have done without you, do we, Dor?'

'No, our Connie. But you have to do a show tonight. Will you be all right?'

With a wry smile, she said, 'The show must go on, I'm sure you've heard that expression. I have a job to do, that's what I'm paid for and Dad wanted me to continue to do it, so I can't fall at the first hurdle, can I? He'd never forgive me.'

But later that night when she was back in London, having given her performance, she shut herself in her room at Irene's, broken-hearted – and shed her tears.

The day of the funeral was bright and cold. The early morning frost had covered the ground in white, but by the afternoon, the sun shone brightly over the Chapel at Hollybrook Cemetery as the funeral cortège arrived. As the family filed in Connie was not surprised to see the place was full. Her father had been well liked in the district. The three women moved along the family pew, with Ben and Eric joining them.

The coffin, covered with a long spray of white flowers, stood on a trestle below the steps to the altar, and despite herself, Connie's gaze rested upon it. She tried not to think of the contents, telling herself that her father was no longer there, that the casket held an empty shell, that the spirit of her father was now with God. No longer in pain, but at peace.

The service was very moving as the vicar knew George well, and instead of the final hymn, Connie stood with the choir and sang 'Ave Maria', which moved several of the mourners to tears.

The Ryan women stood tall at the graveside for the interment. 'Ashes to ashes and dust to dust,' intoned the vicar and at the end, Connie, Freda and Doreen threw a handful of dirt on to the oak casket. They lingered for a moment as the crowd dispersed to allow them some privacy. Then, as they moved away, walking among the many floral tributes, several of George's workmates came up and offered their condolences.

To Connie's surprise, Les Baxter was among the mourners. He shook Freda by the hand and said, 'I'm sorry for your loss, Mrs Ryan. If there is anything I can do, please let me know.'

Connie had laid on a reception at the Bellmoor Hotel and this had been announced in the church, inviting those who wished to come along to do so. Freda, Connie and Doreen with Ben and Eric were the first to arrive and Connie immediately ordered them each a stiff whiskey and ginger ale. 'It'll keep us going, Mum,' she said.

The two hours passed quickly, with friends reminiscing

about various incidents they remembered about George, which revived for Freda pleasant memories, but she was pleased when it was time to leave.

Connie was relieved that Les Baxter hadn't joined them because she didn't know how she would have been able to talk to him after their last meeting, but thankfully she'd been spared such an encounter.

Once home among comforting and familiar surroundings, they were all able to relax. Taking off her hat, Freda said, 'Well, that went off well. I think George would have been pleased to see so many there to see him off.'

'Are you going to be all right, Mum?' asked Connie.

'Yes, we'll be fine, won't we, Dor?'

'Don't you fret,' said her sister. 'You have done your bit, now it's my turn. Mum and I will be just fine. Now I don't want you to spend next weekend here, for once stay in London and relax. You've been up and down like a blue-arsed fly! Take some time to yourself for once, spend it with Ben. Eric will be here with us.' She smiled across at Ben. 'You have been wonderful these past weeks and it's time for you to have a break too.'

'It's been a privilege,' he said.

'In a couple of weeks, you must come up to London and we'll keep that promise and go to the Savoy!' smiled Connie. 'A bit of the high life will do you both the world of good.'

'That'd be nice,' said Freda. 'Just give me a bit of time.'

On the way back to London on the train Connie turned to Ben and said, 'I feel like a piece of chewed string!'

Squeezing her hand he said, 'I'm not at all surprised. A bit of pampering wouldn't do you any harm!'

Snuggling into him she said, 'I couldn't have managed without you.'

'Of course you could. God, Connie! I don't know when I've met a woman so young yet so strong. You've held your family together and that takes some doing under the circumstances.'

'I'm not feeling that strong at the moment,' she said as she began to relax, and her eyes filled with tears.

'Thank goodness for that,' he teased, 'otherwise why would you need me?'

'For sex, Ben Stanton. For sex!' And they both laughed.

'You are incorrigible, Connie darling, but now you must allow me to take care of you. Let me shoulder all your troubles and in time, we'll get married, and we can take care of your family together.'

'Are you proposing to me?' she asked. 'Or telling me?'

He looked at her with amusement. 'I would never dream of telling you, I'm asking.'

Running her finger across his mouth she said, 'I'll have to think about it.'

'Do you have any doubts about us then?'

'None at all, but a girl likes to keep a man dangling just for a bit, you know.'

He pulled her close and kissed her. 'You are a minx.'

But Connie was thinking of the box containing an engagement ring that Les Baxter had given her. She would have to get out of that situation before she dare accept Ben's proposal and that wasn't going to be easy.

She dozed the rest of the journey, which delayed any further conversation about their future.

Chapter Thirty-Seven

It was a further week before Les Baxter made his move on Connie. She was coming to the end of her time at the Palladium and had now agreed to take on a tour of the country. Jeremy was getting the details together, booking the venues and the artists who were to appear in the first half, with Connie making up the rest of the programme. She was absolutely delighted as she was going to make a serious amount of money from the tour, which would provide a nest egg for herself and her family.

That afternoon she was to meet Jeremy at his office to go over the details, but when she arrived, she found the book-maker was also there.

Jeremy's plans were well under way, and Connie was impressed at the list of cities and towns laid on for her. The band was booked, and Ben had already met with them to go over his arrangements; the artists were lined up, and the running order of the show looked great. Connie found herself feeling really excited at the prospect.

At the end of the meeting, Jeremy apologised, saying, 'I intended taking you out to lunch, Connie, but I'm stuck here with appointments for the rest of the day.'

'Don't worry,' said Les, 'it will be my pleasure,' and he ushered her from the room. Outside he said, 'We need to talk, so now is as good a time as any.'

They took a taxi to a small restaurant in the West End, ordered their meal and a bottle of wine, then, whilst they waited for their entrées, Les looked across at Connie and said, 'You look well, and I do realise this has been a difficult time for you. How are you feeling?'

'As long as I keep busy, I'm fine, but you know, I have my bad moments.'

'Well, that's natural.'

'The tour sounds great, doesn't it?' she said, trying to keep the conversation on a business level.

'Yes, and you will be a great success.' He smiled at her and asked, 'Is it everything you hoped it would be, Connie? I mean it doesn't seem that long ago that we were in the Workman's Social Club in Southampton, where you first told me you were going to be a star. Has it been worth it?'

He seemed so understanding, showing the softer side of his character, that Connie in her vulnerable state warmed to him. 'Oh, yes, it's been even more than I could have hoped for. I come alive when I'm on stage performing. I *love* what I do.'

He reached for her hand across the table. 'I'm so pleased to hear you say that. It isn't always the case, and I would have hated it had you been disappointed.'

Connie quickly withdrew her hand. 'Well, I'm not.'

'The tour will be very well publicised and I thought it would be a good time to announce our engagement,' he said casually. She froze. 'What!'

'Now, Connie, don't start being difficult. You have responsibilities: your mother to take care of, your sister. I know you feel that it is your duty now that you are earning such good money, your father would be very proud of you.'

'Don't you dare bring my father into your conversation!'

He didn't falter at her outburst. 'As far as I'm concerned, money is no longer the object.' He shrugged. 'Whether I become a theatrical agent or not isn't important any more, but you *will* be my wife.'

Les Baxter being reasonable was even more menacing than when he was in a temper, Connie discovered, because his tone made no allowance for argument.

'So, if I understand you correctly, you are telling me that if I want to do this tour, I have to agree to marry you?'

'Exactly! How very succinctly put.'

Connie's mind was racing. This time he really meant it. If she was unable to perform, she couldn't earn the money . . . he knew it and had called her bluff. This was emotional blackmail, and she was helpless.

'The announcement will be made in the papers of your forthcoming tour and our engagement, after your closing night at the Palladium – and that night you will wear my ring when you are on stage . . . or you don't work. I told you, I always get what I want.'

'You still want me to marry you even though you know that I hate every bone in your body?' she snapped.

'You'll get used to the idea in time.'

'I'll never get used to it!'

He gave a triumphant smile. 'You don't have a choice.' At that moment the waiter arrived with their dishes and Les said, 'Now I don't want any histrionics, no suddenly rushing away. We are to be engaged, and we're having lunch together as couples do. Try and look happy my dear.'

'Go to hell!'

He totally ignored her outburst. 'I thought we'd hold a party at the Café Royal to celebrate. It has the right ambience and is very classy, after all there will be several influential people there to witness the happy occasion.'

'You've got it all planned, haven't you?'

'Indeed I have, I've been planning it all for some time now. Circumstances delayed it – that's all.'

Connie had lost her appetite and ignored the food on her plate, but she took a long sip of her wine. Christ! What a mess! No one could help her out of this situation. If she told Jeremy and he approached Les, it wouldn't make a bit of difference, she knew that, and she could now no longer hide all this from Ben. Now she would have to tell him the truth, this lovely man who had only recently proposed to her himself. The man she truly loved and wanted to be with. But how on earth was she going to broach the subject?

The matter resolved itself that evening. Ben, coincidentally, arrived at the stage door of the theatre at the same time as she did. He kissed her and gave her a hug, then as they walked towards her dressing room, he was full of enthusiastic news about the rehearsals he'd had with the band, when they had tried out his new arrangements.

'They're a great bunch of musicians, darling, and looking forward to working with you.'

'Good,' said Connie as she took off her coat and hung it up, then sat at the dressing table to do her make-up for her performance. She opened the drawer to take out some tissues.

'What's this?' Ben asked as he removed the small square box from the drawer where Connie had hurriedly put it on the night Les gave it to her.

Feeling sick inside she answered, 'It's a ring.'

Ben opened the box and let out a whistle. 'Blimey, this is some stone, isn't it?'

'I don't know, I've not looked at it.' She stared straight ahead as she smothered her face with cold cream.

'Is it yours?'

'I suppose it is.' She began slowly to cleanse her face.

With a puzzled look he asked. 'Who gave it to you?'

'Les Baxter.'

His voice became distant. 'Oh, and *why* did he give it to you?'

Closing her eyes she took a deep breath and said, 'It's an engagement ring.'

There was silence as Ben looked once again at the jewel, then at her.

She watched his expression in the mirror and wanted to scream.

'What's going on, Connie?' he asked coldly.

She turned in the chair to face him. 'He insists that we

become engaged on my last night here, it's to be announced in the papers the next morning at the same time as the publicity of my tour, and he expects us to get married at a later date.'

'And you agreed?' His voice rose in anger and disbelief.

'Ben darling, I had no choice. If I don't he'll sit on my contract and refuse to let me work! *I need the money!*' She shouted at him.

'You need money so badly that you would sell yourself to that bastard? What about us?'

She caught him by the hand. 'What choice do I have? At least if I work, I can take care of Mum and Doreen.'

He shook off her hold. 'You could do that by working in a shop.'

'What . . . on a pittance compared to what I can earn by singing?'

'They do say that everyone has their price!' He glared at her. 'I thought you were above such things. I thought you loved me.'

She rose from the chair and clutched the front of his jacket. 'I do love you, Ben darling, with all my heart. I'll *never* marry that bastard, but if I pretend to go along with the engagement, I'll get the record contract, the tour of Britain, and I'll make so much money I can tell him at the end what to do with his ring and his bloody contract. It won't matter by then.'

'It will matter to me!'

'Please, darling, go along with this for me. I can't do it without you.'

His eyes blazed. 'You expect me to stand by and see him with you, touching you, kissing you – and do nothing!'

'It won't mean anything to me. I'll never let him make love to me, that I *do* promise.' With a toss of her head she said, 'The rest is nothing.'

Pushing her away from him he said, 'I thought I knew you, Connie, but I don't really know you at all!' and he stormed out of the room.

She sat back in the chair. The box was open, and for the first time she looked at the contents. The large squared-cut diamond with baguettes either side twinkled in the lights as if mocking her with its beauty.

She snapped the lid shut and threw it in the drawer. Ben had every right to be furious with her. What real man would agree with her plan? It was like throwing his love for her back in his face. But she could be stubborn too. She had made her decision and she would have to go through with it, but Baxter needn't think he'd get his own way all the time. There would be no cosy twosomes. He knew she hated him, so she didn't have to pretend. And there was *no way* she would give herself to him. Oh, no! And she would never ever walk up the aisle of a church as his bride. She would do as Irene once said: keep him at arm's length as far as she could.

Taking a deep breath she continued with her make-up and then dressed ready for her performance.

During the final days of her appearance at the Palladium, Ben didn't come near her, which tore at her heart, and when Les called into the dressing room before her final performance, she took the ring from the drawer and, for the first time, she put it on her finger.

He looked delighted and went to take her in his arms, but she held up her hands to stop him. 'You'll mess up my make-up,' she said as she walked past him and made her way to the wings.

Glancing across at Ben, when she walked on stage, she saw the set expression on his face as he looked at the ring on her finger and then at her, before looking down at the keys of the piano as he and the band struck up the opening bars of her first number.

As she sang, she thought of the night her father had sat in the box near to the stage and watched her. I'm doing what I promised Dad, she thought. But at such a price! And she was grateful that he wasn't here to see.

★ ★ ★

Several people came back stage to see her after the show, including her new fiancé who was followed by Jeremy Taylor and Annabel. Champagne corks popped, glasses were filled and then, to her horror, Les stepped forward and tapped the side of his glass.

'Ladies and gentlemen,' he began, 'I'm sure you'll agree that Connie was sensational tonight, as always.' There was a ripple of applause. 'Connie and I would like you, as friends, to be the first to toast our engagement. Darling, come here.'

She saw the shocked expression of Jeremy's face and the mocking smile on Annabel's and she wanted to die.

Les put his arm around her and it was all Connie could do not to move away from the feel of his hand on her bare arm.

'We'll be holding a party shortly at the Café Royal to celebrate, the invitations will reach you all soon.' He raised his glass, 'A toast to my lovely bride to be.'

'To Connie!' they cried and drank.

Moments later, when Les was talking to someone, Jeremy appeared at her side. 'Connie, have you gone mad?'

'No. He won't let me work if I don't do this.'

'What about Ben, I thought that you and he—'

She shook her head and said with great sadness, 'Please, don't ask.'

'Are you really going to marry him?'

'Do you think I'm crazy? I'm just doing what I have to, and believe me that does not include walking up the aisle!'

Annabel sidled over and picking up Connie's hand looked at her ring. 'Well, you are a sly one,' she said. 'Who'd have thought it?' and walked away laughing.

Never had Connie felt more miserable.

She felt a tight grip on her arm, and Les quietly said, 'Look happy even if you don't mean it!' and he kissed her cheek, before turning to talk to someone else.

At last everyone had gone, except for Connie, the bookmaker and Jeremy. Pouring himself another glass of champagne he said, 'Well, Les, I had no idea that there was anything between you and my star – other than business. Don't you think that as partners, you could have told me?'

Baxter laughed heartily. 'That's ripe coming from you! You, who keep all your cards close to your chest, only letting me in when it's absolutely necessary.'

Scowling, Jeremy said, 'I just hope that you realise a wedding is out of the question for a while. Connie will be busy recording and then the tour. She certainly won't have time to sort out wedding dresses and guest lists and such.'

Connie could have kissed him.

'When the time comes, I'll make all the arrangements,' Les said with a broad grin. 'After all, I'm her manager too. I can manage to arrange a wedding, a big one with all the trimmings. After all, it will be good publicity.'

'Very romantic, I must say,' said Taylor sarcastically. He rose to his feet. 'I have to go your way, Connie, do you want a lift?'

But before she could answer, Les broke in. 'No thanks, old man; I want to take my lady home myself. After all I've not been alone with her all evening and it is the night we became engaged.'

'It's all right,' said Connie, giving Jeremy a kiss on the cheek. 'I'll be fine. I'm very tired, I'll be leaving soon.'

And so Taylor reluctantly left.

Connie turned and picked up her coat. 'Ready?' she asked.

'Not quite. I'm pleased you saw sense,' he said, lifting her left hand and looking at the magnificent diamond. 'You looked very beautiful tonight. I was very proud of you.'

Her eyes narrowed as she looked suspiciously at him. 'Les, I'm *very* tired!'

'At least have the good manners to accept a compliment!' he said angrily.

'Thanks. Now can we go?'

He caught hold of her. 'Watch your attitude!'

'Look,' she snapped, 'I played your little game but you know how I feel, so let's stop pretending, shall we!'

'You little bitch!' And he crushed her mouth with his as he kissed her.

Connie stood still without responding or struggling until he released her. 'Now can we go?'

He opened the door. 'I *will* break you of this,' he threatened.

She didn't answer; neither did she speak throughout the journey in the taxi until it stopped outside Irene's house in Maida Vale.

'Goodnight, Les.' She opened the door and got out.

He didn't answer.

When Connie shut the door behind her she saw Irene standing there in her colourful dressing gown. 'Jeremy called and gave me the news,' she said. 'You had better come in. I have a bottle of brandy waiting. I think we could both do with one!'

Chapter Thirty-Eight

Kenny Pritchard was reading the Sunday papers whilst he ate his breakfast, turning the pages slowly. The situation in Palestine was still explosive, 'Well, who cares?' he muttered. On the next page the doctors in the country were arguing about the new National Health Service, saying they would be no more than servants, which was of no interest to him at all, but the headline in the gossip column of the following page caught his eye: BEAUTY AND THE BEAST. *Popular singer, Connie Ryan, 19, to wed her manager, Les Baxter, 40. Miss Ryan has just landed a lucrative recording contract and is soon to start a tour of major cities. Mr Baxter told reporters that the wedding would take place at the end of the tour.*

Kenny couldn't believe what he was reading. Why on earth would she tie herself to him of all people? It didn't make sense, a beautiful girl like that with the world at her feet. The few times he'd taken her out there hadn't been a mention of anyone. There had been that gossip in the newspapers of course, which had been hotly denied. His anger rose as he thought of the fire that had cost him dearly and which was orchestrated by Baxter – of that he was certain. He was on bail because of this bastard. Putting down the paper, he washed and dressed, then drove out to Maida Vale to find out for himself what it was all about.

Connie had just stepped out of the bath and was towelling her hair after washing it, when she heard the front-door bell.

Twisting the towel around her hair like a turban, she marched down the hallway, pulling her dressing gown around her. If this was Les she would send him off with a flea in his ear, she thought, therefore she was more than surprised to see Kenny on the doorstep.

'Hello, princess.' He held up the paper and said, 'Do you want rescuing again?'

Seeing the headline completely ruined her day. 'Come in,' she said.

Kenny made himself at home and sat on the settee. Taking out a cigarette he lit it and asked, 'What's going on, Connie? You're not really going to marry the old man, are you?'

Kenny always made her laugh and his choice of words made her do so now. 'Not if I can help it!'

'Isn't the article true then? It says you are engaged.'

'Yes, that's right.'

He screwed up his face. 'Am I losing my marbles or what?'

For all his brashness, she liked Kenny. Yes, he was a bit rough round the edges, full of himself, but he had a certain charm she had always found, so she told him the truth.

'Jesus Christ! You're the one who's lost the marbles. You are playing a very dangerous game, princess. I crossed the bugger and he had my hostess club torched.'

'What?'

He told her what had happened, the whole story, even about taking Les's mother.

'Kenny! That's kidnapping.'

'No, not really. I took great care of the old girl; after all, I didn't want her croaking on me, did I? I would never have harmed her, Connie.' He puffed on his cigarette and said, 'I brought it on myself really. I was ambitious, I wanted his patch.' He grinned broadly. 'I got greedy, but my God, he made me pay for it.'

'Was anyone hurt in the fire?'

He looked somewhat shamefaced. 'I'm afraid one person died.'

Connie was shocked. 'How did that happen?'

'He couldn't get out.'

'Why not?' she persisted.

Hesitating he said, 'Well, you see he was chained to a wall.' At her startled expression he explained. 'It was what he liked, you see.'

The truth suddenly dawned on Connie. 'It was a brothel you were running!'

He grimaced. 'I don't really like that label. A house of entertainment is better.'

Connie started to laugh. 'Oh, Kenny, you are dreadful. That poor man! What on earth would his family think about him dying in such a place and in such a way?'

'To be honest I didn't give it a thought. I was more concerned about going on trial for keeping the place and living off immoral earnings. I ask you, Connie! If men didn't want these things and there were no such places, there would be more crime on the streets.'

'That's an awful thing to say. I just don't understand you,' she said.

'Never mind me, it's you I'm worried about.'

Taking the towel from her head, she began to rub her damp hair. 'Then don't, I can handle Les. He may have been the person who set me on the road to success, but I'm certainly not going to spend the rest of my life repaying him for that. He's already cost me the love of someone whom I did intend to marry!'

'No chance for me then!' he said, grinning from ear to ear.

'Absolutely not!' But she said it kindly.

'Is there anything I can do?'

'That's very sweet of you, Kenny, but I think you have more than enough trouble on your hands. Now you must go, I've got a lot to do.'

Rising from his seat he kissed her on the cheek and said, 'If you change your mind, give me a call.' At the door he added, 'Take care, princess – and watch your back!'

As he drove away, he was infuriated about the hold Baxter had over Connie Ryan. She was a great girl and a great singer; it was bad enough that she had lost her father, without this as well. He knew to his cost how ruthless the man could be, and it angered him to see the situation that Connie was in. He might get away with a fine when he went to court, but there was a possibility that he could serve time for his misdemeanour, although it wouldn't be for long. But if Connie wasn't careful, she would be serving a life sentence.

Later that morning, Connie received a phone call from her sister. A very concerned Doreen said, 'I've read the paper . . . you can't possibly marry Les Baxter!'

Thinking quickly she said, 'I'm not going to; it's a publicity stunt. Now you're not to take it seriously. After all, our Dor, can you see me being an old man's darling?'

'I thought it was a bit strange when I read it.'

'Has Mum seen it?'

'Not yet, I hid the paper.'

'Then let her read it because others will and they'll have plenty to say about it. She can tell them it's for publicity. Now you're not to worry, do you hear? How are you anyway and how is Mum?' They chatted for about twenty minutes, exchanging gossip, before Doreen put down the receiver and Connie breathed a sigh of relief.

As she told Irene a little later over a cup of coffee, 'It won't be so bad when I'm touring because Les will be too busy to come traipsing all over the country after me.'

Over the rim of her cup Irene looked at her and said, 'But Ben will be with you all the time . . . *that* will be what you find the most difficult, darling.'

'Yes, you're right I'm sure. Poor Ben, how he must hate me.'

'For a while he will – with a vengeance, but give him time, maybe he'll come round.'

Connie doubted that very much, and she was proved right

during the days they spent together in the recording studio. It was like being with a complete stranger. Ben was polite, but cold and distant. Remembering how close they had been before, how he had held her, kissed her, made love to her, Connie found it almost too much to bear, but she grimly soldiered on

On the last day, Les unexpectedly arrived at the studio. He kissed her briefly saying, 'I thought I'd come and give you some moral support.' And despite her coolness, he was solicitous and caring. He sent out for coffee and sandwiches for everyone as the time passed and they were about to take a break.

He sat beside Connie as she perched on a table sipping coffee, and put his arm around her. 'You're not getting too tired, are you? Because if you are we'll stop, and I'll pay for the studio and musicians for an extra day.'

'I'm fine,' she said, moving away. 'I would prefer to finish today, then it's behind me and I can concentrate on the tour.' All this time she was wondering what Ben was thinking and didn't dare look in his direction.

'Very well,' said Les, 'if you're sure, I'll be off. Jeremy and I have some final arrangements to make – and he needs my signature,' he said with great deliberation, reminding her of her position. 'Goodbye, darling,' he said and then he kissed her.

When he'd left Connie looked around to see where Ben was, but he wasn't there.

'He went to the gents,' she was told when she asked after his whereabouts, and Connie wondered just how much he had seen.

When the session was over, she couldn't bear it any longer and walked to where he was collecting the musical scores. 'Did you think the recording session went well?' she asked.

He shut his case and looked coldly at her. 'Fine,' he said and walked quickly away.

Connie sat disconsolately on a chair wondering how on

earth she was going to get through the tour with Ben behaving this way.

Ben Stanton was thinking the very same thing! He'd had to leave the room when Baxter arrived because he just could not stand to see him anywhere near Connie. Touching her, calling her darling. It made him feel sick! He would complete the tour, because it would really establish Connie, then she wouldn't need him and his musical expertise, so when it was over he would definitely move on – start afresh and try and forget her. He told himself that if she really loved him she would never ever have agreed to Baxter's demands. His injured pride brushed aside her more honourable motives, thinking there was always a way round everything.

It was mid April and Connie was packing, preparing for her tour. First stop, Birmingham. Her gowns for the show were to be transported by rail as the petrol rationing made it impossible to do it by road. She had been in rehearsal with the band before leaving and was delighted with them. They were all talented musicians that Jeremy had gathered together and Ben's arrangements were excellent, as usual. They would all be travelling around the country together by rail and had things been normal between her and Ben, Connie would have been really looking forward to it. However, the fact that several of the band were characters, with a great sense of humour, would no doubt help.

Les had insisted that Connie went out for dinner with him the night before she left and despite her excuses that she had a million things to do, he would not be swayed. 'Get yourself organised earlier!' he said. 'I'll pick you up at seven o'clock.'

She made time to call her mother before she went out. She had been down to Southampton at frequent intervals to visit her family but having been so tied up lately, she'd only been able to be in touch by phone.

'Hello, Mum, how are you?'

'Hello, love. All ready for the off?'

'More or less. If I've forgotten anything now, it's too bad. What have you been doing with yourself?'

'Oh, you know, the usual. Been to the pictures with Doreen and Eric. Saw Gene Tierney in *Laura*. It was very good.'

'When I get back, you and Doreen are coming to London for a few days. We'll keep that date for lunch at the Savoy.'

'That sounds lovely, our Connie. Now don't you get over-tired, you need to look after yourself and your voice.'

'I will. Now you take care, love to Doreen.' She gave a half smile as she put down the receiver. Her mother sounded quite chirpy and that was good. She would enjoy spending time with them when she came back. She would really spoil them; after all, that's what it was all about, wasn't it?

Birmingham was a sell out! The applause at the end of the concert was loud and enthusiastic and Connie took bow after bow. She was exhausted but elated. She longed to share her triumph with Ben, but as he passed her all he said was, 'Well done.' It was the same in Nottingham, Manchester and Leeds. The pace was tiring, though: performing, back to a hotel to sleep, off to the railway station the next morning, another performance. And so it went on, until Liverpool, where they were booked in the theatre for two nights, which gave everyone a bit of breathing space with time to relax for at least one day without having to travel.

Connie took the opportunity to have her hair done, then she took a leisurely walk around the shopping centre, but being alone, with Ben in the same vicinity, was making her really unhappy. As much as she tried, he remained distant and businesslike.

Returning to her hotel room after her last performance, she was standing alone in the lift thinking she would have to pack her bags for the morning, ready for Blackpool, and she was tired, so perhaps if she asked for an early call, she could do it in the morning. The boys in the band had gone out for a meal, but she had declined their invitation to join them, saying she wasn't hungry and would get room service to send up something.

When she opened the door of her bedroom, a bottle of champagne was standing in an ice bucket on a side table, beside which was a platter of dainty and appetising sandwiches. How lovely, she thought, and how kind of the band to arrange it. As she took off her coat, there was a knock on her door and she went to open it.

'Surprise!' Les Baxter stood there holding a large bunch of long-stemmed roses.

So shocked was she that she didn't move as he stepped inside, closed the door and took her in his arms. 'Hello, Connie darling.' His lips covered hers, and only then did she move as she tried to push him away, but he held her tightly as his mouth demanded a response . . . without success.

He laughed as he released her. 'I can see you are pleased to see me,' he said with great irony. He threw the flowers on the chair and opened the champagne. 'It's a little ungrateful as I went to so much trouble.'

'You ordered this?'

'Where else did you think they came from?' He poured her a glass of bubbly and handing it to her, said, 'The show was very good tonight.'

'You were there?'

'Yes, I was there or else how would I have known. I wanted to give you a surprise so I didn't visit you backstage.'

'Where are you staying?'

'Here.'

Her eyes widened and she tensed. 'Here?'

'Yes, I have a room down the corridor. Now sit down and eat, then you can tell me about the show.'

Relief made her feel weak. For one awful moment she thought he was going to share her room. Sitting down she discovered that she was really hungry and started tucking in to the food. Between sandwiches she told him about the different theatres, different audiences and their differing responses to the programme.

He listened intently, nodding now and then with approval. 'Your press reviews have been excellent,' he said.

'I wouldn't know,' Connie told him, 'we are never anywhere long enough to read them.'

He gave a benevolent smile. 'Well, take it from me you are a great success and I'm very proud of you.'

'Thank you.' This was so unusual coming from him that in a strange way it really pleased her.

'The band was good and the other acts that came before you were entertaining. The audience must have felt they got value for money. And you – you had them eating out of your hand!'

She grinned and her eyes sparkled. 'I did, didn't I?'

Seeing the delight on her face he laughed. 'You are such a mixture of a girl, you really are.'

With a thoughtful look she said, 'And so are you. You can be such a bastard at times, yet tonight, you're kind and considerate.'

He was highly amused. 'Well, Connie darling, if you didn't waste so much energy hating me, you'd be surprised at what you would find.' Getting to his feet, he said, 'You look tired. I'll leave you to have a good night's rest. We'll have breakfast together in the morning.' He took her gently into his arms and kissed her.

As Les walked back to his room, he felt really pleased. Connie had been through a great deal, but tonight her attitude towards him was definitely different. Maybe he wouldn't have to force her into anything after all. Maybe she would marry him of her own free will.

Chapter Thirty-Nine

In the morning, Les called for Connie and they went down to the dining room together where they settled at a table for two. For once she felt at ease with him and it showed as they talked and laughed together. It didn't escape the notice of the members of the band either, who filtered in after them, in twos and threes, with Ben being the last to arrive.

'Well, that's a change,' remarked the drummer, with a nod in the direction of Connie's table.

'What?' asked another of the musicians.

'It's just that I got the impression that our songbird hated the guy's guts, but look at them now, like two love birds – I wonder what's changed her mind?'

'When did he arrive?' asked Ben quietly.

'I believe he came last night. Makes you wonder, doesn't it?' the other said suggestively.

'It's none of our business,' snapped Ben, which stopped any further speculation. But he cast a surreptitious glance in their direction moments later and he could see what had given rise to the comments. Connie was laughing at something that had been said and there was a complete lack of hostility in her manner as she continued talking. Ben turned away to finish his breakfast, although every mouthful was choking him. Les had stayed overnight, where had he slept? Had it been with Connie? His thoughts were driving him insane.

Shortly after, the two of them were about to leave the dining room, when Connie called over, 'See you at the station, boys!'

337

Ben watched as they walked away and saw Les put his arm around her waist, but he also noted that Connie didn't shake off the arm, as was her usual habit when Les touched her in any way. His heart sank as he jumped to his own conclusions.

As it happened, Connie was the last one to arrive at the station and the musicians were getting worried, thinking she may miss the train. They were hanging out of the carriage windows looking along the platform when they saw her running, Les Baxter, behind her, carrying her bags.

'Come on, for God's sake,' one cried, 'or we'll go without you.'

The door of the carriage opened for her as the guard blew the whistle. Baxter pushed the cases inside for the men to put them up on the overhead racks as Connie scrambled in. She let down the window of the carriage and breathlessly said, 'Goodbye, Les. Thanks for everything.'

He pulled her head down so he could reach her, and kissed her goodbye. 'Take care, Connie.' The train began to move, with Les walking beside it along the platform. 'Look after yourself. I'll try and see you again.'

As she flopped down into a seat, the teasing began. 'And why were you late, Miss Ryan?'

'I had to pack.'

'Why didn't you do that last night then? We all did.'

'To be honest, I was too tired.'

There was ribald laughter all round and cries of, 'What were you up to, you naughty girl? I heard you – thanks for everything.'

'All right, fellows, you've had your fun, and anyway, why the third degree?'

'Well, you know, your fiancé down for an overnight stay. We thought perhaps you were otherwise occupied!'

'Did you now? You lot should stick to playing your instruments!'

She suddenly saw Ben glance over at her with an accusing

stare, and she felt her hackles rise. He didn't want her any more, so what right had he to look at her in that way? She was pleased she hadn't denied any of the things of which she was being accused, even though she was innocent of all of the suggestions. She sat back and started reading the magazine she'd picked up in the hotel. He can think what he bloody well likes, she thought.

After the show that night, Connie went with the musicians to a small Italian restaurant near the hotel for a meal, but Ben Stanton went off alone and got roaring drunk, trying to blot out the ugly pictures that kept flooding into his tortured mind. When the barman refused to serve him any more, he staggered out of the bar.

Connie left the restaurant before the others, saying, 'Thanks, boys, but I'm off to bed. Don't forget you have to leave tomorrow morning! Don't be too late.' And she headed back to the hotel. As she got out of the lift on her floor, she saw Ben staggering along the corridor ahead of her, his room key in his hand, peering at the numbers on the door, muttering angrily to himself. She frowned when she saw his condition and caught up with him.

'Do you want any help?' she asked.

He turned his head and looked at her with bleary eyes, and said, 'Well, if it isn't Miss Connie Ryan who has sold herself to the devil!'

'I haven't sold myself to anyone!'

He gave her a baleful look. 'You have obviously decided to go for the money after all – but what about love, Connie?'

'Don't talk nonsense,' she said. 'Come on, let me get you back to your room and we'll send for some black coffee.'

He refused to move. 'How could you?' he said accusingly. 'How could you choose money and not love?'

'That's enough!'

He caught her by the arm. 'You will *never* in a million years find what we had together with another man.' He gave her a look that tore at her inside. 'Was he better in bed than me, is that it? Did he thrill you more than I did? He's so much older after all, and so much more experienced, but I remember how much you liked it when I touched you and kissed you in those lovely little places, how you would beg me not to stop.'

She slapped him hard around the face and ran to her room, but as she put the key in the lock, Ben called after her.

'You promised me you would never give yourself to him. You *promised*!'

She entered the room, slamming the door shut behind her. Tears running down her cheeks, she slid to the floor and wept.

Ben walked along until he stood outside her room and leaning his head against the door, he called, 'You promised, Connie.'

She covered her ears to shut out his words.

When she woke in the morning Connie felt dreadful. Last night she had been so upset that she shed tears for what seemed an eternity, and when she eventually bathed her swollen face and climbed into bed, she was unable to sleep. Ben's words seemed to be carved deeply into her brain and whenever she closed her eyes, all she could hear were his accusations.

She picked up a glass of water beside her bed and drank because her mouth was dry and her throat felt tight. She rubbed her neck, trying to ease the tightness, drank some more, got out of bed and looked into the mirror. Her eyes were swollen from so much weeping and she had dark circles beneath them. As she studied her reflection, she asked herself, was it all worth it?

Walking back into the bedroom, she picked up the telephone receiver and asked for a pot of tea and enquired if it were possible to have some bread and butter and some honey in a dish. When the tray arrived, she poured some hot water into the cup and added a spoonful of honey. When the water had cooled to a drinkable temperature, she sipped it, feeling the warmth slightly release the tightened throat. The last thing she needed was trouble with her voice.

She stood in front of the window, opened it and took several deep breaths, then she started to exercise her voice. It felt strained. Not wanting to strain it even further, she quickly dressed and went out of the hotel to find the chemist the receptionist had told her was nearby, where she bought some throat lozenges.

On the train later that morning, she hardly joined in the conversation until one of the musicians asked her if she was all right.

'I have a slight cold,' she told him, 'and I don't want to use my voice before this evening if I can help it.' Understanding her predicament, they left her in peace. Ben was in a different compartment so at least she was spared any further confrontation with him.

When they arrived in Blackpool, Connie went straight to her hotel room where she lay in a hot bath, hoping the steam would help, then she crept between the sheets to try and catch up on her lost sleep, asking to be called in time to prepare for the show. But when she awoke, her throat was no better and she asked the receptionist to send for a doctor.

When the man arrived, she told him her problem and he examined her throat. 'I can give you an injection to relax the muscles, he said, 'but how many shows do you have to do after this one?'

'Two. One in Glasgow and another in Edinburgh, why?'

'Because you shouldn't be singing at all!'

'But I must finish the tour!' she exclaimed.

He looked thoughtful and said, 'I'll give you a letter, when you get to your next destination, get a doctor to inject you again, I've written the prescription for you, but when you get home, go to a throat specialist, and when you've sung your last song, don't please speak a word, not one, until you've seen him.'

'You are scaring me,' she said.

'You should be all right,' he assured her, 'as long as you do as I say, but try not to sing at full throttle,' he said smiling at her. 'I'm going to the concert myself this evening, so I'm pleased to have been of help.'

Shaking hands with him, she thanked him. 'I hope you enjoy the show.'

'I'm sure I will, Miss Ryan. Good luck.'

As she waited in the wings of the stage at the Blackpool tower that night, she felt more nervous than she had ever done before. She had practised her exercises and it seemed that the injection had worked, but she was terrified that she might lose her voice in the middle of a song and that made her tense, but as the bars of her opening number were played, she walked on stage with a big smile, to face her audience. Despite her concerns, the show went well, although she was keeping tight control over the volume of her voice, which the audience were totally unaware of. Ben realised what she was doing, however, and he watched her very carefully all through her programme. After she had taken her final bow, he followed her into the wings and asked, 'What's wrong?'

'What do you mean?'

'Don't fool around, Connie, you were not using your voice to its full potential tonight. Why?'

'I have a cold coming and my throat was a little sore so I didn't want to strain it.'

'Have you seen a doctor?'

'Yes, back at the hotel. He gave me some medication.'

With a look of concern he asked, 'Are you all right? Only you don't look well.'

'I'm fine,' she said as she walked quickly away. After the débâcle last night when she had faced Ben's anger, tonight she found it even harder to cope with his concern, and when she returned to her hotel room, she ordered a light meal to be sent up and arranged for a doctor's visit the next morning.

★ ★ ★

The new doctor's opinion concurred with the previous one, and when Connie explained that as their next stop was Glasgow they would be travelling today and not performing until the following night he said, 'That couldn't be better, you have a chance to rest your vocal cords. Please don't talk at all. Write down what you have to say, until you have to sing, say absolutely nothing! It is imperative that you see a throat specialist when you get home.'

Connie was devastated because now she was beginning to realise that things could be serious. 'What are you insinuating, Doctor?'

'Singers are in a vulnerable position, Miss Ryan. A chest infection will affect your breathing, a common cold will cause congestion of the nasal passages, and of course there is laryngitis. But constant use, professionally, also takes its toll. Nodules can grow on the larynx. You need to get your throat checked out.' He paused, 'Nerves can also play a part. Have you had anything lately that has caused you any anxiety?'

If only you knew, she thought. 'My father died recently.'

'That too could have consequences. All you need really is to find the cause, that's all I'm saying. Find the cause, then we can find the cure.'

'Thank you, Doctor,' she said as she showed him out.

'Not another word now, Miss Ryan, until you are warming up for your performance in Glasgow.'

She nodded at him, and put a hand across her mouth.

No sooner had the doctor left than there was a tap on her door. When she opened it, it was to find Ben, standing outside. 'I saw the doctor leave,' he said. 'Are you going to tell me what is wrong?'

She indicated that he should enter, and then searched for a pad and pen, writing down the explanation.

After reading what she had written he looked at her. 'I'm so sorry, Connie. But I'm certain it's nothing serious.'

She just shrugged and raised her eyebrows.

He walked slowly towards her saying, 'I'm very sorry about

last night. I was very . . . drunk.' He stopped in front of her, and, seeing the anxiety mirrored in her eyes, caught hold of her and held her close.

'Oh, Connie. Poor you. You have had such a bad time lately and I haven't helped. I'm sorry. Is there anything I can do?' He held her away from him and saw the tears glittering. 'Please don't cry,' he said, but as a tear trickled down her cheek, he wiped it gently away.

She picked up the pad and wrote on it, *Wouldn't it be AWFUL if I was unable to sing again?*

He read the words, and felt her anguish. He tipped her chin upwards and gently kissed her.

Connie closed her eyes and wallowed in the moment. She was in Ben's arms, his mouth on hers – and it felt like heaven.

'Don't think that way,' he entreated. 'You'll get yourself in a state, probably over nothing. Now get your cases packed,' he said, 'and you and I will take a train together, then when we get to Glasgow, you must rest. We'll have something to eat first and then you can sleep. All right?'

She nodded her agreement.

'I'll find out the train times and I'll come back in an hour. Don't worry; I'll look after you. Whatever happens, you won't have to face it alone.'

Connie bustled around the room gathering her things together, with a feeling of euphoria. Ben really did care after all. She couldn't be happier, especially at this time when she was deeply worried about her future. What if it was discovered that her career was over? What then? She told herself to stop worrying about something that might never happen, as Ben had said. She had enough problems already, with Les.

Chapter Forty

When they arrived in Glasgow, Ben kept his word, getting Connie settled in her room and taking the one next to hers, to be near at hand if she needed him. Afterwards, they went to a restaurant for a meal, and then took a walk.

'You need some fresh air in your lungs,' he said, but he made her wear a scarf around her neck. Being unable to converse made not a bit of difference. They walked hand in hand, keeping away from as many people as possible.

'You don't want to pick up any more germs,' he said.

She chuckled to herself and tried to make signs to convey that he was behaving like a mother hen, which he didn't understand at all, but ended up killing himself laughing at her antics.

'You'd better stop, Connie,' he said, 'only, people are beginning to give you strange looks the way you're flapping your arms like a chicken, and if they discover who you are, they will stay away from the concert in droves!'

They spent an enjoyable day together visiting museums, shopping, drinking numerous cups of tea and hot chocolate – anything that was warm – and in the evening, Ben left her reading in her room whilst he met up with the musicians and prepared for the following evening's concert.

When he returned it was with a deck of playing cards. 'Come on,' he said, 'we'll play Beg O My Neighbour.' Connie was delighted, as she and Doreen used to play this as children.

'We should play Snap,' he teased. 'I would definitely win,

because you can't call out!' She threw a cushion at him.

It was such a restful day. Ben made no demands of her whatsoever, sexual or otherwise. They just enjoyed being together, and as they parted later that evening, she felt rested and deliriously happy. When she eventually went to bed, she slept peacefully through the night.

The following morning after breakfast Connie took a bath whilst Ben prepared to meet up with the band again. 'I'll pick you up later and take you to the theatre,' he said as he kissed her goodbye.

As she was settling down, a messenger delivered a telegram to her room. She opened it and read, *Sorry can't make the last show. See you when you get back. Love Les.* Connie tipped the boy and told him there was no reply, then breathed a sigh of relief. At least she had more time to think about how she was going to approach Les, but at the moment, getting through the two final performances was her main concern.

She was ready when Ben came to her room. He looked anxious as he asked, 'Are you all right?'

She nodded.

He caught hold of her and said, 'You're going to be fine. I'll be on stage with you. If you are in trouble, you just walk over to the piano and let me know. Come here and give me a hug.'

Which she did, gratefully.

Fortunately, the show went without a hitch, but Connie was relieved when it was over. The fear of her voice failing mid-song was always there and she couldn't wait to get to Edinburgh for her final engagement, because then she would have no such worries. Her first concern after that would be the appointment with the specialist, and all that that implied.

It was with a sense of relief that Connie stood in the wings of the theatre in Edinburgh the following night, knowing that this was the final performance of the tour. She pushed to the back of her mind that it might be the last one, ever. The house was packed, without a seat to be had, and she walked on stage determined to give the performance of her life. She had done her warming-up exercises in her room and after yet another injection, her throat felt fine. When the music began she glanced over at Ben and smiled.

Her opening number was George Gershwin's 'Lady Be Good', and the audience loved her. In between numbers she drank from a glass of water on the piano, to lubricate her throat. 'You're Nobody Till Somebody Loves You' went down well, as did the poignant 'The Man I Love' from *Showboat*.

The time seemed to fly by and Connie was in her element, doing what she felt she was born for. She gazed over at Ben as she sang 'Someone To Watch Over Me', and he winked at her. She finished the programme with 'Every Time We Say Good-bye'. As she took her bow, she was delighted to see the audience on their feet.

She waited for the applause to die down and said, 'Thank you so much. This is the end of my tour, but I will always remember the kindness of the people of Edinburgh.' The audience cheered and called for more.

She usually sang a couple of encores, but she felt her voice was beginning to tighten again, so she walked over to the piano and said quietly, 'Just the first song, all right?'

Ben nodded and, looking at the bandleader, mouthed – only one.

Connie stood in front of the microphone and sang one of her favourite numbers, 'Ten Cents A Dance', which didn't strain her voice too much. The perfect rendering of the dance hall girl's sad tale was very moving and at the end of the song she bowed, blew a kiss and left the stage to thunderous applause.

Back in her dressing room, she breathed a sigh of relief because at one point she'd wondered if she was going to make it and that had been a terrifying experience. Her throat felt sore and she slowly sipped some water as Ben entered the dressing room.

'Connie! Are you all right?'

She shook her head and held her throat.

'I'll get you back to the hotel.' He knelt beside her and said, 'You were bloody brilliant tonight, but you worried me to death!'

She pointed to herself and nodded.

He laughed. 'You too?'

She grinned.

'Oh, Connie, what am I going to do with you?'

She held out her arms and he pulled her to her feet and held her. 'You were so brave out there tonight. I was so proud of you. I do love you, you know.'

She indicated that she loved him too, and they kissed each other with a passion that needed no words to describe their feelings.

'Come on,' he said quietly. 'Let's go home.'

Back at the hotel, Connie changed out of her gown into a negligee, removed her make-up and relaxed with a cup of tea whilst Ben ordered a meal to be served to them in their room. Then, walking over, he sat beside her. Caressing her cheek he said, 'You know, without the glamour, your gown and make-up, you look ridiculously young. So different from the sophisticated singer who, earlier on stage, held that audience all through the performance. You never cease to amaze me, do you know that?'

She smiled at him and just shrugged. There was so much she wanted to say. To tell him how much she loved him, had always loved him, and her concerns about her voice – and Les Baxter. They hadn't mentioned the bookmaker once since they had made up, but neither had she worn his ring. That hadn't been mentioned either. There was so much that needed to be said, but Connie hadn't wanted to rock the boat now that they seemed to be sailing in calm waters. However she knew the time would come and it wouldn't be easy.

Getting out her pad and pen, she wrote asking Ben to call

Jeremy and tell him what was happening and to ask him to find a throat specialist for her return. He read the note and said, 'I've done so already. I thought he was the best person to ask.' He paused before saying, 'I didn't call Baxter.'

They looked at each other. This man, they both knew, stood between them and happiness, and both were reluctant to mention his name. Connie just smiled and nodded.

Ben said, 'I'm not going to lose you again, Connie. I'll do whatever it takes for us to be together.'

She was overwhelmed. This was such a strong declaration of his love for her, for him to stand by and wait, knowing the difficulties ahead, and she didn't feel she'd earned such loyalty. Putting her arms around him she just held him tightly and prayed that somehow somewhere, there was a solution – if only she could find it.

Back in Southampton, Les was unaware of the trauma that Connie was suffering. He was a happy man. The time he'd last spent with her had been beyond his wildest dreams. She had actually begun to respond to him, after rejecting him so scornfully in the past. He couldn't believe his luck and was already mentally making plans for the wedding. On her return he would give her time to buy her trousseau, her wedding gown and choose her bridesmaids. He would give her a splendid wedding; show her just exactly what he could offer her as his wife. He would make sure all the national papers were there, as the coverage would be excellent publicity. Connie was a star now after her tour. The critics had raved about her and Jeremy was being inundated with offers, which was terrific news.

Jeremy, unlike Baxter, was a very worried man. After getting a phone call from Ben telling him about Connie's predicament, he rang an eminent throat specialist and made an appointment for Connie to see him the day after her return. His heart went out to her. How dreadful to have this just as she was reaching the pinnacle of her career. The worst scenario would be that her career was over! He brushed that thought aside. The other alternatives were that she had to have an operation if necessary, or that she had to rest her voice for a time. But both would take her out of the limelight and that too was a worry. Show business was a fickle master; people could so easily be forgotten. There were several offers on the table at the moment for Connie and he knew he would have to be smart and keep all the balls in the air until he learned the results of her visit to the specialist. Not one word of this must leak out to the public, or the papers would have a field day. He couldn't breathe a word to Annabel as she was bound to gleefully pass on the information to Rudy, and that would be the end of any secrecy.

In Edinburgh, the band dispersed to go their separate ways. They were unaware of the seriousness of Connie's situation, as, to stop any speculation on their part, Ben had explained that it was just a touch of laryngitis that would pass in a few days. They all bid farewell to Connie with a fondness born of admiration and true affection for her. 'Hope everything goes well, love,' said one. 'It's been a rare privilege to play for you. When you next get a booking, we'll all be prepared to answer your call.'

She was deeply touched. But once on the train heading back to London, her heart sank. Very soon she would know what her future held – if anything. If that was the case, she could tell Les goodbye without any worries, but she would no longer be earning big money, and if it was just a hiccough, she still had a problem.

Ben reached over and took her hand. 'I know you must be worried, darling, but if the worst happens, I can earn good money with my arrangements. We will still be able to look after your family. They won't go without, I promise.'

She squeezed his hand in reply. It was true about Ben. It wasn't only she who had had all the accolades during the tour.

Those who knew about music had praised Ben Stanton for his brilliant arrangements and she knew that several bandleaders had contacted him. She was proud and pleased for him because she knew that he had played a vital part in her success.

At last, they arrived back in London and took a taxi to Maida Vale, where Irene was on hand to welcome them home. She was aware of the situation because Jeremy had called to inform her.

She kissed them both and ushered them inside. Looking anxiously at Connie, she asked, 'How are you, darling?'

Connie put her thumbs up to indicate she was fine, then touched her throat and covered her mouth.

'I know you can't talk,' Irene said, 'but Jeremy has booked you an appointment for tomorrow afternoon. He thought it best not to waste time. And you'll be happy to know that the press know nothing of your ordeal. There hasn't been a whisper.'

'Thank goodness for that!' said Ben. 'That's the last thing we need.' He picked up Connie's cases and said, 'I'll take these up to your room, then I need to go back to my flat to check the post. I'll be back later.'

When they were alone, Irene asked, 'Is everything all right between you two?'

Connie beamed at her.

'I can see it is. And what about Les Baxter? Does he know about your voice?'

Connie shook her head vigorously, and fishing around inside her handbag for a pad and pen she wrote, *If he rings, either tell him I'm out or asleep. I don't want him to know anything until after tomorrow.*

'I understand,' said Madame. 'You look tired after your journey, do you want to sleep?'

Connie pointed to the large settee and indicated that she didn't want to go upstairs.

Irene made her comfortable with cushions and one of her

351

gaily-covered rugs, then sat in one of her armchairs. Within five minutes, Connie was fast asleep.

Irene gazed at her. She looked so young, so innocent and her heart went out to her, knowing that if she was unable to sing it would be devastating news. She'd had enough to deal with already with the death of her father. For one so young, Connie had done so well, but the price had been very high. She prayed that tomorrow would bring good news for the girl she'd grown to love like a daughter.

Early in the evening Jeremy called at the house to enquire after his young star. Feeling rested after her sleep, she was sitting with Ben, reading the reviews that Irene had cut out of the papers and kept.

Jeremy greeted the two warmly and congratulated them on the success of the tour. 'Financially, it has been better than expected and the records are selling well. You are a star, darling Connie. You have achieved your lifelong ambition, and I'm just delighted to have been a part of it.'

She beamed and blew him a kiss.

'Now we just have to wait until tomorrow.' Turning to Ben, he asked, 'Are you going with her?'

'Yes, I am.'

'That's all right then. Otherwise Connie, I would have been there to hold your hand. Now don't worry, Stephen Barrington is the best in his field. I know him and some of my clients have been to him in the past. He'll soon put you right.'

Connie held up her hand and crossed her fingers.

Jeremy got to his feet. 'Good luck, darling,' he said to Connie, kissing her cheek. 'As soon as you know anything, let me know.'

The following day arrived all too soon, and Connie was a bag of nerves. Ben, sensing this, said very little but ordered a taxi. As it drew up before the consulting rooms, Ben paid the driver, then, taking her hand, asked, 'Ready?'

She took a deep breath and nodded.

They mounted the few steps and rang the shiny brass bell. A nurse answered the door and Ben said, 'Miss Connie Ryan for Mr Barrington.'

'Please come in,' the nurse said and led them inside. She knocked on a stout oak door.

'Come in,' someone called, and she opened the door.

The tall man sitting behind the desk rose to his feet and, holding out his hand, said, 'Miss Ryan, how nice to meet you. Please sit down.'

Chapter Forty-One

Les Baxter called Madame Vicario from Southampton and asked to speak to Connie.

'I'm sorry but she's out at the moment. Can I give her a message?'

He declined, saying he would call again later, but he was so anxious to see Connie that he decided to drive up to the city. He had other things to attend to and it would be easier with his own transport. He had a full tank of petrol and a full can in the boot, so he had no worries on that score.

As he drove through the Hampshire countryside, he hummed softly to himself. He would take Connie out to dinner and make plans for the wedding. He wondered where she would like to spend her honeymoon? A lot would depend on what bookings Jeremy had made for her, of course, but he would insist she have a break. After all, she must be worn out from the tour.

Whilst Les was making his journey, Connie was sitting in the surgery in Harley Street, listening to Stephen Barrington. 'I want you to tell me exactly how your problem started, Miss Ryan. For instance, was it before your tour began or midway through? What happened?'

'It was almost at the end of the tour,' she began. 'I woke one morning and my throat felt tight, then when I tried to exercise it, it felt strained.'

'I see. Did you have a cold, a temperature?'

'No.'

'Then I had better take a look,' he said, rising from the chair and walking round the desk. After examining her throat, he said, 'It is inflamed, but I need to take some X-rays before I can tell you anything. I need to know if there are any nodules on your larynx. Come with me, please.'

She followed him to another room where he asked the nurse to X-ray Connie's throat. 'Take Miss Ryan to the waiting room afterwards, until I've had time to look at the results,' he said.

Connie waited with Ben, her heart racing, knowing that in a short time she would be told whether her career was over. She didn't speak but clutched Ben's hand tightly as they waited for what seemed an eternity. Eventually, when Mr Barrington emerged and asked her to return to his surgery, she followed him, feeling sick in the pit of her stomach as she sat down.

He immediately put her at ease. 'Good news. There are no nodules.'

She breathed a sigh of relief.

'That's the good news, but you do have a problem. We must discover the cause of this before we can do anything about it. Now . . . has there been anything in your life lately that could cause you any deep anxiety? Because that could affect your nervous system.'

'My father died a few months ago,' she said quietly. 'That was pretty traumatic. It was discovered that he had a brain tumour and only had months to live.'

'I'm so sorry,' he said sympathetically. 'We all believe that our parents are going to live for ever, don't we?' He paused thoughtfully then asked, 'What about the time when you first had problems, did you suffer any other kind of trauma?'

Connie instantly recalled her scene with Ben when he was drunk. 'Yes, I did. I had a tremendous scene with the man I love, and I'm afraid I spent most of the night in tears.'

'Ah. And the following morning, the problems started . . . am I right?'

'Yes.'

'Herein lies the problem, Miss Ryan. I must ask you, has the situation been solved between you?'

'Thankfully it has.'

He smiled. 'I'm happy to hear it. All relationships are hazardous, but between a man and a woman, it is a minefield of emotions. In your case it started with the death of your father, which took time to manifest itself – call it delayed reaction if you like – and escalated after the scene with your young man. Also there was bound to be a certain amount of tension and tiredness with the tour. Your body and nervous system had had enough and, in your case, it was your vocal cords that suffered.'

'Does that mean I'm unable to sing?'

'For the moment, certainly. You must rest the vocal cords absolutely. They need time and care to recover. I will give you a prescription for a throat spray, but it means you must not speak at all, once you leave my office.'

'For how long?'

'Three months.'

'Three months!' Connie was horrified.

'Miss Ryan, if you wish to continue your career, it will be vital for you to keep silent. I want you to take care of yourself. Don't become overtired, and, above all, no further traumas.'

She thought of Les Baxter and closed her eyes.

'What is it, Miss Ryan?'

'There is one more situation that I have to sort out which will not be easy.'

'Then I advise you most seriously to find a way which will not cause you anxiety. I'll see you again in three months' time . . . unless you have further problems. We are not out of the woods yet, young lady.' He rose from his seat and shook her hand. 'I do hope that this will sort out your problem,' he said. 'I've been reading about your success, it would be a pity if it were all to end. Take care and follow my instructions to the letter.' He handed her a prescription he had written. 'This is for the spray. Follow the instructions on this and renew it when you need to, and I hope next time I see you I'll be able to give you the news you want to hear. Now please, absolute silence, until next we meet.'

She smiled and put her hand over her mouth.

'Good girl,' he said as he opened the door for her.

Outside in the waiting room, Ben stood up as she entered. His face was pale with worry. 'Well?'

She covered her mouth with her hand.

'How long for?' Ben asked.

She held up three fingers.

'Three weeks?'

Shaking her head vigorously she held up her hands, put them together and slowly opened up a small gap between them.

'Three months?' And when she nodded he held her to him and said, 'Oh, my poor Connie. Come on, we'll go back to Irene's and you can write down everything and then I'll call Jeremy and tell him.'

Back at the house in Maida Vale, Connie quickly wrote out the prognosis of the specialist, the reason behind the problem and the worry she had about dealing with Baxter. *What am I going to do about him?* she wrote.

Ben looked at her and Irene and said, 'Nothing at all. I will deal with Les Baxter!' He gazed adoringly at Connie and asked, 'Do you love me?'

She mouthed, Of course I do!

'Do you want us to be together always and eventually marry?'

She smiled at him again and blew a kiss.

'Then we must tell Baxter exactly how things stand. He must realise that he cannot run your life any more.'

She wrote rapidly, *He won't like it. He'll stop me working!*

'If he does he can go to hell! You will be all right for money for a while after the tour, and I will be too, I told you that.'

Irene intervened. 'That's all very well, Ben, but Connie loves what she does, and hopefully she'll get her voice back soon. What then?'

Connie picked up her pen. *But I need to continue working, I've a mother to look after. Perhaps if I pretend that it doesn't matter if he threatens to stop me working, that may take him by surprise, and then when I get my voice back things may be better?* She didn't look entirely convinced. She picked up the pen again. *My other worry is that I know he still wants me! And he was very kind when we last met.*

She couldn't help seeing the hurt expression on Ben's face as he read her words. She grabbed the paper out of his hands and wrote, *I didn't break my promise to you*!!!

He knelt beside her and said, 'No, you didn't and, if I'm honest, I'm not surprised that you turned to him for some comfort, you weren't getting any from me.' He kissed the tips of her fingers. 'Never mind, darling, that's all behind us now.'

'Not until you sort things out with Mr Baxter,' said Irene. 'He called earlier and I said you were out. He said he'd call again later.'

'When he does,' said Ben, 'I'll talk to him. Meantime I must call Jeremy and give him the news.'

The agent was naturally worried, but he realised what a terrible situation it was for Connie. 'Tell her not to worry. We'll have to give a press release of course so I need to think about that, and when I have I'll come round and discuss it with you both first. Give my love to Connie I'll see you tomorrow perhaps.'

Ben told Connie about the conversation and then read what she had written in reply: *I wonder what will happen if he has any bookings for me?*

'They'll have to be put on hold. Let's not worry about all that until you're better, darling. It's out of our hands for the next three months anyway.'

The three of them were sitting in the living room eating scones and drinking tea when the front-door bell rang. Irene rose to her feet saying, 'I'll get it.'

Les Baxter was waiting, clutching a bouquet of flowers. 'Is Connie back yet?'

'You'd better come in,' she said.

Connie froze when she heard the voice in the hallway and looked across at Ben.

Seeing her troubled expression he said, 'Relax. This may not be pleasant, but soon it will be over.'

But Connie wondered, would it? She knew Les so well. She could feel every nerve in her body tighten and worried about the effect this was going to have on her recovery.

Les bustled happily into the room, crossed over to Connie and handed her the flowers, then leaned forward to kiss her. When she turned her face away and offered her cheek to him, his smile faded for a second, then he asked, 'How are you, darling?'

Ben spoke up for her. 'She's not well. When we were away, Connie had trouble with her vocal cords and this morning she went to see a Harley Street specialist.'

'Why wasn't I told of this?' Les asked angrily.

Patiently Ben said, 'It only happened towards the end of the tour and we didn't want the press to find out. I rang Jeremy, who I knew would know the right person to see, and he fixed the appointment.'

'And what happened?'

'Connie is forbidden to speak for three months. She has to rest her vocal cords completely, then she has to go back and see him again. But . . . she *must* have a quiet and peaceful life in between,' he stressed.

Les looked at her and said softly, 'Oh, you poor darling, how awful for you. Well, I can certainly do something about that. We'll take a holiday – the South of France! We'll go to Nice, book into a nice hotel and there you can sit in the sun and do absolutely nothing.'

Connie put her hand to her head. This was going to be even harder than she imagined. She felt very guilty because Les had looked so happy when he came into the room and now . . . she looked at him and slowly shook her head.

'You don't want to go?' He couldn't have been more surprised. 'Why?'

Quietly but firmly Ben spoke up. 'Connie doesn't want to go anywhere with you, Les.'

The good humour he had showed quickly changed to one of anger. 'What do you mean? She's my fiancée, or had you forgotten that fact?'

Connie delved into her handbag and withdrew the square box Les had given her that held her engagement ring. She handed it back to him, then quickly wrote, *I'm really sorry, but I won't be wearing this any more.*

He was livid. 'What is going on here?' he demanded.

'We are in love,' said Ben, in a steady voice, 'and eventually, some time in the future, Connie and I are getting married.'

'Over my dead body!' Les glared at Connie and said, 'You think you can treat me like this and get away with it? You forget that I can put a stop to you working and I will if you don't come to your senses!'

She held out her hands and shrugged.

'What she is trying to say,' said Ben, 'is that it really doesn't matter.'

'Of course it bloody matters! She has a family to keep.'

'She'll have money from the tour and the sale of her records, and I'll be more than happy to help out.' Ben gave him a hard look. 'It will be my privilege.'

'Your privilege!' Les was outraged. 'You'll never work again I'll see to that!'

'Don't threaten me, Baxter. You may have been able to blackmail Connie, but I'm a different kettle of fish. Now I suggest you leave. This is not doing Connie any good, and if you think anything of her at all, surely you want what is best for her.'

For one moment, such was the hatred in the look that Les Baxter gave Ben, Connie thought he was going to strike the pianist. But Ben stood his ground.

Les spoke quietly and coldly, 'You doubt my feelings for Connie? Of course I want what's best for her, but marrying you would be the biggest mistake she could make and I promise you that I will not let *that* happen.' He turned to Connie and said, 'I told you I always get what I want, and I don't think you have ever believed me.' He glared at Ben. 'I make a very bad enemy, as you will find to your cost.' And he stomped out of the room.

Connie's face was white as Irene hurried after Baxter to shut the front door behind him. When she returned she glanced at Connie and said, 'That man is dangerous.' Then she turned to Ben, 'I would be very careful if I were you.'

As Les drove away, he was steaming with rage and muttering to himself. 'That little bitch! She thinks she can play me for a fool – playing up to me, then giving me back my ring. And that bastard having the gall to tell me he was going to marry her.' He wasn't sure which incensed him more. So, Connie had money at the moment but she was going to be out of work for three months anyway. After that, who knew? All these thoughts were racing through his mind. One thing he had learned since he'd been in show business was that the public soon forgot someone who had dropped out of the limelight. If she couldn't work, then she'd come crawling back! Well, it would be on his terms. This possibility calmed his rage. He would have to get in touch with Jeremy and find out what the situation was. He would find a way to spike that Ben Stanton's guns too. He wasn't going to get away with this.

Chapter Forty-Two

Jeremy Taylor presented himself at Madame Vicario's the following morning, bringing with him a bunch of grapes and some yellow roses. Kissing Connie's cheek, he said, 'Hello, my dear, how are you feeling?'

She gave him the thumbs up and mouthed thank you, pointing to the flowers and fruit. 'I didn't think champagne was appropriate,' he said apologetically. 'Is Ben around? Only I want to discuss the press release.'

Connie pointed upstairs and signalled the toilet by pretending to pull a chain.

Chuckling, Jeremy said, 'Very explicit, darling. I can see by the time the three months have passed, you will have invented a new sign language.' Sitting beside her on the settee, he said, 'Nevertheless, this must be extremely frustrating for you.'

She nodded and grimaced.

'I don't want to add to your frustration but I will have to cancel a list of bookings. I can't do that until the press release, otherwise the rumours will get distorted and before you know it, you'll be reading your obituary.'

Connie looked at him, eyes wide, then promptly grabbed her chest and pretended to die. Collapsing beside him.

'Yes, very funny! It's good you still have your sense of humour. Les Baxter rang me yesterday but I was out.'

This brought a frown to Connie's countenance.

'Has he been round here yet?'

She lifted her eyebrows and looked at him as if to say, Has he!

Glancing down at her hands he remarked, 'I see you are not wearing his ring, does that mean you've come to your senses?'

'She certainly has,' said Ben who had just walked into the room. He shook Jeremy by the hand. 'I told Les that Connie was going to marry me.'

'Bloody hell! I bet he didn't like that!'

'No, as a matter of fact he threatened me. I will never work again, etc.'

With a look of concern, Jeremy said, 'Did he now? No doubt he'll bend my ear about you both when I see him, which I must soon, to tell him what's happening on the business side.'

'He has threatened to stop Connie working when she gets her voice back.'

Jeremy glanced in her direction saying, 'Well, that's not the first time, is it? But I'm getting just a little sick of all this from Baxter.'

Connie wrote on her pad and passed it to the agent. *His threats really scared me this time. Especially about Ben. He's so possessive. I'm sure he's dangerous.*

It worried Jeremy too, but he wasn't going to add to her concerns. 'I shouldn't fret, Connie. I'll have a word with a lawyer friend of mine. There must be a way to stop him, lawfully. This is threatening behaviour after all. I'll look into it – now about this press release . . .'

Two days later the headlines in a national newspaper read, SONGBIRD LOSES HER VOICE. *Connie Ryan, whose success has been phenomenal, has been advised by an eminent throat specialist to rest her vocal cords for three months, in the hope of saving her voice. Will she ever sing again?* It then went on to tell her story, as did the other papers, all writing in a similar vein.

Kenny Pritchard read about it and was horrified. He got into a taxi and rushed around to the house in Maida Vale.

Connie was really pleased to see him, as both Irene and Ben were out and she was getting bored and frustrated. She beckoned to him to go into the living room.

'Well, princess, a fine old mess this is, isn't it?'

She nodded vigorously.

'Is that right, you can't talk for three months?'

She held her throat.

Grinning broadly at her he said, 'No point in having a row with you then?' and she laughed.

'There wasn't anything in the paper about Baxter and I wondered how things were?'

She grabbed a pen and started writing quickly, telling him everything that had happened. *I'm scared, Kenny*, she finished.

He got to the end of her notes and said, 'I bet you bloody well are, princess. I know that bugger.' Taking out a cigarette from his case he said, 'Now you listen to me: you stop worrying. Baxter isn't going to do anything, you have my word.'

Her eyes narrowed and she wrote, *Why? What are you up to?*

Laughing, he retorted, 'Me, Connie? Nothing. I'm up in court next week, but I'm telling you to stop worrying, all right?'

She shrugged and made the thumbs up sign.

'Do you know where he is? Is he in London?'

He was here yesterday. Why? she scribbled.

'Just wondered if I need to post a couple of my men on your door, armed with tommy guns,' he joked, then, rising to his feet, said, 'I've got to go, Connie. You take care, you hear? I'm really sorry about your voice, but don't you worry, you'll be back on stage afterwards, and I'll be there with all the others, cheering like mad.'

She pointed to him and crossed her fingers.

'Thanks, princess. If they send me down it won't be for long, but my brief thinks I'll get a fine – no criminal record, you see.' He kissed her cheek. 'If they do send me down you can bake a big cake with a file inside.'

She hit him playfully, and walked with him to the door. Then in her own sign language told him she'd see him soon.

He grinned broadly. 'Hey, you're good at that. I can understand you perfectly. Look after yourself.'

She watched him leave, smiling at the cockiness of his walk. Whatever his faults, she felt he had a good heart and hoped he wouldn't be put behind bars. As for not worrying, what on earth could Kenny Pritchard do to solve her problems?

Les Baxter eventually caught up with Jeremy Taylor in his office the following day. Taylor looked at the anger reflected in the other man's eyes and waited.

'Have you seen Connie yet?' Baxter asked.

'Yes, I have. What a terrible thing to happen to the poor girl. I expect you've read the papers. I've been busy ringing round cancelling engagements. Such a pity because I could have booked her well into next year.'

'You can forget about all that!' stormed Baxter. 'She won't work again until her contract with me runs out. By then she will be forgotten!'

Beneath his calm exterior, Jeremy was seething. This jumped-up little man without a shred of breeding was sitting lording it over one of his brightest stars, all because of his damaged ego. He looked at Baxter and said, 'That makes you happy, does it? Holding this girl to ransom, just to make you feel big and important.'

Baxter glared at him. 'I won't be treated like a piece of dirt by a chit of a girl.'

Jeremy sat back in his chair and said, 'You amaze me, you really do. You should be proud that you discovered such talent, that *you* instigated her success. You could have earned her undying admiration, but that wasn't enough for you, was it?'

'What are you getting at?'

'Your treatment of Connie – and your unhealthy obsession. Good God, Les, you're old enough to be her father, yet you

366

even blackmailed her into becoming engaged to you, knowing it was the last thing she wanted. You can't go around threatening people to achieve your own aims. It isn't done. It isn't cricket, old chap.'

With a sneer, Les said, 'Old chap! Isn't that just typical of your class! Look at you: public school education, wealthy parents. You have never had to scrimp for anything in your life. How can you be expected to understand me?'

'Ah, now we are getting down to your feelings of inadequacy. It isn't money and education that makes a real man, Baxter: that comes from inside – and inside you are all twisted. If you want something and can't have it, you try to buy it, and if that doesn't work, you bully and threaten. Well, I'm not going to let you do that to Connie, or Ben Stanton.'

'And how are you going to stop me?'

'The law of the land will deal with you, my friend. If you persist in this insidious behaviour, I will go to the law. Threatening behaviour, blackmail, and who knows what else, may rise to the surface. Your line of business can be suspect in itself.'

'Now who's threatening who?'

'I'm not doing any such thing, I'm just warning you. Stop your treacherous games or I will be forced to do something about it.' He smiled sardonically. 'And of course, with all my contacts, it wouldn't be hard. You could find yourself behind bars and you wouldn't like that. Think of your mother – what a disgrace for her in the twilight of her years. The shock could kill her!'

'You bastard!' stormed Baxter.

'You have no idea, old man. I can be equally as ruthless as you if I'm pushed, the only difference being that I'm doing it for the good of everyone, whereas you . . .' He just gazed at Les and let him digest his warning.

For once Les Baxter had met his match and he knew it, but such was his obsession that all he craved was revenge. But he would be clever about it. 'I'll talk to you again when the three months are up, Taylor. Until then – get off my back!'

'That will be entirely up to you, my friend.'

Getting to his feet, Les glared at him. 'I'm not, and never will be, your friend!'

'I'm always grateful for small mercies,' the agent replied. 'Heed my words, Baxter. I wasn't joking.'

Les left the office, feeling less than satisfied. He had expected Taylor to be really worried when he knew that, as far as Les was concerned, Connie Ryan wouldn't work for another three years, but the other man had come back at him with his own solution.

Driving back to Southampton, Les thought about Jeremy's words, and he didn't doubt the validity of them. If he thought Connie was in danger, he would go to the law, but that barb about his mother was strictly below the belt. Bastard! Well it made no difference. Connie Ryan and her fancy man were finished. And if he couldn't have her, no other bugger would, he'd make sure of that!

Two days later, whilst working in his office, Jeremy Taylor took a call from Kenny Pritchard. He listened intently and then said, 'I think we should meet immediately.' He rose from his desk, telling his secretary he'd be back later.

Kenny was waiting in the saloon bar of an old pub in the East End of London, impatiently chewing on his cigar when the agent arrived. Raising his hand, Kenny called, 'Over here!'

'Pritchard?'

'Yes. Call me Kenny. What's your poison?'

'Brandy and soda please.'

Carrying their drinks, they sat at a table in a corner. 'Your call intrigued me, Kenny,' said Jeremy. 'Now tell me more.'

'Well, it's like this,' he began, 'me and Connie Ryan are mates and I believe she's having trouble with that bastard Baxter, right?'

Taylor nodded in agreement.

'Nasty piece of work. I crossed him and he burned down a

business of mine, causing the death of one of my punters.'

Leaning forward, Jeremy became very interested. 'Really?'

'Really! And because of him I'm up in court for keeping a house of ill repute, etc.'

'How do you know it was him?'

'It's a long story; sufficient to say he was settling a score. He didn't start the fire of course – he made bloody sure he was miles away – but I have the proof that he was behind it all. Now Jeremy, you mix with the top shelf. You must know a clever brief that could put this bugger behind bars if I get the proof to you, don't you?'

'Damn right! Let's have another drink, then you can explain.'

Kenny filled Jeremy in on all the details of his past dealings with Baxter.

'You took his mother?'

'Yes, I know, it's kidnapping, but the old girl was well looked after. The point of all this is that one of the blokes who did set fire to the place is in the shit. He's in trouble with some very nasty villains. He's into them for a deal that went wrong and he's spent their money. Now I have offered to give him the dosh to settle but he's scared they'll still come after him, and he would welcome a spell in the clink. Thinks he'd be safe there.' He paused to sip his drink. 'Now for all this, he's happy to finger Baxter.'

'But if we do this and Baxter is arrested, when he's in court wouldn't he bring up the kidnapping of his mother and make it worse for you?'

Shaking his head, Kenny disagreed. 'No, he wouldn't put the old girl through a court appearance. Besides, it would start unravelling too much more that he doesn't want investigated. Bookmaking is a dodgy business, you know. Well, the way he runs it.'

And so the ball started to roll. Taylor got in touch with a lawyer friend of his, who met with Kenny Pritchard, and after a long chat with him and the man who was prepared to stand in the dock and accuse Baxter, the police were called in. Two days later, a warrant was issued for the bookmaker's arrest.

'All right, I'm coming!' Baxter called as he walked towards the door after the loud knocking disturbed him. He was very surprised to see two uniformed policemen on his doorstep and, before he could say a word, one of them spoke.

'Leslie Arthur Baxter, I have here a warrant for your arrest.'

'You what?' he blurted out.

'I'm arresting you on a charge of being an accessory to murder. Anything you say . . .'

Les didn't hear the rest of the arraignment, he was so shocked. Before he knew what was happening, he was being bundled into a police car and driven to the local police station, where he was closely questioned by two detectives about the fire in Kenny Pritchard's premises. What the hell was going on? He wondered. But he was smart to realise that he wasn't there by chance.

'I want my solicitor,' he demanded.

Jeremy called on Connie and Ben the day Baxter's arrest hit the papers and told them what had transpired. 'Your friend, Kenny Pritchard, has done you a favour,' he said to Connie, 'because if Les is sent down, I can get you out of the contract.'

Is there any doubt that he'll be sent to prison? she wrote, glancing anxiously at Taylor.

'Not much, according to my friend,' he assured her. 'He's charged with being an accessory to murder. His case comes up next month.'

Poor Mrs Baxter, she wrote. *As for Les, he could have been the cause of other deaths that night; they were lucky to get out of the building.*

'You're well rid of him, Connie,' said Jeremy quietly. 'He was a very dangerous man.'

'We ought to go down to see your family and explain all

this,' said Ben. 'When they read about it in the papers, they'll only worry. I'll pack a bag and we'll catch a train later this afternoon.'

She and Ben stayed at the Polygon Hotel overnight, which enabled her to spend time with her family in comfort. They had invited Freda, Doreen and Eric over to the hotel to dine with them that evening.

When all the explanations about Les Baxter were out of the way the evening became a happy occasion, with family stories being exchanged between Connie's mother and sister, to Eric and Ben's amusement, especially as Connie was unable to quieten them. She gazed fondly at the people she loved most in the world, but she still had a black cloud of uncertainty to contend with regarding her vocal cords, and that she tried to push to the back of her mind.

That night in their room, Ben took her into his arms and tried to brush her fears away. 'It won't be long now, darling. And whatever the result, we'll cope with it.'

As she lay there, in the curve of his body, Connie knew that she would be devastated if she could no longer sing. It wasn't a case of earning a living any more, but a primeval need within her, and she was scared out of her wits as the time drew ever nearer.

Her three months of silence were up, and that morning she was to return to Mr Barrington's surgery. As she waited at the front door with Ben, she was trembling, and when she was invited in to see the specialist, she felt faint.

'How nice to see you again, Miss Ryan. Have you followed my advice to the letter?'

Gripping her hands tightly together to steady herself, she nodded.

'Good. Well, let me have a look at your throat.'

After his examination he said, 'The inflammation has gone, of course. I'd have been very concerned if it hadn't.' He sat back behind his desk and said, 'Talk to me, Miss Ryan.'

Her eyes were wide with apprehension and she was too frightened to utter a sound for a moment, then taking a deep breath she said, 'Hello,' in a whisper.

'You can do better than that,' he coaxed.

Straightening her back she said, 'Hello, Mr Barrington.' Then burst into tears.

Outside in the waiting room, Ben was beside himself with worry. He tried to read a magazine, but not a word registered. He got up and started pacing, wondering how Connie would be if the news was bad. How would she cope? How would he cope with her? The door opened and she walked out, the specialist behind her. Ben stood, rooted to the spot.

Connie walked up to him, put her arms around his neck and said, 'Hello, darling. I do love you so much. When are you going to make an honest woman of me?'

He picked her up in his arms and spun her round. Kissing her he replied, 'Whenever you name the day.'

Stephen Barrington watched the touching scene with amusement and when Ben eventually turned to him he said, 'Miss Ryan can go back to work after a few weeks spent with her vocal coach, getting her voice back to scratch. She'll know when she feels ready.' He held out his hand to Ben and said, 'Congratulations on your recent engagement!'

Connie laughed with happiness. 'I'll send you tickets to my first concert,' she told him as she walked towards the door.

'Thank you, Miss Ryan, I'd like that very much.'

This time Jeremy Taylor arrived at Irene's house with two bottles of Bollinger. He had hurried over there when Ben had phoned him with the good news. As the champagne corks flew, he said, 'Now there is really something to celebrate. My God, Connie, I have aged ten years since I became your agent!'

Giving him a big hug she apologised. 'I am sorry; I think I've gained a few myself. But now I promise to be a good girl!'

There was great rejoicing all round and Irene said, 'Now you are not to be in too much of a hurry. I know you, you are impatient, but this is the time to be really sensible.'

'I know, and you're right, but I am so happy I want to tell the world!'

'I'll do that tomorrow,' said Jeremy, grinning from ear to ear. 'I'll release the good news to the press. It will be good publicity.'

'Listen to him!' teased Connie. 'He's thinking about his ten per cent already!'

Sitting dejectedly in his cell at Pentonville prison, Les Baxter was looking at the paper, reading all about Connie Ryan and her appearance at the Palladium. He gazed at the smiling face of the picture before him and cursed beneath his breath. What a bloody fool he had been! But he couldn't help the way he felt about her. Even now as he looked at the paper – he wanted her. But by the time he got out of this hole, she would have been a major star for many a year and he wouldn't have shared in her success, despite being the one to discover her talents. And what was even worse, she would be married to Ben Stanton.

He took out some tobacco and cigarette papers from his pocket and rolled a cigarette. As he lit it he gave a rueful smile. Not really his style, but cigars were a rare treat for him these days. He stood up and glanced at the small window high above him, covered with an iron grill, and wished with all his heart that he could be sitting in the audience on the first night of Connie's performance.

'Come along, Baxter!'

A prison warder stood in the doorway of the cell. 'It's time for your exercise.'

Connie's come-back concert was a complete sell-out. Her dressing room was festooned with flowers from her well-wishers, including one large bouquet from Kenny Pritchard.

The card read, *Good luck, princess, I'm not behind bars, I'm out front cheering as I promised. And, as you know, I always keep my promises*. She smiled fondly as she replaced the card. Because of him, she was free of Les Baxter. He had been found guilty and sent to prison for fifteen years and, through Jeremy's lawyer, she was no longer under contract to him. Now Jeremy was her sole agent and she knew she was in safe hands. But, despite everything, she still was grateful to Les. After all, he had given her her chance and she would always be mindful of that.

As she stood in the wings of the Palladium Theatre, she breathed in the atmosphere, knowing she was where she wanted to be. Beside her, holding her hand, stood the man she loved, the one she would be marrying in a month's time – the man she very nearly lost. She had it all – money and love, but if she had to choose . . . she gazed at Ben . . . it would be the love of this man. There would come a day when she would have to give up singing professionally, but Ben would always be at her side, and that was priceless. Absolutely priceless.

Now you can buy any of these other bestselling Headline books from your bookshop or *direct from the publisher*.

FREE P&P AND UK DELIVERY
(Overseas and Ireland £3.50 per book)

Across a Summer Sea	Lyn Andrews	£5.99
A Pocketful of Silver	Anne Baker	£6.99
Candles in the Storm	Rita Bradshaw	£6.99
The Pride of Park Street	Pamela Evans	£5.99
Strolling With The One I Love	Joan Jonker	£6.99
Out With The Old	Lynda Page	£6.99
Pride and Joy	Dee Williams	£6.99

TO ORDER SIMPLY CALL THIS NUMBER

01235 400 414

or visit our website: www.madaboutbooks.com

Prices and availability subject to change without notice.
